HUNTED

ANNE FOX

Hunted: Book 19 of The Unit Series
COPYRIGHT © 2021 Anne Fox

First edition 2021
Printed in the United States of America
10 9 8 7 6 5 4 3 2 1

ISBN
978-1-950389-42-1(ebook)
978-1-950389-43-8 (print)

Cover design by Momir Borocki
Cover images: Sue Critz, Shutterstock
THE UNIT logo by Michael Critz

❀ Created with Vellum

OTHER BOOKS IN THE UNIT SERIES

"The whole world can become the enemy when you lose what you love."

~ Kristina McMorris, *Bridge of Scarlett Leaves*

G ood evening. Heading our news this evening: A tragic death occurred today when a round from a rifle struck and killed a Makinen woman while she was filling a bird feeder in her yard. According to her neighbor, Holly Fay had just gone out to the back yard to refill the feeder when she was seen to fall to the ground. MaryBeth Moe, long-time friend of Holly, rushed over after seeing her fall and noticed blood coming from Ms. Fay's mouth. After calling 911, paramedics arriving on the scene found that Ms. Fay wasn't responding. She was rushed to the emergency room at the Fairview Range Medical Center where she was pronounced dead. Investigators have no leads as to who may have fired the rifle.

"GOOD MORNING, EVERYONE."

"He's like the Soup Nazi," Cloud informed his fellow teammates as Spud took his place to give the morning intelligence briefing. "Only he's the Intel Nazi. *No more crash day for you!*"

"What the hell are you talking about?" Crow asked him.

"It's an old thing from some old sitcom," Cloud said.

"Figures. Something that aired before any of us were born?"

"I guess we now know who ties up Hal's processor time watching old reruns during crash days," Hank smirked.

"Intel Nazi or not, here we go," Spud said. "And this is no bologna. It seems CBP is interdicting quite a few interesting things these days, including lunch meat. Specifically, five hundred pounds of Mexican bologna."

"That *is* bologna," Voice asserted.

"And it's no bologna that it's bologna," Spud said.

"Moving on, we have a story that you just can't make up."

"Aren't we a little early in the briefing for You Just Can't Make This Shit Up?" Amigo asked.

"This isn't the usual stuff. A quarter of a million dollars in counterfeit bills arrived from China, got caught in Ohio, and was headed to Oklahoma," Spud said. "The fact that it got seized shows you can't make up fake currency, nor have it made for you."

"Or you'll be out your ten bucks," Edge quipped, initiating a round of laughter from his fellow operatives.

"On a more serious note, we have a manhunt going on right now spanning three states. The suspect is wanted for murdering three people."

"Yeah, well we have a guy we're looking for who has murdered two hundred and nineteen. He probably should take priority," Edge grumbled, prompting his teammates to initiate a vigorous round of knuckle-tapping on the conference room table.

"I'm betting my lovely wife would like UniPerp to get nabbed as well," Spud said.

"It's a given, but—"

Hank cut Edge off with, "Every time we get news of

another UniPerp event, for some reason I have a nightmare about Spot."

"You do?" Crow asked.

Hank and Spud both nodded.

"Did you have one while we were at Remote Base New Area 51?" Voice asked.

Nods again.

"What happened? In your nightmare, I mean?"

"Spot grabbed you from behind, cut out your bum ticker, and declared himself Wizard of Hal," Hank summarized.

Voice stared at her. "I don't *recall* you eating anything weird before going to bed."

"It's always something like that," Hank said. "I don't know it's Spot until he smiles. It's when I see his two missing teeth that I realize it's him."

"Uh... forgive me for asking this," Voice began tenuously. "But have you talked with Doc Andy about your nightmares?"

"More than once," Hank revealed. "He says they'll stop when Spot gets apprehended."

"We need to think about finding *him*, too," Crow said.

"Only one problem with that," Spud said. "It's still the U.S. Marshal's case, and they haven't asked for our help."

"And just how much do you think they're doing on it?" Crow demanded. "It's been over two years."

"If you believe the U.S. Marshals are going to slack off on a case involving a fugitive who murdered one of theirs, I suspect you are quite wrong," Spud asserted.

"They probably want to get the bastard worse than we do," Edge agreed.

"That's language a little uncharacteristic of you," Amigo noted.

"Any animal who tries to rape a woman needs to be put in a cage," Edge said.

"I don't really have anything else," Spud revealed. "Did we want to take some time to examine the UniPerp case?"

"Do we have anything new to examine? Other than the fact that he just killed seven more people?" Hank asked.

Voice was shaking his head. "You all can probably guess that I didn't really spend my crash days crashing. Four of the people he murdered were friends of mine. They were good guys. Didn't ever hurt anyone. Then UniPerp decides they should be his victims for who the hell knows why. But there's nothing new to know."

"Any bullets recovered?" Cloud asked.

"More than one. The forensics reports say the ones recovered all came from the same gun."

"Is the gun a match to the rifle he stole from one of the gunsmiths?" Hank asked.

Voice shrugged. "I guess that can be assumed."

"Never assume anything. Let's see if we can make a request through the FBI to get one of the bullets sent here so Doc Sue can see if it matches up."

"I'll put in the request," Voice said. "Like Edge said: this time it's personal. I want this guy so bad I can taste the blood."

CROW HAD ACCOMPANIED Hank to the York airport. Finding the Seneca standing ready on the ramp, he asked, "Downsizing a bit?"

"No. I want to go through some of the commercial maneuvers. We haven't done that in a while. Lazy eights, chandelles, steep turns, emergency descents, precision landings."

Crow chuckled. "Precision landings? Can anyone do a precision landing in a Seneca? They float like crazy in ground effect."

"They do, but back when I was taking 103UN more on my own, I learned a few tricks."

"I never have quite figured out why Piper didn't try a semi-tapered wing for the thing."

"It probably would have resulted in a wing too long to fit in a typical t-hangar," Hank postulated.

As she completed the preflight inspection and preparations, she reflected on how, when she'd first encountered the Seneca, she had felt it beyond her: too much additional speed, the complexity of flying an airplane with two engines... Now, with a considerable amount of time flying the unit's Latitudes, she considered the Seneca a pussycat. If it wasn't for her additional experience flying the unit's helicopter, she'd likely consider it to be a bit too slow as well. But given the H155 and the Seneca had similar airspeeds, the difference in speed between the Seneca and the Latitude didn't seem to count for as much. She would still take the Seneca out on occasion though, finding a flight rewarding and relaxing from the standpoint of being able to absent-mindedly watch the scenery pass by.

Today would be different, however. Though she found the commercial maneuvers challenging, certain of them left her with a feeling of foreboding. Steep, spiraling descents—a valuable maneuver to be proficient in for quickly escaping altitude in the event of something like smoke or fire aboard the aircraft—always left her a bit breathless. Smiling, she considered, though, that were there an actual fire aboard the aircraft, she'd be left a bit more breathless if she didn't feel she could get the airplane on the ground quickly. *There's only one way to escape a burning airplane, and that's by jumping out,* she considered. *It's a lot less messy when you're on the ground.* She also chuckled, remembering Cloud telling her at one point, "Air Traffic Control will consider you've declared an emergency if you use the 's' word or the 'f' word. Also if you say 'shit' or 'fuck'," the inference being that in aviation the 's' and 'f' words were 'smoke' and 'fire.'

"Alright, Captain. Let's see what you can do," Crow said once they'd gotten to a good altitude for the performance of the maneuvers.

"What do you want to see first?"

"Let's try the chandelles."

Hank did a mental review of the maneuver, then set up the twin-engine airplane at maneuvering speed. Using a roadway below her as a reference point, she swung smoothly into a banked turn and maintained the bank angle until ninety degrees through, then gradually rolled out until the wings of the Seneca were once again level and she was one hundred and eighty degrees away from her entry heading. The stall warning barely hinted at sounding, demonstrating that she had successfully bled off the airspeed as the Airman Certification Standards required as well.

"Good job!" Crow enthused. "Now drop back down and show me one in the opposite direction."

Hank did as requested, again completing the maneuver to the standards required for a commercial pilot.

As he had her drop down once again to work on a different maneuver, he remarked, "You should work on getting your ATP."

"Why do I need an *Airline Transport Pilot* certificate?" she groused. "It's not like I'm going to go fly for an airline. Not now, not ever."

He leaned toward her. "It's a challenge," he prodded.

Hank started to mutter. "You guys always snooker me into doing additional training by leading me along with that 'it's a challenge' stuff."

"You noticed?" Crow said, his eyes twinkling at her.

Hank just grumbled.

"We do the same thing to Spud, you know."

"No you don't. With him, it's always, 'You don't want Hank to completely outclass you, do you?'"

Crow laughed. "You noticed that too."

"*He* noticed, then mentioned it to me."

"So... you'll get the ATP?"

"Oh, for fuck's sake! Quit twisting my arm!"

"Edge said he'd work on his..."

"You're not going to cajole me into doing it that way either."

Crow shrugged. "Suit yourself. After all, I don't mind seeing a man gloat about being ranked higher than a woman at something."

Hank glared at him.

"Just sayin'."

"Oh, alright! I'll work on it!"

"Good. You and Spud can go off places so you can get the flight time in. Take our little birdie here. It's slower, so you can get more flight time in per trip. Maybe go visit some place with a nearby hotel so you can get some private time together."

She was still glaring at him.

"Just a suggestion."

She rolled her eyes. *Men!*

HANK WATCHED as Cloud and Crow whispered to one another conspiratorially.

"Did she bite?" Cloud asked.

Crow chuckled. "What do *you* think?"

"I'm not deaf, you know," Hank told them with a scowl from where she sat across the table from them at lunch.

"What?" Voice asked, having been somewhat self-absorbed.

Spud leaned to him and whispered, "Crow and Cloud are pressuring Hank to get an ATP."

"What's an ATP?" Voice whispered back.

"Airline Transport Pilot certificate."

Amigo was ignoring the entire exchange, focusing instead on examining what was on his plate. Edge was doing likewise.

"Mama Rose, what's this stuff?" Edge finally asked.

"What stuff?" she queried from the kitchen.

"These little thin noodle-y things."

"Those are rice noodles."

"What's sitting on them?"

Hank could tell that Rose was instantly exasperated.

"It's chicken, snow peas, shitake mushrooms, and beansprouts with oriental seasonings an' *why you gotta question everythin' I put on your plate?*"

"I've never had anything to eat that looks quite like this before, Mama Rose."

"Didn't I hear you ate a raccoon stew recently?"

"That was a survival exercise, Mama Rose."

"So is this," she asserted.

"How is this a survival exercise?" Edge asked, his tone full of indignation.

"This is an exercise to teach you to quit questionin' what

I feedju so I don't slap you in the head enough times to *kill* you," Rose promised.

"Don't fuck with Mama Rose," Hank quietly advised him.

"Language, Hank."

"I see I'm not the only one gotta put up with that big snowflake," Rose observed as she made her way back to the kitchen.

"Better watch out," Hank advised him. "If she ever gets to chatting with Amigo, she's likely to find out how *his* mama would slap him with a flip-flop."

Edge looked at her wide-eyed. "For heaven's sake, Hank —don't give her any ideas."

"Hank had a great flight review today," Crow announced in a bid to change the subject before Rose got riled up again.

"She can still do all the maneuvers," Spud concluded.

"To the standards, with no assistance from me," Crow related.

"I don't think I could learn how to fly," Voice said.

"I don't think I could learn how to program a quantum computer," Crow said, balancing the scales.

"I play with a sim sometimes," Voice revealed.

Crow looked at him and said, "If you can fly a sim, you probably wouldn't have a hard time with an actual airplane."

Edge disagreed. "You don't get the same feel that you do with a sim that you get in a real aircraft."

"What's the game plan for this afternoon?" Spud asked, likewise wanting to change the subject. He wasn't looking forward to having the present conversation segue to 'when do *you* want to go get some refresher training, Spud?'

"Hank and I had some training planned. It was put on the calendar," Amigo pointed out.

"I saw, but was curious about just what the training would involve," Spud clarified.

"We've got some new training guns in," Hank said. "Actually, conversion devices that we can retrofit our regular MK25s with so that they project a laser dot rather than shoot a bullet."

"What's that going to accomplish for us?" Edge wondered.

"Unlike a bullet that just pokes a hole wherever the bullet ended up, you can see the movement of the laser dot as you're pulling the trigger. Better yet, we can have Hal record it, and you can see the playback of what your shot looked like on your tablet, thanks to a little programming Voice did. You can tell if your trigger pull is smooth and whether or not you've got a shooting error going on. Then you can work at correcting it. Because the trigger pull will be the same as what you normally experience with your handgun, it will be a good way to determine if your trigger pull needs work without having problems masked by recoil."

HAVING FINISHED THEIR LUNCH, the team was now gathered in the Level 5 shooting range. Each was closely examining their issued SigSauer MK25 pistols that each now sported a bright yellow slide. Mounted where they might mount a tactical light was a small battery pack with a thin wire leading up and into the replacement slide. As each took Amigo and Hank's invitation to point their handgun down-range and pull the trigger, they all noted a bright red laser dot appear on their target downrange.

"Neat thing about this is we don't have to keep going down and stripping off shot-up targets," Crow remarked.

"Just do a little extra workout to make up for the exercise you're not going to get," Hank quipped. "Voice, can you let everyone see what was happening with their aim while they were pulling the trigger?"

Voice intoned, "Hal, display pointer movement to all FT tablets, one-half speed."

They all looked down at their tablets, noting that what they had thought was a steady dot actually was a dot with a bit of movement. What kind of movement, the direction, and the magnitude all were displayed, along with an analysis rendered by Hal of the probable trigger pull error that had created each along with potential corrective measures.

"This is pretty sweet," Spud said.

"Isn't it?" Amigo replied. "Hank and I have been coming down here to work on this system and get Voice to perfect the programming. You can come down, practice your trigger pull, and no need for Luigi to be up in the booth. No headset required either, nor safety glasses. Or come in your SWAT gear, or any of the unit wear. This system looks *only* at trigger pull, so you can isolate a trigger pull problem and work at correcting it without any of the other things involved."

"Too bad we don't have systems for those things as well," Edge bemoaned.

"Why? Do you feel you have problems with handgun skills?" Hank asked.

"You can always be better at anything you do," Edge pointed out.

"True, this will only help you with trigger pull," Hank said. "But for evaluating your stance, try running to a mark, aim, close your eyes, pull the trigger. If your shot is off, it's likely stance or grip. If you stand perfectly still, same thing. If you keep your eyes open and the shot is off, it's likely aim, breath control, trigger pull, or follow-through. Of course, we have to be able to accurately acquire our target and hit it, so it pays to pay attention to everything and make a conscious effort to correct any errors we discover so that getting it all correct becomes muscle memory."

"With the only problem being that with only six shooting fundamentals, it seems like there are at least a dozen things that can go wrong with each one," Crow observed.

"True. You'll chase the errors around and around, and about the time you think you've got them all, you discover there's another one out there or one you thought you'd eliminated is back like Freddy Kruger," Hank admitted. "That's what makes marksmanship such an interesting sport, though. There's always *something* to work on."

She walked to her own firing position. "Another good thing about this little system is that you don't need anyone standing over your shoulder. Hal is already there, and he can watch all of us at once." She grinned. "Meaning you can fire at will."

"WHAT ARE THESE?" Spud asked, sitting down next to Hank in the reading nook. He eyed a plate of what looked like squares with oatmeal in them.

"Oatmeal cookie bars," Hank replied, taking his offer of a mug of herb tea from him.

"What's in them?"

"Oatmeal, whole wheat flour, organic sugar, nuts, dried fruit, applesauce, and a few other things."

"Like what other things?" Spud persisted.

"Baking soda, salt, cinnamon, vanilla extract... stuff like that."

"What aren't you telling me?"

It was at this point that Hank realized Spud was playing "Edge."

She waited until he picked one up and took a bite. "Well, I wasn't going to tell you about the arsenic, but seeing as you asked..."

Spud grinned and gave her a kiss.

"Would you really bump me off?"

"Nah. I need *someone* who doesn't complain too much when I put my cold toes against his toasty balls to warm them up at night."

He mockingly took his pulse. "I think you went a little too light on the arsenic."

Hank pulled down her book from the bookshelf. Spying the cover, Spud asked, "Now *you're* reading about Ted Kaczynski?"

"This book is by another guy who also seems to think Kaczynski was some kind of modern-day philosopher rather than a slightly twisted murderer."

"Why read it?"

"I want to understand the mindset," she said. "Understand how Miller felt the need to cripple the Utah Data Center in the name of Ted Kaczynski." She sighed. "Reading about the stuff does make me weary, though."

"Then why read it?"

"Again, to understand the mindset."

Spud shrugged. "To each his own."

"You don't find wading through the news just as mind-numbing?"

"Mission First," he said unenthusiastically.

Hank dropped her book on the coffee table, turned, and straddled his lap. "I always warm your balls up for you again." Leaning toward the window, she pulled the shades shut and said, "Hal, hide Hank."

"Right here?"

"Why not?"

"Right now?"

"Again, why not?"

"I still have to prepare for the intel briefing tomorrow."

"If you do that afterward, it will take what? Forty-five minutes? An hour?" She leered at him. "That's enough time for you to be ready for Round Two."

He raised an eyebrow. "You're a bit..."

"Are you looking for a word? Try 'horny'."

He gazed at her.

"Are you complaining?" she asked, tugging at his belt.

"Hal, hide Spud."

TWO MEN SAT at the bar inside the Timber's Edge Bar and Grill, enjoying a late-night beer.

"Saw something funny today," one said to the other. "A guy came flying out of the woods out there along Bodas Road with a rifle in his hand. Had a truck sitting there by the edge of the road. Chucked his rifle in the back seat, climbed in and hauled on outta there like his pants were on fire."

The second guy laughed. "Bet he got caught poaching in the game preserve and had a ranger on his tail."

"I'd-a thought that, but he came from the south side of the road, not the north side."

"Really."

"Yep."

One of the other patrons had taken all of this information in. In his mind he was connecting some dots. He scowled, downed the last of his beer, and laid some money down on the bar saying, "Keep the change." Then he pulled on his jacket and left, not saying a word to anyone.

2

"You know what we should be planning?" Hank queried the rest of the team over breakfast. "Another hunt."

"You want to sneak down to Remote Base Roswell for oryx and feral hog?" Voice asked.

"Or another elk and bison trip to Wyoming?" Spud wondered.

"Yeah, so everyone who decides to stay and fish gets pickled again," Hank scoffed. "I was thinking more like moose."

"Where can we find moose?" Amigo asked.

"I was thinking Montana. Do we have a remote base anywhere in Montana?"

"Remote Base Lake Frances," Edge revealed.

Hank's face went straight to scowl. "So anyone who isn't hunting moose can stay and fish and get plastered again? Same shit, different remote base?"

Adopting as close to a Russian accent as he could, Edge snickered, "Maybe ve vill be hunting *squirrel*, Natasha. Besides," he continued in his normal voice, "we weren't at a remote base when we got plastered."

"Yeah, right. Like that makes a difference. Maybe you'll be out with me and Amigo, hunting moose. They're a big animal—lots of meat. Two people can't haul one back all by themselves. It'll likely take the entire team."

"Is it moose season in Montana?" Edge asked.

"If it isn't, I'm sure we can get the fish and game people up there to make an exception for a Homeland Security or FBI or DEA or even, given they're right on the border, a BORTAC unit to hunt a single animal."

"Bending the rules a little, aren't we?" Crow admonished.

Hank squirmed a bit.

"I think you just want a moose head on the wall in the den. Am I right, Love?" Spud asked. He was envisioning the thing. *Moose have got to be the ugliest big game animal on the planet.*

"When I was a kid, the family took a trip to Yellowstone for vacation. We went to one of those campfire lectures the rangers give. The ranger said that when God got done making everything else, He took the leftover parts and made a moose with them," Voice said.

That got the rest of the team laughing.

"So what if I *do* want a moose head on my wall?" Hank complained. "You all realize that before I got thrown out of a helicopter to join the unit, I had an elk head, a mulie head, an oryx head, a javalina, and even a *bear* head up on my wall. I bagged every one of them."

"Did you eat them?" Crow asked.

"Every one of them."

"Probably all by herself," Edge jested.

"I might have had a little help from a guy like you if he wasn't so squeamish about eating anything that didn't come out of a grocery store," she countered. "I also hear that moose is good eating."

Voice had been tapping on his tablet. "Not moose season

in Montana," he said. "As a matter of fact, it's not moose hunting season *anywhere* right now."

Hank slouched sullenly in her chair. The little angel on her right shoulder was saying, *That's the way it goes. You'll just have to wait until next time moose season comes up.* The little devil on her left shoulder was saying, *Do you think some state game agency is going to say no to an elite team, no matter **what** agency they say they're with?* She was leaning heavily toward the little guy on her left while the one on her right kept yelling, *Integrity, Hank! **Integrity!*** louder and louder. She sighed.

"Can we just make an inquiry and find out if they ever make exceptions?" She was well aware of the pleading tone in her voice.

"Do the honors for us, Voice," Spud suggested, knowing *no one* would hear the end of it until Hank got a definitive *no* for an answer—and not from the six of them, but from some official source.

Voice did some tapping on his tablet. "Sending a message directly through to Montana Fish, Wildlife, and Parks," he mumbled.

"Let me see that before you send it," Hank demanded, feeling certain there might be some language Voice was using that would guarantee that 'no' would be the answer.

The Department of Homeland Security would like to inquire as to whether an exception is ever made to conduct a hunt outside of the established hunting season for moose, she read after Voice had handed her his tablet. *Our Special Operations Unit is making the request.* She looked questioningly at Voice.

"If it's acceptable to you, hit 'send'."

She smiled and poked the 'send' icon on his tablet. "Now what?"

Voice shrugged. "We wait for them to answer."

"SIT. STAY," Spud said as the team gathered for the morning intelligence briefing. He noticed that Chip obediently complied. "Now if the rest of you dogs would follow suit?"

"Are you calling me a bitch?" Hank asked, arms crossed defiantly.

"I was referring to the other members of the team. I know that *you* will submit to me, wife."

"Last time I embed in an extremist group with *you*," Hank grumbled as she sat.

"First up, we have a search for two children aged two and three in Oklahoma."

"Let me guess: a parent is suspected," Voice said.

"Give the man a quarter. They have the mother in custody."

Spud consulted his tablet again. "We have a story of an interesting attempt at divorce. It seems that the potential victim has artificial knees and has to take a dose of four antibiotic pills before any dental surgery. He had also had a recent surgery, and was given four doses of a very powerful pain killer."

"Let me guess," Amigo said. "The wife saw an opportunity as he was getting ready to go to the dentist and swapped the pills in the bottles. Am I right?"

"Give Amigo a quarter, too. The only problem was that although he should have died from the four doses of painkiller, he didn't. When his medicine cabinet was searched, they found the four doses of antibiotic in the antibiotic bottle, but they also found a little residue of antibiotic in the pain killer bottle. Upon closer examination, they also found a little pain killer residue in the antibiotic bottle. It seems the mister was very suspicious of the missus, given she had actually threatened to kill him on numerous occasions. Thus, instead of getting his retirement account, she gets three hots and a cot in a women's penitentiary."

Hank was sitting looking off in the distance, strumming her fingers on her cheek. Spud eyed her, and she quickly folded her hands on the table and looked up in the air.

"Love?"

She looked at him and grinned. "Did I make you nervous?"

He gave her a sideways look.

"We have an unusual vehicle theft that got thwarted by the Border patrol in Maine. Make a guess; maybe you can win a quarter too. I'll give you a hint: the vehicle came from Canada."

"A bus," Edge said.

"Sorry, buddy—no quarter for you."

"A plane?" Crow asked.

"You may stay seated. No need for any sort of celebration," Spud told him.

"A boat," Voice said.

"Our fucking genius is cleaning up today. Indeed, it was a boat: specifically, a fishing boat. No mention of why the fine citizen of Canada believed he needed it, nor why he needed it in the U.S. of A., but there you have it."

"Then how come I haven't seen any quarters coming my way yet?" Voice asked accusingly.

"Did you really expect anyone to hand over a quarter to you?" Crow asked.

"*I'm needy!*" Voice protested. "Dog treats aren't cheap, y'know."

"Yeah, right. Like Gil or Chandra makes you pay for them," Edge said.

"Here's an unusual story for our CBP guys out there.

They recently had to help extract a hunter with a broken leg from the middle of Nowhere, Texas."

"CBP does a lot of search and rescue work," Amigo said. "A lot of areas on both the northern and the southern border are in the middle of nowhere."

"This guy wasn't out there trekking around on his own, I hope," Hank said.

"Apparently, he was. When he became overdue for returning home is when the missus decided to call in the cavalry, and the cavalry decided to ask CBP for assistance with a helicopter."

"I'm glad he's ok, but that wasn't the smartest thing to do," Hank asserted. "Go with a buddy and make sure someone knows where *both* of you went."

Voice took a glance at his watch, then activated his own tablet. He scowled.

"Whatcha got?" Hank asked. "UniPerp?"

"No. Montana Fish, Wildlife, and Parks."

"Ooo! What do they say?"

"Not much," Voice said, giving the tablet a shove away from him.

Before he could protest, Hank grabbed the tablet and got a look. She then gave it a kiss. None of the men knew if this meant they should be happy or not.

"Ordinarily, we do not grant requests for hunting outside of established hunting seasons," she read. "In this case, however, we may be able to accommodate you. We have an aggressive moose that has necessitated that we close one of our more popular hunting and fishing camps on Hungry Horse Reservoir. If you would like to come to the area prior to our usual booking period which begins in May in order to assist in the elimination of this moose—"

"Shit," Cloud said, interrupting her.

"What the fuck, Cloud," she protested. "We get a *ton* of meat and help out the folks in Montana as well. What's your problem?"

"It's barely making it above forty degrees and overnights are subfreezing in Montana right now."

"How the hell do *you* know?"

"I looked it up after you mentioned this harebrained idea at breakfast."

"You're just pissed because you can't go fish and... get pissed," Hank said, pointing her finger at him.

"Maybe we should ask Doc Wright if he wants to be on the medical away team this time," Edge said.

Hank glared at him.

"You're just upset because last time you weren't able to... massage away Spud's stiffness," Cloud noted, getting an angry glare from Hank.

"I think that was the problem," Voice said. "Spud was so drunk he didn't *have* any stiffness."

That got him a glare from Spud as well as Hank.

"That's enough," Edge said. "Hank's right. We have the opportunity to get a lot of meat and help out the folks in Montana, too."

"And you don't have a problem just being a Sherpa to haul a moose back into camp?" Cloud asked.

Edge stood up and casually flexed his chest. "I happen to like to eat, and Hank hasn't steered us wrong on a hunt yet." Relaxing, he added, "Doc Rich is happy as can be with us eating game meat, too. Says it's better for us than just about anything other than the organic stuff we get from Gil."

"You're taking her side."

"Yes, I am. I'm more than ready to spend a little time outside the Mole Hole without it being on a mission. Our last training exercise got cut short, in case you don't remember."

"I was sleeping in a hole in the ground. How could I forget?"

Edge just looked at him, his blue eyes boring holes in the former Army man.

"You Army guys—"

"Let's not even go there," Spud cautioned.

"Let's not. Let's go to Montana instead," Hank said with a smirk.

"Ok. We head to Montana to hunt down a rogue moose," Spud said, wondering if he should try emulating Boris Badenov as well. He discarded the notion by a vision of Hank's back, clad in a t-shirt and gym shorts, given she had no pajamas or nightgowns, on the other side of the bed from him. *Do not ruffle the wife.*

Hank was looking at him closely. "Decided not to say that, didn't ya?"

"It would have been a bad idea," he replied to the curious looks of his teammates.

"It's your exercise, so you get to plan it," Amigo said, hoping she would relent.

"No problem. Which campsite is it that they had to close?" she asked of Voice.

"Emery Bay."

"Is that on the water?" Edge asked.

"Dunno. I didn't check that out," Voice admitted.

Hank was doing so, however.

"Oh, this is going to be so incredible. It's right on the water, and pretty remote."

"What are the amenities?" Edge asked.

"Um... Water, pit toilets." She paused, scouring the campsite information for more. "Looks like that's it."

"Another survival exercise," Edge said. "Making up for the one we didn't finish?"

"Not at all," Hank said, smiling. "There's an RV rental place in nearby Kalispell." She grinned broadly. "We're going to camp in style."

"Really? You're thinking about renting RVs?" Crow was gaining some enthusiasm for this trip. "I've seen some of those. Some of them are just like living in a house. Some of them even *cost* as much as a house."

"I figure if we rent four of them, we can have Crow, Cloud, and Amigo in one, Edge and Voice in another, the medical team in another, and Spud and I get the last one."

"Naturally. You'll hunt, and Spud will keep you warm at night," Voice poked.

"We can have Page come along instead of Doc Frank," Hank suggested.

"Page and I made a pledge that if at all possible, we'd avoid being on a mission of any kind together," Voice revealed. "Besides, I'll have Chip along—"

"The dog is coming again?" Crow asked.

"Is there a problem with Chip being there? He has to be used to being around the team. Training and missions both."

"Does Page know you love that dog more than you love her?" Edge asked.

"Page and I *both* love Chip," Voice asserted.

"I still think it's roughing it with no electricity," Spud said.

"Those things have generators," Crow said. "As long as you have gasoline, you've got electricity."

"But don't they usually require individual water and sewer hook-ups?" Spud asked.

"They have holding tanks," Crow said. "As long as we're

not out there forever, we can just drive out to a dump station to flush the black water and gray water tanks."

"If need be, we can drain tanks into a pit toilet, too," Hank said. "We'd just probably need to take a turd tote."

"*A what?*" a chorus of men's voices asked.

"It's a thing you can use to drain the tanks and then wheel it over to where you can dump it."

"This is going to be a bit different than accompanying presidents on trips," Spud noted.

"Oh, everyone quit grousing. You haven't lived until you do a hunt from a base camp like the one we'll set up," Hank said. "This is going to be a lot of fun, and the accommodations will beat the Taj Mahal hands down."

HE SAT CONTEMPLATING HIS COFFEE. With some time before he had to head out to work, he thought about what he knew.

She's dead. The love of my life, and she's dead. Why?

He thought of all the people who could be responsible. The other man. The neighbor. The other man's former lover who wanted the guy so badly that she destroyed his marriage.

Holly never hurt a fly.

He remembered, too, Holly talking about being annoyed by someone shooting in the woods behind her house. *Stupid hunters,* she had said. *Don't they look before they start shooting at things?*

He thought about what he knew, and decided he needed to know more.

I'm a God-fearing man. Remember what the Bible says Abraham asked of God: 'Wilt thou also destroy the righteous with the wicked?' Yes, the wicked must pay, just as did Sodom and Gomorrah. And I will find out who did this wicked thing, Holly.

SPUD WAS ONCE AGAIN down in the lowest level of the head-quarters complex, getting some additional pointers from Amigo on tactical rifle shooting. The two of them were standing twenty-five yards from the target line, with three targets set up on the carriers in front of them.

"Let's review all the basics," Amigo said. "Going to start with a single center-of-mass shot from a low ready position. We're looking for accuracy first and foremost, Spud. Remember: slow is smooth, smooth is fast, accuracy is everything. Gonna give you a ready, then a fire about three seconds later. Got it?"

"Sure thing."

"Ready... *fire!*"

Spud brought his rifle up and took a single shot to the target, placing his shot nearly centered in the four-inch circle that defined the center of mass location.

"Good job. Let's do that a couple more times. You know me: I don't like saying that it's time to move on until I'm sure what I'm seeing isn't a fluke."

Repeating the exercise with similar results, Amigo then had Spud move back another five yards, then another, until they were finally situated at one hundred yards from the target. Being satisfied that Spud could perform the simple task with accuracy and reasonable speed, they then moved forward again to repeat the drill, this time from a high ready starting position.

"I'm still surprised you don't practice this stuff with

Hank," Amigo remarked as they moved back to the twenty-five-yard position.

"She's working out with Edge this morning. She still considers herself a hundred-and-twenty-five-pound weakling."

Amigo laughed. "Somehow, I don't think she and Edge are exactly matched."

Spud shrugged. "Her philosophy is that if she takes on the person she believes has the most skill at something she feels she's weak on, it will give her more incentive to improve."

"Así o así," Amigo said. "I take a little different tactic: go against the person I feel is *slightly* better than me until I feel either equal to or superior to him. Or her. I'm still trying to be as good as Hank with a firearm."

"The difficulty you're going to have there is that Hank always considers she needs to be a little better than she is at everything—firearms included. She competes against herself."

"She's driven," Amigo agreed.

They ran through the drill again, this time with Spud starting with the muzzle of his gun pointed upward: the high ready position. Again, he progressed through the drill smoothly and accurately, with reasonable speed.

"Doing well, my man," Amigo said encouragingly. "Let's add a twist. Three targets, one round to each target. Ready for this one?"

"Sure."

EDGE AND HANK stood squared off in the gym, Edge with a training knife in his hand. Hank was unarmed.

"This is going to be good training for you," Edge assured her.

"I hope so. I've been a bit leery of knives ever since Nickell gave me the lovely tattoo I have on my hip."

"Let's see if we can help you avoid getting another one." He flipped the training knife casually in his hand, adopting a grip on it that would allow him to make a stabbing motion straight to Hank's belly.

"This is going to be a simple blocking maneuver. I go to stab you, you block the attack by deflecting the knife to your right. I go to stab you again, this time use your left arm and deflect to your left."

"I tried deflecting Nickell's knife and still got slashed," Hank reminded him.

"Yeah, but he was trying to slash your throat and you got a superficial cut on your hip instead. Take your pick."

"Well, when you put it *that* way..."

Edge started out slowly, allowing Hank to get the blocking motion down. Then he gradually increased speed, requiring Hank to move yet faster. Soon they were both exchanging motions in rapid succession: Edge repeatedly trying to complete a stab to Hank's abdomen, Hank doing her best to keep deflecting the blade to the side alternately with right and left hands and arms.

"That's right—keep moving your arm away from your body as mine slides up on it," Edge said, encouraging her. "The knife will move farther and farther from your body as you do."

"Does this work if you're trying to stab me in the throat as well?" Hank asked, remembering that Nickell had tried a similar move.

Edge worked his stabbing motions up higher and higher with Hank's counteractions also moving higher and higher.

Being able to successfully block the moves even when Edge was stabbing toward her throat assured her the technique would work.

Resting a bit, Hank observed, "The difference, though, is that Nickell was making a slashing motion to my throat."

"And you blocked him, driving his hand downward. That's how he managed to cut you on your hip. But you only need one arm to block an attack. Use the other one for an attack of your own."

"Punch him?" Hank asked.

Edge grinned at her. "This is Krav Maga, little lady. Fight like a girl."

Hank scowled at him. "What the hell is *that* supposed to mean?"

Edge laughed again, this time louder. "You women fight *nasty,*" he said. "Go for his eyes. Jab your finger in a nostril and drive his head backwards. As he's falling to the floor— and he will with you tearing up his face like that—give him a swift one in the balls."

"You want me to try that?"

"Not with me, please," Edge said with a negative wave of his hand. "Maybe just shove on my face. But remember: you've got lots of options. Gouge his eyes. Stick a thumb in his nostril and tear his nose off his face. Head-butt him in the throat, then bite his shoulder."

"Good gawd!"

"Yeah, nasty. But nasty is very effective in hand-to-hand combat."

VOICE WAS ONCE AGAIN in the residence level with James done up in what James referred to as "the Michelin Man suit." Voice had noted that although James complained, he not only never said no to working with Chip but also never was late unless he was doing something for one of the doctors or for Doc Sue in Forensics. He was also getting pretty good at being the "bad guy," giving Chip a merry chase and even trying to fool him by acting nonchalant or offering him treats. *All the sneaky stuff some actual perp would try.*

Chip wasn't fooled. If Voice told him to apprehend James, then that's what he did.

Presently, James had treed himself atop the cargo net climb. Chip was making his way up, and James was maneuvering to the other side of the top of the obstacle. Chip hung by his paws, the cargo net jittering in response to the dog's attempts to ferret out a way to get to James. In the end, Chip opted to finish climbing to the top and dash across to where James was now descending down the net. Jumping down, Chip then began to harangue James from the ground, barking, growling, and jumping in an attempt to grab James. James just laughed at the dog and climbed back up to the top.

"Sooner or later, you're going to get sick of sitting up there," Voice said, smiling.

"Call the dog off, cop, and I'll come down."

Just like the real thing, Voice thought. "Chip!" He gave the command to heel once he had Chip's attention.

While Chip trotted over to take his place to Voice's left, James took the opportunity to climb down halfway and jump down the rest of the way, taking off in the opposite direction. Voice sent Chip after him, Chip easily wrestling the man to the ground after charging full speed in pursuit.

"Don't know what I'd do without you," Voice

commented to James. "You're really helping me to get Chip trained to be a good police dog."

"As long as he doesn't get the idea that every black guy out there is a bad guy," James remarked.

"You've got a point. Black guy, white guy, Japanese guy... woman. They can all be perps. I should get Hank to help me with this too."

James laughed. "Might be dangerous for the dog. She could bite him."

"She growls, but she doesn't bite," Voice chuckled in agreement. "And you're reminding me: I have a little job I have to do, unless I want to keep doing yard work for her until the day I die."

"She's got you doing yard work?"

"Yeah, ever since Chip dug up her flowers."

James laughed. "I've heard she's a little anal about her flowers. And her rocks."

"Ya think?"

"Tell you what: you call off the dog, and I'll help you plant her flower beds."

"For real? After putting you through all this crap?" Voice asked.

"I'm kind-a flattered, really. I never thought the team would ask me to do anything mission- or training-related, to tell you the truth."

Voice reached out for a fist-bump. "Thanks, buddy. I have no idea how to arrange a flowerbed, and I'm sure Hank will give me that look and tell me to do it over if she doesn't like it."

"You're in luck, my man. Planting flowers is something I do myself. Gotta keep up with the neighbors."

"WHAT DID you guys get done today?" Amigo asked as the team sat down to lunch.

"Hank wanted to work on knife skills. Specifically, how to avoid getting stabbed," Edge said.

"Been there, done that once. Once is enough," Hank said.

"Like I said, though, getting a superficial cut across your hip beats getting a good slash across your throat," Edge said. "You did well against Nickell."

"I had a case of wrong-thinking," Hank admitted. "I never thought he'd actually try to kill me. We were partners, after all."

"I imagine things don't go all that well for disgraced FBI agents in prison," Edge remarked.

"You know the saying. He made his bed and he had to sleep in it. Though he took the only way out he probably thought he had. But he had the choice to just man up and rebuild his life rather than take the path he took in the first place.

"What about you, Amigo? Did you get Spud to do a few rifle drills?"

"Yeah, and he did fine."

"Hank believes I'm allergic to rifles," Spud said. "I'm guessing Voice isn't allergic to flowers, though."

"Oh, he did a great job getting the flowerbed back in shape after Sir Digsalot got done pulling out all my posies," Hank acknowledged.

"I got some help from James," Voice said with a nod in James's direction, having invited the lab tech-slash-pharmacist to lunch. "You'll notice I have shrubs. Flowers escape me unless they're growing on an azalea."

"What did you guys do?" Voice asked Crow.

Crow looked over at Cloud. Cloud shrugged.

"We went over to Grand Island and grabbed a couple of burgers at Sin City Grill."

"You didn't."

"It's not far from the airport, and they have a crew car they let pilots take to get something to eat."

"So... while we were polishing up on our skills, you two were polishing off burgers?" Edge asked. His menacing look didn't bring a sense of comfort to the two senior aviators.

"Which aircraft did you take?" Spud asked.

Crow looked at Cloud again, getting another shrug.

"One of the Latitudes."

"You guys took a *Latitude* to grab a hamburger?" Hank asked incredulously.

"What's the problem?" Amigo wondered.

"Two thousand dollars an hour operating cost is the problem," Hank said. "Pilots always talk about a hundred-dollar hamburger. The burger is five bucks, but the airplane is a hundred. Only *these two jokers* just had themselves a *thousand-dollar* hamburger apiece. Wait till the committee gets wind of *this* one!"

"The flight required that we maintain our skills," Crow said in their defense. "We shot a couple of approaches before we landed..." His voice trailed off. He could see that five of his teammates weren't buying it. The five who hadn't gone to Grand Island for a burger.

James laughed out loud while shaking his head. "Doc Rich is spot on when she calls you guys 'the children'."

Chip gave out a single bark.

"You tell 'em, Chip."

Edge broke off his steady gaze that he'd been skewering the two pilots with. Giving them both a stern look, he said, "I guess I'm going to need to give *you two* a little extra attention during the gym session this afternoon."

"Is that going to be some kind of *retaliation?*" Cloud asked.

Edge sat back. His face was one hundred percent Marine drill instructor.

"You just said that after breakfast, the two of you went over to Grand Island and ate burgers. I'm imagining you didn't skip the fries. Then you come back here and eat lunch. Part of *my* job in the team is to make sure everyone stays in peak physical condition. You can't stay in peak physical condition if you're going to down three thousand extra calories a day. You're going to have to work those extra calories off."

His look could rival anything Doc Rich had ever rendered to a team member. They were both having instant regrets.

HANK CAME into the reading nook, a plate of cookies and two mugs of herb tea in her grip. Setting them on the coffee table, she sat next to Spud and took up her tablet.

"Done with your book on Ted Kaczynski?"

Hank scoffed. "More a book on how the author agrees with him. These people are just plain nuts."

"You don't believe that technology is taking over the world," Spud said.

"The tech has *no ability* to take over the world. Ultimately, it's dependent upon humans to maintain it. Do repairs, provide electricity, provide raw materials... the list goes on and on. I won't argue that there are *people* who would like to use technology to take over the world, but even there you will always have someone who is willing to reveal that they're doing it, and just *how* they're doing it."

Spud smiled. "What are you reading now? Another crime novel?"

"This thing is a crime in and of itself," she said, still scoffing.

Spud raised an eyebrow. "What is it?"

"A dystopian zombie novel."

This time Spud raised *both* eyebrows.

"Why are you reading it? Because if you tell me you want to understand the mindset, it's simple: zombies want to eat your brains."

"And apparently, according to this author, zombie hunters are immortal—like zombies, I guess—and just want to spread zombie gore all over the countryside." She scowled even deeper. "Plus, the ego he instills in his main character is enough to make you gag."

"You don't have to finish it."

"Yeah, I do. It will make me appreciate the next book I read much better. *Nothing* could be as bad as this one!"

She read on for a bit and then shut down her tablet.

"Thank *God* I'm done with that!"

Spud chuckled. "I told you: you didn't have to finish it."

"Maybe I always hold out hope that something good will come in the end. In this case, it was misplaced hope."

She reached up for a print book from her shelf.

"What's next?" Spud asked.

"Another book on technocracy. This is a small treatise. I could probably finish it tonight."

Spud grasped her book and pulled it gently from her hands.

"I'm done with checking out the news, and would like to move on to something else."

"Like what?"

"Like making you submit to me, wife."

"I'm going to hurt you," Hank warned him.

"No, you're not. You're going to submit to me."

"Why would I do that, Neanderthal?"

"Because you love it as much as I do."

She gazed at him. He smiled. She gazed some more. He reached out and drew her near, giving her a gentle kiss.

"Bible says a man should love his wife."

"I don't think what you have in mind is what the Bible intended."

"Sure it is. Bible says, 'Be fruitful and multiply'."

"We can't multiply. We've both been sterilized, remember?"

"We can try." His eyes were twinkling.

"We will fail. At least we'd *better* fail."

"We'll never know until we try." He began to caress her. "You want to try, don't you?"

"I should hate you."

"But you don't."

He could see her softening up.

"You're right. I love you."

"I thought so." He got up and picked her up. As he carried her off to the bedroom, he added, "I love you too. Very, *very* much."

3

"We'll go through the newsworthy items first, then Hank will fill us in on the Mission to Murder Bullwinkle," Spud said.

"This mission might be a little *rocky*," Edge remarked.

"Keep it up, guys," Hank complained.

"We can't go fishing," Edge pointed out.

"You can't go drinking beer until you're five sheets to the wind," Hank countered, pointing at the five guilty parties from the last hunting trip. "And *you*," she said, looking directly at Edge. "Didn't you tell me you'd never taken a drink?"

The rosy color Edge's face turned was in stark contrast to both his blond hair and his blue eyes. Sheepishly, he amended his prior remarks to, "Before the unit, that is."

"Yup. And then it was only once. Once was enough," Hank concluded.

"I am not about to break that rule," Spud announced. "And with that, let me get to the news."

He sat back and activated his tablet.

"We have an interesting apprehension that was made by the Border Patrol in Arizona. It seems they made a vehicle stop and discovered a couple of men heading southbound. The men declared that they were illegal immigrants, and because they had been unable to obtain work were asking to be immediately deported back to Mexico. Upon running the tag of the vehicle they were driving, it was determined that it was stolen. It was also determined that the two men had recently escaped from a prison in Utah. The U.S. Marshals thanked the CBP profusely for not swallowing the 'we just want to go home' line."

"Aw. Their families down south of the border will be heartbroken, I'm sure," Hank said.

"Given that they are both U.S. citizens, it's more likely that their families *north* of the border will be the heartbroken ones," Spud said.

"Some other folks who will be heartbroken due to a CBP seizure will likely be the ones whose eight-hundred-and fifty thousand dollars got confiscated before it could head south as well."

"That's a boatload of loot," Edge commented.

"Literally," Spud said. "They were attempting to get it across the Rio Grande when a CBP Air and Marine unit boat interdicted them.

"We have a story from ICE. It seems one of our brothers in blue went bad."

"What did he do?" Crow asked.

"He got caught with a boatload of something, too. In his case, it was child pornography."

"Oh, they *love* guys with 'short eyes' in prison," Hank said. "And a cop to boot? That guy wasn't thinking. *Not at all!*"

"He wasn't the only one caught for child porn," Spud said. "They got a pastor too."

Hank laughed. "Then the pastor can pray for them both, because they're going to need it."

"You can reveal a downright mean streak when you hear news about these kinds of guys," Voice observed.

Hank looked at him. You know, with *that* look. "You don't think they deserve anything and everything I can think of?"

"Didn't say that," Voice admitted. "I think of someone doing that to the kids I hope I have one day and it twists my stomach into one giant knot."

Hank got that other look. The smug one.

"And taking the place of You Just Can't Make This Stuff Up this morning, we have something from the 'oddly coincidental' department," Spud announced. "It seems that a neighborhood in Utah had an unwelcome visitor."

"You're not going to tell us it was a moose," Crow ventured.

"I *am* going to tell you it was a moose," Spud replied. "And it seems he was a rather unhappy moose as well."

"What'd he do?"

"He went down the street knocking over garbage cans, kicking down mailboxes, and blocking unhappy workers in their driveways, making them late for work. The police arrived and attempted to collar said moose, whereupon he took off across front yards, back yards, over fences—basically giving the cops some good exercise to work off their morning donut calories. The Division of Wildlife Resources got involved, declared Mr. Moose to be 'grumpy', and settled him down with a nice tranquilizer dart before relocating him to a neighborhood far from the one he was in. A neighborhood with pretty much nothing but trees. They're hoping he'll find his new digs a bit more amenable than the neighborhood he trashed."

"Has anyone asked if the folks in Montana have tried relocating the moose that's giving them fits?" Edge asked.

"I did," Voice said. "They say they've tried relocating him

several times. No matter how far away they release him, he always manages to find his way back."

"See what happens? When you drug a moose, he just comes back for more. Drugs are bad," Hank asserted.

"Gonna *really* be bad for our Montana moose," Amigo said, "given we're gonna shoot him."

"That's what I've got. Now I'll turn it over to my lovely, if not somewhat possessed wife, so she can fill us in on what she's been doing for our moose hunt," Spud said as he simultaneously stuck his thumbs against his temples and spread his fingers as if to adorn himself with moose antlers.

Hank gave him a narrow-eyed look. "Funny guy."

Sitting back after stuffing one of Rose's goodies in her mouth, she said, "Haow, dispway FD Seven pwee– pwee—" She gulped down what was in her mouth. "Presentation."

"Good thing Hal understands Mouthful Hank," Voice said as the monitor sprung to life.

"Bite me."

"Now that the *lady* has spoken..." Edge remarked.

Hank just looked at him. She wasn't about to apologize.

"First, my thought is to go directly into Kalispell. Well, nearby La Salle, actually. Glacier Park International Airport. They've got nine thousand and seven feet of runway and an ILS, so no sweat getting one of the Latitudes into it. I've arranged for rental of four pickups."

"What do we need four pickups for?" Edge wondered.

"To haul the four travel trailers we're picking up in Kalispell," Hank answered.

"We're hauling trailers?"

Hank gave him a look. "Do you have a problem with hauling a trailer?"

"Not me," Edge said. "But how many other guys here have hauled a trailer before?"

Cloud and Amigo both raised their hands. Hank looked over at Spud, grinning.

"Don't look at me. I could barely handle the little trailer we took into Shining City."

"Should have seen his knuckles," Hank said conspiratorially. "White as the new driven snow."

"Who'll haul the fourth trailer, then?" Edge asked.

"You're looking at her."

"You can haul a trailer?"

Hank sighed. "Do I have to say it again? Yes, I can haul a trailer. My dad was an aviation mechanic. We had to haul lots of stuff. I can drive a stick, and I can haul a trailer. Before you even ask, yes—I can back one up too."

"There are lots of jokes out there about women backing up trailers," Crow remarked.

Hank jabbed a hand into a pocket and withdrew a quarter. Slapping it on the table, she said, "One try. Anyone care to put some money on it?"

She could see her teammates pondering that one. Then they all gave a glance to Spud, who was rendering his best Secret Service face. They all pondered some more, trying to decide if the neutral expression on Spud's face was to hide the fact that Hank *couldn't* haul a trailer or that she *could*.

She took out five more quarters and stacked them atop the first one. "That's one for each of you," she said. "Ante up or shut up."

"What the hell," Voice finally said, taking out a quarter and sliding it over to her stack of them. "It's just a quarter."

"It's not *just* a quarter," Crow emphasized. "It's a *principle*."

Voice shrugged. "Maybe she's good at one of those little flatbed things. But this is going to be a *camping trailer*."

Crow considered that before adding his quarter to

Voice's. It wasn't long before five quarters stood next to Hank's pile of six.

Spud reached out and took the topmost quarter off of Hank's stack and handed it back to her. "Given I have knowledge of your ability or lack thereof for hauling a trailer, I have to recuse myself."

"Can she haul a trailer?" Edge asked.

As his teammates all looked for the answer on Spud's face, he began to look around behind himself.

"Whatchya lookin' for?" Amigo asked.

"The idiot in the room," Spud replied. Looking at the five others, he said, "Oh, *there* they are. Because if anyone thinks I'm going to piss off my wife and get to sleep on the couch for a week, then you must be idiots."

"Ok. Then you hold the quarters," Hank concluded.

She continued with, "We drive the trucks into Kalispell and pick up the four trailers I've rented. Then it's off to Emery Bay, where we'll set up camp. Get a good night's sleep, and then spend the rest of our time hunting our pesky moose for the good folks in Montana."

"No stay at Lake Francis?" Edge asked.

"Is there anywhere close by where we can get a Latitude in?" Hank asked.

"Great Falls International," Edge replied. "It's almost as far away from Lake Francis as Kalispell is, but the route is mostly via Interstate 15, with a bit on local roads once you get to Conrad. Conrad has a dinky little airport, but no services we could use. No jet-A for sale, for instance."

"Ok, then. After the hunt, we'll head to Remote Base Lake Francis and rest up a bit, then back here," Hank said. "Sound good?"

"If we can go fishing," Edge said.

"Is it fishing season in Montana?"

"You can fish in lakes year round," Edge replied.

"And all you want to do is fish."

Edge gave her his typical exasperated look. "The beer last time was Doc Wright's idea."

"You didn't have to take him up on it," Hank said.

Edge hung his head.

"Who's on the medical away team this time?"

Hank noticed everyone slide down in their seats a bit.

"Oh, for fuck's sake. Don't tell me Doc Wright volunteered."

"Ok, we won't tell you," Voice said.

Hank glared. "Medical 1."

"How can I help you, Hank?" he replied.

"You won't be prescribing anything not absolutely medically required while on this trip. Am I correct?"

"Not knowing who would kill me first—you, or Doc Rich—the answer is no."

With that, Hank was satisfied. "Alright. Pack your fishing rods."

HE HAD a little time before he had to get back to his job. Picking up his phone, he called a reporter for the Duluth paper.

"I was wondering if there was any more news on the shooting death of Holly Fay."

He paused while the reporter answered him.

"Do they have anything new at all? The caliber of weapon that killed her, for instance? Anything like that?"

Waiting for the answer once again, he said, "A .243 Winchester. And they still have no idea who the killer is?"

After getting the reply, he thanked the reporter and hung up.

"Not exactly an uncommon round," he mused. "It might be harder to track down who killed Holly than I thought."

"I NOTICED you all had a good lunch. Now let's work it off," Edge said.

The rest of the team had noticed Edge smile as he said this. It wasn't a comforting smile, either. More like one that foretold of how much pleasure Edge was going to get from watching his teammates sweat.

"First, we'll do a little exercise designed to give you flexibility in your ankles, hips, and shoulders. Going to get down so your left leg is at ninety degrees, thigh parallel to the floor. Right knee is on the ground, and right toe is flexed like this."

Edge assumed the position.

"Now hands behind your head like I'm about to frisk you. Twist your body so you're facing left, then back to center. Left again, back to center. We'll do this six times."

"I thought last time you had us do this exercise, it was five times," Hank pointed out.

"Maybe it was." Edge in fact *knew* it was, but he was intent on continually bringing the team to an even higher level of fitness than they currently exhibited. "One more won't kill ya."

Spud was smiling just enough for Hank to notice.

"Quit that," she admonished him.

"What?"

"I know what you're thinking," she whispered just loud

enough so only he could hear. It made no difference. Crow snickered anyway.

Doing the six repetitions and then switching which leg was kneeling on the floor and doing six more, Edge then moved on to another exercise.

"Now we're going to do a bridge. Lie on your back, knees bent, feet on the floor, arms out to your sides. Raise your butt off the floor so that you're supported by your shoulders, arms, and feet. We'll do seven repetitions of this one."

"I thought it was six last time."

Edge gave Hank a look. "It's seven this time."

Crow once again looked over to Spud and snickered.

"Is this one how Hank hurt her back that time?" he asked.

Now the rest of the team snickered. Everyone except Edge.

"That's enough."

Spud chuckled and began to quietly sing a tune. "You make me feel so young. You make me feel like spring has sprung..."

"Spring ain't what you're wanting to get sprung," Voice surmised.

"That's enough," Edge said. "You guys are acting like a bunch of oversexed teenagers."

"Gonna yell at us for talking in ranks, Gunny?"

Edge went over and planted a foot on Voice's stomach. "One more for you, little buddy."

Try as he might, Voice couldn't lift his hips from the floor. Not with the extra weight of Edge's leg on top of him.

"Weakling. Ok, now let's try ten elbow push-ups. Plank position, hands in front of your face, toes flexed. Push up..."

"I thought—"

"Yeah, we did eight last time. This time, we're doing ten."

Finishing that exercise, Edge announced, "Let's try the bird dog. Hands and knees, feet flexed, left arm out along with right leg. Back to the starting position and right arm plus left leg out."

"Chip!"

Chip trotted over to Voice. Voice then signed 'watch' and went through a single repetition of the exercise. Then he signed 'you do'.

Chip joined in, watching Voice and alternating balancing, trembling, on one hind and one front paw. The entire team was doing their best not to laugh. Except, of course, Edge.

"What's with you guys today?"

"Just getting revved up about the moose hunt and fishing trip," Voice said.

Edge had to admit that he was also looking forward to a little time above deck. Much as the Mole Hole was designed to mimic the above world, it really wasn't quite the same—not in anyone's book. Not even Edge's, and as a marine he'd spent a lot of time below deck on ships.

"Frog squats," Edge announced. This immediately precipitated a round of his teammates dropping to a squat, then springing back to standing with feet shoulder-width apart. Chip joined in by bouncing on all four legs at once, getting the team members laughing and goofing around with Voice's partner.

Edge was beginning to wonder if he should just give up. Instead, he continued through the exercise regimen, deciding that having a dog join in wasn't a bad way to keep Hank from constantly reminding him that he was adding repetitions to the exercises. *Besides, the dog needs exercise too.*

HANK HAD ENSURED that all of her gear was ready and packed during the remainder of the afternoon after Edge's fitness session. It would be her and Edge up front in the Latitude on the way to La Salle as well, with Edge having won the captain's chair. Still, she took the time to calculate the Latitude's flight time and had noted that not only was it a fairly short hop of only about two hours and twenty minutes, they would also pick up an hour due to the time difference between Nebraska and Montana. That also led to her conclusion that an eight AM departure would have them arriving in Kalispell in enough time to conclude all of the arrangements for renting the trailers as well as taking on some provisions and even grabbing lunch. She was presently checking out just where lunch could be grabbed.

"How does the Winchester Steak House sound to you?" she asked Spud, who was busying himself with making tea in the kitchen.

"For what?"

"For lunch in Kalispell."

"We'll be there in time for lunch?"

"And then some. We'll be there in time for finalizing all of the arrangements, checking out a tackle shop for the fishermen, *and* lunch."

Spud returned to the reading nook and set Hank's tea in front of her.

"Are we going to be able to park four trucks hauling four trailers at the restaurant?" Spud figured Hank may have overlooked one *teensy* detail.

"Not at the restaurant, but there's a grocery store across the street with a big ol' parking lot," Hank assured him. "I don't think they'll mind us parking there when we go in and buy enough food and other essentials for nine people for a week. Or more. We might have to come back out and get more if we haven't bagged our ornery moose by then."

"We drive the campers back out?"

Hank resisted shaking her head. "No, we leave them set up and drive a truck back out. You've never done this kind of thing, I take it."

"Have you hauled something as large as a camping trailer?"

"As a matter of fact..."

"You were a regular tomboy," Spud observed.

"Mom and Dad never told me, 'This is something girls don't do.' So, I never had the idea that there were 'girl things' versus 'boy things'. I just followed my heart."

"It's odd, then, that they didn't let Doug follow his."

"I've thought about that a lot myself. I didn't really notice it until after Mom died. I think Dad was really just trying to hold on to Doug. He seemed to start worrying about the 'dangers of my job', as he put it around that time as well. No matter how many times I told him that a good portion of my existence was spent doing reports, he still felt I was in constant, imminent danger. Of a paper cut or a broken fingernail from hitting a computer key too hard maybe, but I never felt a sense of danger."

"Really? You never had a situation where you were looking down someone's gun?" Spud asked.

"Sure I did. But I never reacted by feeling scared. Just did what my training told me to do. It was *after* that I'd get the shakes."

Spud reflected for a bit. "I guess I *always* had a sense of danger, but it wasn't danger for my own sake. It was fear of something happening to the president on my watch. You know there are plenty of people who want to take a pot shot at the president because they talk about it. But it was the ones I knew were out there that *weren't* talking about it that gave me the willies."

"And yet you calmly told the last president you served that you would take a bullet for him without hesitation, even if you weren't wearing your bullet-proof vest."

"It was my duty to protect him. No matter which of the *hims* I served it was."

"Do you ever regret leaving the Secret Service?"

"Do you ever regret leaving the FBI?"

"You know, you've put a bug in my brain on that one. The idea that I might have been recommended for the unit because the FBI felt I wouldn't make a good agent in the long run." She ran her hand through her hair. "I never considered that. One day, I think I might just ask Stan point blank if that was the case."

Spud silently considered that she didn't have to ask Stan —she could ask Hal. But he opted to remain silent rather than have her potentially discover something she might not really want to know.

"Well, if they felt your sense of integrity would get in the way at some point, and they chose to short circuit that by recommending you for the unit, then they forgot something important. They forgot that we don't just help them solve cases. We also watch what they're doing. We know more about them than they know about us, and we have no incentive to keep information about improprieties quiet."

"Yeah, but how can we expose them? Whatever agency it is, the agency head will likely deep six any bad news."

Spud smiled. "It's all a matter of knowing which agencies would like to get a dig into the agency we're seeing sneaking across the line. We take advantage of agency infighting. We, in short, drop a hint—along with a little

damning evidence, of course. Anonymously. We're the ultimate whistleblowers."

"And the gunnies never get the idea that the unit is the
one hinting?"

"They can suspect we're involved all they want, but they
can never prove it. We're sneaky bastards as well."

Spud was giving Hank the widest grin she'd ever seen
him render.

"Why do I get the impression that you somehow enjoy
that process?"

"Let me assure you: I *do* enjoy that process."

*ONE THING about being in a one-horse town: you know where to
find everyone that wants to ride it.*

He stepped into the bar and sat at his usual spot. It was a
bit later than usual, but he'd heard on his scanner that the
local officers of the sheriff's department that were on patrol
had been tied up responding to an accident, and as a result
were taking a late meal break. He was hoping a little eavesdropping would give him a tidbit or two of information on
just who might have shot his Holly.

He wasn't to be disappointed.

The two deputies were sitting at their usual spot as well,
having their usual repast of cheeseburger with the works,
accompanied by a big mound of fries, and topped off by a
diet pop. *To keep those svelte figures,* he thought sarcastically,
noting how both had a nice padding of natural flab trying
its best to stay inside their bulletproof vests and not spill
over everything attached to their duty belts. He also casually noted that one was a "drencher," and the other was a
"dunker" when it came to fries, one drenching them in

ketchup by pouring it all over the pile and the other pouring out a big puddle of the stuff and dunking his fries into it.

He hadn't even considered how these observations were born of a mind steeped in boredom. Which was the other thing about being in a one-horse town.

He watched as Deputy Drencher stuck one end of a fry in his mouth and chomped it down, the fry disappearing an inch at a time into his mouth as he propelled it in with his lips.

"Still no clues on who killed that woman," he remarked to his partner.

Deputy Dunker dipped a fry into his red puddle and popped the entire thing into his mouth, chewing thoughtfully on it before saying, "Yeah, but my bet's on the husband."

"What makes you say that?"

"'Cuz it's usually the ex. When things get bad between a man and a woman, one of 'em ends up hurting th' other one of 'em. The nice way is one just takes th' other to the cleaners during the divorce. The not-so-nice way is one takes a gun to th' other." He dipped another fry and popped it in his mouth while examining his plate.

It's fish or cut bait time, the man thought to himself, figuring Deputy Dunker was trying to decide between a bite of burger or another fry. He was wrong on both counts: it was a sip of pop.

"Hey, Yolie," Deputy Dunker said, calling over the waitress. "I'll take a piece of that apple pie you've got there, too."

"Ice cream?"

He looked down at his bulging middle.

"Nah. Gotta watch my weight."

Too late, the man thought.

"I'd heard Chris was trying to get back in with her," Deputy Drencher said.

"Likely story, but *I* heard she was makin' it with another guy."

He tried not to react to that one, wondering how the rumor got started. *She couldn't have been seeing someone after they separated, could she?*

Deputy Dunker made a dismissive motion with his hand. "Rumors like that always start to circulate when something like this happens. I wouldn't be surprised if *that* one got started by the ex as well. Great way to take the heat off-a ya."

It is a great way to take the heat off ya, he thought.

4

"That's a switch for you," Crow remarked while looking over at Voice. "A book? A *book* book?"

Voice looked up from the print book he had in his hands. "Yeah, I grabbed it out of the library."

"Interesting title. Why are you reading it?"

"It talks about things this guy thinks are leading to the downfall of the United States. It's full of weird crap. I guess, though, that I'm starting to agree with Hank that you have to understand the mindset of these people. Even more, see how they're convincing others to adopt the same mindset. It might give valuable clues as to how an individual can end up as the leader of an extremist group or a cult like Shining City."

Hearing this bit of conversation in her earpiece, Hank perked up a bit from the typical boredom an uneventful flight entailed—especially as first officer. Her only real responsibilities were running the checklist and communicating with the various air traffic control facilities they would encounter along the way. While en route, there really wasn't anything to do as far as checklist items, and communication was reduced to a brief exchange as the Latitude progressed from one Air Route Traffic Control Center to the next. She had just completed one of these "handoffs", and was leaned back with just an occasional scan of the instruments in front of her to assure herself that neither she nor Edge had failed to notice a developing problem.

"What kind of weird stuff is it discussing?" Crow asked.

"Name a conspiracy theory and it's in here," Voice replied.

Edge had also honed in on the conversation. "It might be an interesting exercise to examine each one of those conspiracy theories and see if there's anything to any of them," he intoned over the team's comm link.

"Or at least track down where they originated," Hank agreed, likewise taking advantage of the comm link to do something other than stare out the window at the scattered cloud deck below 101UN in between brief instrument scans.

"True enough," Voice agreed. "This book is a regular encyclopedia of conspiracy theories, so it might make a good starting point for such an exercise."

"I wonder if it's easier to eliminate some of the false narrative if you go back to the beginning and work it from the bottom up rather than try to whack it away from the top down," Hank wondered. "Maybe if it's pointed out that people have been adhering to a lie from the beginning, they'll be less inclined to continue."

"If it's one thing bad about computers and the Internet," Voice said, "it's that a falsehood never dies. People will believe what they will, and ignore anything that runs contrary to that belief. They'll also repeat what they believe, whether it's pointed out to be false or not."

"It's called 'confirmation bias'," Hank noted.

"Exactly."

"Starting our descent into Glacier Park," Edge announced. "You might want to stow that book—at least temporarily, little buddy."

HANK WAS WATCHING with amusement as Cloud tried for the third time to get the ball on the truck he was driving aligned with the hitch on the trailer he would be hauling. She had had no such difficulties, getting the ball aligned perfectly on the first try and seeing the hitch on the trailer thump satisfyingly into place on it when she cranked the foot on the trailer down to lower it onto the ball. Amigo and Edge had commented to each other that either she really did have the experience required to haul the recreational vehicle or she'd been incredibly lucky.

"It's been a while since I've done this," Cloud remarked as he finally got the hitch aligned.

"Guess so," Hank commented.

"Don't be so smug. We aren't there yet," Cloud reminded her.

Hank stuck a hand into her pocket and jingled the quarters that were there. "They sound so lonely," she said, sadness in her voice. Then she grinned. "But they won't be lonely for long!"

Once Cloud had managed to get his trailer hitched, Hank proceeded to lead them in a convoy to the supermarket. With the others poised to just pull through and occupy two parking spaces, she instead headed as if she was going back out a side entrance.

"Um... You overshot, didn't you?" Spud asked.

"Nope. I'm going to put the rig *right there*," she proclaimed, pointing over her shoulder to two parking spaces that ordinarily would have two cars parked nose-to-nose.

"Uh..."

"Just watch. And I hope you have those quarters ready."

Rolling down her window and leaning out, she steered the trailer and truck so that they were perfectly centered in the parking spaces. She turned to Spud and grinned. The audience of her teammates watching the feat didn't grin.

"I think we just got beat by a girl," Voice concluded.

Crow waved at Spud.

"What are you waving at him for?" Voice asked.

"I'm not. I'm waving 'bye-bye' to my two bits," Crow answered.

As Hank and Spud walked up to the others, Edge told Spud, "Just give them to her."

"You can hold on to them and pay me later," Hank said.

Amigo chuckled. "I didn't know husbands paid wives for that."

Hank looked at him with eyes like daggers. "I don't really need a spotter, and this is grizzly country."

"Aw, ya know I love ya. Gimme a smooch," Amigo said, leaning toward her.

Spud put a hand out and stopped him. "She doesn't really need a spotter, and this is grizzly country. Meaning it would be a shame if you got eaten."

They walked across to the steak house Hank had discovered when researching Kalispell.

"Smell the meat," Hank said appreciatively.

"I don't think we're going to walk away from this place hungry," Edge admitted.

Finding a location where two tables had already been placed together, the team sat down and began to look over the menu, then placed their orders. While they waited for their food, Hank returned to a discussion of the book Voice was reading.

"You say that thing is an encyclopedia of conspiracy theories?"

Voice shook his head in disbelief. "I wouldn't have expected to see so much utter nonsense in one place, no. How does anyone believe even *one* of these things he's talking about?"

"Like?"

"Like everything is manipulated."

"To an extent, everything is."

"Not you too," Voice said with dismay.

"The thing about any conspiracy theory is that they are all born of a fact somewhere," Hank said. "You take a little fact, and you embellish it with a little falsehood. Then a little more. Let it keep going, and pretty soon you have more falsehood than fact, but there's still that *teeny* bit of fact in there that makes it seem that it's *all* fact."

"The problem with that is then you get people who are willing to go to war for the whole pie: teeny fact and bigger lies together," Edge observed.

"That's how you get extremists," Crow concluded.

"I think I'd really like to see just how much of what this guy claims is fact and how much is fiction," Voice asserted.

"Give us a for instance," Spud requested before grabbing a roll from the basket of them that had been left on the table and tearing off a bite.

"For instance, he says that America is in the same throes of collapse that the Roman Empire underwent, to the extent that he claims a third of the population is slaves."

Crow resisted laughing for the sake of not spitting his iced tea across the table. "One third of the population slaves? Was this book written in the eighteen hundreds?"

"Hold back that smirk for a second," Edge advised. "How many people in this country are really self-determining versus how many answer to a boss?"

"It's not like they have to stay at that job," Spud pointed out.

"So they quit and go answer to another boss."

"Maybe they start their own business."

"Then they answer to the bank they get the loan from to start the business," Edge asserted.

Seeing her food being delivered, Hank said, "Too much philosophy for me at the moment." She gazed down at the slab of prime rib that had been set in front of her. "Besides, you guys always criticize me for talking with my mouth full, and gauging from the chunk of meat on this plate, it's going to be full for a while."

SPUD GOT out and moved aside the barricade at the entrance to the campground. On it was a sign reading "Area Closed." He allowed the four trucks and their towed trailers through, then trotted back to where Hank idled in wait to lead the team to the campsites she had chosen for them. Again, she had no problems backing the trailer into a site. The others also had no problems, and all were soon setting up the trailers for their camping stay.

"This will spoil us," she told Spud with a wink. "It'll be just like a hotel room on wheels, with the exception that we'll also have a kitchen."

"I noticed there's a queen size bed in there," Spud observed.

"I hope you noticed it's a *full* queen size bed—not what they call a 'queen short'. You won't find your feet hanging over the edge of the mattress."

After getting the trailer level and setting the stabilizers, she climbed in with Spud on her heels and set about putting away the various provisions that had been purchased: everything from toilet paper to food. After that task was done, she headed back out with a folding saw in her hand, ready to gather some dead wood for building a fire in the provided fire ring.

"What's the game plan for tonight?" Spud asked.

"Relax. Get a good night's sleep so we're ready to find where our moose has been hanging out tomorrow."

She went to the kitchen area and began to look over the things they had brought to eat.

"What do you want for dinner?"

Spud caught himself before laughing out loud. "I think that plate of prime rib you had for lunch was enough to feed two people. How can you even be hungry?"

"I dunno. Maybe I have a hyperactive thyroid."

"Not according to Medical. It would have disqualified you."

"Maybe it's all the extra calories I burn satisfying an oversexed husband," she said.

"In that case, you'd better hope we don't run out of food by tomorrow morning."

She looked through what was in the camper's small refrigerator. "I've got some chicken breast tenders in here, and vegetables. How about a sheet pan dinner?"

"Keep it light. I'm still stuffed," Spud said.

"Chicken with a light panko crust, broccoli, and carrots."

"Sounds good."

As Hank went about preparing the meal, Spud asked, "What do you think about this book Voice has been telling us about?"

"I think he has the right idea of reading it to try and understand the mindset of extremists. I think Fred Miller threw him a bit. Voice is our programmer and even Hal's engineer, if you will. It probably unsettled him to see someone adamantly against computers."

"I notice you haven't said much about having to shoot Miller."

Hank sat across from Spud at the small dinette table in the camper. "On one hand, if it had only been the facility at risk, I might have hesitated. I'm not sure myself that I like the idea of the government spying on its citizens, and I don't have a lot of confidence that each and every agent who sees the data analyzes it solely with the purpose of thwarting terrorism. As we've seen, lots of terrorists get through the net. Look at us: we have more capability than even the NSA, and we've been chasing UniPerp for two years without any luck."

"Perhaps one of the things that will come out of Voice's reading of his book is that he'll program Hal to detect any malfeasance on the part of the analysts or their bosses."

"How?" Hank wondered.

"The usual thing is someone living beyond their means. It's how a lot of criminals whose motivation is greed get caught. If, between spending, investing, and banking, you've got more money than you make, it's a pretty good bet you're into something illegal. The other thing would be someone moving up the ladder a little quicker than others. That can be benign; some people just have the kind of talent that leads to them being able to advance quicker than their peers. On the other hand, it could mean they've found something juicy about their boss that they're willing to keep quiet for a raise in pay."

"In that case, they'd better also know that there's something juicy about their boss's boss that they can exploit," Hank said. "Otherwise, it's a sure bet that someone will put an end to that particular attempt to climb to the top." Hank reflected a moment. "You'd think, though, that everyone in the chain of command realizes that danger if they're working for an entity like the NSA. If your coworker is beyond reproach, he'll blow the whistle on you. If your boss is beyond reproach, he'll make sure you get canned, and likely jailed as well. And so on up the line."

"Unless everyone is corrupted," Spud pointed out. "All it would likely take is the top guy to be corrupted. The buck stops there, so if he's corrupted then the guys under him will see corruption as being a way to advance. Make the boss happy by ensuring he gets a slice of the pie, and you can likely get a slice of the pie yourself. Then it becomes a matter of 'I won't rat on you if you don't rat on me.' Then the only thing that corrects the process is if one of the rats believes that another rat is getting too much of the cheese."

Hank grabbed an oven mitt and placed the sheet pan of food in the center of the table. "True," she agreed, handing Spud a spatula so he could serve himself. "It's more difficult, though, when you're just going after one person like we did with Miller. He didn't talk to anyone other than Oscar, and really we're pretty fortunate that Oscar's little voices were telling him that something was off about Miller. Otherwise, he could have very well carried out his plan before anyone even knew he'd left Cambridge. I don't know if you saw the analysis of his rockets. They very well could have taken out the power supplies to the data center."

"That would have been a setback, but likely not totally crippling," Spud said. "Once they got power back into the facility, even if the data was corrupted, they could have recovered it all from their backup locations and their corporate partners that cooperate with them."

"Insidious, isn't it?" Hank said as she served herself. "It seems there are only seven people in this entire country who don't have some sort of electronic eavesdropping going on."

"Oh, we do, too," Spud informed her. "The only difference is that Voice has programmed Hal with a big eraser, so when some computer somewhere gets a hint about us, *poof!* It's gone."

IT WAS LATE, and the owner of the pawn shop in Duluth was a bit annoyed to see the guy walk in with a gun sleeve in his grip. *Probably another clapped-out rusty piece of garbage he found in Grandad's closet after the old geezer kicked the bucket,* he thought.

"Getting ready to close here," he informed the guy.

"Yeah, sorry. But I have this gun I'd like to pawn."

The shop owner sighed. "Ok, let's see it."

"I think you'll like this," the guy said as he laid the gun sleeve down on the counter and unzipped it. "A nice deer rifle chambered in .243 Winchester."

"Yeah, that's a good round for deer," the shop owner admitted dryly. He watched as the man pulled the gun from the sleeve, his eyes getting wider.

"That's a sweet gun," he said, his tone a bit more enthusiastic now that he'd seen the rifle. It was indeed a gem. "Why are you pawning it?"

"It was my dad's. He just passed, and I've got his estate to take care of. I'm not into guns myself, so I just want to get a bit for it. I really don't want it around the house—I've got young kids and you know how a curious kid can be."

Anti-gun. "I see. I can't give you what it might go for, understand. You might get more for it by selling it to a gun shop or just selling it yourself."

The man shrugged. "I figure a gun shop will take a bit off the top as well. Just like you, they have to make a profit. And I just don't want the hassle of trying to sell it myself. So, what will you give me for it?"

"Let me look up what the *Blue Book* says it's worth," the shop owner said, pulling out a copy of *The Blue Book of Gun Values.*

"*Blue Book* says this gun goes for about eight fifty. Mind you, I've got to make a profit, so I'll give you six hundred for it. More if you want to throw in the scope on it."

"Is that a good scope?" *Can't let this guy know I'm aware of exactly what that scope costs.*

"It's a decent scope. I'll give you an extra fifty with the scope."

Robbery. That's a five-hundred-dollar scope.

"A buddy of mine told me a scope like that goes for five hundred bucks."

The shop owner scratched his chin. *He's right about that.* "How 'bout I give you another hundred, then? Seven hundred total."

The man considered this while the shop owner did his best to keep a poker face. It was a good deal for him. He knew he could get a lot more for the rifle.

"I'll have to hold it for thirty days before I can sell it," the shop owner prodded. "Not like I can make money off it right off the bat."

"Why hold onto it? I won't be coming back for it," the man said. "I just want it outta my life."

"Then I'd still say seven hundred is a good deal. I don't think you'll find another shop willing to give you more."

Is it worth haggling with this guy? If anyone ever links this gun to me, I'm going to jail for killing that woman. Reluctantly, he said, "Ok, you've got a deal."

The pawn broker smiled. Going into his cash drawer, he took out five one-hundred-dollar bills and ten twenties. Laying them on the counter, he invited the man to count them. The man thought it might look suspicious if he just grabbed the money and walked out, so he counted the bills.

"Just one more thing. I've got to see some ID," the pawn broker said. "No offense, but if this gun comes back stolen, the cops are going to want to give you a visit."

I figured as much. He went into his wallet and pulled out a driver's license. "Here ya go."

The shop owner turned and made a copy of the driver's license, then handed it back to the man. "That's all I needed."

The man smiled. "I'll make good use of the seven hundred. I guess you'll make good use of the gun."

The pawn broker smiled as well. "Then I suppose we'll both be happy."

Taking his leave of the shop, the man grinned as he shoved his wallet back into his back pocket. *That fake ID has stood up for me pretty good. And when the cops he cooperates with run the serial number on the gun, it won't come back to me, either. You just have to appreciate private sales from people who don't ask for ID.*

SPUD AND HANK were lying together in the camper. Unlike their home in the Mole Hole, they could hear the subtle sounds of wind and wildlife filtering through the walls. It was giving Hank a feeling of nostalgia.

"Dad and I would occasionally go camping after Mom died," she said. "Rent a trailer like this and go do a little hunting. I don't know which we enjoyed more: hunting, or just getting away and getting back to nature."

Spud nearly chuckled at that remark. He was also wanting to get back to nature, but was certain it wasn't the variety of nature Hank enjoyed with her father.

"I miss my dad sometimes."

"Just your dad?"

"Mom too, but Dad especially. The roles for his children were a bit reversed: I was the one who didn't mind crawling in the back of an airplane to adjust cable tensions, and Doug was the one who liked to paint scenery and wildlife. Dad just took it in stride until after Mom died. In a way, I wish he had kept it that way. He'd been fine with an artist for a son and a special agent for a daughter. But he started getting a little protective of me after Mom died and started being a little critical of Doug's artistic inclinations, saying it 'wasn't a real job'." Doug was getting recognized for his art, though. That shop you went to for the portrait he did of me was hot for every painting he did, so he was making good money. His creativity knew no bounds. He did a whole series of paintings of flowers at one point that weren't any bigger than postage stamps. They were incredibly detailed. People paid twenty bucks apiece for them." She sighed. "Doug would have loved painting this place."

An owl hooted as if agreeing with her.

"Do you think maybe that was a message from your brother?" Spud asked.

"You know I'm not much of a believer. I'm pretty sure all of the religions have it wrong. But I do sometimes wonder if there isn't something beyond this existence. If there is, then I would hope that was a message from Doug telling me that he's ok."

The owl hooted again.

"Believe," Spud urged her. "Believe. I have to believe. You should too."

"Why?" Hank asked him, a bit amused.

"Because I never want to leave you—not even in the event of my death. I always want to be with you, even in spirit." He stroked down her side, feeling goosebumps rise. "I love you so much, Hank. When we're done with this, with being in the unit, I'm going to marry you."

Hank chuckled. "We're already married."

"Actually, we aren't. Not a full-blown recognized by law marriage."

"You want to be tied into a contract?"

"Hell yeah."

"I don't need to be tied into a contract," Hank said. "What I feel for you is stronger than paper."

He drew her closer to him. "You know what else this camper has? A shower."

She knew exactly what he was thinking.

"You're incorrigible."

5

Hank woke early and took a shower. *I can already see this is going to be a bit different than a survival camp,* she thought. *Nature Boy back there in the bed apparently is in rut. Better tell him how to conserve water while showering or the gray water tank will be full by tomorrow.* She smiled remembering their late-evening activities before sleep took over. *Not that I mind.*

She decided that rather than use water from the fresh water tank they had filled when they arrived that she'd haul some water back to the trailer for cooking as well, given the almost certainty that they'd run out of fresh water, too. *And then we'll hear no end of it from the other guys.*

As she closed the door to the camper, she noticed that a sheet of paper with a message on it had been affixed with duct tape:

> *If the trailer's a-rockin'*
> *don't come a-knockin'.*

"Very funny," she muttered. She positioned her watch so that the message showed on the watch's camera. "Hal, identify handwriting."

Hal almost immediately returned with, *Analysis of handwriting indicates high probability that author is FT5.*

She peeled the sheet of paper and tape off the door of the camper and went over to the campsite where Crow, Cloud, and Amigo were camped. They were already outside, lounging in folding camp chairs and drinking coffee around a small campfire.

"'Mornin', Hank. Want some coffee?" Crow asked.

"What I'd *really* like is a piece of hide," she answered. She held up the paper so they could read it. "Anyone know anything about this?"

"Not I," Cloud replied all too quickly.

"So... It just managed to get stuck on my camper door by a gust of wind or something?"

"Maybe."

"Or maybe the moose pasted it there."

"He'd be one intelligent moose, but that's always a possibility. But I saw the ranger around this morning. Didn't you guys see the ranger around this morning?" Cloud asked, turning to his compadres for support.

"Sure, yeah—we saw the ranger in the camp this morning," the two of them chorused together.

Hank gave them a collective glare.

"That shows evidence of collusion that I hadn't necessarily assumed, but somehow expected," she said. "Because *Hal*—you know, our good buddy Hal that knows all and has a *ton* of data at its command—says this handwriting belongs to a Field Team member. One FT5, a.k.a. Cloud, a.k.a. Kasey Parker."

"Sorry, buddy—but you're busted," Crow whispered.

"Yes, indeed you are, *Cloud,*" Hank said. "And so are your little friends here. Let me guess: one got the duct tape, one provided the sheet of paper, and you just happened to have the black Sharpie."

"No, no—it wasn't quite like that," Cloud denied as Spud also walked into their campsite.

"Oh? You had the paper, Crow had the Sharpie, and Amigo had the tape?"

"What's going on, Love?" Spud asked.

She held the paper for him to see.

"If the trailer's a-rockin', don't come a-knockin'," he read.

"It was taped to our door this morning."

"Look. We all distinctly heard 'oo-oo' last night," Cloud said in his defense.

"That was an *owl*, you moron!" Hank asserted.

Spud's face had gone straight to Secret Service Neutral. Everything except his cheeks.

"If that was an owl, why is Spud blushing?" Crow asked.

"I'm not. It's chilly out here," Spud said, rubbing his cheeks as if they were cold.

"Yeah, right."

"Besides, how would you guys know if the 'oo-oo' came from inside or outside the trailer?" Hank demanded.

"It was a lucky guess?" Amigo offered.

Hank growled.

"I think I just heard a grizzly," Cloud said, getting up as if to dash back into their camper.

"Sit," Spud ordered.

Cloud decided obedience was preferable to being hunted down by an angry former Secret Service agent seeking to avenge his wife.

Spud gave them all a one-eyebrow-raised looking over. Then he reread the little sign.

"This looks like rather good advice, actually," he concluded. "I'm going to put it back on the door of our camper. But be advised: it's going to be like those bumper stickers you see on the backs of cars that say, 'If you can read this, you're too damned close.'"

"And if we get close enough to read it?" Amigo asked.

"You know," Hank began, "there's an unfortunate thing that happens sometimes when hunters are out hunting. One can get really enthusiastic about filling his tag. So enthusiastic that when he hears something rustling in the underbrush, he takes a shot, even though he can't see what he's shooting at. It's called a bush shot, and often results in his hunting buddy getting a hole somewhere in his body. And you all know that I'm a *very* enthusiastic hunter."

The three did a collective gulp.

"I guess you guys failed to notice that our camper is a little farther away from all the rest of you, too..."

No one wanted to admit that they had, nor that they had deduced the possible reason.

Hank growled again.

"Bad enough I haven't had coffee yet."

She strode off to get the water she had originally intended to get, leaving her three teammates facing Spud's half-stern, half-stoic, you'd-better-believe-I-mean-business Secret Service face. He gave them one last look, and turned to follow Hank.

The three sat silently for a while. Then when both Spud and Hank were safely out of earshot, they collectively snickered.

"You weren't the only one got busted," Crow remarked to Cloud. "Red-faced because he's chilly my ass!"

WITH EVERYONE UP and having eaten breakfast, the group set out with Hank in the lead, Voice and Chip right behind her, on a hunt for any sign of their renegade moose.

"Don't you feel a little guilty about hunting down a wild animal?" Voice asked her.

Hank gave him a sideways glance.

"Is there a reason I should feel guilty?"

"I mean, we have domestic animals that are raised expressly for food. These animals are part of nature."

"Let me show you a side of hunting that perhaps you don't know about," Hank said. "First, do you know what the Pittman-Robertson Act is?"

"Uh..."

She noticed that her other teammates were now paying a bit more attention as well.

"Pittman has been around since 1937," Hank began. "Depending upon what it is, it provides for either a ten percent tax or eleven percent tax to be applied on anything hunting-related: rifles, ammunition, bows, arrows.... The tax is collected by the manufacturers, so any time you buy something hunting-related, money goes into the fund. The fund is then divided up among the states, and goes for three different things: habitat preservation, wildlife conservation, and hunter education—which includes the development and maintenance of shooting ranges. Basically, the fund allows the states the funding to manage wildlife.

"One of the things the fund does is give funding to state game wardens to assess the health of both an animal's habitat and the numbers of animals utilizing that habitat. This is important to conservation of a species. If the habitat is in good shape and the numbers of animals using it aren't too great, then everything's in balance. In a situation like that, the game wardens will recommend that perhaps only a few animals should be hunted that year. Depending on the animal and how well they reproduce, they may recommend that *none* of the animals be hunted that year. This is why states issue tags to hunters. They only issue so many tags so that only the correct number of animals get hunted.

"If you didn't do that, if no animals were hunted then what would happen is that you'd get too many animals for the environment to support. When that happens, *all* of the animals are affected, and they all could die out. Every game animal has natural predators, and humans have always been one of those predators. The key is to not allow too much predation, whether from humans or other predators like mountain lions, for instance."

"Yeah, but you're killing an animal when you don't need to," Voice protested.

"Maybe so, but hunting still helps maintain a healthy balance between wild animals and their habitat. Besides, have you stopped to consider the life of a game animal versus the life of an animal in a production facility? The steer in a feedlot, for instance, is eating an artificial diet. In fact, the diet they feed steers in feedlots is so unhealthy for them that it can actually kill them if they're fed it for too long. Gil's operation is different, because he allows his cattle to graze in open fields so they get a more natural diet, but there aren't a lot of ranchers that raise their cattle that way. They allow them to free range, then round them up and ship them to feedlots to be fattened.

"A game animal in the wild lives a free life and eats a natural diet for its entire existence. It's the ultimate organic meat."

"Still, it's got to be painful for them when they're shot."

"You don't think it's painful for a farm animal when it's slaughtered?" Hank asked. "But this is where the shooting ranges come in. Because there are two things at play. First, if you hunt, you want to make a clean kill. A shot that kills the animal immediately. You don't want the animal to suffer, if for no other reason than it changes the way the meat tastes. But it's considered unethical to cause an animal to suffer when you hunt it, so you spend a lot of time at the range to make sure you can hit the animal with a shot that kills it immediately. Not only that, it's illegal to shoot an animal and leave it in the wild, so if your shot doesn't kill the animal almost immediately, it will run off. Then you have to track it so you can take it in. In my mind, that's a terrible situation, knowing you shot the animal and it's suffering while you track it down. Plus, I don't think it's ethical to shoot an animal purely for sport. You shoot it, you eat it."

"I guess you guys don't see what Hank does after she shoots an animal," Amigo said quietly.

Edge piped up. "I have. She consoles it. Thanks it for the food it will give her."

"All life is sacred," Hank said. "When you take the life of an animal, it has to be for a purpose. In this case, we have an animal that has become a dangerous animal. Our hunt will serve to remove that danger, but also provide us with meat. Just because this guy has become a nuisance doesn't mean his death should be entirely wasted."

She stopped for a moment and gazed at the ground.

"What are you looking at?" Crow asked.

"Scat."

"Fine, I'll leave. But what are you looking at?"

She turned to him with a huge grin on her face. "Animal feces is called 'scat'. I'm looking at moose poop."

"No accounting for the things my wife takes an interest in," Spud commented.

Not able to resist taking the dig, Voice turned and looked

at him, saying, "We know." Hank resisted the urge to chuckle herself, but her teammates didn't.

"Why is it interesting?" Voice asked.

"Consider, oh ye who are good with computers but bad with hunting. Where there is moose poop, once upon a time there had to have been a moose," Crow replied.

"Uh, well, yeah... I guess that makes sense."

"Not going to have the doggo learn to track our elusive moose?"

Voice got the hint and walked Chip over to the pile of grape-sized and shaped droppings. Chip gave them a sniff and let out a low howl. Voice gave Chip the hand signal for "track," prompting the dog to circumnavigate the pile of droppings with his nose to the ground. When he'd done a thorough circuit, Chip looked back at Voice and let out a plaintive whine.

"I wouldn't have expected him to pick up a scent," Hank said. "These droppings have been here a while. See how they look like little balls of shredded wheat? If they'd been fresh, they'd look more like shiny black grapes."

"I'll never eat shredded wheat or grapes again," Edge grumbled.

"Wussy."

"Ok, so we know our moose has been in the area, but at some time in the past," Spud said, his voice taking on an investigative tone. "What now?"

"We look for fresher sign," Hank said.

"Like hoof prints, or shiny black grapes," Amigo added.

"Note to self: do not eat shiny, black, wild grapes," Edge muttered.

"That's good advice you just gave yourself, big guy," Hank agreed. "Especially if you find them in a pile on the ground."

The team continued on, skirting the water's edge where Hank felt it would be more likely to find some sign of the moose. In spite of devoting a couple of hours to the search, they came up empty-handed.

WITH LUNCH CONSUMED, the team replayed their morning search, only this time heading in the opposite direction along the shore. Everyone was now keeping a close eye out for signs of moose. Except Chip, of course. He was keeping his nose to the ground, literally, while leading Voice along at the full length of his lead.

"Got some fresher scat here," Edge announced from an area at the fringe of where the water's edge had given way to sand and sand had given way to brush.

"Good eye, my man," Hank said, getting a look at the shiny black scat at Edge's feet. "Those turdlettes look pretty fresh."

"Turdlettes?" Crow questioned.

Hank shrugged. "I don't know if there's an official name for the individual bits. I call them 'turdlettes'. Moose are in the same family as deer and elk. They all drop turdlettes. Small little black beans for deer, bigger black kidney beans for elk, bigger black grapes for moose."

"Two more things I'll never eat again," Edge griped.

"I thought you'd never hunted moose before, though," Spud recalled.

"Never have. Which is why I carefully researched the topic before ever proposing this hunt. For instance, we're not likely to find our moose actually roaming around at this time of day. They usually bed down shortly after dawn. But if we do find a moose resting, we can wait him out. When he gets up, I could get a good heart shot."

"How will we know if it's *our* moose?" Amigo asked.

"The rangers affixed ear tags to him," Hank said. "It's how they know he keeps coming back to be a pest."

CHRISTOPHER FAY PICKED up his phone from where it was buzzing on the end table next to him. Getting a look at the screen, he noted the caller ID.

"Hey Lionel. What's up?"

"I just got in a sweet gun I thought you might be interested in," the pawn broker told him. "A nice deer gun chambered in .243 Winchester with a good scope on it. Guy said he inherited it. Acted like a real anti-gun type. This gun is beautiful. Care to make the trip in to see it?"

"Text me a picture," he said. He waited for the notification that the text had arrived. Giving the picture a look, he said, "Yeah, I could be interested in it. You want to hold onto it for me until I can get in and see it? Bites, but I've got to work a half day tomorrow. But I can be there by the afternoon."

"Sure thing. I'll keep it in the safe until you get here."

"Thanks, Lionel. See you about one o'clock."

"See you then." *He's always good for top dollar on a descent gun,* Lionel thought. *If I can interest him in it, I can probably make eleven hundred for it. Nice little profit of four hundred.*

HE SAT EATING dinner at the usual place in his usual spot. If anything, he was predictable. That predictability was probably why Holly never paid any attention to him. Predictable, unassuming, not pushy and would never think to be—especially when it came to Holly. *A man has to be gentle with a woman he loves. Not come on too strong; just gradually let her see that he loves her. I never got the chance.*

"What's happening with that shooting of your neighbor?" he heard a man ask behind him. He didn't turn to see who was talking. Just began to pay very close attention.

"Who gives a shit?" he heard another man answer.

"That's kind-a unkind, don'tcha think?" the first man said. "After all, the woman *is* dead, and it looks like someone might-a murdered her."

"Well, I hear she wasn't popular with quite a few people," the other one said. "She sure as hell wasn't popular with me. Always giving me grief, saying I was stealing her land. Ever since I moved in, she'd been saying that. There's a fence, fer God's sake! If she didn't like where it was, why did she wait until I moved in to contest it? But you know what they say: You shouldn't say anything bad about the dead. She's dead. Good!"

He glanced over his shoulder quickly to see the first man shaking his head. "I think it's time you let that one go."

"Like I said: I can't cry a single tear for the bitch."

The scrape of a chair alerted him to one of the two getting up from the table. As the man approached the bar, he saw it was the one who had spoken ill of his Holly. He etched the man's face into his brain.

*If you killed her, you'll pay. I'll send you straight to hell. And if that means I go straight to hell as well, then it means I can continue to chase you down and make you pay **there**, too!*

Doc Frank walked up to where Doc Wright was sitting on a log, his fishing pole in his hand. Dressed in hip waders, Doc Wright was concentrating on tying a fly.

"Catch anything?" Doc Frank asked.

"Go take a look in my creel."

Doc Frank walked down to the water's edge and took a peek inside the wicker creel that was partially submerged there.

"That's a nice bunch of fish," he said, returning to where Doc Wright was now attaching the newly-created fly on a leader. He grinned. "You make your flies on the fly?"

"Usually," Doc Wright admitted. "When I catch a fish, I'll usually get a look at the contents of its stomach, then make flies that mimic what they're eating."

"A fisherman through and through," Doc Frank remarked.

"Always have been, ever since I was a kid," Doc Wright confirmed. He stood and waded into the water at the edge of the reservoir and began the rhythmic casting of the fishing line out in front of him, soon laying a stretch of line atop the water. Watching the newly-made fly float lazily on the surface, he found himself with but a single thought: *I wish I had a beer to go with this.*

"Did you happen to notice the sign taped to the trailer Spud and Hank are in?"

Doc Wright chuckled. "I guess those of us in Medical aren't the only ones who have noticed that they're a very physically active couple after the lights go out."

"*They* didn't paste the thing up there?"

"From the discussion I overheard this morning, Cloud did."

"Cloud's still alive?" Doc Frank asked, amused.

"He escaped unscathed. At least for the time being."

"You know, I'm still trying to figure out the team's dynamic," Doc Frank admitted. "It seems like there's always some kind of little war going on between them. You'd think it would interfere with their ability to work together effectively as a team."

Doc Wright chuckled as he reeled in a little line, then let the fly drift some more. "You have to understand, Frank. They're like a couple, only there are seven of them. They have their tiffs, but they always kiss and make up."

"I'm amazed that the guys rough it up with Hank the way they do."

"You know how she got that code name, don't you?"

"No."

"She insisted on it. It's based on her former identity. Her last name. She had them truncate it to 'Hank' because she said she wanted to just be considered as if she was another guy." He gave his rod a little tweak to make the fly dance on the water. "She probably works the hardest to make sure they *do* just think of her as another guy."

"I'd think that Edge would have a hard time getting aboard with that. Big guy, ex-Marine Raider..."

"They spar together a lot. He doesn't hurt her," —Doc Wright chuckled— "and she doesn't hurt him."

"She could?"

"Oh yeah. You know she knocked a couple of teeth out of a guy's mouth early in her tenure in the team."

"Yeah, I heard about that. But Edge is twice her size."

"You see," Doc Wright said, turning to him, "Hank is one of two team members that serve the role of odd man out. You want at least one person as odd man out, otherwise the team can get into the dangerous situation where they all agree to do something they shouldn't because no one questions it. Hank is an odd man out simply because she's a woman. The other odd man out is Voice. He never served in the military or in law enforcement. He was brought in for his technical skills. The guys who were in the military all had to learn different rules of engagement, if you will. Had to learn proper police procedures, including little things like you try *not* to kill your adversary," Doc Wright said with a bit of emphasis. "The guys from law enforcement had to learn a whole new set of tactics that border more on military tactics than civilian ones. Voice had to learn both—is still learning both. His questions may make it seem that he's not quite a part of the team, but in fact they make the rest of the team revisit the hows and whys of the ways they do things. So, Hank brings a different viewpoint to the team whether she wants to recognize it or not, simply because she's female, and Voice brings a different perspective because he's a civilian—both in the military sense and in the law enforce-ment sense. Don't get me wrong about Hank, either. She's tough, but she's reluctant about using the strength she has. She moderates the response of the men that way."

"I'd think that would create problems, though, if they aren't always on the same page."

"You might think so, but I can tell you from my experi-ence since being with the unit that this has got to be the best team we've ever put together. It's tit for tat. The guys will poke at Hank and Spud mercilessly simply because they're essentially married, and enjoy all the perks of married life, if you will. Hank and Spud? They flaunt it just to make the other guys jealous. Voice is so incredibly smart that no one dares cross him, and his involvement with Page puts a new wrinkle on that. Edge is a giant, so no one dares cross him, either—even though he's probably the most mild-mannered guy in the group. The other three are fluid about whose side they're on at any particular time. But when the shit hits the fan and the scramble call goes out in the facility, they're all in it together, and that's all that counts."

"DIS IF *PUFFICK!*" Hank exclaimed through a mouthful of fresh trout that had been cooked over a bed of coals back at the camp.

"What'd she say?" Doc Frank asked.

"This is perfect," Crow translated.

Doc Frank grinned. He'd heard how the team occasionally had to translate 'Mouthful Hank', and failing would have to rely on Hal to do so.

Hank leaned forward toward the fire and carefully lifted the lid on a Dutch oven with a tool specifically made for handling the hot cast iron. "Biscuits are done, too," she announced, using the same tool to remove the entire oven from the fire. She walked around the men encircling the small fire that nonetheless warmed everyone with its glow, letting each of them reach in and grab a hot biscuit, each juggling one between their hands before dropping it on their plate of fish and vegetables.

Hank was stuffing the meal down like a ravenous tiger while her teammates savored the fresh fish. Voice occasionally snuck a little chunk down to his four-pawed buddy, who likewise was enjoying his share, meager as it was. They had opted to eat the meal down by the water's edge, keeping the smell of the cooking fish away from the camp in the event that an equally hungry bear might decide to come for a serving.

Hank leaned back in the camp chair she'd brought and patted her stomach. "If I'd known you'd be catching enough fish for a meal like this, I'd have let you bring a few beers along, Doc Wright."

"Now you tell me."

"You really didn't miss having a beer while you were fishing..."

"No." *Yes.*

Hank leaned back for a look at the stars. With a clear sky, the Milky Way spilled like a jeweled path across the heavens, illuminating the ground in deep azure shadows and giving a twinkling appearance to the surface of the water with the slight breeze causing it to ripple ever so delicately.

"This brings back so many memories," she sighed.

"Thinking about your dad?" Spud ventured.

"Yeah. We'd do trips like this. Never here to Montana, but up in Colorado. Spend the day hunting... Build a cozy fire and just lean back and see if we could count the stars or how many constellations we could identify. Sometimes, we'd rent a trailer like the ones we've got back in the camp. Other times, we'd put up a couple of tents, or even just sleep under the stars if the mosquitoes and no see ums weren't biting and it didn't look like it would rain. We'd pack fresh meat back home and gorge on it until we were sick of it. Mom always thought it was some sort of voodoo we had that would allow us to eat so much and not gain any weight. Then the rest would go into the freezer. Those were good times."

"Your dad was thin like you, I take it," Doc Wright said.

"I think we both had pretty active metabolisms. Dad could work a twelve-hour day and then come home and putter around the house for another hour before hitting the hay. Between shooting and helping him out after school when I was younger and then the PD followed by the FBI after I graduated, I always stayed pretty active too. You can't be too sedentary when you've got the occasional bad guy to run down."

"Ever have a guy try to fight you?" Voice asked.

"Oh, hell yeah. All the time. Some would be a little reluctant to take on a woman, but others had no problems with it if they thought it meant they could escape."

"Did anyone ever escape from you?"

"Nope. Had some try, but usually a taser would dissuade them."

"Ever have to draw your weapon on someone?" Crow asked.

"It was a rarity, but yeah. First time was a domestic. He thought he'd choke his wife to death in front of me, so I convinced him it wasn't worth getting a hole in his head. I hated responding to domestics. They were always nasty affairs with everyone throwing everything from fists to chairs. And if you think *I* cuss, you haven't heard *anything*."

"It seemed like we always went into a situation with guns drawn," Crow said. "More often than not, the drug dealers and the guys guarding the stash houses were armed to the hilt."

"I don't envy you," Hank remarked. "Ever have to shoot anyone in the line of duty?"

"Once. He wanted to shoot me, but I was faster," Crow said.

"I never had to shoot anyone before the unit," Hank said, her expression going hollow.

"It's a tough deal for sure," Crow agreed. "I think I see the face of everyone I ever pointed my gun at. But especially the one I shot. His face never goes away."

THE HUNTER WAS LYING in bed, staring at the ceiling. He'd never had a hard time getting to sleep before, but ever since that day he'd found it harder and harder to drift off. He kept seeing it in his mind's eye: stalking through the trees, keeping each footfall as quiet as he possibly could, looking for that good bird, his trusty .243 in his hands. Yeah, you didn't want to hit a bird wrong with a .243, but if you were good—and he considered himself good—you could head-shoot a tom and come home with a nice bird for your table. So when he'd come across a nice, big tom sitting in the low boughs of a tree, he'd decided it was his lucky day and he'd be taking home a nice turkey for Easter.

How had he been that far off? He couldn't conceive of it until he looked at his scope settings. *Forgot to adjust the settings!*

He could see it again: the big bird sitting low in the branches of the tree, how he slowly and stealthily raised his rifle and aimed in, then the shot and the big tom flying off unscathed as he continued to watch in horror as the woman fell to the ground, the bucket of bird seed she had been filling her feeder with scattering. He'd been so focused on getting that damned bird that he hadn't seen her in his line of fire. But he saw her now: lying supine, unmoving, blood flowing out of her mouth.

He ran and he ran and he ran. But he couldn't get away from the sound of the shot and the woman falling to the ground and the knowledge that he had just killed another human being. The gun was gone, but his guilt was still there as he lie and stared at the ceiling, instead seeing the woman fall to the ground, over and over and over again.

6

Hank rolled over in bed.

"Whuh?"

"Wake up, Love. We've got something going on in the camp."

Groggily, Hank suddenly became aware of the commotion outside. Some sort of horrific banging was coming from one of the other campsites. Pulling on her clothing and grabbing her .308, she ran from the camper and arrived at the campsite where Crow, Cloud, and Amigo were camped, just in time to see something big and dark lumber off into the shadows of the trees.

She watched as Cloud first peeked out of the door of their camper, then climbed down the stairs, looking around apprehensively. She snickered. He was butt naked.

"What the hell was *that?*" he asked, fear still tinging his voice.

"From the size and stature, I'd say it was our moose, nature boy," Hank said, wishing he could see her smirking in the dark.

"What time is it?" he asked, still sounding a bit out of it. He reached down and scratched.

Hank shook her head, then glanced at her watch. "About three in the morning."

Cloud rubbed his arms, suddenly realizing he was standing naked in front of the team's only female member. He quickly hid the area he'd just scratched with his two hands, making Hank reflect that *that* was something Spud couldn't do.

"Why don't you at least go pull on a pair of pants?" she advised him.

While Cloud retreated inside his trailer, Hank pulled the tactical light off her .308 and began to get a look at the camper. When Cloud arrived back outside, his two bunkies making their appearance as well, Hank was examining the outside of the RV.

"The good news is that there's no serious damage," she said. "The bad news is that there *is* damage, so the other good news is that we paid for the renter's insurance." She shined her light on a large dent on the side of the trailer. "I see why this guy is considered a nuisance."

"Are you going after it?" Cloud asked.

"Not in the middle of the night," Hank replied.

"Why not?"

"A, because it might be tough to track him without a moon in the sky—or even with one, for that matter. B, because if I get a little turned around out there in the dark, I might not realize I'm shooting back in the direction of the camp. And that could be a *bad* thing."

"So, what are you going to do?"

"*Pfft!* Go back to bed. I don't know about you, but it's cold out here—which I think you would have noticed." She shined her light on him indirectly so as not to blind him with it, noticing the red glow of his cheeks. "Your cheeks are plenty red," she observed. "That's from the cold, right?"

"Uh... I guess."

"Yeah, right." This time, she turned the light in her own direction so she could be sure Cloud could see her smirking.

"We'll see what we can find in the morning. Mr. Moose knows we're here, and has let us know he's here as well. Go back to bed."

As Hank and Spud nestled back in their bed, Hank started chuckling.

"Well, *that* was interesting."

"Oh?"

"I've never had a guy stand in front of me stark naked and scratching his balls before."

Spud chuckled as well. "Yeah, that was an eyeful."

Hank laughed. "Not quite."

"Oh, cut him a break, Love. It's cold. Shrinkage."

"I bet even with shrinkage you wouldn't be able to hide behind your hands."

Spud reflected that this was likely a compliment, Hank-style. And perhaps a prelude to something else.

"Have *you* got some place I can hide it, then?"

Hank rolled toward him, gave him a kiss, and chuckled seductively. "You know I do."

THE TEAM HAD OPTED to set up an outside eating area under a tent and were busy cooking and chatting.

"What is it this morning?" Spud asked Hank, given she was doing the cooking.

"Coffee is ready over there on the other camp stove. I'm doing up pancakes and sausage."

"Links or patties?" Spud asked.

"Links. I got inspired last night," she said, giving Cloud a cheery grin and a wink. He immediately tried to hide his face behind his mug of joe, but not before Hank noticed his cheeks turn red again.

"Voice, you've got dinner duty tonight. Can I put in a request?" Hank asked him.

"I guess so. What would you like?"

"Spaghetti and meatballs." She was still grinning at Cloud.

Cloud put down his fork and gave her an exasperated look.

"Alright, Hank. I was a little disoriented last night, ok?"

"What you were was a little underdressed."

"Where that *moose* you're so interested in getting kicked the trailer was right outside where my *head* was."

"And *still* didn't knock enough sense into you for you to put on a pair of pants before you came outside to investigate," Hank declared. "Bet you don't sleep *au naturel* for the rest of the trip." She held up a sausage link on the end of the two-pronged cooking fork she was using, gave it a look and then looked at him before putting it on a plate for Spud along with a couple of pancakes.

With this revelation, the four remaining members of the team were now aware of just what the conversation between Hank and Cloud was about. "It's not often Hank gets an opportunity to inflict a little karma on those who delight in poking fun at her and Spud," Doc Wright quietly related to Doc Frank.

"I guess we're going back out to see if we can find the brute?" Voice asked, segueing the conversation away from any kind of discussion that might get Edge's ire up.

"That's the plan," Hank said. "Your doggie might have an easier time tracking Bullwinkle down this morning, too."

"Great! It's tough getting in some good tracking experience for him. I've tried having him track the cats, but they wander all over the residence level, so he just gets confused."

"Maybe he can track us down another raccoon too," Edge said.

"You want another raccoon stew?" Spud asked incredulously.

"It wasn't bad at all," Edge replied.

The rest of the team stared at him, having never heard him show a liking for anything that wasn't absolutely identifiable as having been strictly a product of modern food production—and quite a few of those items were off-limits for him as well.

"Speaking of raccoon, where's your hat?" Amigo asked Spud.

"I haven't had time to get it together yet," Hank admitted. "The hide is stretched and tanned, but I have to get it off the stretcher and work with it a bit more to get it supple enough for sewing."

"You should have seen how she skinned that thing," Edge remarked to Doc Wright and Doc Frank.

"Pioneer woman?" Doc Wright asked.

"Gotta make my man a hat," Hank said. "After all, he's a lumberjack."

Spud hung his head to hide the fact that he was smiling and looked askance at Hank. The rest of the team chuckled.

"I take it there's an inside joke involved here," Doc Wright determined.

"Just a little one," Voice revealed. "But back to the topic of tracking the moose, ok if Chip and I take the lead this morning?"

"Sure thing," Hank said. "If it will get him a little better at the kind of work we need him for, I'm all for it."

"This is going to be interesting working with our canine cop," Crow said. "Can he tackle a moose?"

"I would not advise that," Hank declared. "If Bullwinkle thinks he can take out a camping trailer, I have no doubt he'd not have an issue with a dog that's only a tenth his size at best."

"That could be an issue," Voice mused. "Chip thinks he can take on anything."

"You've got him well enough trained so that he'll obey you, right?" Edge asked.

"He should. But this will be a novel situation for him."

"If you have any doubts, Voice..." Spud began.

"Yeah. We don't want anything to happen to our doggo," Amigo agreed.

Voice ruffled Chip's ears and took out a pull toy for him to grapple with a bit. His pride in the concerns his team-mates were showing for his canine partner was evident.

"He's a good guy," Voice said. "He'll obey."

THE TEAM SET OUT, Voice and Chip in the lead. Chip was energetically dashing back and forth, bounding through the trees and then down to the water's edge and spending a fair amount of time sniffing at the ground before returning to Voice. Voice had him fitted with his vest, his doggy bum ticker stuck in a pocket on the inside of it next to his fur and his canine earpiece clipped to his ear. Voice would occasion-ally quietly command him to come, and there he'd be, bouncing back to greet Voice and get a scratch on his neck, his ears rubbed, a tug-o-war session, or a treat before Voice would give him the hand signal to seek once again.

"How do you keep up with him?" Crow asked, watching

Chip dash off into the trees again, then cross their path on his way to the water's edge.

"I don't," Voice admitted.

"I don't think any of us could," Crow conceded, watching Chip come galloping back to make a circle around the team as if to herd them forward a bit faster.

Coming around a bend in the path they'd been walking on, they saw Chip in the distance, sitting on the trail. When the dog saw Voice, he let out a plaintive *rowr-ow!*

Voice signaled him with *what?*

Chip stood, pawed at the ground, then sat back down.

"He's got something," Voice announced to the rest of the team. "That's his alert signal."

Voice trotted forward to where Chip sat, prompting Chip to stand and sniff at the ground.

"What's he got?" Edge asked as the rest of the team neared.

"Looks like some fresh scat," Voice said. He pointed for Hank to get a look. "Is that moose?"

Hank got a look herself, and pronounced the oval, black droppings the size of jumbo black olives too big to be anything but moose.

"Good dog!" Voice praised Chip, who immediately got up and started a back-and-forth survey of the immediate area with his nose to the ground. Letting out a single bark, he sat again.

"He's got a hoof print here too," Voice announced.

Hank came up and judged the hoof print with an outstretched hand.

"That's got to be our moose too," she confirmed. "It's too big even for a good-size elk."

Chip sniffed and sprang along the trail, then turned into the trees, continuing to follow the scent of the moose. The team trailed along behind him with Chip occasionally halting to allow them to catch up with him. His path meandered among the trees, then headed back down toward the water when suddenly he let out a single bark followed by the sound of something crashing through the underbrush.

The team ran toward the sound of Chip's bark in time to see their quarry bound off across the trail they had originally been walking on and head toward the water.

"Oh shit!" Hank exclaimed. Gun in hand, she ran after it, but was no match for moose nor dog. Arriving at the water's edge, she stood next to Chip, who was barking his frustration as the moose swam off toward the other shore of the elongated reservoir.

The rest of the team arrived to find Hank standing dejectedly, heaving her shoulders in a sigh.

"Aren't you going to shoot it?" Cloud asked as he watched the moose swimming away.

"No."

"Why not?"

She turned to him with an annoyed look on her face.

"Because we don't have a boat."

"What's a boat got to do with it?" Cloud demanded. It was obvious to all that he wanted his revenge for what he now blamed the moose for: his all-too-revealing exit from his trailer during the wee hours of the night.

"If I shoot yon moose who swimmeth in the water, that's where he dies," Hank explained with exasperation. "We can't let him just float out there—we have to recover the carcass. I know you have a good tolerance for cold; you proved that last night," she smirked. "But that water is even colder than the air you tolerated in your all-together. I doubt you want to swim out and bring that beast back."

The team stood and watched as the animal reached the

other shore and climbed out, then turned and looked back at them. Defiantly, they all imagined.

"Our moose is a pain in the butt," Spud concluded.

Hank adopted a Russian accent and proclaimed, "Don't vorry, Boris. Ve shall get moose. Maybe not today, but ve shall get moose!"

You can't shed a tear for her, eh? he thought as he made his way through the trees to the back of the house. *Let's just see if you deserve what you gave her.*

He had watched from Holly's yard until the neighbor drove off, then waited a while longer before assuring himself that the man had headed to work and wouldn't be back any time soon. Then he had made his way through the trees from Holly's yard to the neighbor's.

No wonder she had a dispute with you, he thought, reflecting on the contrast between Holly's prim yard with the house nestled back against the trees and her garden plots already being tilled in anticipation of planting some early cold weather crops. The bucket that had held the bird seed she was filling her birdfeeder with still lay on the ground, the seed already consumed by the wildlife that doubtless visited the house to take advantage of her generosity. He had wept when he noticed not only the bucket, but the brown and crusted patch in the lawn that showed where her lifeblood had drained from her as she lay dying.

His own blood seething, he regarded the derelict and rusting cars and piles of debris in the neighbor's yard that abutted her rear property line. *What a slob! I'd be surprised if her well wasn't contaminated by all this shit!*

He made his way to the back of the house, noting that the back door was one of those sliding glass patio doors. He lifted upward on the outer panel and was rewarded with the door coming off its track.

Dumb ass! It's surprising you've never been robbed. But then, if you're too cheap to get someone to haul all this garbage off to the landfill, then I guess you're too cheap to spend a couple of bucks on screws to put in the tracks so someone else couldn't do what I just did.

He set the door aside and walked in, then went methodically through the house, being careful to leave no evidence of his having been there. He wasn't interested in anything else the neighbor had. He was searching for one thing and one thing only: a gun chambered in .243. He took his time, knowing the neighbor wouldn't arrive back until at least lunchtime, and with no real work to be had in Makinen other than at the post office, was pretty sure he wouldn't even return then. *Probably works in Duluth, given how early he left.*

He had no intention of confronting the man, much as it would have satisfied him to do so. He just wanted to find the gun and then drop a dime to the county sheriff. "I overheard the neighbor saying he couldn't care less that she was dead, and he's got a gun with a caliber that matches the one she was shot with." He imagined himself composing the note a hundred times since he'd heard what the neighbor had said.

But even with a thorough sweep of the house, he was coming up empty. No gun safes, no guns. Not in the closets, not in the bed stands, not even between the mattresses. None. Nichts. Zilch.

He went back through the house, giving careful attention to everything he had examined and making sure everything was exactly as he had found it. He then went through again, making sure he hadn't tracked any dirt, mud, or grass in on his shoes. Going back out the door, he reset it on its track and closed it. Then he stood outside with his hands on his hips, his lips fused together in consternation.

"He doesn't even have a gun of any kind," he muttered to himself. *He may have hated her, but he wasn't the one who killed her.*

He walked off back into Holly's backyard, carefully ducking under the crime scene tape, then back out through the woods to the west side of the house and to where he had parked his truck. Climbing in, he took up the small notepad he'd brought with him and turned to a page of notes. Taking his pencil, he scratched through what was written on one of the lines.

It was the neighbor's name and address. But there were others, and he intended to investigate them all.

Whoever you are, he thought, his anger rising, *you better hope the cops get to you before I do!*

"So now what?" Voice asked after the team had finished eating lunch. "Go back out and see if we can find the moose?"

"I doubt he'll be back today," Hank said. "Chip probably surprised him as he was bedding down, so I imagine that right now he's bedded down on the other side of the reservoir."

"You think he'll come back to this side?" Crow asked.

"According to the rangers, he's made it a habit to come back to this spot and be a pain in the ass," Hank said. She was annoyed that so far, the moose had evaded her.

"Then what's the game plan?" Crow asked.

Hank picked up a small stick and tossed it dejectedly into the campfire ring. "I guess we all go down to the water's edge and watch Doc Wright fish," she groused. "Or go read a book. Or something."

"I think I'll do a little more work with the Chipster," Voice said.

"I guess we can gather some firewood," Edge suggested.

"Maybe hunt up another raccoon," Spud added.

"I'm gonna catch up on some sleep," Amigo decided. "Cloud wasn't the only one got woke up by the damned moose."

Hank hugged her knees to her chest. "This is not how I envisioned this hunt going." She plopped her chin on her knees, clearly bored.

"Come on, Love. We can see about gathering some firewood too. Then come back, have a nice lunch, and take a nap in case Bullwinkle decides to pay us another visit in the middle of the night."

Hank rocked herself to her feet and trudged after him.

The duo soon fell into walking along the way they might when rockhounding, Spud thinking that if perhaps Hank found something interesting in the mineral realm it would brighten her spirits. Hank trudged along, her disinterested countenance a reflection of the fact that she didn't even find the local geology of significance. At one point, she stopped and took out a throwing knife and propelled it at a tree. Hitting in the wrong orientation, it simply bounced off and fell to the ground. Retrieving it, she said, "I've got to get Edge to teach me how he does it." She leaned back against the tree and stared at her feet, totally unimpressed with anything and everything.

Spud walked up and put a hand against the tree next to

her head. Gazing at her, he said, "You know what we've never had?"

"No. What?" she asked, her tone reflecting the ennui she felt.

"We've essentially been married twice unit-style, but we've never had a honeymoon. Aren't we overdue?"

She looked up at him. "Is that why you've been so hot to trot every night?"

"I thought I was always hot to trot. At least according to you."

"You've seemed especially hot to trot ever since we got here. Almost as much as our first night together."

"Is that bad?"

He saw her starting to warm up. "I wouldn't say *that*," she proposed.

He moved closer, effectively pinning her against the tree.

"You're not thinking right here."

He looked all around. "I'm not seeing a soul. Just my beautiful wife."

"You are totally incorrigible."

"More like totally in love. Submit to me, wife."

"You're out of your mind. It's only what? Forty-five degrees out here?"

"All I've got to do is unzip."

"Not me, fella. I've got to drop my pants. I think the appropriate song would be 'Blue Moon'."

Spud stood up straight. "Everyone's out of the camp right now, and there's a warm bed in a warm trailer back there that I know will be good for what I have in mind because I've used it every night since we've been here for that purpose."

"You are completely and utterly incorrigible."

Spud pinned her back against the tree and proceeded to

give her a ravenous kiss. When he finished, Hank stayed leaned against the tree with her head against it.

"So, which will it be? Here, or back in the trailer?"

Hank didn't say a word. Just stood up and headed back to the camp, Spud smiling and following her.

CHRISTOPHER FAY WALKED into the pawn shop in Duluth, Minnesota.

"Hey, Lionel. How's it going?"

"Going well, Chris—going well," the pawn broker proclaimed. "I think there's a certain gun you're interested in, isn't there?"

"I believe there is."

The pawn broker went back to his gun safe and brought out the hunting rifle he'd recently acquired. Bringing it to the front counter, he said, "You're going to fall in love with this." He pushed the gun sleeve toward Chris and invited him to open it up himself.

Unzipping the case, Chris laid it open and whistled at the sight of the gun within.

"That's a sweet one."

He picked it up and gave it a careful looking over.

"Looks brand new."

"It's not. They don't even make that model anymore," Lionel said. "This is a gun that's seen a lot of loving care. Hardly a nick on it, and not a speck of rust anywhere. I put the bluing at ninety-nine percent as well. The guy said it was his dad's gun. Dad must have kept it in a safe and never touched it."

"I doubt that," Chris said while holding it and looking

through the scope. "It's been fired recently. I can smell the fresh residue. And the scope is a new model."

Lionel shrugged. "Maybe his dad put the new scope on before he died, and Junior took it to the range and fired it once."

"Whatever," Chris said. "I agree it's a nice gun. How much are you wanting for it?"

"In that condition? I'd say right about at *Blue Book*."

"Condition or no, it's still a used gun. Hand me the *Blue Book* so I can get a look for myself what they say this gun is worth."

Lionel reluctantly handed over the *Blue Book of Gun Values* and waited patiently while Chris looked up the gun.

"With the scope, I make it worth about eleven hundred," Lionel said as Chris looked at the data.

"I agree," Chris said. "Tell you what: make it an even thousand, and you've got a deal."

Still gives me a nice profit, Lionel thought. "Sure you won't give me eleven hundred? I'm betting I can get someone to give me that."

"You've got a bird in the hand," Chris said. "I can give you a thousand right now, or you can take your chances that no one else will make you a good offer and I'll change my mind."

"You drive a hard bargain," Lionel said, taking the rifle back and zipping it back inside its sleeve. "Alright, I'll take your thousand."

Chris smiled and went for his wallet, pulling out ten one-hundred-dollar bills. "You won't even have to pay a credit card fee," he said.

"Yeah, but I've got to get the state's cut, so I'm going to need sixty-eight dollars and seventy-five cents more from you."

Chris took another hundred from his wallet. "Gonna take the change and have me a nice celebratory steak dinner," he proclaimed. "Right after I take this home and put it in my gun safe."

"You do that. Take good care of that gun and I'm sure it'll appreciate in value, too."

"HOW DID YOUR NAP GO?" Crow asked Amigo.

"Not so well."

"Why? What happened?"

"It was a bit noisy in the camp," Amigo explained. "It seems a couple of people forgot I was there trying to get a little extra shut eye."

Hank nearly choked on the barbecue pork rib she was eating. She gave Spud a look that had *I thought you said no one was in the camp* written all over it. He just looked over top of his own pork rib and gave a little shrug.

"Who might that have been?" Edge asked, knowing full well who it *had* to have been.

"The trailer was a-rockin', so I didn't go a-knockin'," Amigo replied.

Doc Frank was grinning while listening to this exchange. He reflected that his experiences serving the unit were a bit different from his experiences while in the Navy.

The fire the team sat around while eating crackled invitingly. Spud had his feet up on one of the stones while he finished off his plate of food by sopping up barbecue sauce with a piece of bread.

"Don't look now, Spud. But your shoes are on fire," Edge advised him.

Spud pulled his feet away from the fire to see that

indeed, the soles of his shoes were smoking. Hank chuckled and decided she could make great play of the situation.

"That's not from the fire—that's from him chasing me back into the camp this afternoon."

The rest of the team looked at her, mouths gaping, before breaking into laughter. Chip bounced and twirled, expressing his delight at the joviality of the team members. Voice gave the dog a sign and pointed at Hank, prompting Chip to go over and give her a big lick up her face.

"Chip loves you, too," Voice said as Hank wiped dog slobber off her cheek.

"And don't I feel special," she said.

"What's the plan for tomorrow?" Edge asked.

"Second verse same as the first," Hank replied. "We go out early and see if we can't locate our miscreant moose." Switching to her Natasha voice, she continued with, "Ve must find moose!"

The rest of the team chuckled.

"Maybe ve are goink about this wrong vay," she continued. "Maybe ve should be looking for *squirrel*. Ve find squirrel, ve find moose."

"Excuse me, sir," Voice said, leaning toward Cloud. "You haven't seen a squirrel flying around here lately, have you?"

"No, and I didn't see the moose that bashed in my camper this morning either."

"Well, we saw plenty of *you* this morning," Hank remarked. "Although there wasn't a whole lot to see, actually." She held up her pinky finger.

"Cut him a break, Love," Spud admonished her.

"Yeah, I know. Shrinkage." She leaned over and got a look at the truck that Cloud and his trailer companions had driven into the camp. "That's not a dinky dick truck, so it must have been shrinkage."

"A *what?*" Spud asked.

"You know: one of those trucks with big tires that's all jacked up. I've always thought that the guys who drive them are compensating, so I call them 'dinky dick trucks'."

"And I thought I was the only one who called them that," Amigo confessed. "Those, and the cars and motorcycles with shotgun mufflers."

Hank pointed an acknowledging finger in his direction. "Those too. Big noise, little penis."

She got up from her seat by the fire and stretched. "I think I'm ready for bed. I want to get an early start tomorrow morning."

"I thought you spent the afternoon in bed?" Edge said, taking one last poke at her and Spud.

"She did. But she wasn't sleeping," Spud stated with his Secret Service face in play. *And you guys can eat your hearts out,* he thought as he followed Hank to their trailer.

7

He sat and drank his coffee while staring at the small notebook open in front of him.

The neighbor didn't do it. Who did?

He looked at the list. *Her ex. Isn't that what the cop said? 'It's usually the ex.' But I heard that he was trying to get back with her. Not that I wanted that. I also heard that **his** lover wasn't too happy with being jilted. Maybe **she** did it. And then there's this rumor that Holly was seeing someone. If she was thinking of going back with her ex, could the person she was seeing have done it?*

His mind swirled with the possibilities as the remainder of his coffee gradually got cold. Taking an absent-minded sip from his cup, he grimaced. *Cold coffee. Ugh.*

Looking up at the clock, he got up with a start. *Late for work. The boss is going to have my ass!*

LIGHT WAS BARELY COLORING the sky as Hank finished her breakfast and started getting her gear together for the day's hunt. She was intent on being out in the field during the dawn hours when moose were generally more active.

As she and Spud emerged from their trailer, they found

Voice and Chip were already out, Voice tossing Chip a stick and Chip bounding after it to retrieve it, then running back full tilt to drop it in Voice's hands.

She stood checking out her 6.5 Creedmoor that she had chosen for the hunt while waiting for the others to join them. Hearing Chip bark, she looked up to see him facing away from the camp, ears erect. Then he dashed off.

"Chip!" Voice shouted as the dog ran off into the woods away from the camp. "Chip! Come! Oh shit."

Voice took off after him, anxious to not lose his canine companion to whatever had captured Chip's attention so strongly that he wouldn't obey Voice's command.

"What's going on?" Spud asked.

"Peabody evidently heard or spotted something, so his boy, Sherman, has gone after him," Hank explained with amusement. "I guess Peabody isn't the scholar Sherman thought he was, because he didn't obey a command to come."

Spud chuckled as well. "Hopefully whatever Peabody alerted to isn't too far away, or Sherman is likely to have a helluva chase ahead of him."

"We really don't want to be minus the dog, though," Hank said. "He was an expensive animal to begin with, and now that Voice has done some training with him, he's even more valuable. It would be a shame if we had to start all over again with another canine, not to mention what the loss might do to our man Voice."

VOICE DARTED AFTER CHIP, not wanting his four-pawed partner to get into a bad way. It was the first time Chip had ever disobeyed a command, which he found worrisome. He soon lost sight of Chip, and strained to detect signs of disturbed ground cover that would indicate which way the dog had gone. Continuing to call him, he trotted onward, occasionally stopping to examine the ground in front of him and then continue on. Chip had evidently made a straight beeline to whatever had grabbed his interest.

Voice was soon aided by Chip's energetic barking. Stumbling through some underbrush, he found his dog. But what else he found had him frozen in his tracks. In front of Chip stood the biggest animal he had ever seen in a wild setting, and that animal was both not looking happy and transfixed on his precious partner. He groaned as he noticed the ear tags.

Oh no—he found Bullwinkle!

His head down, the bull moose snorted, sending two jets of misty breath from his nostrils into the chill morning air. Voice correctly concluded that this was the prelude to worse yet to come.

"Chip! *Come!*" he ordered his dog as the moose took a step forward.

Chip seemed just as intimidated by the moose as Voice was when it took another step toward them—especially now that the moose appeared to be deciding which of the two animals in front of him he would charge: the four-legged one, or the two-legged one.

"Whuh-oh-oh..." Voice moaned, then turned and ran, shouting over his shoulder, "Chip! Come! *Come!!!*"

He was somewhat relieved when Chip ran full bore past him until he quickly determined that this was likely because the moose was running full bore behind him as well. Chip seemed to defy gravity as he bounded up a nearby tree, and with its branches low enough to allow it, Voice decided joining him was probably a good tactic. Hauling himself well up into the tree's branches where Chip had chosen to stop, he turned and looked back down at the ground.

Yup—there was the moose, and he was still looking none too happy. His hair raised and his ears laid back, the moose took a couple of steps backward, making Voice think he'd soon just turn and leave.

He was to be disappointed.

Instead, the moose charged at the tree, ramming it with his head and then kicking at it with his front hooves, making the tree shake.

"Haaaank!!!" Voice shouted.

Back in the camp, Hank yanked her earpiece from her ear. Holding it and looking at it for a moment, she could hear Voice's cry coming through her earpiece even with it out of her ear, followed by the cry itself sounding like an echo through the trees.

Tentatively putting her earpiece back in, she calmly said, "Voice, you know you don't have to yell. I'll be surprised if Doc Gillie doesn't tell me I just lost half the hearing in my right ear."

His voice shaking, she heard him say, "Sorry, but Chip found your moose."

"Ok, that's nice. Headed your way," she said, consulting her watch by bringing up the location screen. She put on her hearing protectors, not wanting to lose any more of her hearing than she already felt she might have from Voice's frantic yell and vowing to demand he put some sort of volume limitation on the earpiece.

She walked in the direction where her watch indicated Voice's icon, Spud behind her. Glancing at it again, she puzzled over the fact that her watch was displaying Voice's icon overlapping the 'FTC' that indicated Chip's position. *What? Is Chip standing between his legs or something?*

Getting to a point where she could now see the moose, his head down and facing the tree, Hank scratched her own head.

"Where the hell is Voice?"

She heard Spud chuckle, then noticed Voice herself. He was up in the tree, one arm hugging the trunk of the pine and the other holding the grip on Chip's harness.

The moose charged the tree again, shaking it and its occupants as well as dislodging a shower of needles.

"*Shoot it! Damn it, **shoot it!!!**"* Voice cried.

"Just a minute," Hank said, grinning.

"What the hell are you waiting for?" Voice lamented.

"Are you kidding me?" Hank said, carefully composing a picture with her watch. "I've got to get a picture of this one!"

"Oh, for heaven's sake, Hank! Screw the picture! *Shoot the moose!*"

"Just hold on," she advised him.

His exhortations hadn't calmed the moose any, which rammed the tree again, shaking more needles down and threatening to shake Voice and Chip down as well.

"*I'm trying!!!*" Voice cried. "And I wish you hurry the hell up!"

Hank chuckled and brought her gun up, satisfied with the few pictures she had taken to commemorate the event. Adopting her Russian accent, she said, "Stay calm, squirrel. I am about to keell moose!"

Taking careful aim, she honed in on the region of the moose's body where its heart would be, her little voices congratulating her for being directly to his side and thus making a heart shot easy. Then she murmured "Sending," and squeezed the trigger, feeling the light click of the sear that would start the series of events to send the one hundred and forty-three grain bullet on its trajectory.

The moose jumped, then made as if to run before flopping to its side. After a few feeble kicks, it lay still.

"Did you get it?" Voice asked.

"Nah. He's just sleeping," Hank jested as she walked up. Looking down at the animal, she commented, "He's a big beast." She then knelt beside it and stroked down its neck.

"You were a proud man, weren't you?" she remarked. "These were your woods, and you were their king. It's too bad you had to decide you couldn't share these woods with the people who also enjoy them. Your death isn't in vain, though," she continued as she stroked the animal. "You will feed us well, and the calves you fathered will take your place."

Spud was trying to imagine the huge head adorning the wall of their den back in the Nebraska complex. No matter how he might think Hank would cherish the idea, a big part of him felt it would be one ugly addition to her trophy wall.

"Are you sending the head to a taxidermist?" he asked.

"No. Not this guy. A better trophy would be if he was antlered, but he's shed his." She stood up. "And something just tells me that for this guy, that wouldn't be right. We'll take the meat, but the rest of him we'll leave. The bears and wolves will take care of the rest of him, and his essence will stay here in these woods, which is as it should be."

Any sense of relief at knowing the huge head wouldn't make it to a wall in the residence was overshadowed by the reverence Hank had shown to the downed animal. *All life is sacred,* he heard her voice echo in his head.

HANK HAD RETREATED into her camper to shower, her teammates once again watching her head off with the usual sense of wonder at the woman who had just gutted, skinned, and butchered a huge moose after securing its hind legs to a spreader and winching it into a tree. "Definitely a pioneer woman," Crow had remarked.

Edge and Amigo had volunteered to head into Hungry Horse after ice to pack the butchered meat in the coolers that had been brought. It had already been packed inside plastic and still laid out on the ground so the chill air could quickly cool it.

"I guess this means we get ready to pack up and leave," Voice said. After his highly-encouraged excursion into the top of a tree, he wasn't exactly anxious to spend another night in the woods.

"I think we should take one more day," Spud said. "Just to relax."

Voice didn't want to admit that he wouldn't find another day relaxing.

"You haven't had enough 'relaxation'?" Cloud asked, clearly by his tone indicating that he didn't feel that relaxation was actually what Spud was after.

Spud decided it was time to explain himself while Hank was still showering.

"It dawned on me when we arrived that Hank and I never had the opportunity to go on a honeymoon."

"Ah!" the rest of the men present exclaimed. "That explains a lot," Voice added.

"So, if the rest of you don't mind..." Spud suggested.

"As long as we don't get visited by another moose," Voice ventured.

Spud chuckled. "You guys should have seen that. Voice was up in that tree hanging on for dear life while the moose tried to shake him loose."

"Me and Chip both," Voice said. Chip lifted his head and

came out with a single bark. "That's right, isn't it, buddy?" Voice said, rubbing a hand between Chip's ears, then taking out his tug toy and wrestling with him.

Hank emerged from the trailer she and Spud were sharing. Looking again at the moose meat that had been laid out under the trailer, she said, "Can't wait to get this back and into the meat locker."

"We have a meat locker in Nebraska?" Crow asked.

"Yeah," Hank said, surprised that he didn't know about it. "All the red meat we get is aged. Gil's got a big meat locker that will keep it at just the right temperature for aging. When these chunks we've got here get back to Nebraska, he'll hang them in there for a couple of weeks." She grinned. "Then we eat."

"How good is it?" Voice asked.

"*Really* good if it's aged right," Hank said. "This is the first time I've ever bagged a moose, but I've eaten it before."

"Don't tell me it tastes like chicken."

"It doesn't. It tastes like a slightly gamey version of beef," Hank said. "From what I saw in this guy's stomach, he's been eating the new shoots and buds that are just starting to come up, and you know what they say: you are what you eat. He'll taste a bit like the forest smells."

The men present considered that and decided it wasn't an unpleasant prospect.

"The meat is really, really lean," Hank continued. "You don't have to eat a lot of it to get a good dose of protein. He'll serve us for an entire year, even if we ate some every day. I'm wagering we've got at least six hundred pounds of meat here."

"One animal. Six hundred pounds of meat," Spud reflected.

"We don't eat a ton of meat as it is, not when we're at the

headquarters," Hank said. "Most of what we get is either wild game that we've hunted or the meat that Gil produces, which is all grass-fed. Even the chickens get to roam and eat weeds and bugs, so it's leaner than what the typical American eats. It's probably why we crave bacon. No fat to speak of in the other meat we eat."

"I notice Doc Rich doesn't say much about us wanting full fat milk, cheese... stuff like that," Voice said.

"As long as it's Hamilton Farms," Spud noted. "I'm convinced both she and Gil are in cahoots with Mama Rose. I bet they keep track of everything we eat. And with James poking us on a regular basis, I bet they correlate all of that with how healthy we are."

"No doubt," Cloud said.

"As soon as Edge and Amigo get back, we'll want to get this meat on ice," Hank said. "Then get packed up and ready to leave tomorrow."

"Not tomorrow—the next day," Doc Frank told her.

"We're staying an extra day?"

"Per your spouse's request. Something about a honeymoon," Doc Wright explained.

Hank turned and looked at Spud.

"Just one more day, Love. One day when we're not planning on hunting a moose." He gave her a look. *That* kind of look. "We can even sleep in."

The rest of the men present grinned. They all doubted there would be much sleeping going on between the present moment and the day the trailers were hitched and driven back out of the campground.

HANK AND SPUD walked together along the path for a stretch before Spud steered her into the trees.

"You're not intending on trying the same thing you were thinking about the other day," she cautioned him.

"No. It's still cold, and you'd still have to drop your pants," Spud said, grinning at her. The crunch of their boots through the leaves was one of the few sounds that could be heard, but with buds starting to swell Hank knew from experience that it wouldn't be long before the forest they walked through would be full of life with animals coming out of hibernation and birds returning to their summer roosts.

"Do you think of what our life has been like so far?" he continued. "How many times have we had the opportunity to just walk together like this? Just enjoying each other's company someplace other than in a hole in the ground?" He reached out and took her hand, continuing to walk with her, their hands joined.

"There are times when I imagine what it will be like for us after the unit," he continued. "We'll have time for this, just walking hand in hand. Alone except for each other. Not planning a mission, or a training exercise or anything of that nature. Just time together, when we can walk and share our dreams."

Hank smiled and swung her arm, getting him to swing his as well. "And what do you dream about?"

He stopped and turned to her. "Getting married. For real. Maybe having a kid or two."

"Want to keep me barefoot and pregnant do you?"

"If children aren't what you want..." Spud began, sounding a little disappointed.

Hank hung her head. "I'm not sure if I dare want children. By the time I'm ready to retire, if I stay in the unit for as long as you have, the opportunity will have passed." She looked at him, the pain evident in her face. "Is it wrong to love what I'm doing right now?"

"Of course not," Spud said, resuming their walk. "I wouldn't have stayed in this long if I didn't love what I'm doing. It would be unfair of me to ask you to curtail your time in the team just because... of something I want."

Hank got a sudden sense of foreboding. "You're not planning on retiring, are you? That isn't why we're having this private chat, is it?"

Spud shook his head. "I'm not ready to retire yet."

He felt her hand clutch his tighter.

"That's good. Good," she said. "I'm nowhere near ready to retire. And I'm afraid."

Spud stopped again. Looking at her closely, he asked, "What are you afraid of?"

"That when you're ready to retire, I won't be. You'll go back out into the world without me. There are lots of women to choose from above deck. Maybe you'll get tired of waiting for me."

He put his hand against her cheek. "Never happen, Love. Never. If I retire, it will be because Medical says I've lost my edge and have to. If that happens, I'll make a home for us and be there waiting for you. Haven't I told you that before? And when I do, I'll take that billboard UniPerp has been using and paint a bunch of numbers on it. All you have to do is remember when you decide it's time to leave that those are GPS coordinates."

"What happens if there are no numbers there?" Hank asked, her eyes starting to glaze.

"Then it means you can find anyone you like, because I will have died."

A tear made its way down Hank's cheek. "I couldn't bear to leave the unit and discover that you had died."

He leaned and kissed her. "Then I won't. I'll hang on until we're together again. I promise."

HE SAT on the same log he'd sat on many times before, gazing through the trees to Holly's house.

How many hours did I sit here, just to get a glimpse of her? How many days did I come here? Oh, how I wanted to just walk out from among these trees, Holly. Take you in my arms, tell you how I loved you, feel your lips against mine.

Now it's too late.

The blood within his veins alternated between seething hot and freezing cold: fury over her death, chilling resolve etching his heart.

What does it matter anymore without her?

He got up and paced.

I know that bastard over there with his pigsty of a yard hated her, but he couldn't have killed her. Not without a gun. They said it was a gun. One chambered in .243. He's not the one. But the cops say it's usually the spouse, or the ex. They say her ex was trying to get back in with her, but what if she told him to take a flying leap? Could he have been mad enough to shoot her?

Only one way to find out. See if he's got the gun in his house. I'll have to find out where he's holing up these days. Then it's the same plan: if he's got the gun, drop an anonymous dime to the county sheriff. They can take it from there.

"FIND ANY GOOD ROCKS?" Edge asked as Hank and Spud returned from their walk.

"Believe it or not, Hank didn't pick up a thing," Spud said. He held his hand against her forehead. "Doesn't *feel* like she's running a fever, and I notice neither Doc Frank nor Doc Wright came to check her out...."

Edge chuckled. "I keep telling you: be grateful she likes the kinds of rocks she can pick up for free. Those twinkling colored ones you find usually set in gold aren't free. Not by a long shot."

"I've never been into jewelry," Hank admitted. "It seems like it's more trouble than it's worth. Just these two rings," she added, holding up her left hand.

Edge lowered his head. "Yeah, I guess those two are special."

"What's the game plan for tomorrow?" Amigo asked.

"I thought we'd get Doc Wright to show us the secret of catching trout," Hank said. "I never did much fishing. I was always more into hunting."

Voice was listening to all of this with his chin on his fist, petting Chip with his other hand.

"I wish I'd brought my new toy," he grumbled, getting Chip standing up to console him with a slobbery lick.

"What new toy?" Edge asked.

"My new drone."

"You've put together a new drone?" Hank asked. "What is it this time?"

"Just looks like your typical drone you can buy at a hobby shop," Voice said. "It's what it can do that's special."

"Ok—I'll bite. What can it do?" Cloud asked.

"It can watch an entire area at one time. With video—not still frames. And it has infrared capability, so we could have found Mr. Moose a lot quicker."

"Before he found you and sent you and Chip up a tree?" Edge asked.

"No problem. It could have done it easily. I call it HARVEST."

"Something tells me that's a catchy acronym," Hank postulated.

"It is. It stands for 'High Altitude Relay Visual and Electronic Surveillance Tool.'"

"That sounds a bit Orwellian," Hank remarked.

Voice shrugged. "It's not like the technology hasn't been around for a while. Mine is just smaller and has greater endurance."

"What gave you the idea for this?" Spud asked.

"I read a book."

Spud shook his head. "Not you too."

"I think maybe we shouldn't be so cavalier about Hank's book-reading," Voice said defensively "She gets some good ideas. So, I had Hal check out what's available and read a book on Gorgon Stare and Vigilant Stare."

Edge blinked once and said, "Ok, you've got me curious. What are these 'stares' you're talking about?"

"Gorgon Stare is a surveillance tool used by the military. Vigilant Stare is its civilian counterpart. They're usually pretty big and carried on aircraft. They can watch entire cities all at the same time. You can play the images backwards and forwards from an event and track the perpetrator back to where they came from and forward to where they went after the event. Then you can go to where he or she is and apprehend him. For the military, they were able to track the movements of terrorists in Afghanistan and determine who they associated with, giving them clues to entire terrorist cells."

"Who does this system watch?" Edge asked.

"Everyone."

"Um..." Edge looked over at Hank. "Forgive me if I'm wrong, but isn't that a bit of a privacy issue? Say, of the Fourth Amendment kind?"

"The oddity about privacy is that you have to have an *expectation* of privacy for it to apply," Hank said. "Can you expect that something you do outdoors is private? Certainly not if it can be seen from a public area, and the sky is considered as public as it gets. Unless you make an effort, for instance, to hide your swimming pool from the sky above it, someone can fly a drone over and record you screwing your girlfriend in the pool."

"Figures you'd consider something like that," Spud remarked.

"What's to keep someone from shooting down your drone if you do that?" Edge asked.

"The law," Hank said. "They have every right to fly their drone anywhere they want to, as long as it's something like within four hundred feet above the ground. It's destruction of property, and they can sue. But I take it if Voice's drone is 'high altitude,' we're not talking about four hundred feet. In that case, the issue is different. It's an issue of the FAA's regulation of airspace. Generally, I'm thinking there are exceptions for law enforcement use."

"I'd still think there would be some privacy issues," Amigo stated.

"Precedence has already been set on it," Hank related. "I can't remember the exact case, but it had to do with a couple of cops getting a little distracted during a drone surveillance mission. Seems a couple having sex on a rooftop took priority for a bit." She looked over to Voice. "Just how high up does this thing of yours get?"

"It depends on the atmospherics at the time, but it can get to fifteen thousand feet. At least that's what I calculate."

"How do you keep an aircraft from hitting it?"

"It has the same avoidance technology that the dragonflies have. Basically, it dodges."

"Now I wish you had brought it, too," Crow said. "I'm intrigued."

"I know we were planning on a stop at Remote Base Lake Frances," Voice ventured. "But could we maybe take the moose meat and any fish we get tomorrow back to the HQ first? Then I can pick up HARVEST and we can go play with it at Lake Frances."

"I know I begged an extra day here," Spud said. "I admit, I'm intrigued as well. Any objections to pulling out of here tomorrow and heading to Lake Frances after dropping off the meat in York? It won't cut into your fishing will it, Doc Wright?"

"Plenty of good fish in Lake Frances," Doc Wright said, always the consummate fisherman. "Walleye and pike. I'm all set up to try some cold weather fly fishing to see if I can get a pike to strike when the water is cold as well."

"Love?"

"I've never seen the Lake Frances facility," Hank said in agreement to the plan.

"Any objections?" Spud asked, raising his fist above the log he sat upon.

No one raised their hand to tap their objection.

"Then it's a slight change of plans," Spud concluded. "We head back to York tomorrow, then turn around and come back to Montana for test flying of Voice's new toy."

8

Spud and Hank won the honors of the flight back to York and then out to Great Falls, Montana, making a simple swap of 101UN for 102UN as Frank had pulled out the second Latitude and had it fueled and ready for the trip. The trip itself would take two hours in the air, and with the time difference only being one hour the team had determined that the ensuing drive from Great Falls to the Lake Frances facility wouldn't put such a dent in their time that they couldn't get the facility shipshape and provisioned. That would give them enough time to relax and get settled in before starting the next day with a briefing by Voice on his 'new toy,' as he put it. Afterward, he'd put it through its paces, with the team assisting him.

With Spud in the captain's seat and the FMS engaged, the flight was reduced to the typical monitoring of instruments and the occasional Air Traffic Control communication, leaving Spud and Hank to chat.

"You know, Hank—I'm not afraid of dying," Spud said.

Hank whipped her head to look at him.

"What made you say that?"

"That talk we were having on our walk yesterday. You said you couldn't bear to retire and find that I'd died."

Hank inwardly groaned. "Do we have to pick up the conversation from there?"

"I'm not afraid of dying," Spud repeated. "What I *am* afraid of is leaving you alone. You have to promise me that you won't just grieve for the rest of your life if something happens to me. If something happens, I want you to find happiness again." He reached over and put a hand on her thigh. "I want you to find love again."

"I hope you'll do the same should something happen to me," she replied.

"Nothing will happen to you."

"Something almost already did!" Hank declared. "Kat Hamburg damned near did it. If it hadn't been for Amigo seeing her aimed in and shoving me before she pulled the trigger, the shot she got off would have caught me right in the head. With it being a 6.5 Creedmoor round, there's a good chance it could have penetrated my helmet or snapped my head back so hard that it would have broken my neck."

"It wasn't to be. I know you don't believe in God, but God had more work for you to do."

"It's not that I don't believe in God," Hank asserted. "It's just that I don't know what God *is*. I have a hard time believing that an all-knowing omniscient being can let people suffer. Innocent people. I have a hard time thinking such a being can let evil exist." She fingered the medallion of Saint Michael that Luigi had given her. "Why banish Satan from heaven only to let him exist in hell and keep visiting that hell on Earth? Why not just destroy him?"

"It's called 'free will,' Hank. God wants us to choose on our own: Him, or Satan."

"And then He takes the ones who choose poorly and sends them into eternal punishment? No chance at redemption? How is that just?"

Spud gave a slight nod of his head and said, "Religions vary on that score. Catholics have Purgatory, where less than perfect souls get purified before moving on. Buddhists believe that you're reincarnated to have another go at it until you finally attain enlightenment."

"What do you personally believe?" Hank asked.

"I believe we don't have to worry about going to hell, because this is it. We have to work our way *out* of hell. If we fail, we get sent back here to try again."

"It sounds like you're a bit within the Buddhist camp."

"Maybe a bit. But I still believe that God decided to come live among us in the person of Jesus so that He could know exactly what we're going through—right down to feeling abandoned by God."

"That's a novel idea."

Spud shrugged. "It's a biblical idea. Jesus said, 'The spirit is willing, but the flesh is weak.' How did He know that? Because He Himself was a being in flesh. He had been tempted in the desert. He had all the urges men have, I'm sure. No one likes to talk about that—least of all preachers from their pulpits, but I'm sure He reacted physically to attractive women. While He hung on the cross, he cried out and asked, 'Why have You forsaken Me?' He felt abandoned, and not by just anyone. By His own Father. By God. We can identify with Jesus, because He went through everything we might go through—including an agonizing death."

"Do you believe that the Shroud of Turin is the burial cloth of Christ?" Hank asked.

"I don't know what to think about the Shroud of Turin," Spud said. "I'd imagine, though, that someone would have been prompted to save Christ's burial cloth. For a believer, it would be a powerful relic."

"You know what the problem is with the Shroud of Turin, though?"

"I know it's been studied a lot."

"Yeah, but they overlook the simplest clues."

"Being?"

"The blood. The amount of it. Dead people don't bleed, remember?"

Spud thought about that before Hank added, "So, either it's a fake, or Jesus was still alive when He was wrapped in the shroud."

"I guess I'll have to think about that a bit," Spud admitted. "But back to the original topic, I want you to remember what Edge promised: that if something happens to me, he'll take care of you. And I meant what I said when I told you that if that happens and you and Edge decide you want to be more than friends, you have my blessing. You both do."

Hank couldn't help but chuckle. "We'd make one odd couple. He's nearly a foot taller than I am, and weighs twice as much. People would call us 'Beauty and the Beast'."

Spud ran the back of his hand down her cheek. "You finally admit you're beautiful."

Hank held up an index finger, then said, "Contact Approach one-two-eight-point-six, one-zero-two-Uniform-November. Thanks for the ride, Center." Completing the handoff and notifying those in the cabin of their impending landing, she turned to Spud and said, "I guess that's enough philosophy for one day."

HE SPREAD out his lunch on the seat next to him. Parked at the side of the road, he was the only one there. Usually, he'd head out to find a bite to eat somewhere near where his route took him. But he no longer had time for that, prefer-ring to bring a bag lunch and do a little research on his cell phone while eating his sandwich and bag of chips, and downing a can of cola.

Fay... Fay... Who would imagine there would be that many Fays in Minnesota? I wonder if I can narrow this down. What the heck is his first name? Chris. Probably short for Christopher.

He you are. He popped the address into Google Maps and got a look at the satellite view, then smirked. *Got your-self a nice trailer to live in over by Lost Lake, I see. Bet your neighbors in those fancy houses really **love** that place of yours. Is that why you wanted to get back with Holly? Tired of slumming it?*

He leaned back. "This one ought to be pretty easy," he muttered to himself. "They don't exactly make those tin cans with a lot of security in mind. After all, how much does trailer trash have that's worth stealing?"

Now to spend a little time scoping him out. Find out when he's there and when he isn't. Then see if the ex did it after all.

"THERE'S A HELIPAD HERE," Amigo remarked as he pulled into the access road to Remote Base Lake Frances. "Why didn't we bring the helicopter?"

"Because there's only so much my butt can take," Hank said. "Seriously, the flight would have taken around five hours, and we would have had to make a fuel stop."

"I agree with Hank. Better a two-hour flight, and the drive really isn't that bad. Just a little over an hour. Gives us two extra hours to get situated and goof off," Edge said. "We really don't need the helo for this one."

"Besides, Voice might want to use the helipad as a

staging area for his test flights, and we wouldn't want it occupied by a helicopter for that," Hank said.

Amigo drove up to the entrance to the above-ground facility while everyone grabbed the gear they had brought from between their feet. Making their way inside, Voice remarked, "Not much has changed." He reached out to a nearby table and drew a little "Kilroy" with the message, "Voice was here, but where was our caretaker?" in the dust.

"Yeah, this is why we needed the extra two hours," Cloud lamented. "So, we can move the half of Montana that came to squat here back outside where it belongs."

"I take it there's a decent facility under the dirt, though?" Hank queried, looking around.

"Yes, there is," Edge declared. "You just need to grab a shovel and dig down to find it."

As they went about setting down their gear so they could pitch in and get the place cleaned, Hank sneezed.

"This place is one huge allergen," she complained.

Hearing a vehicle screech to a halt outside, Spud remarked, "That will be our caretaker now."

True to his prediction, the door flew open and a middle-aged woman burst inside.

"I'm so sorry!" she exclaimed. "I didn't get the word that you were coming until this morning."

"And there's the usual excuse," Spud whispered to Hank.

"I'm so sorry, Spud," the woman continued, walking over and starting to fawn over him. "Really. If I'd have known you were coming...."

Hank was looking disapprovingly at the woman, who had now taken up a stance next to Spud with her arm around his waist. For his part, Spud was looking distinctly uncomfortable, and those who had been in the unit long enough to have spent some time at Remote Base Lake Frances already were wearing twisted grins.

"Let me introduce you to our new people," Spud said, his tone reflecting the same demeanor as his stoic Secret Service face. "Over there is our new spotter and Sniper Two, Amigo. And here to my right is our new firearms expert and Sniper One, my wife, Hank. Amigo, Hank, may I introduce Barb Keiner."

Barb slid her arm from around Spud's waist.

"Wife?"

"Wife," Spud confirmed.

"But I didn't think team members could marry."

"They can now," Hank said coldly.

"And you're the team's sniper?"

"She's damned good, too," Edge pointed out.

Barb took a few steps away from Spud, Hank watching her every move like a hawk, keeping her eyes leveled on her.

Edge whispered over the team's comm link, "It looks like Spud isn't the only one with a jealous streak."

The rest of the team tried not to laugh.

"Well. Let me help you all get this place cleaned up," Barb said.

"I think we can handle it," Spud said.

"Oh, I wouldn't think of it! After all, this is supposed to be *my* job," Barb said, smiling saccharinely at Hank.

Spud had stuck his hands in his pockets. Looking at his feet, he said, "Barb, you know that the facility is supposed to be ready for us to occupy on a moment's notice."

Hank smirked at her.

"Yes, of course, Spud. I'm so sorry. I've just been so *busy*."

"You know that *we're* very busy as well. You're supposed to stop in on a regular basis to ensure everything is always prepared for our arrival."

Barb was now hanging her head. "I know."

"Perhaps we need to discuss this," Spud said. His tone inferred that the discussion might entail the terms of Barb's contract with the unit, and whether or not it should be broken.

"No no. No," Barb declared hurriedly. "I know I haven't been able to get here, but if you all just take a seat, I'll have this place cleaned up in no time."

Hank walked over to an upholstered chair in the common area and patted it, raising a cloud of dust.

"Where do you suggest we sit?" she asked, clapping the dust off her hands.

Barb hurried into the kitchen area, diving into a cabinet below the sink and coming back up with a can of furniture polish and a dust cloth. Quickly spraying and wiping first the tables, then the chairs in the adjoining dining area, she said, "Just take a seat right here. I'll put on a pot of coffee so you can all relax while I get the place cleaned up. I promise, Spud," she added, putting a hand on his arm and winning another icy look from Hank, "this won't happen again."

She hustled back into the kitchen, taking a coffee maker out of another cabinet. Hank noted with a sigh that at least it had been enclosed in a plastic bag so she'd be drinking coffee and not Montana's Finest Farmland. Coffee filters were likewise enclosed in a plastic bin that she thankfully noted was wiped clean and hands washed before the filter removed. Giving a sniff to an open can of coffee grounds, Barb threw it out and opened a fresh can.

Hank sighed again. It was going to be a long afternoon, and not the one she'd planned, for she was certain as she watched Barb take the vacuum cleaner from a utility closet that it would be some time before she could settle in, snuggled next to Spud, for what was rapidly becoming a much-needed nap.

GUIDED by a GPS and the coordinates he'd pulled from Google Maps, the man had walked a couple of miles through the forest until reaching the ex's trailer home. He sat in a location where he could barely see the front of the trailer, feeling confident that if he could only see a small portion of the property it sat on, likewise he would not be seen.

He watched as the ex left his house, got into his truck, and drove off. He glanced at his watch. It was two PM. He'd already done his homework there—the guy was a shift worker at one of the mines and would be working from three until eleven on the security detail.

Perfect!

He sat and waited for another half hour, just to be sure the guy didn't realize he had to come back for something. Then he made his way to the trailer. Taking out a bent paperclip from his pocket, he went to work on the lock to the door, but then stopped and grinned when he realized it was a simple spring lock. So instead, he took out his pocket knife and slid it up behind the latch, popping the door open.

Too easy. This guy better feel lucky I'm not here to rob him blind.

He walked in and looked around. *Shabby, shabby, shabby. No wonder Holly ditched you if this is the way you like to live.* He reflected on how Holly's house always looked: her yard well-trimmed, always mowed, neat flower beds and her cute little ornaments, her bird feeders in the back and her tidy vegetable gardens. Even when he'd seen inside the house, it was always neat, clean, and organized. Not so the place he was standing in. Even the dishes in the sink looked like they'd been accumulating for a while. *Holly would never put up with that!*

Walking into the bedroom, he noticed first that the bed wasn't made. And there was a smell. *That* kind of smell. A mixture of dirt and sweat and sex, like the sheets hadn't been changed in weeks. *What a pig!*

Then he noticed it. Laying across the arms of a chair was one of those padded rifle cases that zip up. He went over and unzipped it, not an easy task with gloved hands. Opening the case and not daring to touch the gun, he looked it over. It was laying so that the serial number, maker, and chambering could be read.

.243.

He fumed.

The bastard did it!

He imagined himself killing the man.

No. He's not worth it. Not worth jail time. Just drop a dime to the sheriff's office. Let them know he's got the gun that did it. Then sit in the gallery during his trial. He'll get his! We may not have the death penalty in this state, but we've got plenty of horny bastards behind bars that will give him the punishment he deserves for the rest of his goddamned life. Just the thought of it makes me wanna dance.

AMIGO HAVING READ the handwriting on the wall had convinced the others that waiting on Barb to get the remote base cleaned up—or, as he put it, get the potatoes harvested —would likely take them well through lunch and possibly through dinner as well. Hank wasn't in disagreement, but suggested that they find a place with something other than burgers and fries, given what they ate might have to suffice them for the day if the kitchen wasn't cleaned up enough to cook in.

"You're not going to find much outside of burger fare in Valier," Edge had advised her.

"What else is close by?"

Voice was investigating the possibilities on his tablet as she made her inquiry.

"It looks like there's a decent place in Cut Bank."

"Which is where?"

"'Bout a forty-five minute drive from here."

Hank clapped her hands. "*¡Vamos!*"

They all bade Barb a farewell, informing her that they were going for lunch, and exited the remote base, first circling around one end of Lake Frances, then making their way north.

"Hey, there's an airport here," Cloud pointed out. "Why didn't you two just fly into here?" he asked Hank and Spud accusingly.

"Besides fuel, no real services to speak of."

"It says it's an international airport."

"Maybe if you're bringing your bug smasher in from Canada and know enough to ask Customs to show up. But otherwise, no hangar space for something the size of a Latitude, no catering—though I suppose we could go without coffee, and most importantly, no vehicle rentals. It's a long walk from here," Hank pointed out.

"Take a right; follow US 2 into town," Voice directed Edge, who was driving.

"Ok. So, where is this place?" Edge asked.

"Right there," Voice said, pointing. "Across from the pet store." He rubbed Chip's ears.

As the team piled out of the van they'd rented, Voice announced, "Grab a table—I'll be right there. Chip!" He signed 'come' to the dog, who stood patiently while Voice attached his lead, then trotted along heeling to Voice's left as they crossed the street to the pet store.

"Gotta get something for his kid," Hank remarked, grinning.

The rest of the team and the medical personnel went in and found seats, having the wait staff put them in a room with large tables and pushing two of them together so all nine of the unit members could sit together. As their drinks were being served, they could hear an argument start back where they had entered.

"Someone ain't happy," Amigo remarked.

"Don't look now, but that someone sounds like Voice," Hank observed.

The entire remainder of the team got up and went to see if indeed it *was* Voice. To their consternation, it was. He was holding the handle on Chip's vest, saying, "This dog is staying *right with me!*"

Edge walked forward and asked, "Is there some kind of problem?"

Noting his size, the waitress figured she'd found an ally. "This *gentleman*," she began indignantly, "is insisting on bringing his dog into the restaurant. We don't allow pets."

"Look again, lady," Voice said, his demeanor a bit more aggressive than anyone on the team had ever heard him address someone. "You see the vest? See where it says 'POLICE K9' in big, fat letters?"

Hoo boy, Hank thought. *The fight is on!*

Voice reached into his pocket and drew out the Credentials of the Day: his FBI creds. Nearly shoving them in the gal's face, he repeated, "This dog stays with me."

"Calm down, Ben," Edge advised him. "She didn't have a way of knowing what the situation is."

"I would have thought she could *read,*" Voice said in his defense. He turned and found himself looking directly at Spud, whose Secret Service face was skewed slightly toward the negative.

Spud did a twirl of his finger to indicate Voice should turn back around and face the waitress. "An apology is in order, Agent Ito."

"Sorry," Voice said, turning to the waitress.

"Just sorry?" Spud asked.

"*Very* sorry," Voice said grudgingly.

As he went to say something else, Spud said, "An apology will suffice, Agent Ito." He then turned to the waitress and said, "The K9 needs to remain with us. He's not a pet—he's a trained police dog, and his handler will make sure he's on his best behavior while here."

"Thanks a heap," Hank snarled at him as Voice went with the others to their table.

"What's the big deal?" Voice demanded. "She wanted me to leave Chip out in the van. That would not have been good, huh, Chip?"

"What might not be good is finding spit in your food," Hank pointed out. "Not everyone likes cops—especially pushy ones."

"Oh, crap."

"I think maybe you should get Chip to stay and go make your apology sound a little more genuine," Hank advised.

Voice gave Chip the command for 'down' followed by 'stay' and went back out to where the waitress was. Arriving back, he announced, "Hopefully, I got it taken care of."

"She didn't seem like she was still miffed?" Hank asked.

"She still seemed a little miffed until I gave her ten bucks and promised her a good tip on top of that."

Spud nodded approval. "There ya go."

HAVING EATEN A MORE than adequate lunch and then killed time in Cut Bank, the team finally decided the inevitable trip back to Remote Base Lake Frances was in order. Each held a sense of not-so-eager anticipation at what they might find upon their arrival, not really wanting to spend additional time completing a clean-up job. Noting that Barb had left, they were dreading having to do just that. However, when they walked through the door, everyone's jaw dropped. Everyone except Spud and Edge.

The entire facility was spotless.

"How did she do it?" Hank wondered aloud.

"See, this is the thing with Barb. Whenever we show up here, it always looks like she hasn't been here since the last time we were. But once she knows we're here, the place becomes miraculously clean," Edge explained.

Hank was on her knees.

"Giving it a Marine Corps inspection?" Edge asked.

"No. Wondering if she neglected to clean up all the magic powder. I'd like to take some back with me."

Voice backed Chip out to the door mat. 'Wipe paw,' he signed, prompting Chip to vigorously wipe his paws on the mat.

Cloud laughed aloud watching the dog. "Just what have you been teaching that animal?"

Voice shrugged. "They say a Malinois can learn over a thousand signs and commands. I've been seeing just how many Chip can manage."

"Do you have a little better appreciation for Barb now?" Edge asked Hank.

"I still don't appreciate her putting her hands all over my man," Hank growled.

Edge chuckled. "Barb has been sweet on Spud ever since she first saw him."

"The feeling has never been reciprocated," Spud hastened to add.

"Seems like she would have been willing enough," Hank grumbled.

The other team members were all smiling with amusement at Hank's obvious jealousy.

Spud hesitated a bit, then said, "It would have gotten us both tossed. But truth to tell, I just wasn't interested."

"She was in the unit?" Hank asked.

"In the team," Edge confirmed.

"Really. What did she do?" Hank asked, sounding dubious.

"Undercover work mostly," Spud said.

Hank scowled at him and asked, "And did she ever go undercover with you?"

"Like I said: not the way you're thinking. Otherwise, you and I would have never had the opportunity to meet."

"Why did she leave?" Amigo asked, curious.

"She was asked to," Edge said. "The rest of us who were in the team at the time felt it would be best."

"Not because..." Hank ventured.

"Yes, because," Edge said. "She was obviously not very capable of keeping it professional, and it was putting a lot of strain on all of us—especially because Spud didn't want her advances."

Hank leveled a look at him. "So why did you all lobby for the fraternization rule to be changed?" she asked.

"It was a different situation," Crow said. "We could see that the two of you were wanting to be... *involved*, shall we say? And that it wasn't one-sided. And..." He shrugged. "I dunno. We just felt that the two of you would be stronger working together, I guess. That instead of detracting from the team, it would be an asset to let the two of you stay on as a couple. Were we wrong?"

"Not at all," Spud said, putting his arm around Hank's waist. "She's really good for me—even when she *is* acting insanely jealous."

HE WROTE out the message he wanted to send and looked it over.

No, I don't want to say it that way. 'He owns the murder weapon'? No. That would raise questions: how does this person know it's the murder weapon?

He scratched that out and wrote, 'I know he has a gun...' then scratched that out as well.

How would he know he has a gun that matches the murder weapon? That's what they're going to wonder.

'I heard he has a gun that's the same caliber as the murder weapon.' *Yeah, that's better.*

'I heard him say he could just kill her.' *Yeah, everyone says that about their ex, but in this case maybe he meant it— that's what they'll think. Didn't one of those cops say it's always the ex, or the spouse, or someone close to the victim?*

He looked over the brief note, what words remained after he'd struck out some, replaced others, totally rewritten other places.

"Now to print it out," he murmured. "Don't want it in my handwriting."

He began typing it out on his computer, adding at the end 'I'd come in, but I don't want to get involved—he's a dangerous man.'

Yeah, that should do it. Tomorrow when I go to work, I'll drop it off in one of the mailboxes outside the post office. That should make it tough to have this come back on me.

HANK LAY IN THE BED, a print book opened in her lap.

"What is it this time?" Spud asked.

"A book on government spying on citizens," Hank revealed.

"What's got you reading it?"

"We just got done with a mission where the guy's big beef was NSA spying. I want to know more of why this is a beef."

"Probable cause," Spud explained simply.

"Yeah, that's pretty much my conclusion as well. It's not the spying, it's gathering all sorts of data on *everyone* without probable cause when few people are intent on engaging in any kind of illegal activity."

She read a bit more of her book, then without taking her eyes off the page asked, "When were you going to tell me about Barb?"

"You're cute when you're jealous," Spud said.

"If you're not careful, I'll get cute with my boot."

"I really didn't think Barb was a person of any consequence," Spud said honestly. "I wasn't interested in her when she arrived in the unit, I didn't become interested in her at any time she was in the unit even though she was obviously interested in *me*, and I'm definitely not interested in her now."

"It seems she's definitely still interested in *you*, though."

"There was a reason I introduced you as my wife. I was hoping, and am still hoping that she heard 'back off!' loud and clear."

"Better hope she got the message. Sometimes, unrequited love can take strange twists. Even dangerous ones."

Spud considered that. "If it continues to be a problem, then I'll have to talk with Medical about it when we get back. It would be easy enough to get her terminated as the caretaker here on the basis of the facility not being in inhabitable shape when we arrived. It's one of the conditions of the caretaker contract: the facility must be continuously ready for use."

"Would that put her in a hard way?"

Spud reflected. "She didn't last long in the team, so it could. No big nest egg like many of us have."

"I guess as long as you stand there like a stone statue the way you did when she started to paw at you, I wouldn't want to put her in a state of hardship. Though she said she was *sooo busy!*" Hank mimicked snidely. "She must have other pursuits, then."

"Hopefully of the male variety," Spud wished aloud.

Hank snickered.

Spud reached over and took her book from her, placing it opened face down on the nightstand next to him. He drew her to him and nestled his face against her neck.

"You always say I have a 'man smell'. You know you have a woman smell, don't you?"

"I do?"

"Mmmm... yes, you do."

Hank grinned. "What do I smell like?"

"Well, when you've just showered like you are right now and haven't dabbed on perfume, you smell a bit like..." He took in a deep breath through his nose. "...A bit like a hint of vanilla and nutmeg."

Hank chuckled. "You make me sound like a cookie. Or a donut."

"Definitely good enough to eat," Spud said suggestively. "What do I smell like?"

Hank put her head against his shoulder and inhaled through her nose. "You smell like a hint of musk mixed with a fine leather that's been rubbed with saddle soap."

"And you like that smell?"

"Mmm," she replied, taking another whiff. "It gets stronger when you're aroused, too."

"It does?"

"I can always tell when you're horny. You exude man smell everywhere."

"So, Edge is right: it's pheromones."

"Who cares what it is? It turns me on."

"And your notes of nutmeg get stronger when you are."

"Really."

"Uh huh. You're starting to smell very nutmeg-y."

"And what does Barb smell like?" Hank wondered, giving him a stern look.

"When she subjects me to being close enough to notice, a bit like all the dust she vacuumed up today."

Hank laughed. "How romantic!"

9

E dge's mind hovered in that odd space most people
find their minds in when they are not quite awake
but not still asleep. He had been dreaming. Half
dream, half reality.

Yasutomi? Yasutomi! I'm home! Where are you?

Why is she hiding from me? Her car is here...

Through the house... Not in the kitchen... Not out back...

No, don't go in the bedroom. Stay out of the bedroom.

*Like a force I can't fight, and I'm there. And there she is—my
Yasutomi. She's staring in the mirror at my reflection.*

Turrrrrn arrrrrounnnnd.

No words. Can't speak. This. Don't want to see this.

Howwww farrrr alonnnng arrrrre yooooooou?

*How many months? But I've been in Afghanistan for... Not
mine. Not mine.*

*There are a lot of things a man can forgive, Yasutomi. This
isn't one of them. I was never unfaithful to you. I never even
looked at another woman.*

*Of course you weren't unfaithful! But where were you, Hal?
Why is it that when you come home, you don't come home to me?
No—you have to hang out with your buddies. Big, bad Gunnery
Sergeant Halton Fryberger is more in love with them than he is*

with his wife! Well, maybe I discovered I was more in love with one of them than with my husband.

The guy who got medicalled out? Schmitt? It's Schmitt's baby?

Just turn around, Hal. Just walk away. Go to the JAG office. They'll help you with a divorce....

He opened his eyes, swung his legs off the side of the bed, sat up and ran his hand through the military haircut he still preferred even though it had been some time since he was in the Marine Corps.

Schmitt was my best friend, he reflected. *And that's the one thing I've never told anyone here: that my best friend shacked up with my wife, and that's why I didn't hesitate when I was offered the opportunity to leave the Marine Corps by joining the unit. How does a guy do that to his best friend?*

HE WALKED UP to the mailbox just outside of the post office in Makinen. He held his brief letter in his gloved hand, neatly printed from the flash drive he'd taken to one of those copy joints, and after a second of hesitation opened the mailbox and flipped it inside.

Now we wait. I wonder who will haul him off, Dunker or Drencher?

"YOU'RE LOOKING a little worse for wear," Hank remarked to Edge as the team sat eating breakfast.

"I had a little trouble sleeping last night."

"Hank and Spud kept you awake?" Cloud poked, noting that Edge was bunked in the room next to theirs.

"Very funny," Hank said, giving Cloud the kind of look that made his teeth want to hide from her boot.

"Not breakfast table conversation, but it had nothing to do with Hank and Spud," Edge returned somberly. "Just an unpleasant walk down Memory Lane."

Hank surmised that it must, therefor, have something to do with Yasutomi, and gave Cloud a subtle sign any aviator would know as 'cut engine'.

"I hope everyone is as excited as I am to be doing the test run on HARVEST today," Voice said, his enthusiasm very evident to the rest of the team. Chip let out a single bark as if he was in agreement with his handler. "Just keep in mind, Chip—this isn't a toy." He then signed 'retrieve no'.

"I take it you're all prepared to give us both a briefing and a demonstration," Spud said.

Voice clapped his hands. "Ready and raring to go."

The rest of the team had to admit that he was confirming that with the speed he was putting away the breakfast of pancakes and sausage that had been chosen as the morning fare.

"Are you over your first impression of Barb?" Edge ventured to Hank.

"Spud has convinced me that she possesses all the wrong pheromones," Hank assured him with a grin.

Edge chuckled. "So, you had a discussion on what makes him want to... mate with you rather than her, I take it."

The medical duo was trying to feign disinterest in the topic, but Doc Frank couldn't help saying it. "I thought this wasn't a breakfast topic?"

"I thought I wasn't being quite as graphic as Cloud," Edge explained in his own defense. "I should have known better when it comes to him, though. You know what they say: you have to have a lobotomy in order to fly helicopters."

That was met by protests from both Cloud and Crow, while Hank merely pointed a fork at Edge and noted, "You also fly helicopters."

"And so do you, so I guess that qualifies us to comment. What kind of pheromones does Spud think Barb has?"

Spud was also feigning disinterest in the conversation in a valiant attempt to not turn the shade of the sunrise. He was losing.

"He says I smell like nutmeg and she smells like a fine Montana haboob."

Doc Wright spit orange juice and tried to hold at least some of it inside his mouth in spite of the rivulet that ran down his chin.

"Nutmeg, huh?" Amigo commented. "Then that explains why I'm not attracted to you. You don't smell like tacos."

VOICE BROUGHT out a case that looked all the world like some of the cases Hank had for her rifles, except smaller and square in shape. Opening it, Voice extracted a drone that looked like the same kinds found in hobby shops.

"This is HARVEST."

"Didn't you say this thing can go up to fifteen thousand feet?" Edge asked. "I thought those drones could do a few hundred at best."

"It only looks like a hobby drone," Voice explained. "It's considerably lighter, and it has some unique features." He held it so they could see the top. "First, it has a film-type solar cell. This solar cell can provide all of the juice needed to operate HARVEST and all of its systems, even on an overcast day. It also recharges a set of batteries that can operate the systems for nighttime operations."

"I take it that it can see in the dark," Cloud concluded.

Voice turned the drone so that the bottom could be seen. On it was a circular array of what looked like tiny water droplets.

"It can. See how some of these lenses look blue, and others look red? The red ones are infrared cameras; the blue are daylight cameras." He turned the drone back over and pointed at a tiny area in the very center of the drone's body. "This sensor gives the software information on which cameras to use and whether the sensitivity of a set of cameras needs to be augmented."

"Where did you get the tiny cameras?" Edge asked.

Voice grinned. "From a bunch of these." He pulled a cellphone from his pocket and tossed it onto the coffee table in the center of the group of chairs in the common area.

"You're kidding."

"When did I ever kid around about my tech?" Voice asked. He was obviously not annoyed. More like gloating.

"The trick isn't really snagging the cameras from cellphones, but getting them and their sensors to all work together," he explained. "That's not a hardware thing, that's a software thing. These cameras all overlap each other quite a bit, so what the software does is determine the overlap on the images and then does pixel averaging."

"And right there is where I heard the whooshing sound of your explanation soaring over my head," Hank admitted.

"Here's what the software does. First, it determines where the overlap in the images is by readjusting each camera's image with respect to the camera images from cameras next to it in the array. Hal, display graphic, HARVEST camera array, monitor RBLF1."

The monitor on the wall of the remote base's common

area came to life, showing a line drawing graphic of the circular camera array on the bottom of the drone.

"Take this camera here," Voice said, pointing one out. "It has this group of cameras around it that I call its constellation. There's considerable overlap between this camera and all the others in its constellation. The higher the drone is flying, the more distant the cameras in the constellation get. So, if this camera is overlapping with these six in a low-altitude constellation, it might be overlapping with all of these others" —he tapped on his tablet as he spoke, highlighting more and more of the cameras surrounding the one he'd first indicated— "at a higher flight altitude. The software then looks at the overlapped pixels, pixel by pixel. By averaging the spectrum from each pixel, it can highly refine what that pixel actually looks like. That gives greater definition to the overall image seen by HARVEST, meaning you can see finer details."

"Does that mean that the higher HARVEST is off the ground, the better picture it can render?" Hank asked.

"Not exactly. What pixel averaging does is compensates for the pixel spread."

Hank looked at him with the deer-in-the-headlights look.

"You only have so many pixels available on any one camera sensor, meaning that the higher you go, the more any single pixel 'sees', if you will," Voice explained. "The pixel itself is recording an average of the wavelengths that are hitting it, so really pixel averaging is averaging the averages each pixel sees already. The higher you go, the fuzzier things get."

"Just how fuzzy do things get?" Spud asked.

"That's what I want to find out," Voice said, grinning.

"I'm taking it the actual data is all your device gathers, and then it's sent off to Hal?" Spud asked.

"Yeah. The heaviest item in the drone, aside from its purely structural components, is the BTD."

"I'm betting that stands for 'bum ticker in a drone'," Amigo put forth.

Voice tapped his nose with a forefinger.

"How do you keep the circuitry light?" Crow queried.

"Do you have to ask?" Edge said. "Everybody: one, two, three…"

"Graphene," the rest of the team answered in unison.

Voice chuckled. "What else? The rotors on the drone are also graphene laminate, with a fine wire running down the leading edge. That wire makes contact with a band of conductive material, making the rotor arrays serve as antennas for communicating with Hal. HARVEST streams the data it gathers to Hal via the usual relay, the same way our bum tickers do. The body is reinforced with a graphene coating as well, given it's made of graphite foam. I devised a way of injecting air into the same sort of graphite structural material used in aircraft. Or should I say, other aircraft. So it's tough, but light."

"The way structural components of other aircraft have holes in them to lighten them without compromising strength," Edge concluded.

"Exactly."

"So it takes pictures. Why not just use your typical camera?" Cloud asked. "You know, on a typical airplane or helicopter? What's the HARVEST advantage?"

"It doesn't really take pictures, per se," Voice said. "Unless you want to talk about the way video cameras take pictures. HARVEST takes pictures at the same frame rate as your typical video camera: twenty-four frames per second. I know I can get that higher, and that's my goal. Get it to a high-speed camera rate of two hundred and fifty frames per second."

"Why bother going that fast?"

Voice grinned again. "So you can track Hank's bullet back to where she fired it from."

"Is that practical?" Hank asked.

Voice shrugged. "Dunno. Unless maybe you want to find out where the bullet that assassinated the president came from, and you need to know *right now* so you can catch the assassin."

This caught Spud's attention.

"This is more like a real-time video," Amigo noted.

"Yes. You can take an event, like our hypothetical assassination of the president, and then basically play the video backward to find the assassin, or forward to watch the assassin's escape route and then follow him to where he's hiding," Voice said. "But there's more."

"There usually is," Crow said seriously, showing his respect for Voice's accomplishments.

"This same video can see a wide area. A large city and its surrounding environment. If this had been available when McVeigh bombed the Murrah Building, he could have been stopped without having committed any traffic violation whatsoever just by watching him drive away from the scene. Further, if he had had an accomplice there on that day, the same video could have tracked *him* as well. It could have seen everyone who ran a stop sign or red light, everyone who did a beer run on a convenience store, and with enough resolution, everyone who spit on the sidewalk in Oklahoma City that day."

The team members were staring at him.

"This is nothing new, guys. This is just Gorgon Stare miniaturized and on steroids."

"This is George Orwell," Amigo said. "This is *1984.*"

"The technology actually started in 1935," Voice said. "So, what's the big deal?"

"Aside from the fact that we just got done with a mission where the guy was obsessed with government data-gathering, what kind of shit do you think will hit the fan when someone finds out about your new-and-improved eye-in-the-sky tech?" Crow asked.

"Who's going to tell them?" Voice protested.

"I think what you're really asking, whether you know it or not," Amigo began, addressing Crow, "is whether *we* can be trusted with this technology."

"If I couldn't be trusted with this tech, you'd know by now," Voice protested.

Amigo turned a hand palm up and indicated Voice with it. "Behold the Wizard of Hal."

"We hash this over all the time," Cloud said wearily. "But who do we always say we are? Aside from the guys who solve the cases others either can't, don't have the resources to do in a timely manner, or for whatever reason don't want to address. But beyond that, we're the ones who watch the ones who are watching everyone else out there." He turned to Voice. "I'm more interested in something a bit more practical. If this thing is operating at fifteen thousand feet, how do you keep an airplane or other aircraft from hitting it? You can't rely on the 'big sky' theory—aviation found that out early on, which is why we have Air Traffic Control. Your gizmo is small, but the damage it could do to a jet engine it gets ingested into could take an airliner down in the middle of a city."

"I thought about that," Voice said. "It has the ability to

detect anything within a half mile sphere of its location, and it can move quickly enough to avoid your typical aircraft—even military ones. About the only thing that could hit it is a bullet or a missile. A missile might be the biggest threat, because it does have an electronic signature that a properly equipped missile could home in on. The default is to simply drop by braking the rotors and letting gravity do its thing, but the rotor assemblies can also gimbal to direct it in any direction three-dimensionally."

"So I couldn't hit it with a Latitude."

"I won't say 'can't happen,' but I can say 'the probability is very, very small.' Besides, we'll always know where it's operating."

"I'm more concerned with a close encounter of the civilian kind," Cloud said.

"The most likely scenario there is another aircraft doing surveillance, and for that we just avoid the altitude they're using," Voice said.

"Another aircraft doing surveillance?" Cloud asked.

"Yeah. Vigilant Stare, Gorgon's civilian brother."

"I guess we've been living under an Orwellian system for a while. I know we used surveillance tech in war zones, but I didn't think this was a home-side phenomenon."

"Think again. All kinds of agencies use aerial surveillance of one kind or another. The FBI, the DEA..."

"Border Patrol," Amigo added. "It's one of the things I did in CBP."

"They usually use soda straw technology, which can only track one thing at a time, but yeah," Voice confirmed.

"See, the difference here is that this tech doesn't just watch a person of interest," Hank said. "It watches *everyone in its view*—innocent as well as guilty. It's the same reason people don't like NSA data-gathering. They feel that if they're not doing anything wrong, then what they're doing is nobody else's business—especially the government's."

"What you're saying, though, is like saying 'you can't look at my house from the street'. The street is available to the public, so if your house is visible from the street then anyone can see it. The sky is also public. Anything visible from the sky is fair game," Voice said.

"You sound all too certain of that," Cloud pointed out.

"I'm *dead* certain of that," Voice said. "I researched the law on it."

"Well, I suppose we should let Voice show us if it's really as great as he says it is," Spud said. "It's really a moot point about how intrusive it might be if it really doesn't see that well."

"Which brings me to one last point," Voice said. "It has its limitations. Anything that can scatter light will degrade the image. Clouds, fog, haze, dust... You're not going to get good images, if you can get images at all. High winds make it difficult to control as well. Thermal effects like ground radiation—mirage—can mess with images too."

"I have to ask. Are you conveniently not mentioning something?" Hank asked.

"Uh... like?" Voice asked, suspecting he knew what she was referring to.

"Uh... like, it's called high-altitude relay visual and *electronic* surveillance tool."

"Yeah, well... It can gather electronic signals, too."

"Like?"

"Cellphones, radios, and WiFis."

"Oh, for fuck's sake, Voice! Why don't you just call yourself the NSA?"

"If we're supposed to watch the watchers, how can we

watch them without the *tools* that allow us to watch them?" Voice asked, once again on the defense.

"He has a very valid point, Love," Spud said.

"What HARVEST does is completely legal," Voice said. "It doesn't get information by putting a tap on a cable or pulling it from a data center or anything like that. It picks up stuff literally out of the air. There isn't a law anywhere that regulates that."

"You're sure."

"I checked."

"It's creepy. But I guess I have to concede the point," Hank acknowledged.

"You say it's creepy, I say it's cool," Voice said.

"That's because *you're a geek*," Hank said.

"At this point, I think it's time to go off to see the wizard, the wonderful Wizard of Hal give us a demonstration of this thing," Spud said.

THE TEAM STOOD out at the remote base's helipad. Voice had commanded Chip to lie down, and was now unpacking the HARVEST device. Setting the drone on the ground, he took up his tablet and clipped two controllers to each side.

"Am I mistaken, or are those like video game controllers?" Hank asked.

"They are," Voice said nonchalantly. "But I'm working on using my fingertip controllers and a set of specialized glasses that use OLED technology. It's tech that's been out there for a while. If it works, I'll be using the same tech to improve our present goggles by incorporating augmented reality."

"Augmented reality," Cloud echoed.

"Yeah," Voice said, sounding a bit distracted as he powered up his tablet and readied the drone for flight. "You'll see your data overlay right in front of your eyes while still seeing your actual environment there as well."

The team members all looked at each other.

"What can we say? He's a fucking genius," Edge said in spite of his aversion to cursing.

"When I get HARVEST fully perfected, I'll be able to control it just by looking at where I want it to go," Voice murmured as the drone eased up into a hover. "Everything you see on my tablet will be displayed on augmented reality glasses."

Everyone gravitated to a position behind Voice so they could try to watch what he was seeing on his tablet versus what the drone was doing. Pushing a joystick with his thumb, the drone zipped straight up, hovering above the group.

"One hundred feet," Voice announced. "Swat the fly away from your hair, Hank."

"That thing can see a fly on my head from a hundred feet up?" she questioned, swatting above her head and seeing the fly Voice had spotted from the image being sent by the drone fly off.

"Replay that, and the fly flew off to your left."

Hank turned and gave Spud a surprised look.

Voice commanded the drone higher. "Two hundred feet, and not here, Spud." Everyone looked at him to see him quickly pull his hand away from where he'd rested it on Hank's behind.

Hank chuckled, gave Spud another look, and said, "Busted."

Voice sent the drone up higher. "Five hundred feet, and that's gross, Edge."

This time, all the rest of the team noted when they turned to look at him was a quick lowering of Edge's hand.

"What was he doing?" Spud asked.

"See for yourself." Voice was backing up the video recording, and then played it forward again, revealing that Edge had been picking his nose.

"I think I might not like this tech," Edge complained.

"Probably for the same reason our average citizen won't like this tech," Hank said. "Get a guy out mowing his lawn who doesn't feel like heading back into the house, and I guarantee you'll catch a guy watering his lawn as well."

The men didn't know whether to laugh about that one or not.

"Somehow being caught with my dick in my hand isn't what I'd like to know some cop caught on video," Cloud said.

"Or maybe standing in front of a woman scratching your balls?" Hank asked.

"That too."

"The thing about that is this: if they don't know the drone is up there—and we're quickly getting to the point where you won't be able to see it, they won't know it's seeing anything," Voice commented.

"Unless you get some unscrupulous person who decides they'll make it public, even if just at the neighbor's barbecue," Spud said.

"Yes, but this is *our* tech," Voice asserted. "For us to reveal anything it sees compromises the unit."

"If you have it now, how long before someone else has it?" Spud asked. "They don't have a fear of compromising their organization."

"Unless laws are passed regarding release of the images

to anyone outside of the agency using the tech," Amigo pointed out.

"Outside of the investigative team using the tech," Voice amended. "If you want to keep secrets, you need to limit who knows them." He nudged the controller again.

"Twenty-five hundred feet. We can see the entire complex now in the wide shot. IR is picking up all of us as well." He zoomed the image in on a spot on the roof of the remote base's building. "IR is showing that there's an area of the roof that's apparently not well insulated. Hal, send still image to Allen Chelon, Chelon Contruction with notation 'RB Lake Frances roof needs work here.'" He moved a cursor and added, "Mark location."

In addition, he tacked on, "Wave, Crow."

The entire team watched at Voice zoomed the image in on Crow, who could clearly be seen not only waving his hand, but could clearly be seen to be Crow and not just a nondescript person on the helipad.

"Heck, let's go for it," Voice murmured, nudging the controller again.

The team watched as a bar-type altitude display on the right side of the tablet's screen showed the drone in a rapid climb that ended at fifteen thousand feet.

"You can see just about all of Lake Frances and about half of Valier," Voice said. "I can move HARVEST laterally so we can see all of the lake." He tweaked with the controller, centering the lake on the tablet. "HARVEST is now directly over the lake. Did Doc Wright say he was going fishing when he headed out with the van?"

Edge chuckled. "What else? The guy's a fishing fool."

"HARVEST is integrated with Hal, the same way everyone with a bum ticker is. And Chip, of course. Hal, find Doc Wright."

A blinking green icon showed up on Voice's tablet, and he then zoomed in on it.

"HARVEST is still at fifteen thousand. The icon is Doc Wright." He then zoomed in some more. The flashing icon remained the same size relative to the screen, but the image magnified until Doc Wright could be plainly seen standing in the lake in his hip waders. Though slightly fuzzy, he was still recognizable, as was an area on the lake's surface where water was being disturbed.

"He's caught something," Voice said.

"Let's see if he can land it," Hank said, watching the doctor battle with the fish.

When he bent toward the water, they all surmised that he was netting his catch.

"Medical 1, what did you catch?" Edge asked over the comm link.

They couldn't see Doc Wright's surprised jump and frenzied look up, scanning the sky.

"Hold it up so we can see."

As he did, Voice lowered the altitude of the drone to eight thousand feet. It was still too high to be seen from the ground, but Doc Wright and his fish were now quite clear, the doctor holding a huge fish in both hands, his hands at shoulder width.

"What is that?"

"A nice pike!" they all heard the doctor report over the comm link.

"Want a nice picture to document your catch?" Voice asked.

"Can you do that?"

"Sure." Voice decreased the drone's altitude farther, soon getting the drone hovering in front of Doc Wright. Doc Wright stared at it.

"Try to look a little less 'deer-in-the-headlights'," Voice advised.

They watched as Doc Wright grinned for the camera array. Voice then sent the drone back aloft. Stopping it at ten thousand feet, he tapped a command. From his tablet's speakers, the team could hear a hissing sound.

"What is that?" Hank asked.

"SIGINT," Voice said. "What you're listening to is the simultaneous broadcast that HARVEST can receive from every active cellphone and radio within range. I'd have to get a lot closer to pick up wifi signals."

"What good is it?"

"No good at all until Hal separates the signals."

Hank began to feel very troubled. "This is too much," she said.

"Isn't it?" Voice said, thinking she was praising the tech.

"No, I mean, *this is too much*. It's too intrusive."

"Hank, I'd never think to use this for anything other than an investigation we're involved in. Nothing else has any relevance."

"Then why not limit this to what you were calling 'soda straw' capability? Just follow *one* image or *one* communication."

Voice brought HARVEST down to a hover in front of himself and plucked it out of the air as he shut it down.

"Let's take a scenario," Voice said. "You have a group of people who are surrounding another guy. They all attack the guy. Maybe it's a gang. They beat him, kick him, and stab him. Then they scatter, leaving him on the ground to die. You can only watch one of them. Which one are you going to watch? With HARVEST, you can watch *all* of them, find out where they all went after they scattered, and get all of them for murdering the guy."

"I can see the good that can come of this, but I can see the bad as well," Hank said. "The bad scares me."

"I think what scares you is the idea of someone else getting this technology," Amigo pointed out. "Do we have any reason to distrust anyone in the unit?"

"Of course not," Hank said.

"Then this tech is ours, and not to be divulged," Crow said. "All of us have an unlimited Top Secret clearance. It's as high as you can get. And we're like Vegas: what happens in the unit stays in the unit."

"How do we explain what we get with this tech?" Hank asked.

"Maybe we don't," Amigo said. "Maybe we just give a big, strong hint to whoever's case it is that we're working that perhaps they should watch this guy, that guy, and that other guy."

"You will not seek to analyze the communications feed you got," Hank said. "Right?"

"I'll ask Hal if it can separate the signals. I'll ask to hear one, only to determine if it's intelligible. I will not listen to any others if it can," Voice assured her. "Unless I just listened to a hit being ordered?"

Hank thought about that. "For now, not even that. I think we all need to consider just what we should use this for. Agreed?"

With no table to serve the purpose, everyone made a knocking motion in the air with their fist.

AFTER A FEAST OF FRESH PIKE, the team all made their way to their quarters to sleep it off. Hank slid into bed next to Spud and picked up her tablet.

"Another book?"

"Yup."

"What is it this time?"

"You know, I could make out a reading list whenever I'm reading something and you could just look at it to tell what it is...."

"Could I tell from the title?"

"Uh... maybe not."

"Then tell me what it is."

"It's a novel."

"I figured that, given you're reading it from your tablet," Spud observed. "What kind of novel?"

Hank muttered something unintelligible.

"Love, are you reading another crime novel?"

Hank got an exasperated look. "In case you've never noticed, I happen to *like* crime novels."

"I'm beginning to think you're obsessed with crime. If it isn't the real deal, then it's a novel."

"This one's a bit different. It's got an unusual twist."

"Just what kind of twist?"

Hank adopted a highbrow British accent and said, "The principal investigator is a high-ranking officer in a U.K. police department. He is also a nobleman," she said, stretching out the 'o' in 'nobleman'. "Further, he is enamored of a subordinate who is much younger than he, and worse—she's a" —Hank sniffed— "*commoner*. They are investigating the death of a man by poisoning. Strychnine, they do believe."

Spud laughed. "You and your British crime novels."

"What I like about them is that they're not all blood and guts," Hank said. "They focus usually on the investigation and the investigators. They usually also do a very good job of discussing" —she slipped back into her British accent—"proper police procedure, I dare say."

"You are insane."

"Not according to Doc Andy, and he's the authority on insanity," she pointed out.

"Have you ever let him know how many crime novels you read?"

"No."

"Why not?"

"He's never asked about my reading habits."

Spud shook his head. "And naturally, you wouldn't volunteer that you consume crime novels, nor that you like to read them right before bedtime."

Hank got a determined look and returned to reading her novel.

"You know, you've been smelling especially nutmeg-y lately," Spud ventured.

"You realize that nutmeg is psychotropic?" Hank pointed out. "The druggies call it 'spice.' They say it affects your mental state."

"Is that what it is? You're drugging me?"

Hank slapped him with her tablet. "You're *impossible.*"

"No, I'm incorrigible."

"You're incorrigible *and* impossible."

Spud began to nuzzle her neck.

"Will you stop that? Let me read my book!"

"Spoilsport."

10

"I understand we have one more day of miniaturized helicopter flight training for Voice," Cloud said.

"Yeah," Voice confirmed, sneaking a treat to Chip so he'd quit whining for a bit of everyone's breakfast.

"Be careful. Chip's training *you* now," Edge commented, noticing.

"What's on today's agenda with the drone?" Hank asked.

"I want to check the avoidance capability. Most hobby drones are maneuvered by slowing or speeding up the individual motors to the rotors. I built HARVEST a bit differently. The rotors can actually gimbal in their housings, which allows the drone to make more rapid sideways maneuvers."

"Sounds a bit complicated," Hank observed.

"Only marginally so. The main thing is that it needs to work, otherwise the scenario of the drone being hit by a plane may make utilizing HARVEST problematic." He chewed thoughtfully. "What are pilots trained to do to avoid other traffic?"

"Depends," Edge said. "If you've got it, you follow what the TCAS tells you. Otherwise, what our senior aviators taught me was a climbing turn to the right."

"What's TCAS?"

"Traffic Collision Avoidance System," Spud translated.

"And how does it work?"

"The TCAS unit interrogates the transponders of aircraft operating around it," Edge explained. "Its computer determines where those aircraft are in relation to your aircraft and displays those on a display in the cockpit. If the computer determines that the other aircraft will collide with yours, then it issues an advisory. Something like 'climb, climb'."

"Ok. Sounds a lot like what I've done with HARVEST."

"But you let HARVEST be a lot closer to an airplane than TCAS does," Spud pointed out. "TCAS determines the threat based on closure rate. Usually something like twenty seconds will get it to issue a Resolution Advisory: Edge's 'climb, climb'."

Voice scratched his chin while considering this. "I used distance, but maybe time is more appropriate," he considered. "I think I'll change that. Just a matter of reprogramming."

The others noted that he was now not as concerned with breakfast as he was with tapping out commands on his tablet. Once again, they had to inwardly express their amazement at how Voice could reprogram something on the fly.

"That should do it. Too bad I can't test this with actual aircraft."

"Don't ask me!" each of the aviators quickly said practically simultaneously. None of them relished the idea of potentially being involved in a crash should the aircraft they were flying hit a drone—even one as small as HARVEST.

"Was Hal able to untangle the electronic communications HARVEST picked up yesterday? Amigo asked.

"As a matter of fact...."

"What did Hal untangle?" Crow asked.

"A cellphone call."

The look on Hank's face told everyone that she wasn't particularly happy with this news.

"What was the call about?" Edge asked.

"A robbery in progress."

Hank immediately regretted telling Voice that the team shouldn't get involved.

"What got stolen?" she asked.

"Some laundry."

Everyone stared for a moment.

"Run that one by me again," Edge requested.

"It seems that a squirrel was stealing socks off this woman's clothesline and using them to line a nest. She was telling her bestie about it."

Hank visibly relaxed while the rest of the team laughed. "I guess that's 'You Just Can't Make This Shit Up' for today," she concluded.

"HERE'S SOMETHING INTERESTING."

The dispatcher was doing one of her less case-related activities: opening the mail.

"Yeah? Whatd'ya got?" the desk sergeant asked.

"Letter, no return address. The guy says he has info on the Fay shooting. Says her ex has the right kind of rifle for having made the shot."

Deputy Alex Gray (a.k.a. "Dunker" in Holly's wannabe paramour's mind) turned to Deputy Robert Fishback (a.k.a. "Drencher") having heard the Dispatcher's reading of the letter to the Sarge and said, "What'd I tell ya?"

"Hold up," the sergeant said. He snapped his fingers at

the dispatcher, indicating for her to grab some paperwork. "Once we get the paperwork done, you two are going to run this warrant request over to the magistrate in Duluth and get a warrant to search" —he shuffled some paperwork and yanked a folder out— "the residence of one Christopher Fay for one rifle, caliber .243 Winchester, and ammunition for same."

"THIS SHOULDN'T TAKE LONG," Voice announced as the team gathered at the helipad. Once again he had commanded Chip to lie down and stay before extracting the drone from its carrying case.

"Typical drones," he began, "maneuver by differences in rotor speeds. Less speed for any particular rotor equals less lift, so if you reduce speed on a rotor or combination of rotors, the drone tilts to the side slightly, causing the drone to drift to the tilted side. I didn't think that mechanism would be fast enough for avoiding traffic, so instead of using that mechanism, HARVEST uses a different one."

He held the inactive drone in one hand while activating it, then released it into a hover in front of him.

"What HARVEST does is adjust the pitch of the rotor blades as well as the tilt of the rotor assembly. That will sound simpler than it is, as everyone who flies probably already knows—especially the helicopter pilots."

"You made a miniature swash plate assembly?" Edge queried.

"Well, not me. The drone design is Oscar's. I just did the electronics and camera."

Everyone chuckled.

"From little green men to covert surveillance. Oscar

knows he's got a job waiting for him, doesn't he?" Hank asked.

"And he's really excited about that," Voice revealed. "He's excited enough to be a year ahead of schedule for graduation. He's been taking an enormous course load, and he stayed for the summer session as well as kept up with everything during NovoRo."

"I'm not sure the unit can tolerate two fucking geniuses at once," Hank said, prompting chuckles to turn into laughter.

"Get used to it. He's been told that this project falls under our nondisclosure agreement, and further that it's information that falls into a Top Secret category well above anything he's ever heard of, with the penalty for discussing any information whatsoever about it a life in jail rather than a life with the unit."

"I guess he had practice with keeping secrets both as our Roswell caretaker and while spoofing an entire city," Hank reasoned.

"These housings you see protect the rotor mechanisms," Voice said, pointing them out. "Oscar made them fairly robust, but because of their small size and the requirement to keep HARVEST light so it can make the altitude, we both felt that a little collar around the rods would keep the potential for a catastrophic failure due to an encounter with something like a large insect in flight—a beetle with a hard exoskeleton, perhaps—to a minimum. They're made of the same thing the body of the drone is made of: sponge graphite with a graphene armor layer."

"I take it that sponge graphite is what you're calling your graphite with air cells within it," Spud said.

"Yeah. Like it?"

"It's certainly descriptive of what you say it looks like without a shell of outer material on it," Spud confessed.

"Ok. Time to see if HARVEST is as maneuverable as Oscar says it is." He watched the drone for a moment, then announced, "Zero to ten thousand."

The team watched in amazement as the drone zipped upward.

"Where is it?" Edge asked, searching the sky above them.

"It will be too far away for you to see it with the naked eye," Voice said, prompting everyone to gather behind him to get a look at his tablet. Zooming in on the group, they could all see the tops of their heads as they peered over Voice's shoulder. Anticipating their next actions, Voice intoned, "Hal, record."

True to his prediction, everyone looked upward, then back down at his tablet.

"Hal, replay last fifteen seconds."

Once again, they were amazed to see that not only had the drone recorded them looking skyward, it could also clearly record each of their faces recognizably.

"This should demonstrate a word to the wise," Voice said. "If at any time you might find yourself being taken captive and you're outside, make your best effort to look skyward. We don't really need that with the bum ticker, but it will serve as confirmation that you're alive and well, and not incapacitated in any way. Incapacitated or not, that information can help the rest of us determine the best way to recover you."

He got a look at the altitude bar on the right side of his tablet. "Station keeping at ten thousand, and compensating for winds aloft. Avoidance test, dodge up..." he announced, giving a shove to the control sticks on his controllers. "Both sticks up is the upward dodge test command, and

HARVEST is now stable at eleven thousand feet. Dodge down..." —he gave another shove to the control sticks— "HARVEST is back at ten thousand, holding steady. Dodge left... HARVEST is now offset from directly above by a thousand feet. Dodge right... HARVEST is back on station."

"The thing is quick," Edge remarked.

"Any traffic dodging maneuver is done at full throttle and full deflection of the rotors," Voice said. "That was just a test, and a simple one. I could have done it closer to the ground, but HARVEST at the moment isn't a cheap item, and if one of the tests had failed, I wanted the altitude to get it back under control rather than risk losing the drone." His face got a satisfied smile. "I can report to Oscar that it works as advertised. He'll be happy about that. He was expressing reservations. The kid always second-guesses his talent. He also wishes he had it while he had Roswell convinced that aliens had returned."

The team watched as Voice maneuvered the drone over Lake Frances.

"Now what?" Hank asked. "Doc Wright isn't out fishing without us, is he? He promised us a fishing trip."

"Nope. He's still at the building. But he asked me to get a look at the water before we go."

"Any special reason?" Spud asked.

"Yeah. He says pike like to hide in the weeds and ambush other fish. And..." He studied the images coming back to him via HARVEST. "It looks like the best place is right where he was the other day."

DEPUTIES GRAY and Fishback arrived at Christopher Fay's trailer home in Lost Lake, and noting his truck parked outside went up, paperwork in hand, and knocked on his door. They stood and waited for a few minutes before giving the door a more vigorous rapping.

"Alright, already!" they heard from inside. "Can't you read the sign says 'Day Sleeper'? I've gotta work tonight! I'm warning you, if you're some damned solicitor, I'm going to wring your stinkin'—" He cut his threat short when he threw open the inner door and stared through the screen door at the two deputies. Squinting at their name tags, he apologized with, "Sorry, Deputy Gray and Deputy Fishback. I work nights and you wouldn't believe how many people don't take that into consideration when they pound on my door. I take it this has something to do with Holly's death?"

"Yessir. I take it you're Christopher Fay?"

"That would be me."

"Mr. Fay, we have a warrant to search your premises in connection with possible evidence in the death of Holly Fay."

Christopher opened the door to the two officers. "You're free to come in and do any looking around you want," he said. "I don't have anything to hide."

"You're telling us we have your consent to a search of your home and yard?" Deputy Fishback asked in order to confirm that consent was given and a warrant not needed.

"Sure. Come on in."

Christopher stepped aside so the two lawmen could come into the trailer home. Deputy Gray handed him the search warrant. "I know you've given your consent to a search," he informed Fay, "and I suspect you might know that you can withdraw that consent at any time. However, this search warrant means we don't need your consent, and you cannot ask for the search to be terminated. So, I hope you'll remain cooperative while we get this done."

"No problem!" Fay answered. "Like I said, I've got nothing to hide. I figured I might get pegged as a suspect at some point, but I can assure you that I didn't shoot Holly. I was trying to get back together with her."

"That's what we heard," Deputy Fishback said as the two officers proceeded to search the trailer home, methodically examining closets, under furniture, and any other place where a rifle might be concealed.

"Hey, Bob," Deputy Gray called from the bedroom.

"Whatcha got?"

Deputy Fishback made his way to the bedroom, where Gray stood by a chair, his hands in nitryl gloves. He was pointing.

"Got a rifle here chambered in .243."

Fishback looked over his shoulder at Fay. "Is that so?" He walked over and gave it a good look. "It looks like we just might have our smoking gun."

"Look, I just got that gun. A buddy of mine runs a pawn shop in Duluth, and he called me about it. Asked me if I wanted it. You've got to admit: that's a nice rifle."

"It is. I can tell from the smell that it's been recently fired as well. So, Mr. Fay, if you could turn for me and put your hands on the wall. Spread your feet apart. Before I search you, do you have anything on you that I should be concerned about? Any knives, guns, sharp objects, hand grenades?"

"What? *Hand grenades?* Of course not!" Fay scoffed as Fishback began to pat him down.

"That's good. We'd have had to confiscate the hand grenade," Fishback said with not a hint of humor. "Let me take your right hand, and no resisting, alright? I'm placing you under arrest as a suspect in the death of Holly Fay."

Fishback took Fay's hand and put handcuffs on him,

bringing his left hand down as well behind Fay's back while Fay continued to protest. As they walked him out, Gray taking the rifle in its case as well and placing it in the trunk of their cruiser, Fay objected with, "Don't you have to read me my rights?"

"No need for that, Mr. Fay," Gray said. "We won't be asking you any questions. There will be plenty of time for that once we get you over to the county jail in Duluth."

"But I've got to work tonight!" Fay protested.

"Better call in and let your boss know you're not going to make it."

THE TEAM STOOD in a stretched-out line along the shore of Lake Frances, fishing poles in hand.

"Dad and I never did any fishing," Hank said as she looked at the lure dangling on her line at the end of her pole prior to attempting another cast. She had been none too successful at the venture, casting her lure first no more than ten feet from shore and then struggling to get it in through the weeds, then managing to get the line wrapped around the end of the pole. At one point, she even managed to snag the rear of her pants so that now they sported a small hole where Doc Wright had extracted the hook from the fabric. It hadn't escaped her notice that her teammates to either side of her had put a bit more distance between themselves and her than they had between themselves and their teammate to their other side.

"It shows," Doc Wright said, then regretted the remark.

"At least you're honest," Hank sighed in agreement.

Even Spud had maintained his distance from Hank, and was now casting his line once again. With a heavy spinning rod, braided line, and a steel leader, he had chosen the brightest, gaudiest fishing lure Hank had ever seen, though admittedly she hadn't seen many. A bright green body was mated with an equally fluorescent orange belly with both separated by a bright silver midline. She had no idea why any self-respecting predator of any kind would want a taste of the thing. Spud had adeptly cast it to a point just at the edge of a stand of weeds and grass, and was now reeling it back in when he felt a strike.

His companions watched as he played the fish, alternately reeling in line and then pulling the rod upright to draw the fish in to where he could net it. Smiling, he reached into the net and held up a good-size pike.

"Pretty fish," he remarked as the others admired it. "Too pretty to keep." He gently unhooked the fish with a set of forceps and held it by the tail upright in the water he was standing in until the pike signaled its desire to not hang around any longer.

Edge likewise was reeling in a fish—in his case, a nice perch. Hank, being unfamiliar with which fish was which, asked, "What do you call that fish?"

"Dinner," Edge said.

As the afternoon wore on, Hank began to feel a bit dejected. She hadn't caught anything, and was beginning to conclude that fishing was just not her forte. Reeling her line in one more time with the plan to make it her last fishing activity of the day, she was surprised to see something glimmer on the end of her line.

"I got something!"

Spud glanced over and asked, "Do you need a net?"

Chagrined, Hank said, "I don't think so." Pulling up her line, she revealed her catch: a four-inch minnow.

Doc Wright resisted the urge to even chuckle, not

wanting to turn Hank into a person who would shun fishing for the rest of her life.

"That's a nice spottail shiner," he said. "I'm surprised you didn't get a pike to hit it while you were reeling it in."

"Hold it up! Let's get a picture!" Amigo exclaimed, winning him a look much chillier than the water they were all standing in.

Spud smiled and gave her a nod. "Keep it, Love. Everyone has got to start somewhere, and the good news for you is that you have nowhere to go but up when it comes to fishing."

Voice leaned over to Spud and quietly asked, "Just what can you do with it?"

Spud just smiled. He wasn't going to be the one to rain on Hank's parade.

Not hiding his thoughts on the matter, Crow announced, "She goes hunting. She brings back an oryx. She goes hunting again. She brings back a buffalo."

"Bison," a chorus of his teammates corrected.

"Bison. She goes hunting again. She brings back a moose. She goes fishing. She brings back a minnow."

"Just for that, I'm having it mounted," Hank pouted. "It should contrast well with the oryx and buffalo heads I already have."

Voice had to act quickly to suppress a guffaw.

"You're going to have to have it skin mounted," Doc Wright advised.

"I thought they just painted a form," Spud said.

"First, it's tough enough to find a taxidermist who will skin mount a fish these days, but unless you do it that way no one is going to believe she caught the thing, never mind kept it."

"See? I told you it was the ex."

He sat and listened to "Dunker" and "Drencher" while they both consumed fries and ketchup with a side of something else.

"I admit it's looking pretty good, but we won't have ballistics on the rifle for a while," Drencher said.

"What'd you think of his story?"

"What? That he didn't even own the gun until after she'd been shot? It'll be easy enough to check out. In the meantime, he's safe and secure over in Duluth and won't be going anywhere soon."

Good, he thought. *Let the sonuvabitch rot for as long as possible.*

"We did find that receipt from the pawn shop that seems to back him up," Drencher said.

"It'll put an interesting wrinkle in this case if it turns out to be legit," Dunker observed.

"You've got to ask, though, why Fay would put the whole thing on a pawn broker."

"First thing we do is see if the pawn broker has got matching records. Don't put it past this guy to have faked that receipt."

"You really think he could have done that?" Drencher asked.

"People alter numbers on documents all the time," Dunker said. "Maybe he doesn't know the kinds of records pawn brokers have to keep on guns, though. We check his FFL book and his 4473s he's got on file to see when he took possession of the rifle and when he sold it. We can even double-check with the FBI to see from his sales authorization through NICS when the exchange was done. Sure, he's a security guard and this isn't the first weapon he's purchased, but that doesn't mean he knows all the ins and outs of it."

HANK PACKED the last of her gear and set it by the door to their quarters in the remote base next to Spud's gear. Staring at it, she said, "Why don't we just take this stuff out now and put it by the front door so all we have to do is load it up in the morning?"

Spud shrugged. "I see no reason why not."

They lugged their laden duffle bags out, trying their best to not make any noise that might wake any teammate who might already be sleeping. As Hank stood and considered how much more they would have had to load with the large coolers of meat they'd already delivered back to Nebraska, she remarked, "That was a good hunt."

"I'm still surprised at two things, though," Spud said. "First, that you didn't ask for that moose's head for your wall, and second that Voice hasn't sicced Chip on you for leaving him up in a tree while you had to get a picture."

Hank chuckled. "It was a definite Kodak moment. I should get a print done and framed to put on the wall of The Restaurant. We could start a tradition: Great Field Team Moments, memorialized on a wall there."

Spud was glancing over toward the end of the building.

"Ever been down in the launch control?"

"Is there a reason to go?" Hank asked. "We weren't here long enough to need to get anything out of storage."

"It's kind-of interesting," Spud said. "You get there via elevator. It's a hundred and twenty feet down to it."

"That's almost as deep as one of the Atlas F silos," Hank said.

"Come on—I'll take you for a little tour."

Spud strode off to the end of the building where the entrance to the elevator that accessed the launch control and subterranean equipment module were. Letting Hank go ahead of him, he got into the elevator and sent it down to the level below.

"This way is the equipment room," he announced, directing Hank to her left as they arrived in a tunnel junction. "It's pretty much the same as it was when this was an operating Minuteman launch control facility."

Hank looked around briefly.

"My guess is that eventually, Allen will convert this into the same sort of equipment bay we have in the other former missile facilities so that we're off-grid."

He indicated she should walk back out, and pointed her in the other direction.

"This is the former launch control. The equipment has been removed to make space for our storage. But there are a couple of things left over from when this was a launch control."

"Like what?" Hank asked as she took in the racks of provisions stored along one side of the module.

Spud pulled aside a heavy curtain.

"A bed."

Hank gave him a suspicious look. "Is that why you brought me down here?"

Spud grinned.

"You know you're nothing but a forty-something naughty teenager, right?"

Spud approached her and put his hands on her hips,

then began to sing. "You make me feel so young. You make me feel like spring has sprung...."

"Something has sprung alright," Hank commented with a glance at his straining pants.

"That, my dear, is my missile."

Hank's face got a wrinkled grin. "Oh?"

"Yes. It takes two to launch it."

Hank glanced upward to where her other teammates slept—she hoped. "The other missileers seem to handle launching their missiles solo just fine," she commented.

"My missile requires a silo, and I do believe you're in charge of that," he insisted, pressing his hips against hers and holding her face to render a kiss.

"For someone who always manages to render that 'don't screw with me while I'm guarding the president' look, you're totally insane. How have you kept that hidden from Doc Andy for so long?"

"I didn't have anyone around me who brought it out before you arrived." He chuckled.

"What's so funny?"

"I'm just remembering when you *did* arrive. I don't think you uttered a single sentence without a four-letter word in it."

"I was a bit nervous when I first arrived."

"Are you nervous now?"

"I... make noise. What if I cry out? Our compadres are sleeping right over our heads."

"Correction: a hundred and twenty feet over our heads, most of it solid dirt. Plus, we are surrounded by the typical shell of reinforced concrete, and the entire area we're standing in rides on shock absorbers. Which might be a good thing."

Hank suddenly realized that he had been gradually

getting her to step backward toward the bed. Involuntarily sitting down as he pressed her backward into the edge of it, she said, "But don't missiles explode?"

"Yes. Yes, they do," he said, slipping into the bed with her.

"You're incorrigible."

11

Christopher Fay sat up on the edge of his cot in his jail cell. He never thought he'd see himself like this: dressed in a set of bright orange scrubs, and more disturbingly, separated from the outside world by a locked door. About the only thing he was grateful for was his lack of a "bunkie". He wasn't sure how being a security guard would go over with someone else being held.

He put his head in his hands. "What's going to happen to me? What about my job? I'm innocent. Will that matter to my boss? Will I even be able to prove it?"

DEPUTIES GRAY and Fishback walked into the pawn shop in Duluth. Looking up, Lionel got an instant sense of apprehension. It wasn't often that the cops came looking for stolen property, but each time made him immediately run through all of the transactions he could recall in case he'd neglected to follow the exact letter of the law. He was always careful to do that; after all, his livelihood depended on dotting every i and crossing every t. But you only needed to slip up once....

Deputy Gray walked to the counter and asked, "Are you the owner here?"

"That would be me," he said, holding out his hand. "Name's Lionel. How can I help the sheriff this morning?"

Gray pulled a copy of the receipt that had been found in Fay's trailer and showed it to him.

"Does this look like one of your receipts?"

Lionel recognized it immediately. "Yeah, that's one of mine. This guy is a regular customer. Likes firearms, and doesn't drive too hard of a bargain if I can offer him a nice one. This looks like the receipt for the rifle I sold him recently."

"How recently?"

"Three days ago, if I recall." Lionel looked at the receipt. "Yeah, I'd say that was the date."

"Do you keep a copy of your receipts?" Fishback asked.

"For firearms? I'd be an idiot if I didn't. The ATF would have my FFL in a heartbeat if I didn't." He pulled out his FFL record book. "Right here, I bought the gun from this guy. Checked out the serial number to make sure it wasn't stolen, and the gun came back clean." He was pointing out entries as he spoke. "Sold the gun to Chris here... See? The date matches the receipt. Ran him through NICS, though I knew he'd come up clean as well. He works as a security guard and would lose his job if anything ever made him unable to carry a gun. Here's the number of the 4473 he filled out. You want me to go grab that? I keep them in the back."

"I'll be damned," Gray said. "His story checks out."

"He in some kind of trouble?" Lionel asked.

"We thought he might be involved in the shooting of his estranged wife," Fishback explained. "But the rifle you sold him is the only firearm he had chambered for the correct caliber. From the dates you show here, it looks like even you didn't have the rifle until after the woman was shot."

"Oh, hell—you don't think the guy who sold me the rifle was the one who shot her, do you?" Lionel asked.

"The rifle is at the BCA forensics lab in Saint Paul right now, but I'm thinking it will be a real coincidence if it's the right rifle," Gray said. "Just in case, though, can you make copies of all the paperwork you have on this rifle for us? If nothing else, we have to be able to show cause for releasing your pal."

"Aw, man. He's in jail? Chris is about the straightest shooter I know!" Lionel declared.

"The good news for him is that it doesn't look like he's the kind of 'straight shooter' that shot his wife," Fishback said.

SPUD OCCUPIED the pilot-in-command's seat, Edge in the first officer's seat next to him as they winged the Latitude back to the York airport.

Edge had just completed the handoff from the Salt Lake City Air Route Traffic Control Center to Denver's. Settling back, he turned to Spud who was just monitoring what the FMS was telling the plane to do and asked, "Did you and Hank enjoy yourselves last night?"

"What are you talking about?" Spud asked innocently.

"I heard talking outside the door to my room last night. Sounded like the two of you were getting your gear at the front door, ready to load up this morning. Then a little later, I hear the elevator go down to the old launch control center.

Then *much* later, I hear the elevator come back up, and then I hear the shower running in your room. All of these things lead me to believe that you gave Hank a tour of the bed that's still down there in the launch control."

Spud maintained silence, along with a stoic Secret Service face.

"That's what I thought," Edge continued. "What do you think Barb is going to think when she discovers she has to change the sheets on that bed?"

"I hope what she thinks is, 'Spud's taken'," Spud replied.

"Aw. You're breaking her heart, you know."

"You want her? I hear she's available."

"I didn't say that."

"Would you?" Spud asked.

"No. She's a little too clingy for me."

Spud laughed. "And you don't think she's too clingy for *me?*"

Now it was Edge's turn to laugh. "Given that you're in love with Hank, I'd say just about any other woman might be too clingy for you. Hank's pretty fiercely independent."

"Also, not afraid to call me to task," Spud said. "About the only thing she doesn't do, which would irritate me no end if she *did* do it, is" —Spud poked Edge with his fore-finger in the chest three times. "She does put her hands on her hips, though, and give me the 'woman lecture'."

"That's gotta be the one that starts with, 'You know, if you...' Then fill in the blank for about five minutes."

"You *were* married, weren't you?"

"Oh yeah," Edge said.

In the back, most of the rest of the team was trying for a quick nap. Voice was working on ideas for improvements to HARVEST, and Hank was finishing up reading her book.

When she snapped it shut and took up her tablet, Voice asked, "What was it this time?"

She held out the book to him. "You want to read it next? It's a book about the events that happened with the FBI around the time of the 2016 election."

"Ancient history," Voice said.

"Maybe, maybe not," Hank asserted. "There were lots of mistakes, the principle one being Comey acting autonomously at one point rather than sticking to the usual protocols or conferring with his superiors at the Justice Department."

"Hasn't that stuff been resolved?" Voice asked.

"Who knows? Things like that don't usually trickle down to the rank and file. But it has me wondering about your new toy."

Voice sat back and lowered his tablet into his lap. "I don't see why you're so concerned."

Hank sighed. "It's because of the power of the thing. It would only take *one person* with a HARVEST to grab anyone in power by the short hairs."

"It's only a problem if they have something to hide," Voice said.

"That's the problem, Voice. *Everyone* has something to hide. It might be something as innocent as having shoplifted a piece of candy when they were a kid to having an affair as an adult. Maybe the candy theft wouldn't be considered a problem, but revealing an affair can have devastating consequences for lots of people: the spouses, the kids, perhaps their job, and with no opportunity for the affair to stay a thing of the past—which it might well be."

"It might be having been involved in a serious crime which can't be uncovered any other way," Voice said, as usual defending the role of technology.

Hank sighed again. "I know. I'm just trying to decide if the benefits of using a tool like HARVEST outweigh the risks."

Voice looked at her and replied, his face showing absolute sincerity. "I considered recently that with Hal I could do that kind of thing: blackmail people. People in power. I decided the same way I've decided every time I consider the power of the technology I can command. Power may corrupt, but I'm not going to let power corrupt me. Right now, I'm looking at something else, though: UniPerp. UniPerp is still out there. The last time he struck, he killed people I worked with, people I knew. Good people who didn't deserve to die, let alone by the hands of a mass murderer for what apparently is no stinking reason. Think about it: if we could crack the method behind his madness, we might be able to predict where he might strike next. But he's a slimy bastard who manages to slip away every time. Maybe not in the future, though, because we've got HARVEST overhead, watching the entire place he's targeting. When he strikes, we've got him. We can track him back to where he came from, and forward to where he went. We can get him before he kills again."

"Mr. Fay, gather any belongs you have. You're being released."

Chris Fay looked at the jailer. "For real?"

"That's what the judge says, and there are a couple of officers here that are going to take you back to your house."

"That's a switch. I thought the most you got was a free phone call for someone to pick you up."

The officer looked at hm blankly. It didn't surprise Fay; it was typical that anyone brought to jail was thought to be guilty, even though that was for the courts to decide. He hoped his boss would understand that last.

He was handed the clothes he'd been in when delivered to the county jail. Changing out of the orange scrubs, he began going through everything he might endure as a result of being wrongfully accused. The possibilities were sobering: everything from the loss of his friends to the loss of his job. If he'd considered his situation was bad before, he wasn't considering that it was much better now.

Walking out, he saw that it was the same two deputies who arrested him who had come to collect him. He glanced at their name tags to refresh his memory of their names.

"We meet again," he said. "Deputy Gray and Deputy Fishback." He tried not to chuckle at Fishback's odd name and his conclusion that the fish was likely battered and deep-fried, with a side of fries, everything swimming in ketchup—all accompanied by a diet cola, of course, to keep the calories down. He, too, had noted the size of the two deputies, concluding that their girths likely equaled their heights.

"The sheriff extends his apologies for the mistaken arrest," Gray said. "But you have to admit that you looked good for it. Estranged husband, in *discussions* with the wife, owning the right caliber of gun...."

"And I told you, I was trying to reconcile with her."

"These things get based on the evidence we have," Fishback said contritely. "In this case, the department was mistaken."

Fay bit his tongue to not say *because I couldn't be believed, in spite of a spotless record.* Instead, he considered his good fortune that there actually had been evidence that exonerated him.

"What about my rifle?" he asked as the deputies walked him to their cruiser.

"It was sent to the forensics lab in Saint Paul for ballistics testing," Gray informed him. "The department will contact them to get it back. Might take a few days for them to get it shipped."

12

"I think the expression is 'back to the grind,'" Edge commented as he sat. Seeing Hank nose down in her tablet, he added, "Another book?"

"So what if it is," she replied. She was getting tired of people's pokes at her reading habits.

"What is it this time? Must be recreational if you're reading it on your tablet."

"None of your business."

Spud chuckled. "Make a guess."

"Didn't you say she was addicted to crime novels?" Amigo asked.

"It's not a crime novel," Hank said defensively.

This time Spud laughed. "No, gentlemen—it's not a crime novel. It's a *paranormal* crime novel."

"You're kidding," Voice said, leaning to get a look.

Hank shut her tablet down and sent an annoyed look around the table. "You guys are always telling me—you, especially, my dear husband—that I shouldn't read crime novels because it's too much like work. Well, is a witch that chases demons in the company of a seer, a shifter that turns into a wolf, an illusionist, and a bunch of other weird things not far enough away from a crime novel for you?"

The others were staring at her.

"What's possessing you to read it?" Crow finally asked.

"When you read something that someone else has written, you're looking into their mind. I'm getting an interesting impression of this author by reading this book. Totally not in touch with reality. Likes to live in a fantasy world. But we do have something in common."

"Which is?" Voice asked, not seeing how Hank could have anything in common with the author of a book as she had described.

"The main character has noticed that the shifter, when not shifted, is... *Spudly.*"

Spud's eyes flew open.

"Did you mean that the way I think you did?" Edge asked.

Hank grinned and nodded.

Spud's face went to a reddening version of Secret Service Neutral.

"No need to be embarrassed, buddy," Edge said. "None of us ever got the impression that Hank didn't appreciate *everything* about you."

Hank had slid down in her chair and was now giving Spud a wrinkled 'gotcha' grin.

"Now that my lovely wife has embarrassed me, it is indeed time to get back to the grind. First up, we have more news of racial unrest."

"Why should that surprise anyone?" Cloud asked. "I got a look at some statistics recently that showed that the average wage of blacks is only about half that of whites when you look at most of the major cities. Blacks *still* aren't equal to whites in terms of economic advantage."

"Neither are women, but you don't see the women out there rioting," Hank observed.

Cloud sat back. "Maybe it's just a matter of time before they do."

"Our agents at the border continue to see human smuggling attempts, with many being apprehended stowed in tractor trailers. These are being discovered at inland checkpoints, I'll point out."

Amigo had his chin in his hand. Lifting his head, he said, "Anyone should try doing that job. Every time the head occupant of the White House changes, CBP gets handed a different set of rules."

"On the good side, CBP is also continuing to interdict large shipments of illegal drugs as well as undeclared currency at the ports of entry."

That got a thumbs up from Hank.

"We have a Texas pastor who ICE had gathered up for sexual exploitation of a minor sentenced to twenty-four years in prison."

That got two thumbs up from Hank.

"You *really* don't like those guys who go after the kids," Amigo noted.

"Given during our undercover one tried to rape me after I told him I was fifteen, I even have personal reasons for considering they come from the very bottom of the slime barrel. Besides, look at Chandra and Brianna. I think if you ask Gil or Doc Andy what they think of child molesters, you'd get even stronger language from them than you do from me."

"Speaking of the girls, I haven't seen much of them lately," Crow remarked.

"Chandra is finishing up her veterinary training when she's not upstairs helping Gil with the livestock," Spud reported. He grinned as he turned toward Hank. "Hank keeps Brianna hidden downstairs in the range whenever she has time to practice."

Hank was all smiles. "You should see her. She's a very talented and very disciplined four-P markswoman. She's looking at getting an athletic scholarship to one of the universities that has a shooting team. She could even be Olympics material."

"She's got a good coach," Amigo said.

"Without self-discipline and motivation, you can have the greatest coach in the world and you'll go nowhere in the shooting sports," Hank asserted.

"You didn't have a coach at all," Amigo noted.

"True, but I think I did have the self-discipline and motivation—which just goes to prove that the coach is just there to wave the pompoms on the sideline."

"And last but not least—"

"You just can't make this shit up!" the rest of the team exclaimed with the announcement of their favorite part of the intel briefing.

"This is true, you absolutely cannot," Spud confirmed.

"In this case, we have the mysterious investigation of the hillbilly beer heist, with apologies to anyone here who may have relatives in Arkansas."

"Distant ones, but guilty," Cloud said, raising his hand.

"Favorite cousins?" Spud asked.

"Not by a long shot," Cloud revealed.

"Then I can tell you this one. It seems a little feud of sorts broke out between a couple of neighbors in the great state of Arkansas. One of the neighbors kept an old fridge on his back porch that held one and only one item."

"Beer. Every now and then, I get a real craving for one," Cloud admitted.

"We found that out on a trip to Wyoming, as I recall," Hank said with a scowl.

"I wasn't the only one," Cloud asserted, getting everyone else except Amigo shrinking slightly in their chairs.

Spud cleared his throat nervously. "Exactly. Beer.

"He began to notice every so often that a couple of his beers would go missing. Naturally, he suspected the neighbor. But the neighbor swore up and down that he wasn't swiping the suds, as it were. So, he took his investigation to a higher level. About eight feet up a tree in his backyard, to be exact on how high the level was that he affixed a trail camera."

Hank was starting to chuckle. "Busted."

"Indeed, the trail cam revealed that it was the neighbor who was burglarizing the brew. But the victim felt that for justice to be done, there had to be an appropriate punishment. Given his choice of beer came in long-neck bottles, he very carefully removed the caps from the next six-pack, drank the beer, and refilled the bottles, replacing the caps and putting them back in the fridge."

The rest of the team members were now contemplating what the beer had been replaced with.

"The neighbor, naturally, sought his usual free beverage. But when he took a pull from the pilfered pilsner, he discovered it tasted like piss."

A universal exclamation of "ugh!" went around the table.

"Of course, the offender was offended, and sought remedy by contacting the county sheriff, who informed him that it was not illegal for someone to fill an empty bottle with post-pilsner pee, but it *was* against the law to purloin private property."

The team members groaned and sought out one of Rose's morning intel goodies to toss at Spud. Each taking a look at the small, flaky almond danish that they intended to throw but had already sampled and found to be delicious, they simply popped them in their mouths instead.

"That 'no alcohol' rule has its advantages," Cloud remarked.

"If there's nothing else?" Spud asked, expecting to give his usual dismissal.

"Yes."

Everyone turned and looked at Hank.

"I think we need to discuss HARVEST."

Voice sat back in his chair, looking defensive.

"I take it you have an objection to using it?" Edge asked.

"I wouldn't say an objection right off the bat, but I do have some reservations."

"What are they?"

"Just one, actually. This technology," she began, trying to keep her language as neutral as she could, "is tremendously powerful. This is like the roving cellphone interceptors. What were they called?"

"StingRay," Voice said.

She snapped her fingers and pointed at him. "That's right—StingRay. But along with capturing communications, this can also capture the movements of people. There *might* be a crime being committed that HARVEST picks up, but it picks up *everything*. I'm wondering if it isn't, in a sense, a Fourth Amendment violation."

"The sky is public space," Voice asserted. "Anything you can see from public space has no expectation of privacy. Anything you can *hear* from public space also has no expectation of privacy."

"I'm not so sure—"

Voice cut her off. "Do you mean to tell me that when you

were an officer in the Taos PD that if you were driving along on a routine patrol and saw a domestic assault occurring in someone's front yard that you wouldn't stop and arrest the assailant?"

"That's a bit diff—"

"If you were walking a beat and heard an altercation occurring inside a house, you wouldn't go up and knock on the door to determine if an assault was occurring?"

"I never walked—"

"No excuse! If a call came in that a neighbor heard screaming and crying and things breaking from inside the house next door you would refuse to respond?"

Hank remained silent.

"Well?"

"Alright, you have a point, but—"

"So what's the problem?"

"None of those cases involve also knowing what all the neighbors are doing at the same time," Hank countered. "All the *innocent* neighbors. Maybe the closet gay guy whose business would be ruined if someone knew he had a gay lover. Or the married guy who's getting it on with his married coworker. The people whose lives could be ruined if their little secrets got out and who could find themselves being blackmailed by someone who knew about them."

"You don't trust me," Voice said with a tinge of anger.

"I *do* trust you! But what if word of this technology gets out? Who's going to want it? What will they do with it? Someone's going to wonder at some point just how we got the information we got, and I can see at least *one* person who will be very vulnerable should any inkling of this make its way out of the unit."

"Like who?" Voice demanded.

"Oscar."

Voice fell silent. After a moment, he asked, "But who would reveal the existence of HARVEST to someone?"

"Two scenarios, Voice," Hank said. "One: mechanical failure of the drone, and someone recovers it before we can. Two: You and I and everyone else on this team aren't going to be here forever. We can trust each other implicitly, but what happens if we get someone on the team who isn't quite so trustworthy?"

"We've never had—"

"Spot," Hank said with a note of finality.

The entire team sat stunned.

"She has valid points," Spud admitted after what seemed like an interminable silence.

"I can see the validity of using this technology," Hank said. "I can see how powerful a tool it can be. But in the wrong hands, it can be a disaster. We need some rules with regard to using HARVEST."

"It would only be used for a mission," Voice put forward timidly.

"I would like to see some safeguards. First, I don't think the HARVEST drone should just be sitting around and available for anyone to pick up and use. It needs to be secured."

"You can't get much more secure than down here in the Mole Hole," Spud pointed out.

"If just *one* person can get to it, they can remove it from the Mole Hole and use it for *whatever.* I think we need to have a system like the one Voice and I had to use to regain control of Hal. Two people. Two authentications, and the authentication stations far enough apart so no one person can get to HARVEST by themselves. One person being Voice, the other randomly chosen so there's little opportunity for two people to collude on the use of the drone. For missions, before anyone can remove HARVEST from its receptacle, there has to be one hundred percent agreement from everyone in the team that it's required to meet the mission objectives."

"I'm planning upgrades, though," Voice said.

"Two people to remove HARVEST from its receptacle," Hank emphasized. "And you don't get to work on HARVEST alone. Or whoever in the future might work on it. Someone else has to stand guard over you." She withdrew her sidearm from its holster and set it on the table. "Armed."

"You'd *shoot me?*" Voice asked tremulously.

"If I knew you were going rogue, yes I would."

Voice considered this and grew calm. "I'd never go rogue, but I can see how someone might. So, I agree: two people to remove HARVEST and full agreement from the team that it's a tool that's needed for a mission at hand."

"Everyone agree?" Hank asked, raising her knuckles above the table.

Reluctantly, the rest of the team tapped their knuckles on the table.

"Then it's settled," Voice said. "I just need to make a receptacle for HARVEST."

"Which I felt assured you would do, Voice, and not make it so the rule could be defeated. I do trust you. I trust everyone in this team. But after having someone we thought we could trust and who would be an asset turn out to be a rapist and a murderer, I, for one, feel better knowing there are good rules to protect HARVEST from getting into the hands of the wrong people."

DEPUTIES GRAY and Fishback arrived at the forensics lab in Saint Paul to request the return of Christopher Fay's rifle. Going up to the desk clerk, she consulted her computer and informed them, "The lab is just finishing up with it."

"That was quick," Gray said.

"With an apparent murder case with no suspect, they moved it up." She then made a call back to the lab to let the ballistics group know that the deputies were there for the rifle.

They were soon joined by a forensic examiner in a lab coat.

"I'm afraid you can't have the rifle."

Gray looked at him questioningly. "Our potential suspect checks out. He didn't own the rifle at the time the woman was shot, so it's the wrong weapon."

"That's just it," the examiner informed him. "It's the *right* weapon. We test fired it, and the bullet shows the same rifling pattern as the bullet that was removed from the victim."

Fishback and Gray looked at each other, astonished.

"You're telling us *that rifle* is the weapon that killed Holly Fay?"

"That's what I'm saying," the examiner reiterated.

"Things just got complicated," Gray said. Turning to his partner, he added, "It's time to get the BCA involved."

"I'VE GOT SOMETHING FOR YOU," Edge announced as Hank joined him in the gym. "Got a quarter?"

"Why do I need a quarter?"

"Because you have to pay for these."

Hank chuckled. "Some gift if I have to pay for them."

"I don't know about where you come from, Hank. But where I come from, if you give a person a knife, it will sever your friendship. I don't want to lose you as a friend, so you have to pay for these."

Hank withdrew a quarter from her pocket and handed it to him. "I don't want our friendship to be severed either." Getting a look at the throwing knives, she asked, "Where did you get these?"

"I bought them from Luigi."

Hank smiled. "You don't want to lose him as a friend either, I take it."

"Not on your life. He makes excellent knives."

Hank rolled her eyes. "Guns, jewelry, knives, plaques... is there anything that man can't make out of metal?"

Edge grinned. "Not to my knowledge."

"Now I have to learn how to throw these things. Tell me this is going to be easy."

"It's going to be easy."

"Good."

"Once you get the hang of it."

Hank looked forlorn. "I knew there was a catch. I guess I'm just going to have to stick to a .22 for hunting rabbits."

"Here's the big advantage of learning how to throw a knife," Edge said. He pointed to where a standard archery bale stood against the wall. Taking one of his own knives from a set he had strapped to his right leg, he threw it so it stuck in the wooden target next to the bale. It embedded with a *thunk!* He then withdrew another knife and threw it at the bale. It sunk into the center of the target without much sound at all.

"During World War Two," Edge began, "the Army had a classified 'silent flashless weapon'. You know it as a 'bow and arrow'. Throwing knives are another silent flashless weapon. Much more silent than even a silencer can make a rifle. So, if you don't want to announce your presence to the world, you get good with a knife."

"Or a bow and arrow."

"See here?" Edge said, indicating the remainder of his throwing knives secured in their case. "They take up a lot less room than a bow, or even a crossbow."

"Crossbow…" Hank murmured. "That's another thing to try."

Edge shook his head in disbelief. "You are a dangerous woman."

"Only if you're on the wrong side of the law and refuse to stick your hands up."

"Or you're a moose that's being a troublemaker," Edge chuckled.

"Ok, Hank. Here's the first thing you've got to learn: how to hold the knife."

"You don't just grip onto it?"

"No. Throwing knives aren't meant to be gripped. The knife has to release cleanly from your hand, otherwise you can't get it to go point into the target. It'll hit wrong and just bounce off. So here's what you do: first, find the balance point of your knife. You're going to use your forefinger to direct the blade when you throw it by placing your forefinger at that spot on the edge of the shank, so you need to determine where it is. Just hold the knife on a couple of fingers like this, and move it until it balances there."

He watched as Hank manipulated the knife and got it to balance.

"Now that you have that, put the base of the shank into the palm of your hand, secure it with your thumb like this, and use one or more of your remaining fingers to secure the knife in your hand."

"One or more?"

"I only use my middle finger, but other people will maybe use two fingers or all three remaining fingers. You have to experiment with it to find your own style."

"Somehow I think I'm going to end up using my middle finger a lot," Hank muttered.

Edge rolled his eyes. "Why is it when you start something new, you always immediately jump to the conclusion that you're going to have difficulty with it? Just relax, little girl."

"Don't 'little girl' me."

"Don't act like one, and I won't call you one. Take your knife, get a comfortable grip, gonna stand about five feet away from the wooden target, and throw it."

Hank gripped the knife, drew her hand back, and flung it at the wooden target. The knife clanged against the wood and dropped onto a mat Edge had placed on the floor. Handing her another of her knives, he urged her to try again. Again, the knife simply bounced off the target and fell to the floor.

"What am I doing wrong?"

"You're releasing the knife too late," Edge said. "Try releasing a little earlier." He looked at how she was gripping the knife. "Don't hold the knife with too much pressure. You want it to slip right out of your hand."

"Ok. I can do this," she said in an attempt to convince herself. Giving it another couple of tries, however, resulted in the same lack of success.

"Don't start getting frustrated," Edge admonished her. "It takes practice, and developing a bit of your own style. Plus, I'm teaching you spinless throwing, which is a little more elegant of a technique than throwing with a spin. But I find it more versatile, because you can get results at any distance you want to be from your target, within certain limits, of course." He gave her a pat on her shoulder. "Think you can handle this without me?"

"Yeah, I can plug away at it on my own for a while. Just stop in occasionally and try to figure out what I'm doing wrong."

"Try shifting your feet a little, too," he advised her. "Just like in rifle shooting, stance is important."

Hank went back to practicing with her throwing knives, as Edge wandered off to work on the heavy bag. Listening to the regular *clang!* of yet another failed attempt at sticking a knife into the wooden target, he was at least encouraged by not hearing the entire set get thrown on the floor to the accompaniment of a string of four-letter words. He soon settled into his own workout.

It wasn't too much longer before he heard Hank exclaim, "I did it! *Woo hoo!*"

"Now see if you can be a bit more consistent," he called over from where he stood at the heavy bag. As he looked over toward her, he saw her shoulders droop.

"Hang in there, kid," he whispered to himself.

"WE'RE BACK TO SQUARE ONE," he overheard "Dunker" say as the two portly deputies sat and ate their usual ketchup with a side of burger and fries.

Reagan was wrong, you know, he thought. *Ketchup isn't a vegetable.*

"I would have sworn it was the ex," Dunker continued.

What?! He had the gun, didn't he?

"Yeah, right gun, wrong guy." Drencher said.

The man was seriously resisting the urge to go over and

shake the two deputies, demanding just what they were talking about.

"Good thing for him he kept his receipt," Dunker was saying. "Otherwise, he'd still be a guest over there in Duluth."

He was now listening intently to the two, having felt certain himself that Christopher Fay had killed his Holly.

Drencher sighed. "He told the truth. He didn't own the gun until after she had been shot. The pawn records prove that, and according to the BCA, so does the NICS check when he purchased it."

"Yeah, but what about the pawn records?" Dunker wondered. "You think maybe the pawn broker falsified the records regarding when he purchased the rifle? Seems a little suspicious what the BCA guys told us. The gun was sold by a guy with a fake ID, so that's why the ID checked out? See, that's one of the problems with the system. An ID can match someone in the system who's prohibited from having a weapon, but not someone who's ID isn't in it. It wasn't until the BCA ran it through the driver's license database that it came up as bogus."

"What are you thinking?"

"I'm thinking maybe the pawn broker did it. He said he knows the ex. According to people we've spoken with, both the ex and Holly had extramarital affairs. Maybe she was having an affair with the pawn broker and wanted to call it off with Fay wanting to get back with his wife. So he shoots her, then sells the rifle to Fay to shift the suspicion onto him."

"Then why not backdate the sale of the rifle to him?"

"That would have been too easy to prove," Dunker said. "No way you can fake a date for a NICS check. The BCA would have seen the discrepancy the minute they checked with the FBI."

"Yeah, you've got a point there," Drencher admitted. "Now the problem is, how does anyone find someone who used a fake ID? We've seen the video from the store. The guy who sold the gun's hat kept us from seeing his face."

"Looks to me like this case is headed straight for the cold file," Dunker lamented.

Not if I have anything to say about it, the man thought. *No way will I let someone get away with murdering Holly. I may just be the postman, but it's time I became a detective as well.*

"FINDING ANYTHING good for tomorrow's intel briefing?" Hank asked.

"The usual. Politicians chase after sound bites while the more pressing issues remain unaddressed. That, in turn, breeds extremism. How about you? Finding anything interesting in the sniper manual you're reading?"

"Three chapters, one item: parallax. I haven't talked to you guys about parallax adjustments."

"Do I detect a trip to the Lockridge ranges?"

Hank laughed. "Do I detect a morning intelligence briefing?"

"There's a difference. I at least try to end the briefing with something humorous. I have never known you to end a training session with anything that could be called a laughing matter."

"I do other things to get you to relax."

Spud gazed at her with that steady gaze reserved for moments when he was formulating a retort.

"Yes, but what about the other guys?"

"Voice has Page. The rest have whatever they've recently acquired from Doc Andy's drawer."

"For everyone except Voice, I'm guessing it's not quite the same."

Hank thought about that. "You're likely right. Humans are social animals, and they don't get the kind of close human contact you and I get. Not even Voice, given I don't see Page staying over at his place every night. There's someone I think could use more human contact, too."

"And who would that be?"

"Edge."

Spud gazed at her again.

"The times I've spoken with him, he impresses me as... lonely," Hank explained. "I think he's got a lot of stuff hidden inside him that he wishes he could share with someone, but he's afraid to. Maybe afraid others will see those things as weaknesses."

"I'm sure his Marine Corps buddies would see him as being weak in certain respects," Spud said. "You know he's my best friend. Other than you, that is."

"I know."

"You know he's a pacifist at heart, too?"

"I've gathered that. But I think that's what makes him a good unit operative."

"I agree. I'd rather have him backing me up than some of the others. Not that I think anyone else in the team would lose their head, but Edge is remarkably restrained. I consider it an honor that he's my best friend among all the other men. He's strong enough to break me like a match stick, but in my dreams all I've ever seen him do is grab me and haul me out of danger."

Hank studied him a moment. "You dream about the other team members?"

"I have a recurring dream that involves the entire team."

Hank settled back, waiting for him to tell her more.

"It's almost a nightmare. *Almost.* We're running. Scattering. Someone is after us—someone who wants to kill us all. He shoots me, and I die... but I don't die. I watch him chase you off a cliff and you die... but you don't die. Who gets us all out of there? Out of danger? Alive? Edge does."

"What about the man who's chasing us? What happens to him?"

"I come back to life and kill him. Shoot him. And he disappears."

"And that's it?"

"That's when I wake up."

13

unday. No deliveries. Maybe I can make some progress while the cops are twiddling their thumbs, he thought.

He had done what he usually did: parked away from Holly's house and made his way through the woods to the downed tree that served as his seat for observing her. If he closed his eyes, he could still see her tending her gardens, planting her flowers, sweeping her porch... He tried not to see her refilling the bird feeders and chattering to the birds as they tried to steal a few grains from her bucket before she could scoop the seeds into the feeders. He could only imagine along with that vision seeing her fall to the ground, the bullet having cut her life short, his opportunity to tell her _You don't have to go back to him. I love you. I've always loved you. I'll treat you the way a woman like you deserves: with tenderness and kisses, nights out and cozy dinners, with time for just the two of us. Your past doesn't matter to me; the rumors don't matter to me. I will build you a future where the only thing that matters is that I love you._

He wept. _Now, it's all gone. But I'll get the person that did this to you, Holly. I'll make him pay._

He wandered nearer than he would ever have dared when she was alive, too afraid she would see him there in the woods, watching her. As he neared the edge of the yard, something caught his eye. Going over to a tree, he peered up at the branch. Something had scarred the underside of the limb, a grazing scar that broke off bark and splinters of wood. He stood and looked along it, seeing how it lined up with the back of the house and the small, numbered flags that marked where Holly had breathed her last.

A bullet. The bullet.

Walking around to the other side of the limb, he gazed along the mark. Finding as straight a piece of wood as he could from the fallen branches on the ground, he went back and used it to sight along the scar. A clear sight line went back into the woods, stopping at another tree. He walked from where the scarred limb was toward that tree, watching the ground beneath his feet carefully. It was then he saw it: a disturbed patch of leaves and trampled vegetation. Turning and standing at the spot, he looked back to where the scarred limb on the tree was visible.

It was then that he knew.

A hunter did this. Probably after a turkey roosted in the tree. He missed, hit the limb, and the shot ricocheted off the branch and hit Holly. What was wrong with him? Didn't he have any more sense than to shoot toward someone's house?

"I'll find the guy who did this," he murmured. "I'll find him, and I'll make him pay. You wait, Holly. I'll get justice for you."

"GUESS WHAT TIME IT IS, boys and gal?" Spud asked. He knew he was asking for it, too. But Rose's offering for the intel briefing snack looked particularly good this morning, so he felt assured he wouldn't encounter a snack attack team-style by getting the little fruit-filled crescent pastries thrown at him.

"Time to go back to bed and get another half hour of sleep?" Edge offered.

"Aren't you supposed to be a good friend of mine?"

"Bet Hank could think of something more interesting to do than intel if *she* had another half hour in bed," Edge returned.

Spud narrowed his eyes slightly and looked at Edge askance.

"Don't have to go back to bed to get a little extra shut-eye," Hank assured Edge. "You'll find the intel briefing will put you to sleep right here."

"My own wife," Spud complained.

Picking up his tablet, he announced, "First up, we have a vehicular homicide case of a different kind. This one involved a driver ramming into a crowd of people, killing one and injuring several others."

"Because guns are dangerous," Amigo snorted.

"You've got to admit: he probably could have killed more people with a gun," Voice said.

"What a case like this points out," Crow observed, "is that someone intent on killing people will choose whatever weapon they have at hand. Look at UniPerp. He's used bombs, fire, guns, knives, drugs... Probably has killed more people without a gun than with one."

"You've got a point," Voice conceded.

"We have rioting over police shootings."

"A lot of departments need to clean up their act," Edge said.

"I'm going to point something out for you," Hank said. "Nobody thanks a cop when he helps them out, but they're quick to criticize when a cop crosses the line. It's not an easy job. It wasn't an easy job for me when I was in the Taos PD, nor in the FBI. And the job I've got now? Definitely not easy. The only thing that takes some of the sting out of it is that I don't have the public in my face telling me what a bad cop I am."

"Did you ever have the public in your face? I thought from what we got that you had a really clean record."

"Makes no difference. In many people's book, all cops are bad."

"Our guys working in the Border Patrol are continuing to fund us," Spud reported, hoping to put balm on Hank's currently bruised ego. "They got over two hundred and ninety thousand in undeclared currency recently."

"How much of that comes to us?" Cloud asked.

Voice jokingly pulled out his tablet and asked, "How much do you want?" getting the entire team laughing. Mentally, Spud extended him a thank you. It was the diversion that took some of the strain out of the air that had arisen as a result of the discussion on riots over police shootings.

"We continue to see news of soldiers returning from war zones and then committing suicide—sometimes taking their families with them. Unwillingly, of course."

"They don't do enough to prepare these guys for war," Cloud observed. "They're not ready for the psychological effect of seeing just what war is. It's all just duty, clean and pretty, until they see someone get blown up."

Hank was watching Edge out of the corner of her eye. He was showing no reaction, but she bet herself that inside he was reliving just that kind of event, having witnessed his own friend die that way.

"CBP has also discovered an unusual way for a drug to

get into the country. Specifically, ketamine-laced pictures of Jesus."

"Take enough of it, and if He's out there somewhere, you just might meet Jesus," Hank commented.

"I'm not sure Jesus would like to meet someone who was stupid enough to kill himself," Edge rejoined.

"Something which may be of interest to you, Voice. The Department of Homeland Security is funding research projects for a number of investigative tools."

Voice chuckled. "Yeah, I saw that. But didn't you mention earlier that they are already funding my research?"

The rest of his teammates laughed.

"We have a topic that has sprung up before, but is making news again. The topic is for-profit prisons, and potential corruption both in the prison system and in police departments whose pensions are tied to arrests and imprisonments."

"Who wants to go undercover in a prison to help build a case?" Hank said. "Anyone? A knuckle-tap? Raised hand?"

Everyone stared at her.

"That's what I figured."

"Immigration and Customs Enforcement is continuing to make inroads against child porn and sexual exploitation of children."

"It still seems like it's a drop in the bucket, though," Amigo commented.

Hank was nodding. "But every little bit helps. Hopefully, the publicity discourages some would-be pedophiles as well."

"It wouldn't be an intel briefing if there wasn't something about the environmentalists. It seems a virtual war has broken out, with environmentalists going after their usual targets, and those targets fighting back with phishing attempts."

"This should be interesting," Voice predicted.

"That's it, except for—"

"You just can't make this shit up!"

"It's amazing how alert you all get when the last story of the day is revealed," Spud observed. "Edge thought he might like to give this one."

Edge leaned forward and knitted his fingers together.

"You all know I grew up Catholic, right?"

"Yeah," Amigo said.

"And that I was an altar boy?"

"I hope this isn't going to be..." Cloud ventured.

Edge scowled at him. "No, it's not going to be. But my mom was a very strict Catholic mom. I think she wanted me to be a priest."

Cloud laughed. "I can see that. Penitent comes into the confessional and you reach through the screen, grab him by the neck, and demand he 'fess up."

"The story does have to do with confession, but I don't know why you would say that," Edge said.

"Maybe something to do with you being six foot six and two hundred and sixty pounds."

Edge looked at him coolly. "Back to the story, me and a couple of friends were up in my room playing Scrabble. I just wanted to play a normal game of Scrabble, but my friends? Nope. They want to use the entire unabridged dictionary version. You know, the one with all the four-letter words in it."

Hank giggled.

"That's right, Hank—the one *you* use," Edge continued. "We're playing the game and having a good time when my mother walks in. No time to hide the board. She looks and sees what words are on the board, then starts walking around the room sniffing. I thought she was going a little bonkers until she said, 'I knew I smelled brimstone. Now, where did you hide the devil? Because I know none of you innocent boys would have put those filthy words on the Scrabble board.'

"She then sends my two friends home. After they leave, she turns to me and says, 'What do you think Father Ordway would say if he'd seen what you boys had on that board? Do you think he'd still like to have you as an altar boy?'

"Lord, forgive me," Edge continued, making the sign of the cross, "but for the first time in my life I got smart-mouthed with mom. Told her, 'What are you going to do? Wash off my fingers with soap?' She glares at me and says, 'Father Ordway is going to hear all about this. He'll know because you're going to tell him when you go to confession on Saturday.'

"It's 'aw, crap' time, and I know it. I'm practically trembling when I get in line at the confessional, and I've got tears running down my face when I finally get inside. I tell Father Ordway the whole story, blubbering my contrition the whole way through it. When I finish, at first I hear nothing from him. I'm thinking, *that's it—no more being an altar boy for me.*"

"So *that's* how you ended up in the Marines," Amigo quipped.

"Not quite. Because the next thing I know, I hear him on the other side of the screen chuckling. He tells me, 'I think Jesus knows that boys will be boys. But because I know your mother, three Our Fathers and five Hail Marys. Make sure she can hear them.' From then on, whenever I went to confession, he'd ask me if I'd been playing Scrabble again."

The rest of the team clapped their appreciation.

"You know the drill," Spud said to wrap up the briefing. "Work on your skill sets, see you all again at lunch time, and I believe Hank would like us to reconvene down in the range this afternoon."

"Let's see how your knife throwing is coming," Edge said as Hank strapped her set of throwing knives to her thigh.

Hank pulled out a knife and threw it at the wooden target Edge had mounted on the wall of the gym. She grinned when it stuck, then took out another knife. That one, too, stuck. By the time she had thrown all five knives, she had five knives stuck in the target.

"Pretty good. Now we've got to get you to put a little more power into it. The knives are stuck, but I'm betting I could easily knock them all off. So now, I'm going to teach you a little twist on this."

Hank got a dejected look. "You mean I'm not done?"

"You don't want to just cut the guy, Hank. You need to imbed the knife deep if you want to kill him."

"What if I don't want to kill him?"

Edge looked at her in a way that showed he understood what she was feeling. "Here's the scenario, Hank. You're in close-quarters combat. In your case, the first thing you go for is your rifle. You have a malfunction and the next thing you go for is your handgun. Say your opponent is both sneaky and fast, and you're out of ammo. Yeah, yeah—I know," he quickly added. "You don't run out of ammo. But let's say you do. Maybe you've got multiple assailants, and they just keep coming. You get some with your rifle, you get some with your handgun, but you've still got some closing in. So, you pull out your throwing knives. Why? Because it's your life or theirs, and they're the bad guys. Ultimately, you might find yourself hand-to-hand with them. Which is when you remember that the first rule of a knife fight is?"

"You're going to get cut," Hank finished.

"You really want to get them before they get close enough to cut you. Rifle, handgun, throwing knife, and last resort" —he pulled out his ever-present combat knife— "your pig sticker."

"I don't even have a 'pig sticker', as you call it."

"I'll get you one, but you'll have to buy it."

Hank smiled and pulled out a quarter from her pocket. "I have payment right here."

"Good deal. Now, let me show you how to get a little power from your throw. I'm going to show you how to throw sidearm."

"But—"

"Sidearm. You know, how you'd toss something away from you as you're walking along, only you reorient your feet so that where it lands is in the direction of that guy who's coming at you. Just think 'I'm disgusted with this knife.' Hold it the same way I showed you before, but on the release this time, you kind-of *flick* the knife with your index finger." He was demonstrating the maneuver without a knife in his hand, Hank trying to imitate him. "Watch."

Hank stood aside as Edge threw the knife at the target, embedding it well into the wood.

"See that? Stick a guy like that, and he's not just going to ask for a band-aid."

"Ok. I hold the knife the same way, but instead of over my shoulder like a javelin, to my side. Aren't I going to get him at about the same height as I'm throwing?"

"So? You get him in the gut. I think he'll notice."

Hank gave it a try, with the same result as she'd had starting out the day before: the knife clanging against the target and falling to the floor. She sighed.

Edge put a hand on her shoulder. "Same as I told you yesterday, it takes practice. But you'll get it. Just hang in there. You stay here and practice. I hear the dumbbells calling me."

"Ok," came Hank's lackluster reply. *But I'm beginning to think the dumbbell is right here, standing in my shoes.*

"Just like the usual girlie response," Edge chided as he walked off. "Immediately get the idea you can't do it. That's why women are the weaker sex."

That pissed Hank off, and with a glance over his shoulder he caught her glaring at him. Talking quietly to himself, he added, "It's called motivating you, little lady."

Hank was, indeed, motivated. Vowing to prove him wrong, she set about practicing the new throwing technique, and it wasn't long before Edge began to hear her knives biting the wood rather than bouncing off of it. As he worked out with the dumbbells, he couldn't help but think that Hank was imagining his face on the target.

"So, who were you throwing your knives at?" Edge asked Hank as the team gathered in the Level 5 firing range.

"Who do you think?" Hank replied.

Edge just looked at her, not knowing if he wanted the answer or not.

"Try Spot," Hank answered. "Assuming I don't see him from farther out, that is."

"You've got a real hatred for that guy," Edge observed.

"He's a rapist, a murderer, and an escaper from justice. What's to like?"

"Not sayin' you don't have cause, little lady."

Looking around, Hank noted that the entire team was now assembled.

"I have been remiss in my duties," she informed them. "There is an important aspect of accurate aiming that I've neglected to tell you about."

"Love, why do I get the impression you're trying to train us all to be snipers?" Spud asked.

"Isn't everyone supposed to be trained to fill in when another team member is incapacitated?" Hank asked. "I'm always looking at things with an eye toward anything being possible. If I'm incapacitated, then Amigo steps up to sniper, but he's going to need someone to step up to spotter. One of the roles of the spotter is to watch the sniper's back, so you should all be ready to fill that role. But aside from that, having a well-adjusted scope can be the difference between hitting your target or not, so I need to teach you a few things.

"First is going to be eye relief. You'll notice that Luigi has mounted some traditional glass on your AR10s, and that's what we'll be working with today. Note also that we're a bit farther than the rest of you shoot on a regular basis, which is another reason I want to get into this today. Two hundred meters is fine, but five hundred is even better. With our rifles, Amigo and I regularly shoot out to a thousand meters with a .308 round, so I believe all of you will be equally capable of shooting accurately at five hundred meters once you get the hang of getting your scope set up properly *for you*. 'For you' is the operative phrase: everyone's a little different."

Spud looked from Hank to Edge. "A *little* different?" he quipped, getting his other teammates laughing.

"Hey, don't dis Edge. If I'm incapacitated, he just grabs me and tucks me under one arm while grabbing all my gear with the other arm and runs me out of the danger zone," Hank commented to renewed laughter and a little nod from Edge.

"Eye relief refers to the distance your eye is from the eyepiece of the scope. Your eye relief needs to be adjusted so that you don't get what I call 'tunnel vision' nor semi-circular shadows, but also so that you don't get scope eye."

"Scope eye?" Voice queried.

Amigo chuckled. "That's when your eye is so close to the eyepiece that the eyepiece hits you in your eyebrow when the rifle recoils. You can tell everyone who has ever done it, because they have a scar above their eye right like this," he added, tracing a semicircle above his right eye.

Voice got a good look at him.

"Nope—I don't have one. Neither does Hank," Amigo assured him.

"You'll notice that along with your rifles, you have a small set of tools on your equipment bench," Hank pointed out. "One of them is a torque screwdriver. See the thing with the fat, yellow handle? That's the guy. Your rifles are already set in a gun vise."

"Why is it on the floor?" Edge asked.

"Because there are some tricks to eye relief," Hank said. "In the prone position, your eye is farther away from the eyepiece than it is in any other position, and you'll notice that your scopes are set for the highest magnification as well. This is the situation that would be the most critical for getting the eye relief correct. It means the eye relief won't be ideal if you're shooting from other positions, but it will still give you good results in other positions.

"You're going to lie down at your gun and look through the eyepiece. The scope rings are loose, so you can slide the scope back and forth. Slide it out until you see a black zone around the image. That's your tunnel vision. Then slide it toward you until you don't see that tunnel vision, nor any dark arcs around the outside of the image. When you've got a nice clear image, you've got your eye relief adjusted correctly. After that, the thing you want to do is what you *don't* want to do, and that's disturb the position of the scope in the rings."

Hank and Amigo watched as their teammates lay down at their rifles and each went through the process of determining where their eye relief was optimized. When it appeared that no one was doing any additional adjustments, Hank had them all sit back.

"A lot of people try to do this with the upper segment of the rings completely off the rifle. I'll admit that I did it that way, too—but our guy up there in the rangemaster's booth showed me that it's actually a little easier to have the upper segment loosely attached to the lower segment first. If you ever need to do this yourself, the easy way is to put the upper segment on the lower one, tighten all the screws until you just feel a bit of resistance, then back them off again an equal number of turns. That will let you both move the scope back and forth, and also turn the scope side-to-side in order to get the scope level. You've all got your eye relief in; now we're going to get the rifle level."

Hank and Amigo continued to assist the team members with getting their scopes precisely mounted to their individual optimums. Each was amazed at the amount of time it took. When they were finally finished, however, they all agreed that the scope seemed to give them a better picture of their target than they had previously had.

"Now, we're going to talk about focusing the reticle and parallax adjustment."

"All of this is going to make us shoot better?" Edge asked.

"You can't shoot well what you can't see well," Hank replied. "The mistake people make here with getting the reticle focused is that they will keep their eye on the reticle the entire time they're focusing it. What happens is your eye will attempt to focus the reticle, and it will succeed. What happens next is that every time you use your scope, your eye has to work to focus the reticle, and you get eye strain. So, you're going to focus the reticle, then take your eye away from the scope. Give it a little rest. Then look in the scope and focus the reticle again, until you get to the point where you look in the scope and the reticle is already in focus. This is why there's a white target set in front of you. It's to let you see the reticle easier."

Once again, the team members worked at getting their scopes adjusted, this time manipulating the ring on the eyepiece until they could see the markings on the reticle clearly and crisply.

"Everyone done?" Hank asked. With her teammates tapping their knuckles on the floor, she then continued with, "Now for parallax adjustment.

"Anyone ever play with this knob here?" she asked, pointing out a knob on the left side of the scope.

Amigo raised his hand.

"Put your hand down, smartass. I happen to know that's not the only knob you like to play with."

The other men roared.

"I thought it was a focusing knob," Spud said.

"Not really. This knob is your parallax adjustment. What

it does is bring your target image into the same plane as your reticle. You've all gotten your reticle in focus, so this is the next step to ensuring that where you place your crosshair is actually on your target. If you get yourself situated on your rifle with your crosshair on a blank background—your plain white target downrange, then move your head a bit, you might notice that your crosshair moves off your target. That's due to parallax inside your scope. Adjusting this knob will result in no apparent movement between your target and reticle, no matter where your eye is. So, if you're not following Mr. Cleckner's admonition to be consistent, slight differences in cheeking your rifle won't result in differences in reticle location relative to your target."

She watched as everyone gave it a try. When they'd all relaxed, she announced, "Now it's time for fun. Let's see how much better you guys can do at hitting your target precisely at five hundred meters."

She and Amigo went down the line to ensure everyone had made their rifle safe, then Luigi ran the target carriers forward and the two of them went about mounting targets on the plain backers. Luigi then ran the targets back down to the far end of the range.

"This is going to be interesting, I'm sure. All you guys who thought five hundred yards was a bit far for accuracy with your .308s are going to be pleasantly surprised." She turned to Amigo and held up a quarter. He pulled out a quarter of his own and simply handed it to her.

"Like you ever miss," he said.

WITH NO DELIVERIES, he took the opportunity to go to a gun store in Duluth. Walking in and seeing the racks of rifles on one side and counters with handguns displayed underneath on the other, he walked up and got the attention of a clerk.

"I'm looking for a hunting rifle. Something nice in .243," he told the clerk.

"I've got just what you're looking for," the clerk said. "It's not brand new, but it's in great shape and shoots well. A nice bolt-action rifle."

"That will be great," he said. "I'm just getting into hunting myself, and I've heard that's a pretty versatile caliber."

He watched as the clerk brought the gun down to show to him. The price was right, but more importantly to him, the caliber was right. *I'll kill him with the same kind of bullet he killed her with,* he thought. *The Army got me used to 5.56 NATO, but whoever killed Holly did it with a .243.*

"How about a scope for it?" the clerk asked. "We have some nice ones on sale right now, and we can even get it mounted properly for you."

"That sounds like a deal, too," he said.

Only half listening to the clerk and settling on what was represented to him as a good hunting scope for the money, he waited while the shop's gunsmith got the scope mounted on the rifle for him, filling out the ATF Form 4473 and handing over his Minnesota driver's license for the background check, none of which bothered him. He had never even had a driving infraction.

After the paperwork was done, he walked along the counter, giving a casual look to the handguns there. *Maybe I should buy a pistol too,* he thought. *In case.*

"What about a pistol?" he asked the clerk, who had been

hovering nearby with the thought that he could land another sale.

"You have to have a permit to buy one," the clerk answered. "But we usually get those back in five days. With a clean NICS check, you shouldn't have any problem."

"Which one do you recommend?"

"My opinion? You can't beat a 1911, though lots of people these days are going for semi-auto 9mm-chambered handguns. Less kick than a .45, but not nearly as lethal if you're thinking about something for self-defense."

"How about ammunition?"

"Both are readily available, so six of one, a half dozen of the other."

The clerk brought handguns out for him to handle one at a time. When he found one that felt good in his hand, he settled on purchasing it.

"Like I said, there will be a wait for your permit. I'll set this aside for you with a deposit. If for some reason your permit doesn't clear—and I see no reason why it shouldn't, you'll get your deposit back in full. Otherwise, we can apply it to your purchase when your permit comes through."

"Sounds good."

Seeing that his rifle was now ready, he pulled out his credit card and paid for it, along with several boxes of ammunition so he could practice. Walking from the store, he murmured, "And then get down to the business at hand."

"Love, you look entirely bored."

Hank was, as usual, sitting in the reading nook, still reading through her military sniper training manual.

"I am."

"Because?"

"Because I vowed I would read this whole thing, but a lot of it isn't relevant to us. We use different firearms, we use different ammunition, we use different rifle scopes and other optics. We have no need of communication through setting up a radio—we have the bum ticker and Hal. We have access to Keyhole. We now also have HARVEST, which is likely to be even better, given we can keep it located over our objective area, and it's even still in its infancy. Who knows what Voice will do by way of improvements? The guy is never happy to go with the status quo—he's got to keep tweaking things. And I gather he's got Oscar in on the action."

Spud chuckled. "We have two fucking geniuses at our disposal."

"Yeah, we do."

Hank slid a jar over to herself and reached into it with a fondu fork.

"What have you got there?" Spud asked.

"Hamildon Fahm Oganig Baby Dihw Piggles."

Spud stared at her, then grinned. "Hal, translation."

Hamilton Farms Organic Baby Dill Pickles.

"Eed shih, Spuh."

"Hal, no need to translate that." He gazed at the jar. "Any good?"

Hank swallowed and said, "I told you that you could eat shit."

"So, no good?"

"The pickles are great. You can eat shit if you think I'm going to share them."

"Such a way with words. That's a big jar, and you can't spare even one?"

She speared one and handed it to him on the fondu fork.

Taking it and crunching on the pickle, he remarked, "Those are pretty good."

"And here I thought you wouldn't be able to relate to baby pickles. Or baby carrots, or those fingerling bananas... Not with that great big cucumber you've got. Or is that a zucchini?" she asked, looking at her arm.

Spud stared at her and then sputtered with mirth.

"And you call *me* incorrigible!"

14

"Alright, men! Listen up!" Spud announced as the intel briefing was about to begin.

"Just the men have to listen? What about Hank?" Amigo asked.

"She's my wife. She never listens to me."

The men all laughed, with Edge pointing out that it was a wife's job to ignore the husband.

"There is more discussion on police reform."

"Anyone here who has served in law enforcement knows that you get it from both sides," Amigo complained. "When I was in the Border Patrol, of course everyone trying to get across the border illegally hated us, and the cartels hated us enough to put a price on our heads. Everyone who felt that those trying to cross over were just trying to find a better life hated us because we were duty bound to stop them. Everyone who *didn't* want them crossing over hated us because they felt we weren't doing our job, even though we were doing it to the best of our ability."

"I imagine it's the same for the street cops," Voice said. "The drunks don't want you arresting them for drunk driving, and the people who get hit by drunks don't think you're getting enough of them from behind the wheel."

Hank was nodding her head in agreement.

"It's very difficult to decide exactly how much force you need, too," Crow added. "When you're dealing with drug kingpins and stash house situations, it's a given that they're armed. We always went in with guns drawn."

"As long as you didn't get the wrong house," Voice said, recalling a 'You Just Can't Make This Shit Up' story of Crow's and getting his teammates laughing.

"We have a disturbing case of two black men found hanging from trees. Both incidents occurred in California, and family members of both men say neither was suicidal."

"That *is* disturbing," Edge said. "Have racial tensions escalated to the point where we're now seeing lynchings?"

"Which time period do we want to return to?" Hank asked. "The period just post the Civil War, or the atrocities during the Civil Rights movement of the sixties?"

"Neither," Edge pronounced.

"And for those that think racial tensions are rising, we also have the body of a transgender woman being recovered from a river. Or perhaps I should say 'the body parts', given she was dismembered."

"Can I use a Hankism?" Cloud asked.

"Be my guest," Spud replied.

"Oh, *for fuck's sake!*"

"Here's some better news, and this time it's for Chip."

Chip raised his head off his paws and looked at Voice, who signed 'listen' to him.

"After a K-9 alerted on a vehicle at a CBP checkpoint, they discovered some black plastic bundles that turned out to contain over a hundred thousand dollars in undeclared cash."

"Did you hear that?" Voice asked the dog.

Chip stood up and bounced around in a circle, then sat and thumped his tail on the floor.

"What the hell was *that?*" Hank asked, laughing.

"Oh, that's his happy dance," Voice replied, slipping Chip a treat.

"And that's all *I* have, but Hank has an installment of 'You Just Can't Make This Shit Up' for all of you."

"More from the case files of the Taos PD?" Amigo asked.

"You got it," Hank replied.

Knuckles got vigorously tapped on the table top.

"This one comes to you from one of our famous and ubiquitous mega marts," Hank began. "A call comes in saying they have a customer acting suspiciously in the pharmacy area. I hear one of my male buddies say he's nearest, so hey—I decide I can just stay hanging out at my favorite speed trap location.

"About fifteen minutes later, said male buddy calls for backup. He *specifically* calls for *me*. I take off, lights and siren. While I'm en route, I'm trying to think first of what could be going down and second of why he called for me rather than just the nearest officer. In the pharmacy? Is the guy buying all the rubbing alcohol and allergy medicine? Could we be looking at a guy getting stuff for making meth? Is he buying the kinds of things that might indicate he's contemplating suicide and that's why my bro in blue is asking for the woman on duty? He thinks talking the guy into getting some help would be better done by a woman? He's buying a bunch of stuff like bandages, pain killers, antibiotic ointments? Maybe he stabbed a family member and figures he can fix it himself and avoid jail? But big giant question is, *why me?*

"I get there, report on scene, and my fellow officer asks me to make my way to the area at the end of the aisles, along the wall. I've been to that area. I know what's there. It's nothing any man needs."

Eyebrows were getting raised around the table.

"When I arrive, I find my comrade in blue standing looking bewildered, along with a middle-aged man, also bewildered. My buddy's face says, *'Help me!'* The man's face says, *'Please help me!'* The guy has a box of... feminine products in his hand. And I'm thinking, 'What the hell is a-going on here?' Which is what I ask them, only more politely. I ask, 'What's the problem?'

"Our suspect, who I will now refer to as 'Dad', is the single father of a young daughter who has just discovered there's something else to growing up that dear ol' Dad didn't tell her about. He has already had to assure his young charge that she isn't dying and doesn't need to go to the ER, and he knows *vaguely* what she *does* need, but not *exactly* what she needs. So, I ask him how tall she is, how much she weighs... When he finishes, I take what he's got in his hand and put it back on the shelf because *it's all wrong* and give him a package of something more appropriate.

"I'm also none too happy with my fellow uniformed coworker, so I make him buy me lunch for a week. He, of course, realizes how much I eat just to stay skinny, so he starts protesting. I let him know that if he doesn't cooperate, I'll let the rest of the department know that he couldn't handle sanitary napkins for a teenager with her first period."

"You blackmailed him!" Amigo said.

Hank grinned. "Yes I did."

The men groaned.

"Do you know how unfair that is?" Voice asked. "We don't know anything about that stuff."

"You mean to tell me you're seeing Page on a regular basis and don't know anything about... *that stuff?*"

"Even *I* don't know about that stuff, Love," Spud said. "If you were to send me to The Store for... *stuff,* I'd have no idea what stuff to get."

"We've been married for *two years* and you don't know what I use? Besides, how many women are on the team? I think if you went to The Store and cared to notice, you'd find there's only one variety in there."

"First, you never send me for what you use, and you don't leave it where I can see it. And I've never noticed what's in The Store."

Edge was starting to squirm, some of his teammates along with him. The look on Spud's face told Hank his failure to notice what was stocked in The Store was deliberate.

"You wouldn't think to send Spud—" Edge began.

Hank cut him off with, "No, I wouldn't. I would definitely not ever send Spud to The Store for anything of that kind. I know you guys find it embarrassing."

"Damn right."

"But I would have thought...."

"You don't leave it out in the open, Love," Spud explained. "And I don't snoop. Especially when it comes to that stuff."

Excuses, excuses. Hank shrugged. "Well, I thought it was funny in retrospect. But I see this is probably the kind of topic that's funny to women because of the reactions *men* have. But *you* guys... You guys are supposed to be six of the toughest guys on the planet, and you squirm over women's sanitary supplies? Hell, you can't even say 'tampon'. It's *that stuff.*"

All of the men were looking anywhere but at her. She got the definite impression that they were all squashing the urge to start a chorus of nervous whistles.

"Amigo will be working with you guys down in the range

on spotting," Hank said, given Spud still seemed a bit para-
lyzed. "Work on your skill sets, and see you at lunchtime."

He stood with a fellow postman, sorting the mail he'd be
delivering that day along his route.

"I'm thinking of getting into hunting," he said.

"Really? I didn't take you for the hunting type."

He shrugged. "You know how it goes. I've gotta start
thinking about what happens when it comes time to retire.
With the way things are going, I figure every little penny I
can save... Besides, I hear a lot of guys talking about hunting
and how much they enjoy it. With no one in my life, I figure
I need a nice hobby." *With no one ever going to be in my life,
given someone got careless and killed her.*

"Yeah, I do a little hunting now and then. When I want
to get away from everything."

His mind froze. "Been doing any hunting lately?"

"Not me. It's turkey season, and I'm not much on wild
turkey. Too gamey for me. If I'm going to eat a turkey, I'll bag
it at the grocery store while it's wrapped in plastic with
Butterball on the label."

"I got a nice rifle the other day," he said. "But I need a
place to practice before I decide it's time to go hunting. I
imagine that will likely be when deer season rolls around."

"You're going to have a long wait. Deer season doesn't
open until November."

He chuckled a little nervously. "I have to be able to hit
one, don't I?"

"True enough."

"Where do you go to practice?"

"There's a gun club north of Duluth. Not too far a drive.

They have a long range there that works pretty well as long as you don't show up early in the morning. It faces pretty much east, and you get the sun in your face."

"Sounds like it might be good in the evening, though. After work. Are they open then?"

"Members can go down any time there's light in the sky," his coworker informed him.

"Sounds great," he said. *Sounds great for sure.*

"THIS IS GOING to be the easy lesson in spotting," Amigo announced as the team gathered in the Level 5 range. "We'll get to the hard part once you have some of the fundamentals down pat here."

"What's the hard part?" Voice asked.

"Dealing with the weather," Amigo answered.

"I thought the dragonfly could compensate for everything you might encounter with the weather," Crow said, a mild hint of protest in his voice.

"Hank used to rag me all the time about becoming too reliant on Hal. 'What will happen if we ever lose Hal?' she'd say. I thought she was being paranoid, but we just found out what happens when we lose Hal. Plus, sometimes we don't have time for a dragonfly—we just have to wing it. Winging it, in our case, means making a shot by reference to DOPE tables.

"You guys all have DOPE cards for your .308s and have been taught how to use them. Like anything, though, it needs to be tweaked for the gun, the ammo, the shooter, and the conditions. Down here, the only variables are gun and shooter. As good as Luigi is, I'm sure he'll be the first to tell you that every gun will have its little foibles, and it's for sure that every shooter has their foibles as well. So really, you should have a DOPE card for every gun and every shooter if you're a spotter. It simplifies things when you consistently operate as a shooter/spotter pair."

Luigi was listening to all of this in the rangemaster's booth, and casual glances by the team members in his direction showed him nodding his agreement to what Amigo was saying.

"This is what I think will work well, though. Each *shooter* should hold a set of DOPE cards that are specific to them. Why? Because your rifle is *your* rifle, your optics are your optics, et cetera. The only thing that might change is who's spotting for you. We'll spend some time working in pairs to develop DOPE cards for each one of you as a shooter, moving around just to keep from getting bored."

"You get bored as a spotter?" Voice asked.

"Hardly. The spotter does the hard work," Amigo said.

Edge laughed.

"The spotter *does* do the hard work," Hank said, confirming what Amigo had stated. "The spotter has to do all the computations that make the shot work. The shooter just has to adjust sight settings and hold everything still except their trigger finger until the shot is finished."

"Alright," Amigo said. "Let's get everyone paired up. We'll have one person who will have to stand down, given we don't have an even number of team members here."

"We should get Doc Frank down here," Edge said.

"If I caught what he said at breakfast this morning, he's currently in surgery over in Omaha. Something about straightening a kid's leg," Cloud said.

"Think of this," Hank began. "It isn't going to be too long before we have to put up with *four* doctors."

"He's a good guy," Cloud remarked. "Anyone who can keep Doc Rich in line is definitely a good guy."

"Voice, let's get you with Crow. Edge, you shoot, Hank spots for you. That leaves me to spot for Cloud, and Spud to do the heavy safety officer duty along with Luigi for this first round. I'd get Luigi down here, because I know he likes to do a little shooting himself, but we need someone to make sure none of us gets lazy about safety."

THAT'S one reason to get through your route quickly, he thought as he drove US 53 south. Turning and making his way to the gun range, he checked in at the office and purchased a membership, then followed the small signs that directed him to the rifle range. He had made sure he would have everything he needed: a homemade target frame made of PVC pipe, a large sheet of cardboard snatched from a warehouse store that had been used as a pallet stabilizer, targets, and a staple gun for attaching them to the cardboard. He was also armed with an electronic tablet on which he'd loaded what he was inwardly calling 'The Definitive Course on Rifle Shooting'—a series of YouTube videos describing everything from how to adjust a scope to how to accurately aim and shoot. He didn't really need it except as a refresher, given his Army service. He had reflected as he drove that there could be no missing, and that there would *be* no missing. *None of them will get away. If I have to kill them all to make sure I get the guilty party, then so be it!*

He drove down and set up his target against the backstop, then went back to a spot about two hundred yards away to set up a portable shooting bench. Taking out all of his gear, he readied his rifle and set out his ammunition.

Gotta be good enough to get this done before the end of turkey season.

He settled in to review the first videos on how to zero in his rifle, then set about doing so. When he looked through his binoculars, he could see that the first three shots had impacted off onto the left side of his target. Making an adjustment to his scope, the next three struck closer to the center, but still off to the left. Another adjustment put the three shots in a group very close to the center. He considered that this would be good enough. *All I have to do is get them somewhere in the heart or lungs.*

He then sat on the ground with a set of shooting sticks and tried another three shots. They were more scattered, but still in the vicinity of the center of the target. *Can't expect to be perfect. You haven't shot a rifle since you left the Army.*

He continued to work at it, refining his hold, his sight picture, his breathing—getting everything as good as he could in the time he had before the sun went down and he would have to leave. When he finished and went to retrieve his target, he noticed that he was shooting a nice group, well-centered on the target.

It may not be like riding a bike, but it didn't take long to get to where I can consider myself ready. If I'm closer than two hundred yards, I feel certain I can make a kill in a single shot.

"THAT WAS INTERESTING THIS AFTERNOON, AMIGO," Voice admitted as serving dishes of food were being passed around the team's table. "I think I shoot better with a spotter than without one."

"Gotta agree," Crow said.

"Now you know why Hank and I work as a team," Amigo said.

"Wait until we go outside. You're going to find it's a whole new game," Hank pointed out. "The wind blows. The light changes. Maybe it starts raining."

"Or snowing," Amigo added, remembering Hank's demand to practice under just those conditions.

"Your target moves. That's when a spotter really comes in handy. What you see in the spotting scope is a much greater field of view than through a rifle scope. Your spotter can tell you where your target went and both what direction and how fast it's moving."

"What's the crumbly-looking white stuff in the salad, Mama Rose?" Edge asked.

"It's *good for you,*" Rose answered from the kitchen.

"But—"

Voice slapped his arm cut him short. He glared at Voice.

"If Mama Rose says it's good for you, just eat it," Voice admonished him. "You *do not* want to get on her bad side."

"It's feta cheese," Hank said after sampling some of it.

"What does it taste like?" Edge asked her.

"Kind-of like dry, salty cottage cheese," Hank said. "Try it. It's good."

Edge took a little on his fork, watching Hank warily to see if she'd get an expression that would tell him he'd really not like it. Not seeing any indication of deception on her part, he took a tentative taste.

"You're right—it tastes good."

"What did you eat when you were a Raider in the Marines that makes you such a fussy eater now?" Cloud asked.

"MREs."

Cloud laughed. "And you worry that something Mama Rose makes is going to be inedible?"

"Heev wight. You should jus eed id," Hank said through a mouthful of salad. She swallowed. "So, is everyone up for a trip out to the Lockridge range tomorrow?"

Knuckles got tapped on the table as the members ate their salad.

"What's this other stuff?" Edge asked Hank, not wishing to evoke Rose's ire.

"Stir fry lemon chicken. Serve it over the rice. And it's delicious. Don't you think it smells good?"

"Looks can be deceiving. So can smells," Edge proclaimed.

"Oh, for fuck's sake."

"Language, Hank."

"Sister Edge, if you'd just *eat,* you wouldn't hear any of that kind of language."

"Maybe we can have a little competition tomorrow at the end of the training," Amigo said. "See which team can shoot the best score."

"I smell a rat," Crow announced. "Who are you planning to pair with? Will it be Hank? Gonna be Team Taco?"

"We can make it a random draw, and we can include Luigi. Eight marbles in a pouch, four different colors. The ones who draw matching colors are the teams. The first one to draw a color is the shooter, the second is the spotter. Sound fair?"

"Can Luigi shoot?" Voice asked.

"Yes," Amigo and Hank answered simultaneously.

"Sure about that?"

"We've both watched him shoot," Amigo declared. "He's no slouch with a gun."

"Alright, you're on," Cloud said. He withdrew a pair of

quarters from his pocket and stacked them neatly in the center of the table. "Everyone put in two, seeing as the winning team will want to divide the loot."

With a neat stack of sixteen quarters, Hank and Amigo having placed an extra one apiece for Luigi's contribution to the pot, the team went back to eating Rose's stir fry lemon chicken. Amigo grinned. The bet had elicited the kind of enthusiasm for the task that he hoped for.

HANK CLOSED her book and shelved it, something she wouldn't ordinarily do if she didn't expect to make constant reference to it.

"I take it you found some useful things in your sniper book," Spud mumbled as he panned through the news for things to report during the intelligence briefing the next morning.

"Lots that's *not* useful as well," Hank remarked. "Things like leaving caches of supplies, for instance.

"We have them, Love."

Hank's eyes went wide. "We do?"

"Yes. They're called 'remote bases'."

Hank chuckled. "You had me going for a while there."

"So what's next?" he asked as she picked up her tablet.

"Something recreational."

"Like?"

Hank mumbled something unintelligible, causing Spud to lower his tablet.

"Love, you're not reading another crime novel, I hope."

"It's not a crime novel."

"Then what is it?"

"A mystery," Hank admitted sheepishly.

"Oh Lord. Aren't mysteries usually centered around solving a crime?"

"I don't know that this one is."

"Because?"

"Because I haven't started reading it yet."

Spud rolled his eyes and sighed. "I need to get you to talk with Doc Andy about your obsession."

"I'll read just about anything that crosses my path," Hank protested.

"Especially if there's a crime involved."

Turning on her tablet, she remarked, "I think the only crime that's involved here is the constant harassment I get over my reading."

Spud knew when an argument had taken a turn down a dangerous path and went back to examining the news.

Hank read for a few minutes and then lowered her tablet into her lap. "Oh no—not another one of *these*," she mumbled.

Spud looked up. "Another one of what?"

Hank rolled her eyes. "Another story that, for one, is billed as what it's not. Maybe it's a mystery, but the first thing the author has introduced me to is a ten-year-old seer and a witch."

Spud tried his hardest to get the good old Secret Service face going, but the lips-pressed wrinkled grin made it onto his face before he could stop it. He said nothing until the impulse to laugh passed, then told her, "You don't have to finish it, you know."

"Oh, yes I do," Hank declared. "I have to know what kind of warped mind thinks this stuff up."

15

"**Y**ou're going to be with me this morning," Crow told Edge pointedly. "We have to get you ready for your commercial and instrument checkrides in the helicopter."

"Fine by me as long as I get to finish breakfast. I'm not passing up any of this," Edge replied as he surveyed the eggs Benedict and bowl of fruit with vanilla yogurt topping it that Rose had set in front of him.

Voice was eating his while engrossed in his tablet.

"What have you got on your tablet that has you so interested?" Hank asked him.

"A communication from Oscar on how we can improve HARVEST."

"No work at the table," Edge admonished him.

"Why? Is it hurting anything?"

"It's hurting your ability to relax and properly digest your food," Edge replied.

"For once I can agree with you!" Rose called out from the kitchen.

"How 'bout you come with me and do a little refresher in the Latitude?" Cloud asked Hank. Her mouth full, she raised a thumb upward in reply. Grasping his chest, Cloud added weakly, "Someone alert Medical. Hank just passed up the opportunity to talk with her mouth full, and I think I'm having a heart attack!"

Hank gazed at him. "Eed shih."

"Language, Hank," Edge cautioned.

Amigo laughed. "It's not like it was understandable."

Edge pointed at himself with the handle of his fork and said, "*I* understood it."

"Sheesh, but you are a prude," Crow remarked. "We should change your code name to that. P-R-U-D-E. Fits the six-letters-or-less rule."

"Bug off."

"Boy, everyone is testy this morning," Amigo observed. "Are we all nervous about the little competition this afternoon?"

"Not me," Voice said. "But something had Chip a little restless last night."

"The cats were a little crazy, too," Cloud mentioned.

"Excuses, excuses," Amigo said.

"It's supposed to rain this afternoon as well," Hank said. "I checked the forecast."

"What's that you always tell me when the weather is nasty? 'Oh, we're so sorry, Mr. Gunny, but we can't take that mission. It's *raining*.'"

"It won't bother me, but these other guys are going to hate you."

They were, indeed, already giving him nasty looks.

"Ok. So the rest of you aren't as tough as Hank and me," Amigo said. "I can accept that."

"She's been training him," Cloud said.

"Looks that way," Crow admitted.

"Finish up breakfast, and let's get intel out of the way," Spud interjected.

"See? Right there is the kicker. Not only will we have to

do a range exercise in the rain this afternoon, we've got to start the day with intel," Crow jested.

HE WALKED THROUGH THE WOODS, looking for the person he believed was hunting there. He'd seen the truck parked by the side of the road, as well as the sticker in the window that he recognized as being a gun manufacturer's trademark. His footsteps stealthy and his body clothed in a camouflage coverall, he walked along asking himself if this was really something he wanted to do. Every time the question entered his mind, all he could do was imagine his Holly on the ground, breathing her last breath, forever taken from him, never to know the enormous love he had held for her—*still* held for her. *They are all my enemy now,* he thought.

It wasn't long before he heard the turkey call echoing through the trees. *Real, or is that the hunter?* he wondered. He decided to move in the direction where he had heard the sound.

He grinned. *That's their disadvantage. The law says they have to wear that bright orange. But not me. I'm a warrior. A warrior for justice, justice for Holly. A warrior blends into his environment so he can kill the enemy.*

He crouched and set the forend of his rifle in the bough of a tree. Aiming it carefully, he centered the man's head in his crosshairs. His heart was pounding, his breath coming in rasps, his hands shaking. *I'm close—so close. There's no way I can miss from here. But I'm about to kill a man, and I don't even know if he's the one.*

He tried to calm his nerves. *It makes no difference if he's the one. No difference at all. Holly is dead, and either he did it or another hunter did it. Settle down, settle down. You have to do this for Holly's sake.*

Looking back through the scope, his aim now steady, he took a breath in, then let it out. Another one in, then out again. Relaxing, he held as still as the air hung around him and squeezed the trigger. What happened next seem like it took forever: the snap of the man's head, the bewildered look he could see even from where he crouched, the seemingly slow-motion slump to one side as the man fell to the ground. He watched for what seemed like a long time, the hunter lying unmoving.

He ejected the spent case carefully from his rifle, pocketing it so nothing would be left behind, then walked back to where his own truck was parked using the same stealth he had used as he had entered and walked through the woods. Securing his rifle under the back seat of his truck, he then drove to work. He was anything but calm, his heart having resumed its racing, his chest heaving with each breath.

My God, what have I done? He leaned and looked at his own reflection in the rearview mirror.

You did what had to be done. And from now on, doing what has to be done will be easier.

Voice sequestered himself in his lab right after breakfast. He had been communicating back and forth with Oscar Avila on the drone portion of HARVEST. Oscar was proving himself invaluable when it came to engineering the drones —so much so that Voice found himself often lamenting that Oscar wasn't already a member of the unit. Unknown to him, Oscar also lamented this, largely because he couldn't tell anyone else what he was doing nor who he was doing it for.

Voice had his tablet propped up at the back of his workbench, doing a secure video call with Oscar.

"Using a handheld controller is old school," Oscar was telling him. "The unit has far better capability with linking things through Hal."

"That might be so," Voice said. "But we had a security issue recently and lost Hal temporarily. We can't afford to have that happen while on a mission."

Oscar thought about that for a bit. "Have you thought to have some data storage capability on the drone?"

"Weight is an important factor," Voice said. "The more stuff we want to put in this, the more it will weigh. That might limit the altitude we can get, or force us to go with a bigger drone. If we go with a bigger drone, we won't have as good capability for having it dodge other aircraft."

"More weight, more inertia," Oscar agreed. "How about a downlink to a ground-based device. Maybe even a tablet."

"That's a possibility," Voice agreed.

"We could still use a different control mechanism as well."

"What did you have in mind?"

Oscar held up a pair of glasses. "You've seen these, right?"

"Smart glasses. Yes."

"There's no app for drone control, but uh..."

Voice was grinning. "Your alien mind would be up to giving it a whack?"

"Imagine it, Voice. All you'd have to do is *look* at where you want the drone to go by looking at what's on your tablet. You see something you'd like HARVEST to home in on, just look at it steadily, or maybe tap the screen. Looking at it might get problematic if you look away for some reason."

"Like, say, having to run like hell because someone's shooting at us."

"I don't like to think about that, but yeah."

"Go ahead and get on it. Do you need some funds?"

Oscar laughed. "Programming is cheap, and I can always use this one as a class project as long as it's only for controlling a conventional drone."

"Well, uh, probably best to not discuss it," Voice told him.

"You know that I could blackmail you guys into hiring me right now."

"First, that's a surefire ticket to a cozy prison cell, and second, what you don't gain in an education may come back to bite you later."

"Yeah, yeah—I know. I appreciate everything the unit is doing for me. Honestly. Since NovoRo got Dad, you guys and Mr. Pipes are the only family I have."

EDGE WALKED in and took a seat for lunch. The rest of the team had already assembled at the team's table, but Edge had insisted he had to take a shower first. Hank knew very well why he felt he needed one. They were all awaiting his arrival—even Rose had not set food onto the table yet.

"You guys didn't have to let your lunch get cold because of me," he said.

Hank grinned. "Yeah, we did. Let's see it."

"See what?"

"We all know that you did your checkride today. Your temp ticket, asshole."

"Language, Hank."

"She wouldn't have called you an asshole if you had just pulled out your temp," Cloud observed.

Edge reached into a hip pocket and pulled out his wallet. Opening it, he extracted a small sheet of paper. Giving Hank a dirty look, he slid it in front of Cloud.

"Let's see here," Cloud said, making it look like he was closely scrutinizing the paper. "It says that the holder of this Temporary Airman Certificate is a Commercial Pilot, Airplane, single-engine land and multiengine land... and Helicopter."

Hank grinned.

"It also says he is instrument rated for Airplane, single and multiengine land... and Helicopter."

Hank reached over and punched Edge in the arm. "Congratulations, big guy."

Edge responded by saying, "Ow. Bad enough I had the helicopter and Fred Parloy beating me up. You've gotta beat me up too?" Calling into the kitchen he continued with, "What's for lunch, Mama Rose?"

"Your friends all told me your favorite foods were veggie burgers made with tofu and broccoli."

Edge sent glares around the table. He realized the ruse when Rose placed platters with spare ribs, mashed potatoes, and corn-on-the-cob on the table, though.

"What? You not gonna complain?" Rose asked.

"Heck no, Mama Rose."

"Someone call Doc Rich. I'm-a have a heart attack." With that Rose returned to the kitchen.

"Are you going to be able to get your heartbeat down low enough to do a decent job out at the Lockridge range today?" Amigo asked.

"I think doing a little shooting and spotting is going to

seem dull compared to this morning," Edge returned, making all of the other aviators laugh. Each had sweated through more than one checkride and knew the feeling well.

"It's going to be a chilly one out there," Crow remarked. "Only forty-eight degrees."

"I could have used that in the cockpit this morning," Edge related. "Maybe I wouldn't have sweat so much."

"Are we going to talk about sweat over lunch?" Amigo poked him, getting his teammates chuckling again.

No one had ever seen Edge blush before, but they saw it now.

"I for one am pretty proud of you," Voice said. "That makes four helicopter pilots, all commercial, all instrument-rated. The only holdout is Spud."

"Wings are not meant to go around and around. When have you ever seen a bird with wings that whirled around?" Spud argued.

"I've never seen a wing on an airplane flap," Amigo said to the chuckles of all of the other pilots.

"I made ju a cake, too," Rose announced, placing it in front of Edge. It was a simple sheet cake, decorated on top with a helicopter, befittingly depicting a cloud perched in front of the windshield.

"We've got a special knife for cutting that too," Cloud declared. He brought forward a rotor blade for an RC helicopter.

Edge proceeded to cut pieces of cake, and after everyone had gotten one, slid the rest of the cake in front of himself.

"I thought that was my piece," Hank said.

"WHAT ARE YOU READING, HANK?"

Hank had claimed the "shotgun seat," to the surprise of everyone, given Edge was driving. He'd caught her with her tablet in her lap as he drove the team to the Lockridge range complex for the continuation of the sniper and spotter training Amigo was currently conducting.

"A ridiculous novel," she replied.

Edge chuckled. "What makes it ridiculous?"

"Try mixing a British cop story with witches and seers."

Edge tried not to react, but he managed to give her a quizzical glance just the same.

"You getting into paranormals since dealing with Miss Martha?"

"Not by choice. This was billed as a mystery."

"Maybe it will turn out to be one. Maybe the paranormal angle is just bogus, and the real story is more truthful."

"I thought you believed in this spiritual stuff."

"I believe in the things I encounter. What people imagine is another story."

With a hint of mystery in her voice, Hank observed, "Maybe the author's imaginings are based on some of her experiences."

"Playing devil's advocate?"

"Not really. Just very aware that she dreamt up this stuff from somewhere in her psyche."

"It's all research for you, isn't it?"

"Yeah, you might say that. I want to understand people."

"And you believe that authors write in ways that reflect their inner minds."

"I do."

"If you could understand one person, who would it be?" he asked.

"UniPerp. I want to understand that bastard, because I feel that once I understand him, I'll be able to catch him."

"He's one that needs to be caught for sure," Cloud interjected, having taken an interest in the conversation.

"Maybe this magical stuff can give me a clue about him," Hank said. "Seven is a magical number. Maybe he thinks it's protective, and that's why he started choosing seven victims at a time."

"Is the number seven associated with the devil? Because he's the devil incarnate," Amigo said.

Crow fingered his Sword of Saint Michael that hung around his neck. "Then we're the ones to get him, given we have the Saint of the Sword on our side."

"Do Native Americans have a devil in their theology?" Amigo asked.

"I can't speak for every people," Crow answered him. "But for the Cherokee, we have one creator, Unetlanvhi, who knows all, sees all, and can do all. There is more than one spirit considered to be evil. Probably the closest to a Christian devil would be Uya. Uya is in opposition to anything good or just. A dark spirit, opposed to the light."

"It seems every religion has a dark force opposed to a light force," Voice commented.

"Remember what Miss Martha said? She said we were the brightest people she had ever seen, and Blobel was the darkest she had ever seen," Amigo recalled.

"Guess she hasn't met UniPerp yet," Cloud snarked.

"Well, neither have we," Hank remarked as they drove through the access gate to the extreme long-distance range at Lockridge.

Arriving at the designated firing line, they found Luigi already there. The closest targets he had set were at the two-hundred-meter distance.

"I hope you fueled up," Amigo said as he shook Luigi's hand and gave him a clap on the back.

"You really think these other boneheads gonna be able to hit anythin' farther away?"

"We'll keep moving them out until they can't hit anything anymore, Papa," Hank advised him. "We're hoping for five hundred meters."

"You gonna let them use the fancy dragonfly?"

"Nope. We're all working old school this afternoon."

The team proceeded to set up their gear at the firing line. Asking Hal for a string of random digits, Amigo then paired Crow with Cloud, Hank with Spud, himself with Voice, and Luigi with Edge.

Edge seemed discouraged, which Luigi noticed right away. "I'm bettin' you think I can't do this," he told Edge.

"No offense, Luigi, but—"

"Whatchu think I do down in the Mole Hole when I got no guns to fix and no ammo to make? Sit on my hands?" Luigi laughed. "He don't know me very well, does he, Sweetheart?"

Hank chuckled. "Apparently not."

Luigi looked Edge in the eye, which admittedly took looking upward. "You know how I know how well these guns shoot? It's 'cuz I shoot 'em," Luigi said. "I put 'em through the Luigi Cancio torture test. If they stand up to what I put them through and still shoot accurate, then you get to shoot 'em. And if I can't shoot 'em accurate, how do I know if they can shoot accurate? That's how I know when to stop tweakin' 'em for you, too."

No one in the team had ever considered this. But they all admitted to themselves that it made sense.

Luigi then considered a moment. "Well... with a couple-a exceptions. The two top dogs get to do the testin' on their own weapons."

After a thorough discussion of how to gauge wind by looking at things such as the movement of vegetation and dust and observing the mirage, the four teams commenced practicing. Doing a good job at the two-hundred-meter target, Luigi then drove off downrange to set the targets farther out: first three hundred, then four, then finally at five hundred meters from the firing line, each time with suffi- cient practice for each person to assure themselves that they could both do a decent job of shooting as well as spotting.

"This last set of targets, Amigo announced as Luigi again went downrange to set clean target faces, "is for all the brag- ging rights. When Luigi gets back, each of the pairs will get ten shots apiece at the target: five for each person. First person up shoots five rounds, then swaps and spots for the second five rounds by your teammate. High score wins."

"Yeah, but two of these teams have got ringers," Edge complained, referring to Hank and Amigo.

"You forget," Hank said. "The shooter does very little. It's *the spotter* who will matter—meaning the only one out here with a ringer is Voice." She eyed Spud. "You'd better not let me down."

"I never even considered that pairing the two of you might be bad for your marriage," Amigo said. "Honestly—I just used random numbers."

"He went hunting this morning, thinking he could maybe get a turkey before work. But his boss called and said he never showed up."

The anguish on the woman's face was obvious to Deputy

Alex Gray as he and his usual partner, Robert Fishback, interviewed the woman who had called. She sat on the edge of her couch, wringing her hands.

"Does he often go hunting before heading to work?" Gray asked.

"When it's a hunting season. Sometimes he comes home with something. Most times not. I think he really just likes spending time in the woods."

Like most guys with a wife, Gray thought.

"We have the description of his truck and his tag number, so we'll be on the lookout for both him and his truck," Fishback said. "It's possible he just broke down somewhere."

As the two walked back to their cruiser, the voice of their dispatcher crackled over their radios.

"Unit 98, 10-72." The call continued with the location.

The two looked at each other, then glanced over their shoulders at the house they'd just left. "Report of a body? Do you think...?" Fishback wondered.

"Only one way to find out."

Taking down GPS coordinates, they headed out along Bodas Road, then north on Clyde until reaching the power line easement. Pulling off and driving a short way northeast along the easement, they soon came across a truck. Checking the tag, they confirmed that it was the truck owned by the missing hunter.

Following the GPS coordinates they had been given, they made their way through the woods until they came upon a man dressed in camouflage and decked out in a bright blaze orange vest.

"Are you the man who called in a report of a body?" Gray asked him.

The man was visibly shaken. "Yeah, that was me. He's off this way."

The three men made their way into the woods, and after walking a few hundred yards the hunter stopped and pointed. "He's right over there."

As the two deputies began walking in the direction he had pointed, Fishback asked, "Aren't you coming?"

The hunter replied, "No, thanks. Just a warning for you: it isn't pretty."

Walking farther along, the two began to get an idea of what the hunter had meant. It was obvious that the body wasn't all in one piece. As they got nearer, Fishback leaned over and relieved himself of his lunch.

"Animals got to it," Gray said, stifling his own nausea. "A wolf pack from the looks of it. Or maybe a bear."

"I'm going to suggest we just secure the scene and call in the BCA guys," Fishback said.

Gray had walked closer, then turned around and rejoined his partner. "I think you're right. This guy didn't die from an animal attack."

"What makes you say that?"

"He's got a bullet hole in his head."

His last delivery of the day done, he made his way back to Holly's house. Parking in the driveway, he ducked beneath the crime scene tape and into the back yard.

The bucket that had held birdseed was now empty, scavenged clean by the regular visitors Holly had enjoyed watching as they visited her feeders. An additional rectangle of crime scene tape outlined the area where her body had lain. He walked over to it, a single red rose in his hand.

Laying it reverently down just inside the rectangle of yellow and black tape, he knelt and said, "This is for you, Holly. I wish I had given you this one and many more long before now. This is just the first one of the many I should have given you. And there will be many more—as many as it takes."

He stood and fingered the handgun stuck in his waist-band under his jacket. *There's only one way to be with her now,* he thought. *But I can't join her until I'm done.*

"Sɪᴛ ʀɪɢʜᴛ ʜᴇʀᴇ, Lᴜɪɢɪ," Edge said, the team having invited their gunsmith to eat dinner with them. Though he and Luigi hadn't won the sniper competition, they had placed a respectable second.

Spud leaned forward and scooped the stack of sixteen quarters toward himself. Removing eight, he handed them to Hank.

"Nice shooting, Love,"

"You too," Hank said with a grin. "Nice spotting as well."

Spud gave her a nod.

"Right there was your ringer," Edge commented with a point toward Hank.

"I couldn't have done it without a good spotter," Hank pointed out.

"I didn't dare screw up," Spud admitted. "The couch and I have become familiar enough as far as I'm concerned."

"Would you have made him sleep on the couch?" Cloud asked her.

"You bet your ass."

"That, gentlemen, is called 'motivation'," Spud said, eliciting laughter from the others. "What's on the training agenda for tomorrow?"

"It's been a while since we just did a session in the gym," Edge said. "I asked Mike to look over our training records to see what conditioning each of us could benefit from, and he'll be joining us in the gym tomorrow for some personalized training."

"It sounds like I'd better make sure I've got bath salts for the jacuzzi," Hank said. "Mike's got that 'no pain, no gain' attitude when it comes to workouts."

After finishing off Rose's offering of garlic butter salmon with asparagus and potatoes as well as all of the cake that had been left over from the lunchtime celebration for Edge passing his checkride, the team members made their way to their individual residences. Each had a vow of getting some extra rest before Mike would be putting them through what was certain to be a rigorous workout the next day.

As usual, Hank and Spud made their way to the reading nook. Hank took up her tablet; Spud took up his. Together, they read their respective items.

After some time, Hank shut down her tablet and placed it on the coffee table.

"Done?" Spud asked while still scrolling through potential news for the intel meeting.

"Yup."

"Still rolling your eyes?"

"Believe it or not, it wasn't that bad. A kind of odd mixture of a good police procedural mystery with a touch of the occult."

Spud looked up. "I'm surprised you didn't scoff at the occult stuff."

"A big ton of occult I can't take. But a little occult I have to think about."

"After dealing with Miss Martha?"

"You've got to admit: she was uncannily accurate."

"She used some terms that could easily have multiple meanings," Spud pointed out.

"'You are Seven, the seventh of seven'? That seemed pretty specific."

"Except that there are just seven of us in the team."

"Yes, but there were *eight* of us sitting at the two tables, remember? Doc Frank was with us," Hank reminded him. "Dressed the same way we were, I'll point out."

"I think I'll just continue to cultivate my doubts," Spud concluded.

"I will too, but doubt doesn't always involve looking for eliminating only one possibility."

Hank pulled a new book down from those shelved next to her.

"What's next?" Spud asked her.

"Another book by John Douglas. This one is on unsolved cases."

"We're not in the habit of not solving our cases," Spud said.

"But we've got this *one*," Hank began. "UniPerp. Maybe I can get some clues about how to solve UniPerp by looking at Douglas's profiling of the unsolved cases he looks at in this book."

"This sounds like it won't be nearly as enjoyable as reading a British police procedure mystery with a dash of occult seasoning."

"Maybe not. But just because it's nonfiction doesn't mean it's going to be uninteresting."

16

He hesitated briefly, leaning himself against a tree. It was overcast, so the morning light was more diffuse and lower than typical. Nonetheless, he had noted the truck parked by the side of a rural roadway, and figured that only a hunter would be out on such a gloomy day looking for his quarry.

As he was.

The forecast had called for a chance of rain, but he hardly believed it would rain—not on this day. It was barely above freezing. That concerned him a little. He didn't want his breath to fog his scope if he got lucky enough to get one of the hunters he now considered his mortal enemies in view. He hoped the camouflage gator he wore around his neck would do the trick for him once he pulled it up over his mouth and nose.

For the moment, though, he could see his breath creating small clouds in front of his face, then hanging there until slowly dissipating. The air was still as death, and he calculated that death would be something he could easily deal to the unwary hunter who might show up.

He crouched when he heard the crunch of leaves under someone's feet, then slipped behind the tree when he saw the flash of bright blaze orange show through the trees. Then subdued voices made their way over to him.

More than one. He wondered if it would be wise to try and take down more than one hunter. He slipped carefully along, paralleling the voices. He only heard two. *Are there only two of them?* he wondered.

He continued along keeping his distance from the pair, having confirmed there were only two through observing their brightly-colored vests as they moved among the trees.

A small clearing opened in front of them, and he could now plainly see the two men as they stood and looked around, no doubt trying to determine the best spot to head in order to hunker down and try calling in the turkeys that were the current game being taken. He asked himself again if he wanted to try to get both of them, or if he should perhaps not risk it. His blood boiled. *The more I can get, the more likely I'll get the one that killed Holly.*

Bracing his rifle against the trunk of the tree, he took careful aim, then determined the distance through a reading of their height against the dots on the reticle of his scope. Making the appropriate adjustments to his scope, he settled his crosshairs on one of the men and gave a steady squeeze to the trigger. Once he saw that he had hit the man, he moved slightly to engage the second hunter, who had frozen facing the direction where he was crouched. *Shock can be a good thing,* he thought. *Makes things easier. It's for sure this guy never served in combat, or he'd be diving for cover right now instead of standing there like a deer in the headlights.*

He pulled the trigger once more, his reticle steady on the man's head, once again being rewarded by the sight of the man falling to the ground. He stood up and waited to see if there would be any movement from either of the men. Seeing neither movement nor any sign of the same small clouds of exhaled breath his own breathing was creating, he smiled and walked back out of the woods.

He chuckled as he reached his truck and stowed his rifle back under the rear seat in the crew cab.

I'm a postman. I suppose this is what's called 'going postal'.

"OH WHAT A BEAUTIFUL MORNING, oh what a beautiful day," Spud sang as he entered the conference room.

"It would be much more rewarding if intel was going away," Edge finished for him—only an octave lower than Spud's baritone would allow, given Edge's bass couldn't get that high.

The entire rest of the team roared.

"I didn't know you sang," Hank remarked to Edge.

"Sometimes it takes inspiration."

"Very funny," Spud said. Sitting and activating his tablet, he began the intel briefing with, "This isn't news, but Doc Andy is concerned that we seem to be slacking off on meditating. He would like to remind everyone that meditation is, as he states here, 'an excellent way to combat stress'."

"That's not how *I* combat stress," Hank declared.

Spud put his face in his palm while the rest of the men snickered.

"You guys always let your minds go straight for the gutter," Hank groused. "What do we do every morning after breakfast?"

"Tai chi," Edge answered.

"That's what I do to relieve stress."

"That's what you do to remain flexible enough to relieve stress with Spud after dinner," Cloud countered to renewed snickering from his compadres.

Hank rolled her eyes. "Boys."

"We're *men*, Hank," Cloud protested.

"No you're not."

"Moving on. James would also like to remind everyone that the schedule for autologous plasma collection has been posted. He expects to see us promptly after breakfast on our assigned day for that."

"He only takes blood once a year. But it only lasts for forty-two days," Hank noted.

"He actually takes the blood for the plasma and cryo," Spud said. "Those stay frozen for up to a year."

"Why don't we have banked blood?"

"Edge, what's your blood type?" Spud asked.

"O positive."

"And you, Voice? What's your blood type?"

"O positive."

"Amigo?"

"O positive."

"Are you starting to see a pattern here, Love?"

"Mine is O positive too. You mean to say we all share the same blood type?"

"In order to be blood donors for a team member if needed. O positive is the most common blood type, so all team members are required to be O positive. Just in case."

"I learn something new about this team every day," Hank commented.

"Amigo's former coworkers have had a busy few days, mostly with people entering the country illegally and drugs entering the country illegally."

"That's the usual," Amigo said. "Sometimes, the cartels will try to swamp the guys with so much crap because they can get a whole lot more through while agents are tied up in secondary inspection."

"And one for Chip, also from our friends in the CBP. How does sniffing out a hundred and fifty thousand dollars' worth of meth sound?"

Voice signed 'dance' to Chip, who stood on his hind legs and twirled around.

Voice waggled his ears and let him wrestle with a tug toy.

"No treat?" Crow asked.

Voice reached into his treat bag and offered one to Crow. "Here ya go. Didn't know you liked the things."

"Very funny," Crow grumped as the rest of the team laughed.

"And here's what else is funny," Spud began.

"You Just Can't Make This Shit Up?" Amigo asked.

"It would be difficult, but given that the truth is often stranger than fiction, it must regularly be said that you just can't make this shit up," Spud returned.

"We have one of those odd police calls that likely even Hank hasn't seen while a member of the Taos PD."

"Dunno about that," Hank said. "With the profusion of drugs and overaged hippies, I saw a lot of weird shit."

"Let's see if you ever had one like this. A young teenager —young lady, I should clarify—returned one day to find someone in her room, apparently stealing her clothes. The other young lady was even wearing some of the clothes, specifically a pink, floor-length nightie with matching panties.

"Naturally, this young lady knew a crime when she saw one—or at least *thought* she did—and called 9-1-1. When the cops arrived, she pointed them up the stairs to her bedroom, where they found the perpetrator, who was now dressed in the young lady's ruffled blouse, a *very* short skirt, panties, and matching tights."

Hank started to giggle.

"Are you getting ahead of me again, Love?"

"Probably. Can I take a guess?"

"Lean over here and whisper in my ear."

Hank leaned over and whispered. Spud grinned and gave her a 'thumbs up'.

"The responding officers, of course, were having a bit of a time deciding how to handle the situation. Cuff the perp and deliver the intruder to the county jail as is, or have the perp change back into the clothing arrived in?"

"No, no," Hank said, shaking her head vigorously. "Absolutely *do not* deliver the perp to jail in the clothing being worn!"

"As it turned out, there would be no jail involved. Because even though the officers did bring said perp downstairs in the clothing being worn, the immediate reaction by the victim was, '*Howie?*'"

"Yes, by now you have hopefully guessed that the perpetrator was the victim's brother."

Hank nearly fell off her chair laughing. The rest of the men sat staring.

"You're kidding me," Cloud said.

"The name of this segment of the intel briefing is called what?" Spud asked him.

"You Just Can't Make This Shit Up."

"And I am here to tell you, you cannot."

"Could have been worse," Amigo pointed out. "It could have been, '*Dad?*'"

The rest of the team laughed.

"You know the drill. Skill sets, then rendezvous back in The Restaurant for lunch."

HEARING THE *THUNK!* of a blade imbedding in the wooden target near the entrance to the gym, Edge looked over calmly to see one of Hank's throwing knives stuck firmly near the center of it. Looking at where Hank stood about five meters from the target he remarked, "You're getting pretty good at that."

"Thanks. I keep trying to add a little distance. Start close and work backward from the target."

"That's a good way to do it. Let me see you throw."

After he'd walked to where he could watch her, Hank took another of her throwing knives from their sheath and propelled it sidearm into the target. She scowled.

"I can't seem to hit center."

Edge chuckled. "This isn't a sniper rifle you're handling."

"But—"

"Your adversary will be plenty occupied with the pain of having you hit him in the side or leg rather than the center of his chest. Trust me. He'll likely also be pretty surprised that a woman did it to him."

"Seems a lot of people are surprised when they find out the person on the other side of the rifle scope is a woman as well," Hank said, annoyance in her voice.

"There's a rule I made for myself when I first realized that everyone thought a big guy was a natural-born killer," Edge said. "The rule is: don't let the idiots run your life."

Hank had walked over and yanked her throwing knives back out of the target. "That doesn't sound like such a bad rule."

Edge just put a hand on her shoulder, then said, "Keep at it. You'll get more accurate."

"Think I can get a rabbit during our next survival exercise?"

"Think I can hit a coconut out at a thousand meters next time we head to the range?"

Hank turned and smiled at him. "We cross-train, but that doesn't mean we become equals."

"That's another good rule: appreciate that your team-mates have both strengths and weaknesses."

As Edge made his way over to the climbing wall where Spud stood waiting to act as his safety, Hank went back to not-so-casually throwing her knives. She also went back to thinking about the topic Edge had interrupted when he entered the gym. It was UniPerp, and her mind kept asking over and over, *Why seven?*

"WHAT YOU STILL LACK IS UPPER body strength and endurance," Mike told Hank as he counseled her for the physical training the team would be doing during their afternoon session. "I'm going to suggest that we start you with doing some bench presses."

Hank had a mental vision of Edge, having observed him while doing bench presses with a considerable amount of weight on the bar.

"You think I can bench press?" she asked while trying not to look too closely at her own arms.

"We're not going to be beefing you up like that guy over there," Mike said with a casual thumb cast over his shoulder to where Edge was working out on the lat pulldown machine. "For what you do, you need endurance and *some* strength. You've got that in your legs, but you need a bit more in your arms and back."

"How much weight are we talking about?"

"The bar weighs forty-five pounds. We're going to start with just the bar."

Hank considered that. "That doesn't sound too bad."

"Good. Because whether it sounded bad to you or not, that's what you're going to do."

Hank narrowed her eyes and looked at him steadily, observing that when Mike got on his physical trainer high horse, the ogre he ordinarily kept concealed came fully to the surface.

"Ten reps, then a five-minute break, then ten more, et cetera. Fifty reps total. It's not a race, so don't treat it like one. I've got all these other guys working on something, so I'll stay here and spot for you."

"You just want to see how much sweat you can drain out of me."

"No problem. I still have my broomstick."

"Unit 98, 10-72 east end of Erie, times two," Gray heard over the radio. He glanced over at Fishback.

"Times two?"

Fishback was already calling in their acknowledgement, and activating the light bar while Gray turned their cruiser and headed to the scene. Arriving, they found a man standing in the center of the unpaved road. He looked shaken, and was pointing into the woods while clutching his dog's lead.

"Did you call in the report, sir?" Deputy Gray asked the man.

"Y-yes," the man stammered. "I live just up the street. Was just out walking with my dog when he took off into the woods. When I went to get after him, I found him standing and barking over these two men. I didn't want to get too close, y'know? Just grabbed my dog and got him back on his lead, then called 9-1-1 and got the hell outta there."

"How far in would you say these two men are?" Fishback asked.

"Just a few hundred feet, I'd say," the man replied.

"Do you think you can remember just where you saw them?

"You don't want me to go back in there... I mean, what if the guy who killed them is still in there?"

"I understand your feelings," Gray said, "But it's unlikely." He pointed to where an SUV sat at the side of the road. "With just one vehicle, it's likely whoever killed them has left, and that's the dead men's vehicle."

The man led them back into the woods, stopping and pointing at a patch of blaze orange on the ground the minute he saw it.

"Can I go now?"

"Yes, sir. Just let me get your information in case we need to talk to you again."

After taking down the man's name, address, and phone number, Gray and Fishback continued on to get a look at the scene.

Gray looked over at his partner. "Times two," he said. Pulling crime scene tape from a bag he'd grabbed from the trunk of the cruiser, he and Fishback proceeded to cordon off the area. He then radioed in to his dispatcher. "Better notify BCA."

"You think these two are related to the other one?" Fishback asked him.

"This makes four people dead in the space of just a couple of weeks. What does that sound like to you? Especially being out here in the middle of Nowhere, Minnesota?"

"Guys," Voice called from across the gym. "We need to cut this short."

Hank was on the last of her repetitions when Voice called out to the team.

"Why? What gives?" Edge asked.

"Hal just reported what looks like a developing cluster."

Everyone stopped what they were doing and headed up to the conference room.

"I did a minor reprogramming of Hal for UniPerp events," Voice was explaining as they entered the room. "I figured if we could catch a cluster while it's developing, we might be able to catch UniPerp in the act."

"What does Hal have?" Cloud asked.

"Four killings in a remote area of Minnesota. One woman, three men. The last two bodies were just found. The woman is a bit of an oddball; nothing seems to connect her to the others except that she was killed by a bullet wound to the head. The three men have that same connection: killed by a bullet wound to the head. They were also all hunters, and all found in the woods dressed in their hunting gear. One was badly mutilated post mortem, apparently by some kind of predator. The area is known to have both bears and wolves, so it could have been either of those."

"Where is this place?"

"The bodies were all found in Fayal Township. Don't even try to find it on a map—at least not if you're trying to find some kind of town center. There isn't one."

"Do we have anything nearby?" Hank asked.

"Yeah, but you'll be glad to know it's a three-hour drive away," Voice said.

"Don't tell me. We have a Buckingham Palace to go along with the Taj Mahal and Shangri-La?"

"It's an old Nike site, if that's what you're asking," Voice confirmed.

"Oy."

"This one's in pretty good shape, Hank. It's called Remote Base Golf. Doc Wright will be disappointed that we won't be staying there. There's a golf course right across the street from it."

"He fishes? He golfs? Odd combo," Hank observed.

"He says when you golf the way he does, you need to be able to fish. Says it's helpful for getting the ball out of the water hazards."

The entire team laughed.

"Still, I think it would be better to stay closer, given we might want the helicopter for this one. We could stay close by in Hibbing. They've got an airport just east of town we can get a Latitude into: Range Regional. They've got a Hampton Inn we can stay at, and there's even entertainment close by," Voice said.

"Really? That sounds like fun. What is it?" Amigo asked.

"A Walmart. We can go shopping at night and watch the Walmartians."

"Oh my God," Crow said, face-palming and staring at Voice through his fingers.

"First thing: go into the pharmacy area and see if you can find eye bleach," Amigo said to the renewed laughter of his teammates.

Voice had been consulting his tablet. "On retrospect, perhaps we want to take a Latitude. Like I said, we can get one into the airport, and the flight time is only an hour and twenty minutes. In the helo, more like four hours."

"Definitely sounds like a Latitude is the better option,"

Amigo said. "What's the drive time to where these things are happening?"

Voice tapped on his tablet. "Half an hour."

"Much as I like the H155, I'm definitely leaning toward a Latitude, then," Cloud said.

"Who's handling the cases right now?" Crow asked.

"The Minnesota Bureau of Criminal Apprehension," Voice replied.

"Then it sounds like we'll want to get our FBI gunny to get us involved in this," Spud said. "UniPerp is their case, so it should be fairly easy for Stan to explain the situation."

"It might sound easy, but lots of times if the request goes from the FBI to the locals there's a bit of resistance. They sometimes resent that the feds want to 'take their case'," Hank said, making quotation marks in the air.

"We can get Stan to explain that their shootings appear to be connected to a case that's been two years in the making," Spud said. "A major case the FBI has been trying to crack, and with the help of their Bureau of Criminal Apprehension, might be able to put to rest."

"*OOF!*" Hank said as she picked her book up off of the coffee table.

Spud smiled. *I know what that's about.* "Heavy subject?"

"What's that I've heard Voice say?" She adopted a fake oriental accent. "You funny man. Funny, funny."

This time Spud chuckled. "Mike put you through a bit of a workout, I take it."

"Only fifty repetitions bench pressing a forty-five-pound bar," she said with the sarcasm dripping from her lips.

"Need a massage?"

"Not the kind *you're* thinking about," she said. "Besides, I think that kind of massage takes care of something *you* find uncomfortable—not me." She let her eyes travel the length of his body. "How do you do it?"

"Do what?"

"Stay so evenly toned."

"Mike developed a conditioning routine for me a long time ago, and I follow it. Every so often, he'll recommend a little more of something or a little less, like he did this afternoon. Then he just relies on me to do it." He regarded her for a moment. "You're keeping up with the routine he developed for you, aren't you?"

"Well, uh... sometimes I slouch a bit."

"No slouching. When Mike tells you to do a particular set of exercises on a particular time table, do it."

Hank thought of the excuses she could utter. *I do tai chi every morning. I run the silo stairs on a regular basis. I let the damned obstacle course humiliate me too.* Then she reflected that they were, in actuality, just excuses.

"You're right. I should be paying more attention to the fitness plan he makes up for me."

"There ya go." He glanced at her book. "Still reading about Jack the Ripper?"

"Douglas is making his case for who he thinks did it. Then it will be on to another case."

"What will that case be?"

"Lizzie Borden."

"Ah. The forty whacks gal."

"Actually, it was fewer, but yes," Hank said.

"You read some of the most gruesome stuff, and right before bedtime I'll add."

"Nothing in the news is gruesome?"

"You have a point."

Hank laid her book down on the coffee table. "I also have arms that hurt badly enough to make holding a book an effort. Douglas seems to think some poor Jewish immigrant was Jack the Ripper, but I'm still bothered by the fact that only one of the murders happened during bad weather. The perp was used to being comfortable, so I still say a nobleman or a man with some wealth.

"And with that, I'm going to go sit up to my neck in the jacuzzi so I can try and get the aches out of my arms."

"Would you like me to join you?"

"If you even *think* about making this aching body do anything physical," Hank began, jabbing her sternum with her thumb, "I will smother you in your sleep."

"You don't have to do anything physical. You can just lie there."

Hank walked back over to the coffee table, picked up her book, and threw it at Spud, uttering *"ow!"* and rubbing her arm after sending it flying. Spud ducked and chuckled, then said, "I'll be in to give you a massage later."

Hank just glared at him.

17

"Just a reminder that we have our FBI gunny arriving this morning. He's expected right after the intel briefing, so let's see if we can get through this before he gets here."

The team members sat divided over their attendance—not the usual situation. Typically, they'd rather be anywhere than in an intelligence briefing, but this morning it would be coupled with the discussion of what could be their next mission.

"First up, we have the environmentalists. This time, it's plastics. They want them eliminated."

"What are they proposing to take their place?" Cloud asked.

"Paper made from hemp fiber."

Everyone laughed but Cloud. "They're talking about *industrial* hemp fiber," he said. "Not pot."

"Why not pot?" Hank asked. "It's hemp. Doesn't it produce fiber too?" Her eyes betrayed her, and her next statement confirmed it. "I've always thought some of those environmentalists were high on something."

"Speaking of pot, our brothers and sisters in CBP continue to interdict large loads of drugs, most of which are *not* pot but a nice brew of cocaine, ketamine, meth, fentanyl..."

"Great," Amigo said with sarcasm in his voice. "At least they didn't have to worry about interdicting a load that could kill them with pot."

"Other large loads they're interdicting are tractor-trailer loads of human beings."

"Human trafficking is slavery—pure and simple," Crow said. "If more people understood this, more people would be opposed to illegal entry into the country."

"And last but not least," Spud began, glancing up as Stan was ushered into the room by Gil.

"You just can't make this shit up!" the rest of the team exclaimed happily.

"This one should probably be introduced with the expression, 'never underestimate the power of a woman.' You're going to like this one, Hank."

"I already like the title," she said.

"It seems that one evening, a young lady was sitting on a bench waiting for her ride to pick her up. That's when she was joined by a man, who she felt sat a little too close to her.

"She moved away a bit, and he moved back next to her and asked her for the time. She ignored him.

"He then pulled something from his pocket and, concealing it with his other hand, said, 'This is a gun. Don't shout or I'll shoot you.' Then he stood up and took her by the arm, attempting to lead her off. She demanded to know where they were going, and he said, 'Just over in that alley where we can be alone.'

"You probably all have an idea of what he had in mind."

"You might say that," Hank confirmed.

"Unfortunately, he had not taken notice of the building she was sitting in front of. If he had, he could have noticed two things: first, that it was a dojo; second, that the young lady herself was depicted on a large poster in the window wearing a gi and a black belt."

"Oooo—you're right. I like this one," Hank declared to the chuckles of her teammates.

"After practicing a bit of her art on the guy, it was discovered that his gun was the kind that was loaded with water. His police booking photo also looked like this. Hal, display photo."

"Holy crap!" Cloud exclaimed. "Did she leave even a square millimeter of his face unbruised?"

Spud turned and looked closely at the image.

"It doesn't appear that she did."

Hank had pulled out her little leather medicine pouch and was waving it.

"How many teeth did she get?"

Spud took another close look at the man's booking photos. "The story didn't mention any lost teeth, but from the looks of things I would think she would have had the ability to take home more souvenirs than you have there, Love."

Hank began drumming her hands on the table to voice her approval, being joined by her teammates.

"That's all I have for the usual briefing. I'm sure that you all have felt our FBI gunny's breath on your necks, so if someone will get Stan a cup of coffee, we can begin the next phase of the briefing."

Cloud got up to procure the requested coffee while Stan took a seat at the table.

"Good morning, everyone," Stan said as coffee was placed in front of him and Crow slid the usual plate of intel briefing goodies within his reach. "I understand you've taken an interest in a significant event?"

"Our man Voice did a subtle reprogramming of our

supercomputer which has now identified what could be a cluster event similar to what we've been seeing with UniPerp."

"Ah. UniPerp," Stan said. "Another cluster of seven linked killings?"

"Not seven yet. Four, one of which might be unrelated. Three of which are quite closely related," Voice explained.

"Why only four?" Stan asked.

"The logic goes like this," Voice began. "If we wait for seven events and a message in the Lincoln paper or on the billboard along I-80, UniPerp will have finished his latest event and moved on. But I've reprogrammed Hal to tag three events that appear to be identical with the plan that we could then move to apprehend UniPerp before he has a chance to complete seven."

"Then why did you not get this flag before four killings were done?" Stan asked.

"The last event was a two-fer," Amigo explained. "Two victims in the same event."

"What's joining them is the method," Cloud continued as the team briefed Stan. "All occurred in the same general rural location in Minnesota. All involved a bullet wound to the head. The first victim's wound was positively identified to be from a rifle chambered for .243 Winchester, given the bullet remained in her skull. The others seem consistent with a .243, but the bullets went through-and-through and haven't been recovered."

"The first victim may or may not be related to the others," Voice continued. "She's a bit of an outlier. She's the only woman. All the others are men. She was shot while standing in her backyard; the men were all shot in the woods. The men were all hunters—they were all wearing the standard blaze vest and had a firearm with them. It's turkey season in Minnesota right now, and they were all found with a shotgun—not a rifle. The woman didn't possess any firearms and also didn't have a hunting license."

"In short, we're also not sure if the woman is connected to the others," Spud concluded.

"This could be anyone," Stan said. "A family member, perhaps. Or perhaps some demented environmentalist who likes turkeys and doesn't like hunters."

"She has an ex, who was ruled out. Although he had the murder weapon, he didn't acquire it until *after* she had been shot. An investigation of the pawn shop where the gun was purchased showed that they got it after the woman was shot as well. The ID presented by the seller didn't get flagged during the NICS check, but was later discovered to be fake. Pawn shop surveillance video was also not helpful in identifying the seller.

"The case is currently being handled by the Saint Louis County sheriff's department and the Minnesota Bureau of Criminal Apprehension. With this pattern being so similar to UniPerp's, we'd truly like to assist with this one," Spud explained.

Stan looked over at Hank.

"I've already told them that local authorities often don't like the Bureau butting in," Hank told him.

"The feeling we have is that if the FBI explained to the locals that their case could be part of a nationwide manhunt for a serial killer—a major case that the FBI is involved with —they might be more amenable to allow our assistance," Spud said. "It could be good press for them to be able to claim involvement in a major case that gets solved in their jurisdiction."

"In short, we're wondering if you could butter them up for us," Amigo summarized.

"It shouldn't be hard," Stan said. "And I agree: if this leads to the apprehension of UniPerp, then a two-year chase will be over. I know you guys don't like unsolved cases, and neither does the Bureau."

"We'll wait until you give us the go-ahead to work on this," Spud said. "In the meantime, we'll be doing our usual readiness training and will be sticking close to headquarters while you see what you can do."

With that, the team members all stood and started their way out of the conference room.

"Hey, Stan," Hank began.

"What do you want, Hank?"

Seeing Spud hesitate at the door to the conference room, she asked, "Can I talk with you a moment? In private?"

Spud gave her a questioning look, then turned and made his way through Honor Way along with the others.

"Have a seat. More coffee?" she asked.

"Sure. I'll help you polish off the little goodies, too," Stan said.

Hank poured two more mugs of coffee, delivering them to the conference room table and sliding the plate of pastries to be within reach of both of them. After taking one, Stan asked, "So, what's on your mind, Kat?"

"Someone put a bug in my ear recently," Hank said. "Can you tell me why I was selected for the unit?"

Stan chewed and swallowed a bite of the pastry he had chosen.

"I really have no idea, Kat."

"You didn't initiate it?"

"No. I didn't even like the idea, and made that known. The order for your transfer to Quantico came down from above though, and I was bluntly told that it was a done deal and too bad if I didn't like it."

"Why were you against it?" she asked, her curiosity now aroused.

"I felt they were taking a good agent away from me. Albuquerque isn't exactly everyone's choice for an assignment. In you, I got a dedicated agent who was familiar with the area and who actually wanted to be there." He hung his head for a moment. "I had actually had a private tête-à-tête with the cartel task force folks down in El Paso, telling them I hoped they'd keep their claws out of you."

"*You* were the reason I was denied cartel task force?"

"One and the same. When an SAIC of a Field Office gets a good agent, they like to keep him. Or her. I was no exception. But the people above me were not to be denied, and the order came straight from 935 Pennsylvania Avenue Northwest. It was highly suggested to me that raising a ruckus would not be a good career move."

"So, it really came down—"

"As far as I know, all the way from the top."

"It was hinted that maybe I was chosen because the Bureau wanted to get rid of me."

"What? Nothing in any evaluation *I* put in would have suggested that. I saw you as a real asset. A special agent who could get the job done without bending the rules. It's true that there's still quite a bit of rule-bending done by SAs, and as long as it gets the job done without creating controversy, those in charge tend to look the other way. For an SAIC, having agents bend the rules is always a little nerve-racking, though. There's the pressure to clear cases. That's why a little bending of the rules is overlooked. But there's also the desire to keep your ass out of the grinder. For an SAIC, every agent in their office is someone with the potential to get your ass right down in there. But you? You played strictly by the rules and still cleared cases while keeping your partners from stepping over the line as well. I saw that as a win-win."

"You really felt I was a good agent."

"I really felt you were an *exemplary* agent, Kat. The only thing I worried about was that you might not deal well with other agents bending the rules, and you'd either lose your faith in the FBI's mission or decide to go with the flow and bend rules yourself. A person's integrity sometimes can only go just so far when the people around them are putting pressure on them to do things that aren't right. At first, just a *little* not right and when you cave, then it's easier for the next time to be a little more not right. Then a guy like me has hard choices to make. Can I get this agent back inside the line, or do I have to start making her realize she's not going to get good assignments nor coveted transfers because, frankly, she's fucking up."

She looked at him steadily, her little voices whispering to her about his sincerity.

"It damned near killed me when we got word that you had died in a training accident," Stan continued. "The very first thing I thought was, 'How is it that such a good agent dies like that?' It's bad enough when an agent dies in the line, but like that? And if you remember, I just about crapped masonry when I walked in as the unit's new FBI gunny and saw you sitting at the table. It was surprise enough to learn about the unit to begin with, but to find that you were alive, well, and a part of it? Though as I've considered since that day, it's served as affirmation to me that my judgement of your character was right on the money."

"Thanks, Stan. I really had begun to question why I was here."

"Regardless of why the decision was made, you *are* here.

And you belong here, Kat. Hank. I'm constantly amazed by this team and what it can do, and I see that the guys all appreciate and respect you. I pray for all of you every day, that God keep you all safe and healthy in spite of some of the insane cases you take on. I'm really hoping that this case turns out to be UniPerp as well. It will be a great solve for the team, and of course the Bureau will get part of the credit. But even better, UniPerp will be stopped. How many dead is it now?"

"Two hundred and nineteen," Hank said gloomily.

"Two hundred and nineteen." Stan shook his head. "I sure hope this is it."

"I'M SO SORRY, HOLLY," he said as he placed two more red roses inside the rectangle that had once outlined her body. "I looked for them, but didn't find anyone today to atone for what happened to you. But then, tomorrow is Friday, and I'm betting there will be some out hunting instead of working. That old thing about being unable to work because their arm is in a sling. I'll make them wish that had really been the case."

With that, he returned to his mail route, the placard stuck in the windshield that informed everyone that he was the tiny community's rural delivery postman. He considered how perfect that was, given it gave him a ready excuse for being in any area at any moment in time.

"ONE-ZERO-ONE UNIFORM NOVEMBER, MISSED APPROACH," Cloud announced as he and Crow practiced instrument approaches at the nearby Central Nebraska Regional Airport in Grand Island. It was a common location the duo had been using recently to remain current in operating the Latitudes, and the tower was now used to having them arrive and do multiple approaches before landing. Nor did it impress the controllers as a coincidence that their landings usually occurred around lunchtime, and their departure usually was after lunchtime.

"What do you think the big pow-wow between Hank and Stan was about?" Cloud asked once Crow had become established on his missed approach.

"Not a clue," Crow mumbled, being more occupied with correctly flying the aircraft.

"Think maybe she might be missing the FBI?"

That nearly threw Crow off his game. "What are you thinking? That she might want to retire and head back to the FBI?"

"Not sure *what* to think," Cloud said. "She seemed to spend a bit of time talking with him."

"Maybe just friendly conversation," Crow said. "He was her boss, after all."

"Maybe we should lay off her and Spud." Keying the mike, he announced, "Grand Island Tower, one-zero-one Uniform November inbound ILS, full stop."

Cloud had the ILS coupled and simply monitored the instruments in front of him until taking over for the landing. As he turned onto the taxiway, he said, "Do you really think Hank is annoyed with us?"

"She always gives us that 'water off a duck' routine, but the woman's got feelings. Everyone does."

Cloud considered that as he turned onto the FBO ramp, following the lineman ahead of him to a parking spot. "She wouldn't leave Spud, though. And I don't think Spud is ready to leave the team."

"We have no idea what's going on behind closed doors," Crow countered as the two extracted themselves from the cockpit. "The unit isn't exactly a stress-free environment, and we have no idea what it might be doing to their relationship."

Cloud considered this as well. "I can't even conceive of them breaking up."

"They came close once before, remember?"

"Yeah, but that was completely different."

"You think it never comes up when someone's feeling a little stressed out?" Crow countered.

"Not even going to think about this now," Cloud said. The conversation was making him uncomfortable, not wanting to think about losing a respected team member. "I'm hungry, and that's why we stopped. Hey, Johnny," he called to the lineman.

"Looking for another good place to eat?" Johnny asked.

"You know it."

"I'm going to recommend Tommy Gunz Bistro. They do some awesome pizza."

"Sounds great."

As they walked off into the FBO to hitch a ride, Crow remarked, "You know we're going to hear no end of it when we get back. I can hear everyone now: *You guys stopped to get pizza? Where's ours?*"

"This is something we should be concerned about?"

The two looked at each other for a brief moment, then simultaneously said, *"Nahhhh!"*

"WHAT ARE YOU SNACKING ON?" Spud asked as he entered the reading nook.

"The leftover pizza Crow and Cloud brought back from Grand Island."

"Those guys," Spud said sneeringly. "They always say, 'It's recurrent training.' If you ask me, it's nothing more than an excuse to go indulge themselves. And this stuff? *Really?* A Reuben pizza?"

"I agree—sounds weird. But try it. It's actually pretty good."

"You will eat anything that doesn't eat you first," Spud said while picking up a piece and giving it the evil eye before trying a bite.

"Your verdict?"

"Weird, yes. Bad? I'm afraid to say it, but it actually tastes pretty good," Spud admitted.

"I'm done with Lizzie Borden," Hank declared. "Next is the Lindberg kidnapping."

"Well?"

"They found Lizzie innocent, but she did it alright. I agree with Douglas on this one."

"What do you think about the Minnesota case?" Spud asked.

"I'm troubled by one thing: the woman. She doesn't seem to fit in. According to the case report, she was filling her bird feeders when she was shot. And a second thing: the location isn't anywhere near an interstate."

"We *are* talking about Nowhere, Minnesota."

"Which is another reason I think this might be an environmentalist taking things to extremes by shooting hunters. Just one more reason the woman doesn't fit. Why would an environmentalist shoot a woman who is feeding wild birds?"

"You don't think the woman's case and the hunters are connected."

"That's exactly what I think. Not connected."

"So if this is UniPerp, why would he shoot a woman who has no connection with the others?"

"I'm not thinking it's UniPerp," Hank said. "If we agree that UniPerp is a truck driver, we'd expect to continue to see the events happening near to trucking routes. The interstates."

"If you take a look at that area, you'll see there are no interstates," Spud pointed out. "Interstate 35 ends in Duluth."

"So why would he continue north?"

"Maybe he picked up a load that had to get to one of the mines up there. The location is near US 53, and I imagine there's a bit of truck traffic that goes between Duluth and the mines."

"Doesn't compute for me."

"Well, you could be right. Perhaps this isn't UniPerp. But do you want to risk that you could be wrong?" Spud asked her.

"Not really," Hank conceded. "Whatever is going on, there are three men and a woman who are dead. Perhaps not by our guy, but *someone* is responsible."

18

I see your SUV, and I know that antler logo too, he thought as he drove around making his early morning deliveries. Traveling onward for a small stretch and then pulling to the side of the road, he took his rifle from the spot where it was sequestered under his rear seats and put his camouflage jacket over his postman's uniform. Then he trekked into the woods, careful to stay quiet and to look carefully in all directions while hunting his human quarry.

Hearing a distant turkey call, he made his usual wager to himself that it wasn't a real bird, but a hunter trying for one. He moved in the direction the call appeared to come from.

He heard it again—this time, louder. *He's close.* He crouched and looked all around for the tell-tale blaze orange vest that was required by law for hunters. *But not hunters of men. No law covers that.*

He finally spotted the hunter up in a tree stand. *Don't think I'll miss and hit a branch like you did with Holly.*

Taking careful aim, he focused on the man's head, then waited for him to stop moving around as he gazed from side to side to see if his call had caught the attention of a turkey. Once the man stopped twisting his head to and fro, he settled the crosshairs of his scope on the man's head once more and carefully squeezed the trigger. Just after the shot rang out, he saw the man slump against the safety harness he wore to keep from falling from the stand, dropping his shotgun from his hands to the ground below.

He wasn't interested in the gun. He was never interested in the gun. He stood and watched as he usually did, ready to make another shot if the first hadn't proven to be fatal. But between practice on the range and his former military experience, he smiled with the realization that once again his bullet had found its mark.

And once again he turned, walked back to where his truck was parked, opened it up and placed his rifle back under the rear seats, and calmly got back in to finish his deliveries. He wasn't interested in them, either—only one of them. The single red rose rested on the seat next to him, wrapped in cellophane, the cut end of the stem bathed in a damp plug of florist's foam. There would be no mail to be delivered to the address other than the usual junk mail, but it would be delivered along with the rose just the same.

Arriving at the house, he shoved the junk mail into the mailbox, which was starting to overflow with it and with bills that would go unpaid. Then he walked around to the rear of the house, to what he now considered the crime tape-enclosed shrine to the only woman he had truly loved. Setting the rose down with the other three, he said, "Only one today, Holly. But tomorrow is the weekend, and all the good ol' boys will be paired up with their buddies and their beer, which is just how they'll be found—with but one exception. They will get a red rose, too—directly in the center of their skull—all for you, courtesy of me."

"FIRST UP WILL BE our typical run-down of the news. Then we'll discuss possible mission planning," Spud began.

"Not possible. Plain old mission planning," Voice corrected. "We got word this morning from Stan that we are to make our way to Hibbing, Minnesota to set up a base of operations while assisting in the investigation of five apparent homicides in the area around Fayal Township."

"I thought there were only four," Crow questioned.

"Another one was found literally just a few minutes ago," Voice said. "A hunter walking through the woods noticed a shotgun laying on the ground and went to investigate. When he took a look, he saw there was fresh blood on the ground, some of which was spattered on the shotgun. He looked around and didn't see anyone until he looked up. Whoever has been shooting the hunters got the latest victim while he was sitting in a tree stand."

"Bullet through the head again?" Spud asked.

"Yes."

"Ok. Intel first, then mission planning." Spud activated his tablet. "First up is environmentalists again. This time, global warming which they're saying is responsible for a rash of fires that have been occurring in the Arctic."

"How do they figure that global warming is setting fires?" Hank asked.

"Not so much that it's setting fires, but that the unusually dry conditions in the Arctic at the moment are making fires more prevalent."

"I guess that makes sense."

"We have a twist on human smuggling across the border. This time, it has to do with who was doing the smuggling."

"Pray tell," Crow remarked.

"It was two U.S. citizens—both teenagers—driving a semi-truck."

"Sounds like they're granting CDLs to some very young people these days," Amigo snarked. "I suspect the cartels believed they would get a wrist-slap for their participation."

"And that's all I have, except for a tale from the Secret Service files."

"Of the 'You Just Can't Make This Shit Up' kind?" Cloud asked hopefully.

"I couldn't if I tried.

"I was a little late one day, and" —Spud cleared his throat— "got a little heavy footed in my anxiety to get to the White House. This was during the administration of a president that no one liked and who liked no one in the PPD, so I *really, really* didn't want to be late.

"So naturally, I got pulled over by one of my fine brothers in the Capitol Police Department.

"No big deal, I'm thinking. Just flash my creds and I'm on my way.

"He takes his merry time going back to his cruiser with my driver's license, and when he comes back, he's got his gun in his hand and is demanding that I get out of the car, slooowly, and get on the ground.

"At this point, I'm thinking that one of my practical joker friends in PPD has put some pal in the Capitol PD up to playing a prank. Ok, fine. I'll play along. I get out, and the first thing he does is grab me and prone me out right there on the side of the street.

"This is going a bit too far, so I reach for my badge. He gets really excited and tells me to leave my hands where he can see them. He proceeds to pat me down, and naturally he finds my gun, so now he's super excited, yelling at me and telling me there's a warrant for my arrest and he's going to charge me with impersonating a federal officer as well."

Hank started to giggle.

"Love, you think this is funny?"

"Oh, not at this point, I'm sure. But it's going to get better, because I think I know what happens next." She took a quarter out of her pocket and slid it onto the table. "Anyone care to wager?"

"You've told her this story," Crow said.

"I've never told her this story. She would never have believed me."

"Oh, yes I would. I only have to ask one question: a fairly young guy with a short haircut?"

Spud gave off a hint of a grin. "Maybe you *do* know how this ends.

"As he's slapping on the handcuffs, I tell him in my best 'you'd better believe this' voice that I am a Secret Service agent in the Presidential Protective Detail, and I will make sure that I have his badge in my possession by the end of the day. He informs me that I am about to get free room and board in the PD lockup. I tell him in no uncertain terms that he'd better check that warrant again, and he'd also better ask his lieutenant to show up before he takes me in.

"He calls for his lieutenant and then asks for the warrant to be read. I overhear the dispatcher telling him first my name and then the description: a black male, nineteen years of age, five feet five inches in height... At this point, both of us realize he's just performed the... no other way to put it, sorry Edge... fuck-up of his life. He gets this info just as his lieutenant arrives.

"The lieutenant asks what the problem is, and he sheepishly explains that he has mistakenly detained a six foot, one-hundred-and-seventy pound, twenty-six-year-old Caucasian Secret Service agent who he has mistaken for a five-foot-five, nineteen-year-old skinny black guy. He tells his lieutenant this all while leaving me lying in the street in handcuffs and him in possession of my service weapon.

"I don't know who is less amused: me, or his lieutenant. I do know that his lieutenant is hissing like a snake while saying, 'You will get that man out of those cuffs and off of the ground *right now*, give him back his weapon, and then report to my office. *Is that understood?*'

"Of course, I'm now not only late, but my suit is a mess. When I show up and report in, *my* supervisor takes one look and asks if I tied one on the night before and just now picked myself up out of the gutter. I tell him that I did, in fact, just pick myself up out of the gutter, but not for the reason he believes. I explain the whole thing to him, invite him to verify my near arrest with the Capitol PD, all while thinking he's going to send me for a psych evaluation for telling this tall a tale. Instead, he laughs himself into hysterics and does so every time he sees me for about a week afterward."

The team was now also laughing hysterically.

"That was worth the mental picture alone," Cloud says. "Too bad some passerby didn't take a picture with their cellphone to commemorate the event."

Spud got a dismayed look. "For all I know, someone did."

That got the team laughing even harder.

"Alright, alright. Now you've had some fun at my expense, let's discuss the case in Minnesota."

"I've put in some arrangements for us in Hibbing, as we had discussed earlier. Hangar space for the Latitude, hotel rooms for us. We'll be ground floor, and I've reserved an entire wing for us to keep the curious from asking questions. Nine rooms. Hank and Spud can stay in separate rooms this time," Voice informed the team.

Crow and Cloud whisked their head around to look at

Hank and Spud to see just what their reaction would be to that, having expressed concerns among themselves as to what the stress of unit duty might be doing to their relationship. Hank's immediate reaction of "Like hell we will!" gave them both assurances that their fears weren't well founded.

"I kind-of figured you'd say that," Voice said, grinning. "I actually felt that the spare room might best serve as the remote location infirmary in case anyone gets sick or injured. That leaves eight rooms that can accommodate everyone with one room apiece. Except Hank and Spud."

Spud's eyebrow had shot up. "How much is this costing us?"

Voice pulled out his tablet. "If that's an issue, I can solve the problem."

"You're going to put two people to each room?" Hank asked.

"No, I'm going to hack the black funds for a little more cash."

Now everyone's eyebrows shot up.

"Geez, you guys," Voice said. "You think I didn't do the hacking when we first discussed this case?"

Now protests began to be heard.

Voice laughed. "You guys are really paranoid that I'm going to attempt a global takeover. The truth is that the FBI suggested it and also had no problems with the choice of hotel."

The rest of the team was now staring at him, not sure which story was the truth.

Voice sighed. "If you don't believe me, check with Stan."

Feeling somewhat assured that their tech wizard hadn't gone rogue (yet), they relaxed, giving the cue to Voice that he should continue.

"We'll have two SUVs waiting for us, and the hotel is

reserving two parking spots near the side entrance nearest our rooms.

"We have a day to settle in and rest up. Then we'll meet with the BCA guys, who are admitting at this point that they're stumped."

"Conference room in the hotel?" Hank asked.

"Yeah, they've got a meeting room, and can even arrange to have beverages and snacks in there while we're meeting."

"When does all this happen?" Crow asked. "Specifically, when do we have to leave?"

Voice smiled, cocked his head to the side, and said, "Hal, unit, scramble."

HANK HAD WON the left seat, and with Crow to her right handling communications, was more-or-less kicking back drinking a cup of coffee while the flight management system handled the flight.

"It's nice up here in the sunshine," Crow remarked. "But looks pretty snotty below us."

"We'll have a layer of clouds to punch, but they're reporting the deck at about three thousand AGL," Hank replied. "George can handle it until we get a visual on the runway, which we should get right after we break out. Visibility is reporting good below the clouds. Just be glad we're not on the other side of Lake Superior. With the temperatures and lake effect, it's snowing!"

"Oh, but snow is such fun to fly in... *not*," Crow agreed. He then added, "Hal, isolate to FT4, FT7."

"Got something you need to discuss?" Hank asked.

"Uh... just wondering, Hank. Cloud and I got to talking the other day—"

"While you were eating that crazy-ass Reuben pizza?" Hank interrupted him.

"Actually, while we were landing over in Grand Island. Everything is ok between you and Spud, right?"

Hank looked startled. "What would make you think it wasn't?"

"The job. Stress."

"We both love the job, in spite of the stress," Hank assured him.

"It's just you spent a long time talking with Stan the other day. We thought maybe you were wanting to go back to the FBI."

Hank had just taken a sip of her coffee, and had to fight to not spit it all over the instrument panel. Choking it down, she roared with laughter. "Go back to the FBI? Are you kidding me?"

"Well, what *did* you talk with him about?"

"I wanted to know why I was picked for the unit."

Oh, that sounds like trouble. "And he told you?"

"He didn't know. He said he wanted to keep me and had even sabotaged my efforts to get assigned to the drug cartel task force. Said he liked that I could get things done without bending the rules."

"Yeah, agents bending rules can be a problem," Crow admitted, remembering his Drug Enforcement Agency days. "It's easier when you're dealing with foreign cartels, though. Crooked drug lords working in nations run by corruptible officials. They're all bending the rules as well. With everyone playing dirty, it's a level playing field."

"That might work on foreign soil a lot better than within our borders," Hank said. "At least, I always thought so. Nevertheless, Stan told me that the order apparently came all the way from the top, and that he always gave me sterling performance reviews. Impeccable integrity, and all that. So, either someone at the top felt that made me qualified for the unit or they felt it made me less than likely to succeed in the FBI."

"Maybe they felt your integrity would lead you to become a whistleblower," Crow remarked.

"I hadn't thought about that," Hank said, watching the FMS initiate their descent into Hibbing. "But who do you complain to if the guys at the top accept a little sideways action if it gets the job done? If I'd known everything then that I know now, I would probably have simply quit the FBI and either gone back to community policing or joined a state patrol somewhere. Or maybe start my own training outfit. There are lots of outfits, sure—but few that specialize in sniper operations and fewer still that put an emphasis on training women, in spite of how many women you see at the top ranks of just about all the shooting sports.

"Still, if they thought I might be inclined to be a whistle-blower, they sent me to exactly the wrong place. Who watches the watchers?"

"We do," Crow joined her in answering.

THE UNIT MEMBERS parked in the reserved spots the hotel had set aside for them while Voice went in to get room keys and let them in through the side door nearest their rooms. It hardly seemed necessary to have reserved rooms; the hotel was only sparsely occupied though the unit members concluded it was likely much more popular when visitors came escaping the heat from other locales around the nation later on in the year.

"Any place decent to eat around here?" Hank asked, having not noted much on the drive in.

"There's a sandwich place nearby, but the hotel also provides lunch if you request it," Voice said. "Otherwise, if you want something close, you can eat like royalty."

"Really? There's a really good place to eat near here?"

"Like I said," Voice repeated. "You eat like royalty. Specifically, a Dairy *Queen.*"

"What? No Burger *King?*" Crow asked.

"Sorry."

"You should be. They make good fries."

"The best place I found for eating dinner is a place called the Woodfire Grill."

"That sounds promising," Amigo admitted.

Voice looked around to see how close Doc Rich, who had pulled medical duty along with Doc Frank was, and said, "As long as it passes muster with Doc Rich."

"What's not to like?" Cloud asked.

"The full name is Boomtown Brewery and Woodfire Grill."

"Just tell her it's the Woodfire Grill," the rest of the team said in a chorus.

"Do you think I want to eat at Dairy Queen?" Voice returned.

Overhearing them, Doc Rich said, "I will not allow you to eat at Dairy Queen. Fast food is out. You can just resist temptation at the Boomtown Brewery and Woodfire Grill."

Voice whipped his head to look at her.

"Did you really think I was going to come along on this mission without checking out where we could eat, you little sneak?"

"I thought you might consider microwave meals eaten in our rooms," Voice mumbled to her retreating back.

"I'm old. I'm not deaf," she said without bothering to even turn around.

"Shishu!" Voice uttered in Japanese.

Doc Rich turned to look at him. After a moment of glare, she asked, "Did you just say 'shit' in Japanese?"

"No, I said 'sheesh' in Japanese."

She shook her head and continued to her room.

"I'm going to suggest we ask the hotel to do a lunch for us," Spud said. "We can ask for the meeting room and discuss the potentials for this mission while we're eating."

HANK HAD PROPPED herself up in the bed with her book.

"Still reading Douglas's book, I see," Spud remarked.

"Yeah. Gonna try and finish it in our spare time."

"What case?"

"Lindberg kidnapping still. I think I saw something implicating a guy not long ago, and want to see if Douglas points his finger at the same guy."

Spud slid into bed next to her.

"Comfy."

"It's got a pillow top."

"Does it? Maybe we should get Mike to order us a pillow top for our bed in the Mole Hole."

Spud watched the sly grin develop on Hank's face. "Isn't it nice of the Hampton Inn to let us try it out and see if we like it first?"

"We don't have time to try it out right now," Spud said.

"We'll have time later. By the way, did you know that Crow and Cloud apparently had a discussion in which they concluded that our relationship was suffering the slings and arrows of outrageous unit duty?"

Spud looked at her a moment and then asked, "Where did they get *that* idea?"

"They thought I was thinking about retiring and heading back to the FBI because of the chat I had with Stan."

"I've been curious about that chat myself."

"I asked him if he knew why I was chosen for the unit."

"What did he tell you?"

"That he didn't know," Hank said. "And also that it wasn't his idea. He actually didn't like it and said he wanted to keep me in Albuquerque. Those above him told him he had no say in the matter."

"He was telling the truth?"

"As far as I could determine. And he reminded me that he was pretty shocked to find out I was still alive."

"That much is true," Spud conceded. "You wouldn't actually consider going back to the FBI, would you?"

"Hell no. I like what I'm doing right now."

"Not even if they had tagged you for HRT?"

"*Especially* if they had tagged me for HRT. Those guys have testosterone issues."

"And I don't?" he asked with a smile.

"They have the wrong kind of testosterone issues."

THE TEAM HAD GATHERED in the meeting room of the hotel. As they enjoyed the lunch that the hotel staff had prepared, they settled into a discussion of their mission objectives. At Voice's feet, Chip was enjoying some of his favorite Hamilton Farms Organic Dog Kibble.

Crow looked down at the pooch and asked, "Can you

crunch that a little quieter?" Chip just looked at him and went back to his own lunch.

"Do you have a map of the area with the sites where the bodies have been found marked on it?" Amigo asked Voice.

Voice was tapping on his tablet with one hand while munching a sandwich with the other. The rest of the team sat patiently while he worked until Amigo got frustrated waiting for an answer, under the impression Voice was ignoring him. That's when he decided to start whistling the *Jeopardy!* theme song.

"Give me a bit," Voice said with just a hint of annoyance. "I've got to secure the link to the monitor that's in here."

"Really?" Cloud asked, starting to get impatient himself.

"Yes, really," Voice said after swallowing another bite of his sandwich. "It's a smart monitor and has a Wi-Fi connection to the hotel's computer, which in turn has a connection to whoever has a moderate amount of hacking capability. It isn't secure... yet. And I'm betting if any business group that has ever used this room for a confidential discussion knew that, they'd crap their pants."

Continuing to tap on his tablet, he finally sat back. "Hal, display mission area with locations of incidents."

The monitor flickered and a map appeared with red dots indicating the locations where bodies had been found.

"With the exception of the woman, all of the bodies have been found in wooded areas," Spud observed.

"Her house isn't exactly in the middle of town either," Amigo noted.

"Yes. But I'm beginning to see why Hank believes her case isn't linked to the others. She was found in her back-yard. None of the men lived near where their bodies were found, correct?"

"Hal, mark location of victims' residences," Voice

commanded. This was followed by bright green spots appearing.

"That makes sense, though," Amigo said, noting that only the woman's death had occurred near her home. "The men were all hunters, so you wouldn't expect them to be hunting in their own backyards."

"What's the link with the woman, then?" Cloud asked.

"Let's take a hypothetical that this is UniPerp," Amigo said.

"That makes the woman even stranger. UniPerp's seven-victim MO always has the victims the same sex," Crow pointed out.

"It's not like UniPerp hasn't switched things up on us before," Cloud objected.

"Since he's fallen into the seven victims MO, it's never varied," Crow reiterated. "Seven women, then seven men, then seven more men—all gunsmiths, then seven doctors—all women..."

"She's not connected," Hank said bluntly.

Everyone looked at her.

She shrugged and repeated, "She's not connected. Even if this isn't UniPerp, she's not connected."

"She *could* be connected if this isn't UniPerp," Spud said. "If this is the work of a radical environmentalist, they could have targeted her for allowing people to cross her land to hunt."

"Then why aren't we seeing other people who are granting access to hunters being killed?" Cloud countered. "All the others have been hunters."

"I don't know," Spud admitted.

"The scenarios we have so far are: A, the woman isn't connected; B, the woman is connected and this is the work of a radical environmentalist," Edge began. "Can I hear, the woman isn't connected and the others are UniPerp victims?"

"Then how do we explain the woman?" Amigo asked.

"Coincidence. Someone killed her for whatever reason, but not for any reason that's connected to the hunters."

"I've got to admit, that makes plenty of sense," Cloud said.

"We should be prepared to voice all of these scenarios to the sheriff and the BCA when we meet with them tomorrow," Edge concluded. His teammates tapped their concurrence on the table top.

"What do we want as our first order of business after meeting with the locals?" Cloud asked.

"I want to see the sites where the bodies were found," Hank said. "See if there's anything similar about the sites. Other than being in the woods, that is."

HANK and the rest of the team were all involved in doing the same thing: going over their gear, ensuring everything was still in good order and that they hadn't overlooked anything. It had never happened that they had arrived somewhere and found something missing or damaged, but with the hazards of the cases they handled, each found it reassuring to get just one more look at their gear before having to use it.

"We're missing something we need," Hank said. It was heard by the entire team in spite of them being in different rooms, given team comm had been initiated.

"What are you missing? I've got everything," Amigo said.

"It's not just what *I'm* missing—it's what everyone is missing. No blaze vests."

"Are you out of your mind?" Cloud asked. "We're covert, and a blaze vest is anything but covert."

"The woods are chock full of turkey hunters," Hank pointed out. "In this case, we *want* to stand out like a light-house on a clear night."

The rest of the team could hear Voice chuckle over the comm link. "This gives us an excuse to go shopping at the Walmart tonight and see if there are some interesting Walmartians cruising the aisles."

"Oy," Hank returned.

"It sounds like fun to me, Love. And kudos to our resident genius for making it possible to take a picture with our watches."

"It's not like we can post them on Facebook."

"Sure we can," Voice said.

"What? Since when does a team so covert that everyone thinks the people in it are dead have a Facebook account?" Amigo demanded.

"Since the arrival of your fucking genius," Voice said, having decided long ago that the extra emphasis given by the participle was more of an honorific than an insult.

"Doesn't Facebook sell data to the NSA?" Cloud questioned.

"They do. And when they run a trace on our account, it pops up as Helen Bell."

The team erupted in laughter.

"Why do we need a Facebook account?" Amigo asked.

"In the hope that it could assist in an investigation," Voice said. "It's almost like anyone who doesn't have an account is known by someone who does. Did you know, for instance, that there are truckers' groups on Facebook? I've had Hal watch them to see if anyone who might look like UniPerp shows up there. You know, someone posting about being in the same areas as we're seeing the UniPerp events taking place."

"I take it no joy yet," Crow said.

"Nope. But you never know when it might result in a break on that case, if this isn't the end of the line for UniPerp, that is," Voice said. "This guy has been at it for a couple of years. He's bound to slip up."

"I've been saying that for the past two years," Hank grumbled. "Even though I don't think this is UniPerp, I'm holding out hope that it is, though."

HE FINISHED the last of his deliveries and then made his way back to where he'd seen the truck parked alongside the road with the window decal that read, 'You Have Your Family—I Have Mine' along with a display of the silhouettes of five firearms. The sky was threatening rain, and with temperatures hovering around the low forties, he felt assured that he wouldn't have to chase this one down—just wait for him to come back to his truck. Walking just far enough into the trees to not be seen by the rare person who might drive by, he settled in to keep watch for his latest quarry.

It wasn't long before he saw the man striding along, his blaze jacket testimony to his purpose in the woods.

Sitting duck. He raised his rifle, chambered a round, and aimed in. The hunter was walking directly toward him, and with four kills behind him, he no longer felt the flutter of his racing heart nor heard his lungs seeming to gasp for air. No, he was now practiced at this.

Without a second thought about it, he aimed in and took the shot, which now didn't even sound a loud report after he had constructed a home-made silencer. He figured the silencer would give him more of an ability to operate without detection, and had been more than satisfied with the results when he had tried a few shots earlier.

Watching as usual to see if the hunter was still moving, he once again noted not even the telltale sign of mist from his lips that would indicate he was still breathing. Slinging his rifle over his shoulder for the short walk back to his own vehicle, he looked upward and said, "There's one more for you, Holly. With tomorrow being Sunday, I'll see if I can do better than just one."

He drove back to Holly's empty house and went to the back yard with the single red rose he had bought. Laying it with the others, he told the woman whose spirit he hoped could hear, "I wish it hadn't taken this for me to show you I love you."

He climbed back into his own truck and started the engine, the Bluetooth audio system picking up his music from his cellphone and beginning to play. As one song ended and another began, he realized he was listening to Soundgarden's "Mailman."

Isn't that a kick in the head. Yeah, I'm the most important fool you forgot to see, but it wasn't your fault. It was mine for always just handing you a package and never saying, 'How would you like to have dinner with me?'

As the music continued to play, he found himself singing along with the refrain.

"'Cause I know I'm heading for the bottom... I know I'm heading for the bottom... I know I'm heading for the bottom...."

THE TEAM MEMBERS had all dispensed with their facility uniforms and were now dressed in casual street clothes as they drove to the nearby Walmart. Only a small strip mall separated the hotel from the store, and ordinarily they would have just walked, but with the temperatures hovering just above forty degrees and threatening to go lower turning the drizzle into snow, they opted instead to stay dry. Especially knowing that they might be spending some time trudging through the woods in as bad or worse conditions in the very near future.

"Why did they rent us SUVs equipped with bull bars?" Cloud wondered aloud as they made their way into the store.

Spud got a Boris voice going and said, "You never know, Natasha. Ve might hit *moose*."

"That's not funny," Voice complained.

In the same accent, Spud said, "Next time, maybe you don't pretend to be *squirrel* in *tree.*"

The rest of the team chuckled.

"Ok, where's the sporting goods section?" Amigo wondered aloud.

"These stores are all set up about the same way," Cloud said. With a point, he added, "That way."

The team made their way along the aisles, arriving at the sporting goods section. Finding the clothing, they each began looking for a suitable blaze jacket or vest.

"You'll want a vest, not a jacket," Hank admonished the ones who were looking over jackets. "You'll need access to your weapons... just in case."

Each having picked out a vest in the correct size to fit over their SWAT gear, Amigo asked, "Do we want to raid the food section? Y'know... maybe some stuff they won't serve at the hotel."

"Like a bigger bag of chips," Crow said.

"Like a bigger variety of fruit," Hank countered. "I can only eat so many bananas, oranges, and apples."

"You're just saying that to make Doc Rich happy when we get back."

"Big bag of tostadas," Amigo was crooning.

"With a jar of salsa and another of that gooey cheese dip," Crow agreed.

"That stuff's gross," Hank declared as she headed off to the produce section with Spud on her heels.

"That stuff is guy food," Spud told her while she began to look over the fruit.

"That stuff is why guys die of heart attacks more often than women, then," Hank said. She looked up, then hid her eyes and uttered, "Oh, for fuck's sake—I forgot to look for eye bleach."

Spud looked around to see what she was reacting to. There checking out the bananas was a man entirely naked, with the exception of a G-string.

Hank gave the man a second glance.

"I don't know why I looked away. It's not like he's hiding much."

"Cut him a break, Love. It's only forty degrees outside. Shrinkage. He's nearly naked. Damned near one hundred percent naked, I'd say."

"Maybe he's checking out the bananas to find something to fill that thing out," Hank remarked.

"Now you're just being mean."

"Now I'm just being honest."

"Why are you even looking at the guy?" Spud asked.

"I'm wondering if we should head back to the men's clothing area and see if they sell those. Maybe buy you a few."

Spud's eyes grew narrow. "I don't think they make those in my size."

"They didn't make those condoms that glow green in the dark in your size, either, but you managed to stuff yourself into one."

"You will please spare me the indignity of trying to squeeze into one of those."

"That reminds me—let's hit the condiment aisle. I like those little dill pickles."

"Will you stop?"

"Seriously. I don't think the hotel will have them, do you? And maybe some of those little cocktail wieners."

"Hank..."

"I really would like some pickles."

Spud rolled his eyes, rolling them more vigorously when he noticed Hank taking a picture with her watch. He shook his head.

"My wife."

19

After their meeting with the local sheriff and the officers from the Minnesota Bureau of Criminal Apprehension, the team set out with the BCA officers to get a look at the sites where bodies had been found, starting with the hunters to follow up on Hank's contention that the woman, Holly Fay, was not killed by the same person who had killed the hunters. Spud likewise was beginning to think Holly wasn't connected to the others, and not connected to any of the prior UniPerp cases as well in spite of the apparent similarities.

The forecast promised a cold day with temperatures hovering around freezing. The forecast snow and drizzle hadn't developed, however, so as they drove through the wooded areas they noticed quite a few vehicles parked on roadsides. With hunters only having a week to fill their tags, those who worked were braving the cold in order to bag a turkey during the weekend. With the weather having been nastier the previous day, they were now out in force to get a bird before the sun went down on Sunday's hunt.

"I'm glad we bought the blaze vests," Voice said as they walked to the next site where a hunter had been killed. "Have we stopped at a spot yet that hasn't had at least two vehicles parked along the road?"

"Hunting is a big recreational pursuit in Minnesota, especially here in the northern half of the state," one of the two BCA officers accompanying them said.

"So I hear," Voice returned, having just heard the distant report of a shotgun.

Walking carefully through the site, the team once again found it unremarkable—just a typical forested area.

"It seems there's nothing in any of the areas where the hunters have been killed that could be seen as defining," Spud said. "Not particular kinds of growth, nearby water, or even differences in wildlife."

"Not even distance from the roads seems to matter," Amigo agreed. "The only thing that links the cases is that they're all hunters."

"There wasn't anything illegal about what they were doing, either," one of the BCA officers stated. "They all had hunting licenses and turkey tags, and they were all carrying the correct firearm and ammunition legal for a turkey hunt."

"What are the rules for turkey in Minnesota?" Cloud asked.

"For firearms, it must be a shotgun, ten-gauge or higher, 4.5 shot or smaller," the BCA officer said. "Whoever shot them didn't take the guns. We also didn't find any evidence that the killer walked up to the bodies. Whoever this is can be pretty stealthy."

Hank was standing with her hands in her pockets.

"What do you say, Katie? Get a look at the woman's place?" Amigo asked.

Hank shrugged. "Might as well. I do see how these deaths could be UniPerp, though. Four men, all hunters, all carrying shotguns, and all found in the same general area. The odd one out is Holly Fay. The reports all say the rifle was something like a .243, am I remembering correctly?" she asked the BCA men.

"Holly Fay was definitely shot with a .243, and the guy found in the tree stand also was shot with a .243. We were able to recover the bullet from the tree after it had passed through his skull. Both bullets were pretty mangled, though, so we weren't able to determine if they came from the same rifle. We do believe that it's possible the round that killed Holly Fay was fired from the rifle we have in evidence."

"We have Dr. Sue Pratt as our forensics specialist," Cloud said. "If you'd like, we can contact her to see if she could do an analysis of your recovered bullets to determine if they came from the same gun. She could likely say with more certainty whether the bullet that killed Holly Fay was fired from your evidence gun as well."

"Dr. Pratt has quite the reputation," one of the BCA men said. "I'm sure if she could corroborate that, the case would be strengthened for a suspect we could prove had the gun to be the perpetrator."

"At this point, we're uncertain if the hunters' deaths are from the same person as Holly Fay's killer," Crow reminded them.

"We have no reason to believe that they aren't connected," the BCA man replied.

"We do. There's a lot that doesn't fit. She wasn't a hunter from what we can tell. She was killed in her own backyard, not somewhere out in the woods. Even with our alternative theory that this is a violent environmentalist, she doesn't fit. She was feeding the birds, and was filling the bird feeders when she was killed. And last but certainly not least," Hank concluded, "she's a woman."

"But apparently killed with the same rifle," the BCA officer said.

Hank held up a finger. "Killed with a rifle of the same caliber. We'll let Dr. Pratt determine if it's likely both bullets recovered were fired from the same rifle."

HE CROUCHED DOWN. It hadn't been easy to determine where the hunters were, but he had steadfastly followed the sounds from their turkey calls until he saw it: one of those portable hunting blinds.

No wonder the snotty weather hasn't deterred them. Holed up nice and cozy.

He considered his options. Wait until they came out of the blind and pick them off as they gathered up their gear? Or send a shot into the blind and get them as they came out? *But if I do that, I might hit one of them but not kill him. Then I'd have to go in and finish him off, and I really don't want to risk leaving any evidence at the site. Forensic examiners can find out who you are if even a single hair falls from your head these days. And I can't stop—not until I'm sure I got the one that got Holly.*

Having decided to wait, he remained in a crouch and pulled an apple from his pocket. Munching on it until only the core was left, he regarded it momentarily and then gave it a fling away from him. *The deer will find it, then voila—no more evidence.*

He continued to watch, hearing the occasional sounding of a gobbler call emanating from the blind. Then all fell silent for some minutes. It was when he saw items beginning to be set outside the blind that he realized his opportunity was about to come, the hunters giving up on getting a bird. He was betting they had planned to call in sick on Monday, when better weather was forecast and they'd have better luck. He was also betting that their luck had run out in a way they had least anticipated. He considered that his luck had greatly improved when he saw the beer cans come flying out of the opening in the blind as well, the hunters having finished their hunting day with a little conciliatory brew.

Idiots. Didn't anyone ever tell them that alcohol and gunpowder don't mix? The good news, at least, is that you won't be driving.

He waited until all three of the men who had been in the blind were outside and occupied with collapsing the tent-like structure. Having noted that one seemed more sober than the others, he opted to take him first, figuring he'd be more coordinated and more likely to be able to run for it than the other two. Bracing his rifle against a tree, he aimed in and fired.

The more sober of the three fell, his hunting partners looking down at him, bewildered. When the second one fell, the third realized he was in mortal danger and attempted to run, tripping over the stacked gear and falling flat on his face. He raised his head in preparation to get up and run again. He realized he shouldn't have in the split second between the muffled report of his killer's rifle and the momentary pain of the bullet entering his skull.

The forest was silent. No more turkey calls, no more suppressed popping of the killer's rifle, not even the chatter of a squirrel or chirping of a songbird. The only thing he heard was his own thoughts.

That's three more for you, Holly. Aren't you proud? It makes me proud—proud and happy. One of these bastards who comes into these woods killed you, and the more of them I kill, the more likely I'll get the one responsible.

CROW AND CLOUD had left with the BCA officers, ready to
sign their names in the chain of custody records and make a
quick trip back to the unit's Nebraska headquarters to
deliver one rifle and two recovered bullets to Doc Sue. The
rest of the team had made their way on their own to Holly
Fay's house.

Lifting the crime scene tape that surrounded Holly's
property, Spud cautioned everyone to disturb the scene as
little as possible. "If we find anything we feel the BCA has
overlooked, we'll want to stop and call them to come back in
once they've dropped Crow and Cloud off at the airport."

Making their way around to the backyard while
watching their feet carefully to ensure they wouldn't be
disturbing any kind of evidence, they arrived at the additional taped off area where Holly's body had been found.

Spud held up a hand and stared at the area. "Someone
pull up the crime scene photos," he said.

Amigo pulled out his tablet and called up the photos
that they had recorded in Hal's databanks. Passing his tablet
to Spud, Spud then glanced at the photos and back to the
rectangle of yellow-with-black lettered tape. He reached up
and scratched his head.

"What's got you scratching your head?" Voice asked.

"The roses."

"So? Someone is leaving flowers for her. According to
the report, her ex was trying to get back together with her,"
Amigo said. "It would be reasonable for him to leave a few
roses."

"This is a crime scene, though," Edge said.

"Not just a crime scene, but one in which he was a
suspect—at least for a while. It would be kind-of stupid for

him to come back to the scene, don't you think?" Voice ventured.

"Maybe he came back after they determined he wasn't the killer," Edge argued.

Hank was squatted down looking at the roses herself. "There's more to these roses than meets the eye," she said.

"How do you figure that?" Edge asked.

"They weren't all left at the same time. And it's sort-of an odd number, if you ask me. Why leave five roses? Why not a dozen?"

"What makes you say they weren't all left at the same time?" Amigo asked.

"Take a look. Some of them are more wilted than others. Plus, they're all individually wrapped in cellophane, to be sold one at a time. Whoever left the roses left them one at a time."

"The important thing, though, is that these roses weren't here when the crime scene was originally processed," Spud said. "They've been left since then, perhaps by the killer."

"Why would the killer leave roses?" Edge asked.

"Remorse," Hank said. "Maybe a lover, or an ex-lover. Let's try this scenario: we know she had a lover—that was in the report. He was investigated and cleared, given he had proof he was on a business trip at the time of her murder. But was he the only lover she had? Maybe there was another one out there in the wings that no one knew about. If he had heard that she was getting back together with her estranged husband, he may have shot her in a fit of anger."

"A little far-fetched, Hank."

Hank chuckled. "I don't know about you, but I've seen a lot of far-fetched reasons people do things, from the time I was in the Taos PD to the FBI and now to the unit. When it comes to why criminals do criminal acts, the sky's the limit."

"Far-fetched or not, this is as far as we go until the BCA guys get back. Voice, see if you can get a message to them. Tell them there is evidence that someone has been visiting the scene. At the very least, they may want him questioned as to why he's leaving the roses," Spud said.

"Or her," Voice reminded him. "At this point, it might be unwise to assume this isn't a woman."

"Can we grab some lunch while we're waiting?" Edge asked. "I noticed there's a little bar and grill nearby."

"Sure," Spud said. "Voice, let them know to meet us at that place. It's called Timber something."

"Timber's Edge Grill and Bar," Voice relayed. "I'm on it."

HE DROVE to Holly's house, three more cellophane-wrapped roses on the seat next to him. No one seemed to think anything of his visits to the house, but then it *was* located in a remote area and somewhat hidden from the houses on either side, and it was his responsibility to deliver the mail as it was addressed, no matter how stuffed the mailbox was getting. With it being Sunday though, his intended excuse for being there was to collect the mail that had been accumulating and deliver it back to the post office in Makinen, leaving the required notice that the mail was being held at the post office until it could be retrieved. If anyone questioned why he was doing it on a Sunday, he'd tell them that it was more convenient for him to collect it then and deliver it back to the post office when he went in to work on Monday morning.

He once again slipped around the back of the house, going immediately to the enclosed area where he'd left roses previously, and set the three new roses with the others.

"Three more for you, Holly. I hope I got the bastard that did this to you already, but just in case, turkey season isn't over yet. I love you. I wish I'd had the courage to tell you that while you were alive."

He made his way back to his truck, stopping to clear out the mailbox on the way. Then he made his way to the Timber's Edge Grill and Bar, anxious to see if Dunker and Drencher would be there discussing Holly's case. He knew he had to move cautiously, and figured he could both get information he could use to stay out from under law enforcement's radar and make sure they hadn't given up on finding Holly's killer.

Walking in, he couldn't help but notice the five strangers all gathered around a table eating lunch. They were all notable by their appearance: for the most part young with the exception of one man with graying temples; all with short, almost military-style haircuts—even the woman with them. As he walked past, he heard the man say, "It looks like you might be right, Katie. Holly Fay doesn't seem to fit in with the other victims. But my intuition tells me she's connected somehow—just not in the way we might think."

His curiosity was aroused to the point where he turned and addressed them. "Are you discussing the Holly Fay murder?" he asked.

The five people looked up at him. "Do you have information about this?" one of the men asked. His voice had the slight lilt of a Mexican accent.

"I know about it," he said. "It would be hard for anyone around here *not* to know about it. We may not have a newspaper here, but small communities, you know. Word of mouth; news spreads fast. And everyone talks to me about everything."

"Oh?" one of the other men questioned. He noted this guy seemed to spend a lot of time at the gym.

"Yeah, I know everyone in the area. If you've been around town, such as it is, you may have noticed our gargantuan post office. I'm one of the only two rural delivery postmen who serve this area. All the gossip we've heard said, we do our best not to spread."

The five people chuckled at that: the little poem he had composed himself.

"May I ask your name?" the man with the Mexican accent asked.

"John. John Granger," he said, extending his hand.

The man with the graying temples stood and shook his hand. "Special Agent Spencer Banyon, FBI. We've been called in to assist with the investigation. It seems there have been a number of puzzling deaths in the area lately."

"Oh? I was unaware that there were others," Granger said.

"Four that we're aware of," another of the men said. His facial features hinted of Oriental heritage. *They don't know about the other four,* Granger thought. *It wouldn't be likely they would have found the last three, but I would have thought someone would have stumbled across that other guy by now.* He did a mental shrug. *No matter.*

"Being the postman, I imagine you'd recognize someone who wasn't from around here," the big man who'd already spoken to him ventured.

He looked around the table, mentally putting descriptors to each of the people he saw: *Gray Temples, Goliath, Slanty Eyes, Little Blondie, and Taco Bell. Oh yeah, wait—Gray Temples called himself Banyon.*

"I had you guys pegged for 'not from around here' the minute I walked in."

Hank lowered her face and whispered over the comm link, *"Maybe you should have worn your coonskin cap, Spence. Then we'd have looked like we fit in."*

Spud nearly choked on the coffee he'd just taken a mouthful of.

"Do you recall seeing any other people you don't recognize, or perhaps a vehicle you've not seen before?" Slanty Eyes asked.

"Right now, there are a lot of people in the area I don't recognize," Granger said. "Everybody and their brother is out in the woods trying to fill a turkey tag."

Just then, two more people unknown to Granger walked into the restaurant. They immediately made their way to the table where the five FBI agents were sitting.

"We understand you noticed something—"

Little Blondie stopped him from continuing with a hand held up. He noticed her look in their direction and then shift her eyes in his direction.

The two BCA officers getting the hint, the one who had spoken added, "But we can discuss that after you've finished lunch, unless you think it's urgent."

"Not so urgent we can't finish lunch," Goliath said. "We're just about done."

"Speaking of lunch, I should get mine as well," Granger said. "If I can help at all..."

"We know we can find you through the post office," Taco Bell said. "It was nice meeting you, Mr. Granger."

He walked off to the bar, put in an order, then went and sat down at a table across from where the FBI and other two men were sitting, now talking quietly among themselves while the FBI agents finished their lunch.

This isn't going to be nearly as easy as listening to those two loudmouths, Dunker and Drencher, talk about the case.

"ONE OF THE THINGS WE NOTICED," Spud was saying as the five members of the team met back up with the BCA officers at Holly Fay's house, "is that there are some roses that have been left in the backyard where Holly's body was found. When we got a look at the crime scene photos, we noted that the roses weren't in the original photos."

As Spud turned back to walk up the walkway, he noticed a footprint on the cement. Holding up a hand, he asked the other four members of the team present, "Was that there when we arrived earlier?"

"We all walked in over the grass," Amigo said.

"This footprint is headed back to the curb," Spud pointed out.

Amigo shook his head. "I'm pretty sure we all walked back to the SUV over the grass as well."

"Ben, get a picture of that," Spud said. "It should be easy enough to tell if that footprint is one of ours."

"It isn't," Hank declared. "That's the kind of sole you find on a hiking boot. We're all wearing ordinary shoes. Get a good picture, Ben, and make sure the BCA gets a copy. You guys wouldn't be prepared for this kind of thing, would you?" she asked the BCA officers.

"Have camera, will travel," one of them replied, turning back to their vehicle and retrieving both a camera and photo scales.

The team members stood back while the BCA officers documented the footprint, taking photos both with and without photo scales in place. Cordoning off the location where the footprint had been found and outlining it given the print would evaporate, the team members and BCA officers then made their way around to the back yard, walking over to the area where the roses had been placed.

"There are more of them," Amigo noted, looking at the roses.

Hank was likewise examining the roses. "How many were here when you first got a look?" she asked, turning to Spud.

"Five."

"There are eight now."

"Whoever left them had to have been here between" — Edge consulted his watch— "eleven thirty and when we arrived back here around 1300."

"He was here. *He was here.*" Amigo slapped his leg in frustration.

"Whoever is leaving these roses has to be connected to the case," Voice said.

"Is that a conclusion we can make?" Amigo asked, feeling certain of that himself but wanting there to be no doubt.

"It may be just a person who was close to Ms. Fay," Edge ventured.

"Why not leave the roses all at once? Why some left one at a time, and now three all at once?" Voice questioned.

Edge ran his hand over his hair. "That's a good question."

"It's a man," Hank said as she studied the roses. "A man who loved her. He's commemorating something, but what I don't know. Look closely at the roses: one is practically decaying. Then one more in slightly better condition next to it. Then there are two in about identical condition that are laying across the one that's really gone by. Then one more across those that's only slightly wilted. Then these three that are fresh. The number of roses means something to him.

Maybe times they spent together, or something of that nature."

She stood up and turned to the BCA officers. "I'm going to suggest you get your crime scene techs in here again, and go over this yard with a fine-toothed comb. Not saying they haven't already, but one more pass just to make sure they didn't overlook anything. Get a snippet of the grass as well, and a bit of the soil. Dr. Pratt has made an extensive study of DNA from vegetation and elements of soil composition, so when this person is tracked down she might be able to match grass and soil to things found on his boots or in his car."

"We have a real mystery at this point," Spud declared. "Who is leaving the roses, and why? What's the connection with the case? Is there a connection between this case and the hunters?"

"In short, what the hell is going on here?" Hank summarized.

HANK WAS ONCE AGAIN nose down in her book.

"Done with Lindberg?" Spud asked.

"Yup. Douglas suspects a conspiracy."

"Who's next?"

"The Zodiac killer."

"I thought that one was solved," Spud queried.

"The cypher he wrote was solved after Douglas finished this book, but Zodiac still hasn't been identified."

"And what are you thinking thus far?"

Hank smirked. "That both the local police and the FBI were trying to solve a more complicated case than the one they had in front of them. I don't know who Douglas thinks was the Zodiac, but from what I've read so far, I think there were plenty of clues for them to track him down, and do so rather quickly. He was practically screaming his identity to them."

"Hopefully, this clairvoyance you have concerning Zodiac will slide over to solving the hunter murders as well."

"Is this what we're calling them now? The Hunter Murders?"

Spud thought a moment.

"I hadn't really considered that, but it's as good a case title as any, I suppose."

20

"We have a message coming in from Nebraska," Voice said after consulting his watch.

The team was once again gathered in the hotel's meeting room with Voice's security protocols put in place to keep their conversation classified. Activating the monitor provided by the hotel, it flitted to life with Doc Sue's image.

"What's the verdict?" Amigo asked.

"I've taken a look at three things," Doc Sue began. "I've test-fired the rifle for comparator analysis of the bullets, and used the reconstruction software that Voice developed to get a better idea of what the bullets recovered from victims would look like should they not have been deformed. I've also looked at the x-rays of the skulls impacted by the recovered rounds."

"Everything match up?" Cloud asked.

"Yes and no. The bullet recovered from Holly Fay was badly distorted, and the jacket torn. But the analysis shows that it was likely fired from the evidence gun. The other bullet, recovered from the tree behind the hunter shot in his tree stand was *not* fired from the evidence gun. They are both the same caliber, but fired from different guns."

"You're certain," Crow questioned.

Doc Sue gave him a slight grin. "On a witness stand, I would say, 'My analysis of the bullet recovered from Holly Fay corroborates the conclusion drawn by the Minnesota Bureau of Criminal Apprehension. My analysis of the second bullet recovered from the tree is not consistent with having been fired from the rifle the Minnesota Bureau of Criminal Apprehension is holding in evidence.'"

"You're always careful about how you state something," Cloud observed.

"You have to be in my business," Doc Sue said. "In science, you can prove a negative, but not a positive. I can prove a bullet *wasn't* fired from a particular gun, but not that it was, because I don't know if there's another gun out there that could produce the exact rifling marks as the one I'm looking at."

"Why look at the skulls of the victims?" Crow asked.

"From the appearance of the fractures made as the round impacted the bone, you can generally tell a few things: energy of the round upon impact, and condition of the round upon impact. The bullet recovered from the tree shows deformities consistent with having passed cleanly through the skull and then impacting the tree. The entrance wound is sharply defined; the exit wound less so—which you would expect. The fact that it went straight through the skull tells me the round was fired at close range, maybe only one or two hundred yards.

"The bullet that killed Holly Fay has another story to tell. It was recovered lodged in her brain. The entry wound appears 'keyholed,' meaning it was likely tumbling when it hit her rather than flying straight. The deformation of the bullet suggests it hit something before it hit her. It's a ricocheted round."

"It ricocheted?" Hank questioned. "Then you can't really

determine how far away the shooter was by the degree of impact."

"Correct," Doc Sue agreed.

"Did the BCA determine from which direction the bullet was fired?"

"They did. But from my analysis, I'd say what they determined was the direction from the object the bullet hit on its way to Holly Fay."

"We've got a message here from the BCA," Voice said while looking at his tablet. "Three more bodies found, all believed to have been killed sometime yesterday. All in the same location, and all identified as men who hunted together often. The wives reported them missing last night; they were found early this morning."

"Keep us advised of anything new, Doc Sue," Spud said. "It looks like we're going to have to run."

"Will do," she replied as she signed off.

The men in the team had already risen to their feet, but Hank remained sitting, tapping her fingertips on the table.

"Taking the day off?" Crow chided her.

"One, one, two, one, three," Hank said, her brow furrowed.

Amigo raised an eyebrow and turned to Crow. "One one two one three? Does that mean anything to you?"

Crow chuckled. "Not a clue. Maybe a zip code?"

Hank scowled at them. "The roses. If you had noticed how they were wilting, you'd say that first one was placed, then another one, then two more, then one, then three."

"Why is this significant?" Spud asked.

"The victims. First one, then another one, then two in one day, then one, then three in one day."

"That's one too many roses," Cloud said. "For victims, we have one, then one, then two, then three."

"Or that's one too few bodies," Hank countered. "It's too coincidental. I think it's more likely we've got another body out there that no one has come across or has reported as a missing person."

Her teammates stared at her.

"Voice, ask the BCA if there have been any other reports of missing persons—especially if they had left to go hunting." With that, she stood to join her teammates to go to the scene of the latest attack.

THE TEAM STOOD and watched along with two of the BCA investigators while the crime scene techs scoured the scene of the latest shooting.

"This one sure is grim," Cloud remarked.

"Do we think whoever this is has begun to escalate?" Amigo wondered.

"Maybe just intent on killing every hunter he encounters," Crow said.

"Or she," Cloud corrected.

"Probably a man," Hank said. "Men are more likely to kill with guns than women." She paused a moment. "Present company excluded."

One of the BCA officers turned and looked at her.

"I'm the team's sniper," she explained.

"Ah," he said with an acknowledging nod.

"Still, the person who did this has to be pretty good with a gun to get three in one attack," Crow said.

"I think he was helped along by the beer," Amigo remarked, pointing to where the beer cans had been tossed.

"Not exactly responsible hunting," Crow muttered.

"A lot of guys will pack their gear and then commiserate

about a bad day of hunting with a brew or two," Hank said. "Or three, or four..." She gave a criticizing look to some of her teammates. "Or eight, if the fishing's really bad."

"Never going to let us live it down," Spud murmured.

"Nope."

Cloud watched as one of the crime scene techs ducked under the crime tape and walked away from the scene in a particular direction, scanning the ground back and forth as he went. "I take it they've determined the direction of fire."

"Looks that way," one of the investigators with them said.

The crime scene tech had walked about a hundred yards when he stooped and studied the ground. Standing still and turning, he shouted and motioned another of the techs over. The two conferred briefly, then proceeded to cordon off another area.

"Got where the shooter stood," the BCA investigator said. "They'll bring in a metal detector to see if they can locate any brass."

"Did they find any cases at the other sites?" Edge asked.

"Nope. The guy evidently polices up his brass. It's one of his trademarks," the investigator said.

"He's careful. He has experience—either military or law enforcement," Amigo speculated.

"That would seem to rule out this being a violent environmentalist," Cloud said.

"Not necessarily," Voice countered. "Most environmental protests take the form of either demonstrations or more passive kinds of activities. Obstructing fishing vessels, spiking trees. Stuff like that."

"If you've ever seen what happens to a logger when his chain saw hits a spike in a tree, you wouldn't call it 'passive'," Amigo stated bluntly.

"You know what I mean. They don't hang around, and they don't do something directly, like shoot someone," Voice said.

"In light of what we know, I'm going to suggest we head back to the hotel and throw around some ideas for the best way to proceed," Cloud suggested. "We know what this guy is doing, and it doesn't look like he's inclined to stop soon."

"Before we do that, I'd like to grab our two investigators here and head back to Holly Fay's house," Hank said.

"We've worked that scene pretty thoroughly," one of the investigators said.

"But not with the information we got from Dr. Pratt," Hank said. "There's a bit of evidence out there you didn't discover."

The investigator was giving her that 'oh here we go with the FBI' look. The 'like you can do better' look. Hank knew it well.

"It's not that you simply missed it," she clarified. "It's that you didn't know what Dr. Pratt concluded."

"Which is?"

"The bullet ricocheted before it hit Holly Fay."

JOHN GRANGER HAD SPENT the early morning hours and all of the time along his delivery route to hunt for another man he felt could possibly have killed Holly. Unlike the weekend, he'd not seen a single vehicle parked along a roadway other than what one would expect in areas where a house was nearby.

The news is getting out. They're all afraid to go into the woods.

Disappointed, he murmured, "No one for you today,

Holly. But just wait. Those guys with tags that haven't been filled will be anxious to fill them, and the end of this hunting period is coming to a close. Tomorrow is the last day. Everyone who has a tag for this week will be out trying to fill it. Tomorrow should be a good day."

Amigo, Hank, and Edge took the center positions, with the remainder of the team and two BCA investigators spread out to either side of them as they searched the woods behind Holly Fay's house.

"Up, down, and all around," Amigo had advised them.

Their pace was painstakingly slow as they searched for the telltale scar that would be made by a bullet impacting a stone, tree trunk, or branch.

"Like finding a needle in a haystack," Crow grumbled.

"Which is why we're taking it slow and keeping a sharp eye out," Cloud said.

One of the BCA investigators stopped, looking upward. "I think I've got it."

Hank walked over and looked up in the direction he was looking. "That's definitely a scar from a bullet, and it's fresh enough to be what we're looking for."

"Anyone got a rod of some kind?" Crow asked.

Voice walked over, pulling out his tablet. The first thing he did was take a picture, then another one with flash, then another with a photo scale being held against the branch that exhibited the scar. Then he shut down his tablet and placed the longest edge into the scar.

"Not the usual thing that's used to figure out direction of flight of a bullet, but it'll work," he declared.

Edge walked up and sighted down the edge of Voice's tablet, standing on his toes to do so.

"Points right at where the body was," he said.

"Rock the edge of your tablet in that mark," Hank advised. "We might be able to get the direction the shot was made from if we can gauge the impact end of the scar."

With Voice tilting his tablet, Edge then sighted down it again.

"Lines up with the base of a tree over there," he said while still looking down the edge of Voice's tablet and pointing.

"Everyone spread out again, and let's see if we can find where our shooter was standing when he shot at Holly," Hank said.

"I'm beginning to see how our hunts are aiding us with what we do," Spud remarked.

They walked along, again taking it slowly and getting a careful look at the ground they were covering.

"I think I've got it here," Cloud announced, coming to an area where some of the green vegetation looked to have been bruised and broken.

Everyone carefully avoided the spot. Hank came and stood next to Cloud, then sighted to where the BCA investigators had marked the scar on the tree branch with trail tape.

"It was a negligent shot," Hank announced. "He was aimed at something on the branch of the tree in all likelihood. Probably a turkey, given the hunting season. They'll roost at night and will often still be roosting in the early morning. His shot hit the branch and ricocheted off, hitting Ms. Fay."

"It wasn't a negligent shot," one of the BCA investigators said. "It was an illegal shot."

Hank turned and looked at him.

"You can't hunt turkey in Minnesota with a rifle. It has to be a shotgun. So not just overkill, illegal."

"LET'S sum up what we know," Spud said as the team gathered back in the hotel meeting room. "We have seven bodies of hunters recovered. All were shot with a rifle, not a shotgun. None of their hunting gear was taken. All were shot from fairly close range, all were shot in the head, all were apparently shot with the same caliber of rifle. We have eight roses being left at the site where Holly Fay was hit, so if Hank's theory holds up, we have another victim who hasn't been found."

"The roses are what connects Holly Fay's death with the others," Hank said. "That is, if you believe as I do that the roses represent the hunters who were shot."

"The issue we have right now," Crow pointed out, "is that even though it's a blaze orange needle, it's still a needle—and it's in a very big haystack. Lots of acres of woods out there where our predator could be looking for hunters to kill."

"May I suggest?" Voice ventured.

"What?" Cloud asked.

"This is the perfect mission for HARVEST."

"You brought it?" Crow asked.

"These days, I always have two things with me on a mission. My toys, and my dog."

Chip lifted his head.

"Right, Chip?"

Chip gave out a single bark.

"I knew you'd agree with me. *Good dog!*" He pulled out

Chip's tug toy and started wrestling him for it while the rest of the team rolled their eyes.

"We promised the hotel the dog would be well-behaved. We didn't mention that the handler might be tougher to manage," Hank remarked.

"Right now, the cloud deck is pretty low. Will HARVEST be able to see anything with the sky overcast?" Spud asked.

"I can keep it under the clouds and just fly a search pattern," Voice said. "If you know how they use Gorgon Stare, that's how: they'd fly a racetrack pattern to cover more area. With the clouds being close to the ground, it might make the integrated video from the individual images taken a bit jumpy, but it's better than nothing. Plus, I saw a weather report that said the sky would clear by tomorrow."

"I'm looking at that too," Cloud said. "They're calling for clear skies and visibility greater than ten miles. Maybe some low fog in the morning that should burn off once the sun is up."

"Can infrared see through clouds? If I'm remembering right, HARVEST has infrared capability, doesn't it?" Edge asked.

"It does, but infrared can't see through clouds or fog," Voice said. "For HARVEST to be any help, we'll need to wait for the fog to burn off, though if it's really low ground mist we'd be able to see heat signatures."

Amigo looked toward Hank. "Are you having any objections?"

"Not in this case. I agree with Crow: there's a big area to cover, and *one* man to find before he finds someone to kill. But there is one thing I'll add."

"Which is?" Cloud asked.

"If the roses equal the number of victims of our suspect,

then this isn't UniPerp. Eight roses. UniPerp always stops at seven."

"Unless he's going spree," Voice pointed out. "Unless it's his final stand."

HANK WAS GOING through her gear in preparation for the morning. Her SWAT gear was laid out, her magazines loaded and placed in her tactical vest, her firearms ready in their cases—being kept secure for the moment. She looked at her sheath of throwing knives and considered if she wanted to take them along. Placing them back in her duffle, she opted not to, feeling she wasn't quite proficient enough with them yet to be able to throw instinctively and with accuracy. Knowing the morning would be near freezing, she had even checked her temperature controller. *If I have to make a shot, shivering won't help me be accurate.*

Spud, likewise, had laid out his gear and carefully checked everything over. He sat back.

"I think I'm as ready as I'll ever be."

"Think we'll run into this guy tomorrow?" Hank wondered.

"I guess that will all depend on how well HARVEST really works," Spud said. "We can hope. He's killed eight people already, and UniPerp or not I'd like to not see the death count go up."

"Agreed," Hank said. "Did anyone make any dinner plans?"

"Voice felt it was about time we tried out that Woodfire Grill place. He made us a reservation for their private room."

"Good deal. I could use some rare beef. Something dripping with—"

"Don't make me lose my appetite, Love."

"Sorry. It's just a thing. For some reason, when it's a manhunt, I want my beef to moo when I stick my fork in it. I looked at their online menu, and it says they have a garlic ribeye."

"Garlic? You know that rare steak isn't what I feel I need prior to game day."

Hank gave him 'the look.' You know, the one every married man knows. "Really?"

He leaned over and said, "I want the two of us to behave like a couple of porn stars."

"Oh! So you want to *fake it?*"

This time it was Spud's turn to render 'the look.'

"What if I hurt my back again?"

Spud sighed. "How 'bout *after* we catch this guy?"

Hank grinned. "You've got a date."

"Didn't realize I needed to make a date to have a little sex with my wife," Spud muttered.

"I heard that," Hank said as she headed off to wash up prior to leaving for dinner. "Besides, you don't want a little sex. You want *a lot* of sex."

"Your point is?"

"If I've got to chase a guy through the woods, I need to be able to walk."

"Statements like that just encourage me, you know."

Hank grabbed her coat. "We'd better go meet the guys, or they're going to think we're... *occupied* and leave without us."

The two skipped down the stairs to find the rest of the team and the medical away personnel already gathered at the side entrance. Voice had his tablet in his hand, with the controllers attached to either side. He was watching the display. A glance over his shoulder told Hank that he had HARVEST somewhere in the air over the hotel. As they walked out, she noted the heat signatures from the team members' bodies show up as they exited and moved away from the building toward their parked SUVs.

"Pretty amazing," Cloud said from the other side of Voice. He had also been watching the display.

"How high up?" Crow asked.

"Only about three thousand above the ground," Voice said. "Above that is where the clouds currently are."

"That seems like a lot of visible area for only three thousand feet above us," Amigo remarked.

"You know what kind of field of view you can get with a standard cellphone camera," Voice said. "Now imagine an entire array of them on a dome so that there's overlap only on the edges of each image. You get a little distortion on the composite image toward the edges, but I think I'll be able to program a solution that will correct that. I'm pretty sure that it's because the center of focus of the outer cameras is on an area that's farther away than the center of focus of the inner cameras. And Oscar is working on a very sophisticated way to control HARVEST that will make the current controllers obsolete."

"We need to hire that kid," Crow said as they piled into the SUVs, Voice having retrieved HARVEST and secured it back in its case.

"He's chomping at the bit, but both Dick Pipes and I are encouraging him to complete his education. He'll be an even better unit member once he's finished his studies."

"He's a little ahead, isn't he?" Hank asked before heading off for the second SUV.

"He is, but I'd like to encourage him to get his Masters degree. Maybe even a Ph.D."

Taking her place in the SUV occupied by Crow, Amigo, Spud, and Doc Frank, Hank settled in to just watch the sights go by on the way to the restaurant. Or at least it seemed like she just watched the sights. In reality, she was running through the possible scenarios should they encounter a person they considered a suspect. How would they know they had the right person? What if it *wasn't* the right person? Would she shoot an innocent person? What if it was but they didn't realize it and one of them got hurt? Shot? Maybe killed? What if they got the wrong person and the real perp killed another person? Or two? Or three, as he had done once before? Her head swam with the possibilities. *I wish I had some idea about who this could be. If I did... if any one of us did, we could avoid having anyone else die— including him.*

21

"Where are we going to set up?" Crow asked as the team pulled out of the hotel's parking lot.

"I got a look at the maps last night," Hank said. "The biggest issue we have is the Saint Louis River; there's only one bridge across it that could get us into the areas where attacks have already taken place. If we set up right here at the intersection of 536 and 957, it puts us near that bridge. That should allow us to get to either side of the river without having to take the long way around."

"Good plan," Crow said. "I hadn't taken into consideration the river."

The drive would take them forty-five minutes, but with dawn not quite on the horizon, they would make their objective as the local hunters were entering the area in their last-minute attempt to fill their tags. From the vantage point that had been chosen, Voice would be able to use HARVEST to examine the entire area where attacks had taken place.

The weather had warmed up considerably since the day before, now climbing through fifty degrees, and the previous day's gray overcast had given way to clear and sunny skies. All of this gave hope to the team that they would be able to identify and apprehend the person responsible for the seven, and perhaps eight slain hunters—one rose not being accounted for under the presumption that the number of roses left at Holly Fay's house was equivalent to the number of hunters killed.

Parking off the side of the road when they reached their chosen observation post, Voice brought out his newest "toy" and sent it soaring above them. Although it was soon out of sight, video from its complex camera array was showing clear images of the area below them.

"Am I mistaken, or have you done something a little different with the display?" Amigo asked as he looked over Voice's shoulder.

"These are heat signatures," Voice said, pointing at variously-colored objects. "These ones that are blinking are either cooling off or heating up. These ones with circles around them are stationary. The ones with an arrow are moving. Just a little extra programming I put in last night. So, you see this one: it's showing fairly hot, and is moving at thirty miles per hour. Zoom in on it, and we see that it's a vehicle. Specifically, a pickup truck."

He zoomed back out so they could watch the big picture.

"These dotted lines show the prior track of each of the heat signatures. Here's one that's cooling," he continued, pointing to one that sat alongside of a road. "The dotted line shows this vehicle entered the observation area here. And *this* little heat signature is a human being—the person who got out of the truck." He zoomed in, making the signature obviously human, walking into the woods from where the truck was parked at the side of the road. Zooming back out, he pointed out other heat signatures, then would zoom in and identify them as human or wildlife, giving them a tag so he could keep track of which was which.

"Imagine if ve had had dis vile hunting *moose*," Crow quipped, Boris Badenov style.

"That would absolutely have been cheating," Hank said.

"I've got an oddball here," Voice said. He pointed to one of the heat signatures that was traveling along a road. "This guy is going all over the place."

The team watched his tablet for a while until Voice got perturbed with them crowding over his shoulder.

"Hal, mirror drone display on team tablet FT2 to team tablets one through seven." He turned and looked at the rest of the team, obviously annoyed. "Now you all can take out your own tablets and watch on it."

"Sheesh! Touchy," Spud poked as he pulled his tablet out.

The rest of the team took up a spot to lean on the SUV they had brought into the area, watching the images as they moved and evolved on their tablets.

"See the one that's practically driving along every single road?" Voice asked. "I've got it tagged in green. Drives, stops... drives, stops..."

Cloud consulted his watch. He chuckled. "It's the mailman, out making deliveries. Nothing unusual about his actions."

The team continued to watch as vehicles drove along the roads, with one occasionally parking alongside the road and its occupants walking off into the woods.

"Big hunting day for a Tuesday," Edge remarked.

"Last day for these guys to fill their tags," Amigo said. "They all called in sick to work. They've all got their arm in a sling." He grinned as he mounted his rifle with the sling securing it.

They continued to watch, each one making note of when hunters would enter the woods.

Cloud got a troubled look on his face. "Hey Voice, can you zoom in on the mailman again?"

"Why?"

"He's parked alongside the road by another vehicle, but there's no house nearby."

Voice zoomed in on the mailman's vehicle, everyone noting that indeed there was no house in the area—just another vehicle parked at the side of the road. They watched as he went around his truck and then apparently retrieved something from it, then headed into the woods.

"What's he doing?" Amigo wondered.

"Maybe he knows the guy who owns the truck he parked by?" Cloud proposed. "Going to join him for a little hunting before finishing his route?"

"He's coming up on the guy now," Edge said. "Wait—he stopped short of where the other guy is."

They continued to watch in silence, curious about the mailman's actions. Watching closely, they suddenly saw a brief flash of white, indicating high heat, that quickly dissipated, leaving a dimly glowing line extending from the mailman's hands. Nearly simultaneously, they saw the second man's form outlined on the ground.

"Lord in heaven," Edge breathed.

"Did we just see what I *think* we saw?" Voice asked.

"If you think you saw the mailman shoot the guy in the woods, then that's my guess," Edge confirmed.

"But isn't the mailman the guy we talked to at that place we ate at nearby? Timber's Edge? Didn't he say he would help us?" Cloud asked.

Hank was shaking her head. "I knew there was a reason that made me uncomfortable. It's something criminologists have noticed. Often the perpetrator will try to inject himself into the investigation, both to take suspicion off of himself and to keep an eye on how the case is developing."

"How fast can we get to where he is?" Amigo asked.

"No need," Hank replied. "We can chase him all over this area and not get him, or we can go wait for him at the place we know he's going to go."

"The post office?" Voice asked.

Hank shook her head. "No, my dear techie friend. It seems you know programming better than the human mind. He'll go to Holly Fay's house so he can put a rose there."

Having secluded their SUV out of sight just off of Bodas Road, the team now stood watch behind Holly Fay's house, concealed among the trees. Voice had HARVEST aloft and had noted with a degree of thankfulness that John Granger had simply returned to his truck and continued his rounds, eventually making his way back to the post office and then heading back up to Bodas Road. They were now watching him drive westward toward the house that Holly Fay had called home.

"He's right in front of the house," Crow noted over the comm link.

"Everyone just hang tight," Hank whispered. "Let him come to the back and place the rose. That will be the proof that the roses are linked to the killings and that he is responsible for all of them."

"Here he comes," Amigo said. "Coming around the west side of the house."

"He's got the rose in his hand, too," Crow noted.

As Granger stooped to place the rose, Hank held up a hand to signal her teammates to move in from the trees.

"John Granger, FBI," she announced as she stepped out of the trees and into the back yard. "Do not move, put your hands where I can see them."

Granger stood, letting his arms fall limp at his sides.

"So, this is it," he said.

"You are under arrest for the murder—"

He cut her off. "Of course. I did it, all of them. I can only hope I got the one that killed Holly." He turned to look at Hank.

Hank immediately brought her rifle to bear on him, along with her other teammates.

"No need for that," he said, though it didn't cause Hank to lower her guard. "I only wanted to make sure I got the one who got Holly. The sonuvabitch. He sat out there in those woods, not even thinking about what he was doing. Trying to shoot a turkey with a rifle. *Hmph.* Who the hell shoots a turkey with a rifle? Is that even legal? He got Holly instead. I could stand out there where he had and see her yard... Didn't he look before he took that shot? Don't they say you're supposed to know what's beyond your target?"

"It was a criminal act," Hank said, her rifle still at the ready. "But what you did was just as criminal, if not more so. That's not the way justice works. You make the offender pay—not other innocent people in the hopes the offender is among them."

"I loved her! I love her still," he said, tears in his eyes. "I'd have done anything for her. I know she was having her troubles. I was just... waiting for the right time to tell her I could take her away from all of them. Make for her the life she deserved. I'm not a rich man, but I'd have done every-thing to make her happy. *They never gave me the chance!*" he screamed, then began to openly cry wracking sobs, his shoulders heaving.

Turning back to look at the roses, he said, "There's only one way to be with her now."

Before anyone could move, he pulled the pistol he had bought from where he had it tucked in his belt under his jacket, put the muzzle in his mouth, and pulled the trigger.

"No!" Hank cried.

The entire team ran forward, parting as Doc Frank ran up. He rolled Granger's body over, though he knew he didn't have to. The spray of blood and brain matter on the grass told him that even if by some miracle Granger was still alive, there would be nothing that could be done to save him. He turned back to the team, seeing them all standing stunned, the color draining from every face. "Gone," he said simply to the shocked team members.

In breaking news today, a man believed to be responsible for the killing of nine hunters in the area around Makinen and Fayal Township committed suicide as officers of the Minnesota Bureau of Criminal Apprehension and the FBI attempted to take him into custody. John Granger, a rural postal deliveryman for the area, was seen on surveillance as he committed the last of the shootings, with the attempt to arrest him taking place at an area home. It is believed that Mr. Granger's killing spree was set off by the death of an area woman, Ms. Holly Fay....

He picked up the remote and turned off the television, then slumped back in his chair.

Dead. Nine men dead because of me, because I couldn't face the music after accidentally shooting that woman. Nine men dead. And the woman, too.

He went into the bathroom to wash his face. Looking up into the mirror, he gazed at his own reflection. "You're one sorry hunk of shit," he told the image in the mirror. "At least *he* had the guts to face the music."

He picked up his straight razor from where it sat on the edge of the sink. Opening up the blade, he looked at it for what seemed like a long time, the emotion draining from him. Then he casually reached up and drew the blade across his throat. As he watched his reflection in the mirror, blood gushing from the wound, he dipped his fingers in the pools of red.

He was found later that evening when his wife arrived back from her job at the small grocery next door to the post office in Makinen, lying in a pool of congealed blood. Written on the mirror in that same blood was the message, *I shot Holly Fay.*

22

"I'm glad to see that you are all here," Doc Andy said as he entered the conference room. "I thought we might discuss a bit of what went on in Minnesota."

"I guess our biometrics are telling you a few things," Hank said. Her disheveled look spoke of the fatigue from nights spent tossing and turning rather than sleeping.

"You could say that," Doc Andy confirmed. "You all seem to be deeply troubled by this mission."

Crow was visibly troubled from the moment Doc Andy said he wanted to discuss the Minnesota mission.

"I take it you are having some issues with this, Crow?"

"We don't talk about this," Crow said. "Native Americans don't talk about this. It's bad. It can make others do the same. We don't even mention the person's name."

"Will you have a problem remaining and talking about it among your teammates?"

"Maybe Crow can just listen, and only talk if he feels it's right for him to do so," Amigo said.

"And what about you, Amigo?"

"The predominant religion among Hispanics is Catholicism," Amigo said. "My family was no exception. There is a great fear about killing..." He looked over at Crow, who had crossed his arms and turned his head. "...Killing yourself," he continued. "Catholics believe that taking your own life is an instant ticket to hell."

"I don't know what it's a ticket to," Hank said. "No one has ever come down from heaven, stood in front of me and said, 'Hank, this is what you need to do to get to where I am,' and no one has ever come up from hell and said to me, 'Do this and this is where you'll go.' But there's something inherently *wrong* about killing yourself by my way of thinking. Everyone has a place, everyone has something they're supposed to be doing. If you take your own life, you don't know if what you were here for has been done yet."

"I can't help but agree with Hank," Spud said. "I was brought up a Christian, and I still believe in having a purpose by following Jesus's example. He didn't mean 'kill yourself' when He said, 'Take up your cross and follow Me.'"

"Cloud?"

"He made himself the ultimate failure by what he did. It was a cop-out, if you ask me. He didn't want to face the truth of what he did."

"You sound angry."

"I am. I feel like he cheated his victims out of having a voice. The prosecutor would have given them a voice, and he stole that from them."

"Edge?"

"I was brought up Catholic. What Amigo said rings true for me: you don't go to heaven when you take away the gift of life God gave you. He said he did it to be with Holly, but she died an innocent victim. Assuming her life had any merit, he couldn't be with her in the afterlife by killing himself."

"Voice?"

"Everyone here knows I don't believe in a magic man in the sky, but that doesn't mean what I saw didn't affect me. I've seen what Hank does after killing an animal in a hunt. She's respectful. Reverent. Consoling to the animal, expressing her gratitude to it for the food it will give." He shook his head. "There was nothing reverent about what I saw out there. It was just a waste, with nothing gained from it."

Hank sighed. "It's my job to kill someone when that's required to keep innocent people from dying at their hands. I've had to do it, and I know I'll have to do it again. But as disturbing as having to kill someone is, it's nowhere near as disturbing as seeing a man put a gun to his head and pull the trigger. I've had to deal with it a few times as a first responder when I was in the Taos PD, but always after the fact. Never as a witness to the fact. It's going to take a while to stop seeing it."

"Everyone says anger is a strong emotion," Edge began. "That hatred is a strong emotion. But if you ask me, love is the strongest emotion out there. It will make people strong, and it will make people weak. It will make people do wonderful things or strange ones. It will stabilize some people and it will make others crazy. In this case, it made someone kill—and it's not the first time someone has killed another person out of love. That's the scariest thing about this, and that's what's keeping me awake at night right now."

"I think that I've heard very honest assessments of what you have all gone through," Doc Andy said. "I have recommended, and the rest of Medical agrees, that you all take three crash days. Talk among yourselves, and do your best to help each other deal with the events of this latest mission. If you need me, you know where to find me."

Doc Andy pulled small packets from his pocket and dealt one to each team member as if he was dealing cards in a card game. "There are three doses of a mild sleep aid in each of those packets. I will order that you take one tonight; the others take before bedtime if you feel you need it. Turn in any unused doses to James." He stood up from his chair, and before leaving dropped one other thing in the center of the table.

"Hank finds these a comforting medication," he said before turning and leaving.

"Hershey's Special Dark chocolate nuggets," Hank said. She grabbed the bag and ripped it open, dumping the contents in the center of the table before scooping a handful in front of her. Stuffing one in her mouth, she added, "Twy id—dey's *ahsome.*"

Her teammates shook their heads, then scooped some of the nuggets in front of themselves as well. No one said anything. They just sat and let the chocolate melt in their mouths.

As she and Spud made their way back to their residence and took up the usual locations in the reading nook, Hank began to stare across the living room again.

"You can't keep dwelling on it," Spud said. "It will drive you crazy."

"I don't know how you can just put it behind you."

"Maybe because it's not the first time I've had to deal with this sort of thing."

Hank turned and looked at him. "You're kidding."

"I didn't see it happen, but I knew the person who did it."

Hank's look begged him to go on.

"It was another guy I knew in PPD. He was married. His wife was having problems with the kinds of hours we worked. What can you do? You have a sworn duty to protect the president. One day she told him she wanted a divorce. So he shot her. Killed her. Then he wrote a note, stuck it in his breast pocket, and shot himself. I had to go ID him. The note said, 'It's the only way I can stay with her.'"

"Good God!"

"There was nothing good about it, and I doubt God was involved."

He fell silent, then continued.

"He had told me about his wife's unhappiness. I kicked myself for quite a while after he killed himself. Kept telling myself that if I'd just said something to our boss, he could have gotten some help. Or even just some time off. You know, take the wife for a romantic vacation. But I didn't say anything. I didn't think it was any of my business."

Hank could see that the wound Spud had felt was opened afresh. She slid next to him and nestled against his chest.

"I love you, Spud."

"I know. And I hope you know how very much I love you too."

"I do."

"I intend to get you to say that again one day."

"What?" Hank asked.

"I do."

"You want to domesticate me."

"You're supposed to submit to me, wife. When I say 'marry me', you will say, 'I will', and when the preacher asks, 'Do you take this sorry excuse for a man to be your lawfully wedded husband', you will say, 'I do'. That's the way it works."

Hank's face had adopted a wrinkled grin. "You're full of shit."

"I am. I know I'll never domesticate you. You know it's something that neither of us wants. I need that little flash of fire from you every so often to stay warm." He wrapped an arm around her. "I just don't need you running your icy feet up inside my thighs. *That* is cold."

23

With team activities returning to normal, Hank found herself in that groggy zone where sleep was ending but wakefulness had not yet begun. She was dreaming, or at least she thought she was. The dream was vivid—the sort of vivid encounter in that half-asleep, half-awake realm that makes one question if it actually was real or not.

She was sitting with the rest of the team in a diner in Grand Forks, North Dakota. It was the diner they would eat lunch in before encountering Charles Blobel—the tarot reader, and where Miss Martha would go every day to drink a cup of tea. The only difference was that all seven of the team members were sitting at a single table.

They had ordered pie. The diner billed it on the menu as "Fruits of the Forest," with a filling made of apples, strawberries, blueberries, blackberries, raspberries, plums, and peaches. Seven different fruits. The waiter had come and put the entire pie on the table. It had been cut in seven equal pieces. Each of them had a cup of coffee, a fork, and a dessert plate.

The waiter started serving the pie. First piece to Edge, second one to Voice, third to Amigo, fourth to Crow, fifth to Cloud, sixth to Spud, and the last one to Hank. 'Isn't that funny,' she thought. 'He served us in order of team designation.'

As she put the first forkful of pie in her mouth, Miss Martha came walking up from her table in the rear of the diner. She turned and faced the team where they sat and extracted a tarot card from a pocket in her skirt. Laying it on the table, she said, "The seven of swords. This card has the meaning of using your wits rather than force. Secret planning. The use of the mind and methods not obvious to others. Five are taken back, two are left standing away from the others."

She looked at Hank. "You are Seven, the seventh of seven. He knows you, and you know him though you will not recognize him. He hates all of the Seven Swords, but he hates you most of all."

Hank bolted upright.

"Better get moving, sleepy head," Spud said. "Vacation's over. Let's grab breakfast and get intel over with."

"First up, we have the environmentalists again," Spud said. "This time, it's methane emissions."

"Sorry, Great Spirit—we broke the planet," Crow mumbled.

"Along with that, they're upset about declining numbers of certain sea mammals."

"They're finding some of them with their guts full of plastic garbage," Amigo observed.

"It just washes into the storm water systems and out to sea," Crow said.

"I always carried a stainless steel bottle and just filled it up at home," Hank remarked. "Easy to keep clean, doesn't get skanky, could put hot stuff or cold stuff in it with no fear of it getting all warped."

"Smart girl," Cloud said.

"It goes without saying that our brothers and sisters in CBP continue to pick up large loads of increasingly dangerous drugs, as well as find people smuggling illegal border crossers under dangerous conditions. HSI is also continuing to make cases against human traffickers and those engaged in child exploitation."

Hank tapped her appreciation of those efforts on the table with her knuckles.

"And last but not least—"

"*You just can't make this shit up!*" the rest of the team exclaimed.

"Yes, while we're on a mission, the weirdness doesn't stop to take a breath. This one involves a woman with a unique way of dodging jury duty."

"This sounds like it could be a good one," Cloud remarked.

"I thought it was. The case involved the embezzlement of funds from a local bank branch by the branch manager. The woman claimed that what she did for a living made her ineligible to act as a juror.

"The judge was expecting her to say she worked in a bank, or something of that nature. But when he asked her what she did, she told him she was a psychic."

Edge chuckled. "Did she have knowledge about the case from a higher source?"

"That was indeed her claim," Spud said. "The judge dismissed her, but asked that before she left to share with the court the results of the trial so that the court could save some time."

The rest of the team chuckled their approval.

"Now, I think we should get back to some serious business."

"As in?" Amigo asked.

"UniPerp. We all know that John Granger wasn't our man, but we still need to figure out just who is."

"Geez, Spud—we've gone over this and over it," Cloud protested. "It all hinges on the number seven, but that could be anything. We already know the list of possibilities. Seven days in the week. Seventh month of the year. Seven deadly sins. Seven cardinal virtues. The seven seals on the scroll John mentions in Revelation. Seven could be *anything.*"

Hank sat with a vacant look on her face.

"The seven of us."

"That's impossible," Voice protested. "No one knows about us."

"Yes, someone does."

"What are you suggesting?" Amigo asked indignantly. "That UniPerp is one of our gunnies? One of our past operatives? Maybe one in the committee? These people are *vetted*, Hank. Up, down, and sideways! We monitor *them* far more than they monitor *us.* Am I right, Voice?"

"Absolutely."

"No one can possibly know us other than those people," Cloud asserted.

"You're forgetting someone," Hank said. "It came to me in a dream last night."

"Now we're dreaming up the answers," Edge smirked.

"I dreamt that we were back in North Dakota in that diner. We were eating pie made from seven different kinds of fruit. The pie had been cut in seven equal pieces, and it was served to us in the order of our team designations: one through seven. Then Miss Martha came up and put a tarot card on the table. It was the seven of swords."

Hank yanked out her medallion of Saint Michael, poised with his foot on the neck of Satan and holding his sword in his hand. Then she reached over and yanked out Edge's Sword of Saint Michael from around his neck.

"*Seven swords. **We are the seven swords.** And it all makes sense if you look at the victims since UniPerp started using the seven victims MO. Seven women raped and murdered—seven women who looked like me. Seven men who looked like Spud. Seven marines," she continued, pointing at Edge. "Seven programmers. Seven gunsmiths, like Luigi. Seven doctors like Doc Rich. *Each of the groups of seven victims represents one of the people who were involved.*"

"What are you talking about?" Edge demanded.

"I'm saying I know who UniPerp is." She shook her head in dismay. "I think I've known it unconsciously for a long time. It's the reason I'd have nightmares after the UniPerp events."

Everyone was now staring at her in disbelief.

"Miss Martha in my dream said that he hates all of the Swords, but he hates me most of all. She said he knows me and I know him, but won't recognize him. There is one person out there who knows about us and fits that bill.

"UniPerp is Spot."

PLEASE LEAVE A REVIEW!

If you enjoyed this book, please leave a favorable review where you purchased it, and also at goodreads.com. It's ratings and reviews from readers like you who help other readers find books they may enjoy! Thank you!

ABOUT THE AUTHOR

Anne Fox spends her time traveling, writing, and spending time with her three cats in El Paso, Texas. An avid firearms enthusiast, instructor, and competitive marksman, as well as an FAA-certified commercial pilot, *The Unit* series marries her love for marksmanship and flying via an overly-active imagination to answer the question: "What if?"

CONNECT WITH ANNE

https://www.facebook.com/Anne-Fox-Author-1119777951559223

Twitter: @AnneFox83514907

Goodreads: https://www.goodreads.com/author/show/18917324.Anne_Fox

Bookbub: https://www.bookbub.com/search/authors?search=Anne%20Fox

Instagram: https://www.instagram.com/annefoxauthor/

Interact with Anne Fox on Facebook on the Anne Fox – Author Group.